BUZZELLI
COLLECTED WORKS VOLUME 2

HP

Illustrated by
Guido Buzzelli

"HP" Script by
Alexis Kostandi

"Morganna" Script by
Daniela Vianello

Translated by
Jamie Richards

FLOATING WORLD COMICS

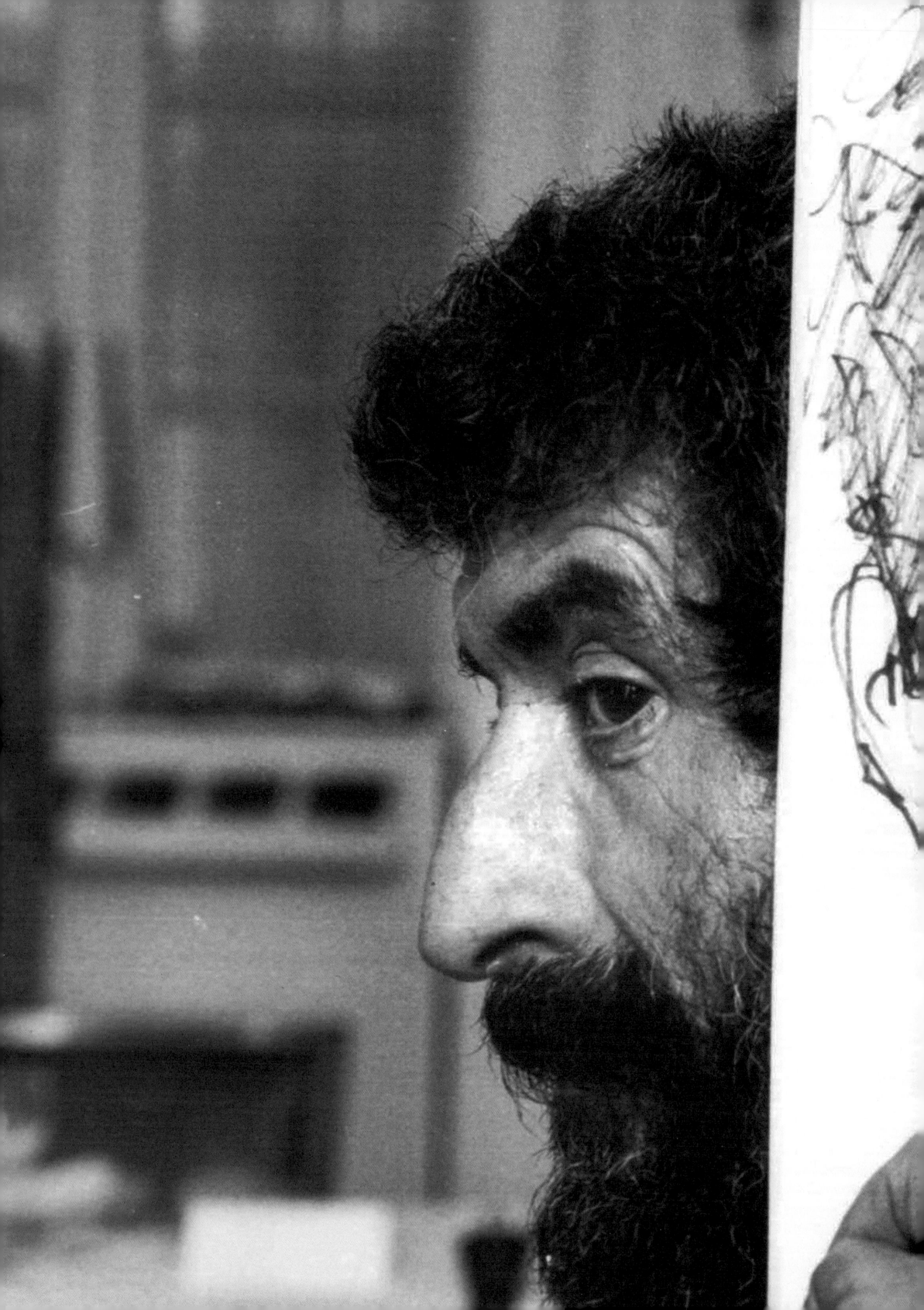

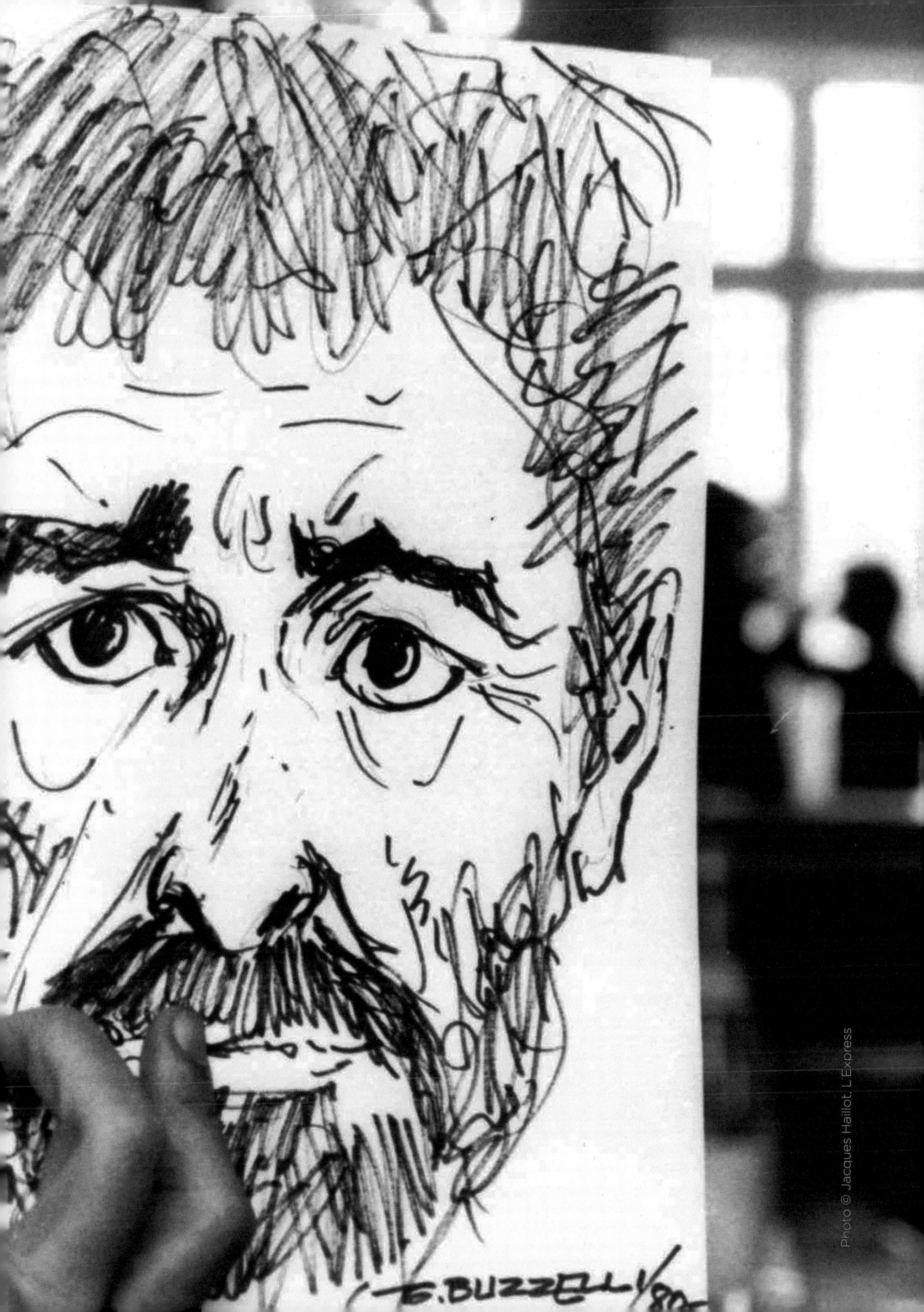
G.BUZZELL

Photo © Jacques Haillot, L'Express

Buzzelli's Future, *Our Present*

Domingos Isabelinho

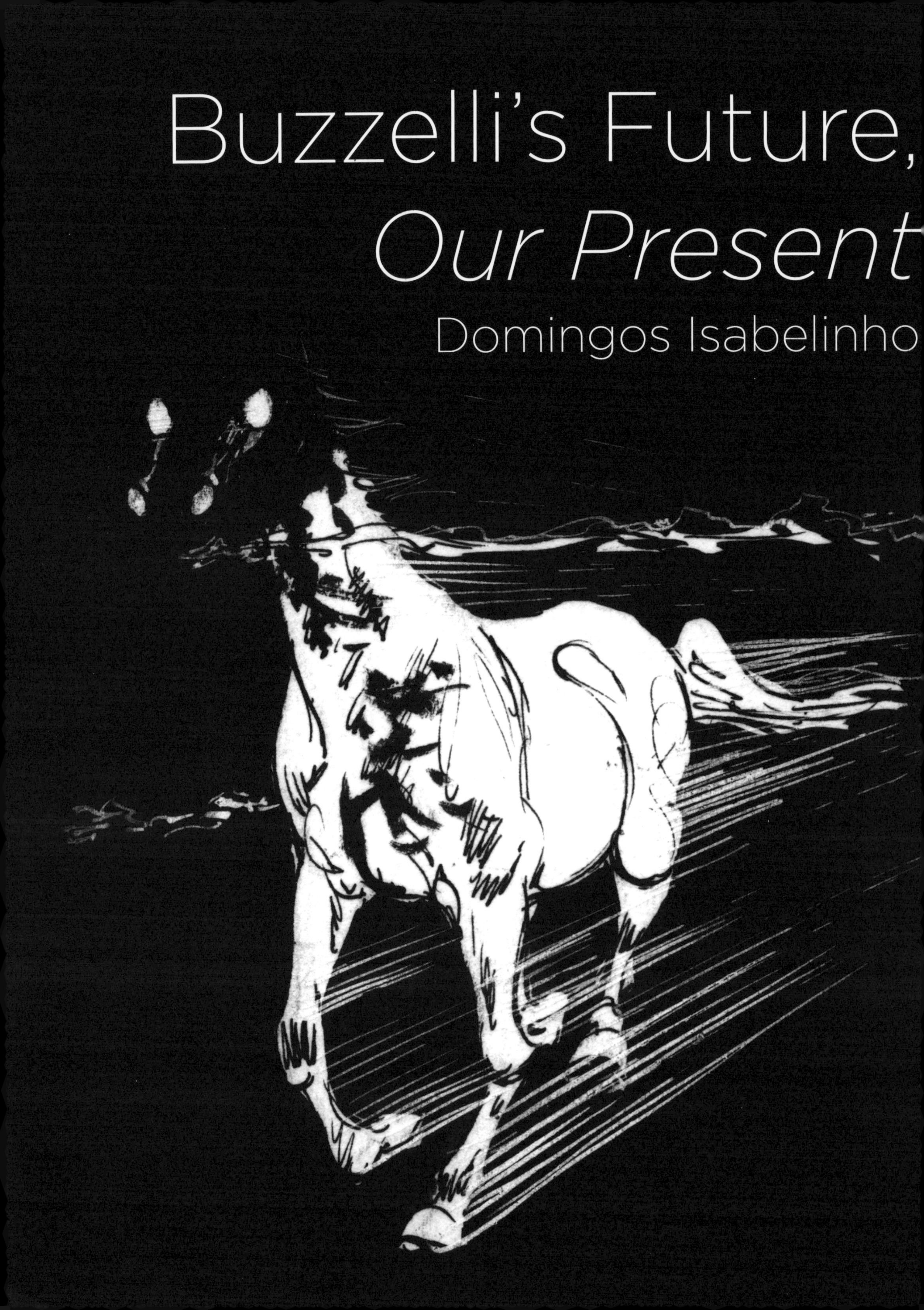

IN THE EARLY SEVENTIES, Guido Buzzelli had completed his auteur trilogy (*The Revolt of the Ugly, Labyrinth, Zil Zelub*) and garnered critical acclaim in his native Italy, winning the Yellow Kid Award at Lucca in 1973. But he was still far more popular and commercially successful in France with his genre comics, including a forgettable Western in 1973 with a script by Jean-Pierre Gourmelin, *Nevada Hill*. At this time, auteur work in comics was virtually unknown and serialized genre comics ruled the market. When he received the proposal to continue drawing *Nevada Hill* as a series, he refused. Shifting his attention away from work-for-hire gigs, he turned toward a series of dystopian future stories, including *HP* and *Morganna*. This marked a shift towards creating genre comics on his own terms, quite subversive and strange ones that brought his obssesive auteur sensibilty to the form.

HP (Horse Power) is regarded as one of his finest works outside of the Buzzelli trilogy. It was published for the first time in France thanks to editor Georges Wolinski, who serialized it in *Charlie Mensuel* magazine in 1974 (May-November). *HP* went on to be published by the Italian press association ANAF (Associazione Nazionale Amici del Fumetto) in 1975, but would not reach a wider circulation until 1979, when it was published as a book by Milano Libri in Italy.

In contrast with the trilogy that he wrote and drew, Buzzelli collaborated with writers on *HP* and *Morganna*. *HP's* script is by Francesco Cerrito (writing here under the *nom de plume*, Alexis Kostandi). Cerrito was a photojournalist who covered the wars in Vietnam, Cambodia and other places. He directed documentaries and published books linking photography and narrative, including *La non-storia* (The No-Story). As a photographer, Cerrito was used to telling stories with his pictures. But what he developed in *HP* was a more complex narrative structure. *HP* is a chorus with multiple points of view. The cowboy, Freeman may be seen as the protagonist, but he is not the traditional "hero" of children's comics, mainly because he does not get more narrative space than the other characters, and because he solves nothing.

Despite the appearances of a Western, *HP* is revealed to be a science-fiction dystopia. A world war has destroyed our civilization and a new world order has emerged with two distinctive and antagonistic camps: the city and the rebels (the "ugly" of *The Revolt of the Ugly*). The city possesses advanced technology and is ruled by ironclad laws. The rebels ride horses and live a tribalistic life, having returned to pre-industrial conditions. Accustomed to the manichean dynamics of children's comics, we could presume that "city = bad" and "rebels = good." Again *HP* subverts these expectations. The characters are complex even when they aren't always given the time to be fully developed. As I said before, this is a chorus - the narrative does not stay long with any of them.

The drama that unfolds in the city of *HP* reminds me of what someone said about the Roman Empire: the worst job to have was Emperor — most did not die of natural causes. Palace intrigue is woven into the narrative of *HP*, along with a brief feminist commentary and an obligatory cameo by Buzzelli. He portrays himself as a frustrated artist who has not be given due credit as a painter. Buzzelli still bore his wounds from identifying as a figurative painter out of sync with an age of hard conceptual art and Arte Povera. He experienced as much difficulty making a living as a painter as he had making a living as a comics artist.

Good science fiction does not talk about the future so much as it comments on the present. In *HP* we see the hippie dropouts of the 1970s with the observation that hippie communes were financially impossible, being supported by someone's rich father. It is clear that to Cerrito and Buzzelli, "Hippyism" was just a fad. Buzzelli places his dystopias in the timeline of our world by including recognizable modernist landmarks. For example, Buzzelli drew the Habitat 67 cube houses from Montreal and a structure inspired by the Theme Building at LAX - repeated in the first panel of *Morganna*, with a monorail added. Habitat 67 was built for Montreal's World Fair in 1967, an exhibition celebrating progress and technology. With these references, Buzzelli subverts the utopian landmarks of his era into his dystopian future.

Morganna was published in Italy in 1975-76 in Sgt. Kirk magazine, with a script by Daniela Vianello. He continues to blend genres with a science-fiction fairy tale disguised as gothic horror, set in the year 2040. If HP was the MacGuffin in *HP*, the "alchemical formula" is the MacGuffin in *Morganna*. It is an intermezzo that gave Buzzelli an opportunity to revel in his admiration for Francisco de Goya, directly referencing the *Aquelarre* of Goya's *Witches' Sabbath*. "The sleep of reason produces monsters," whether the genre is science fiction or horror. Guido Buzzelli's sympathies always go with the monsters.

We conclude with Buzzelli's future, our present. Two prophecies: the citizens in *HP* wear masks reminding us of the recent pandemic; and in Morganna's future of 2040, print books are long gone. Buzzelli even foretells the internet, housed in a gigantic machine. As Miki puts it in *HP*, let's hope Vianello and Buzzelli were failed prophets. I say this because of the generation I belong to, and like Morganna's aunt Alcina, I am a sentimental creature...

HP

(1974)

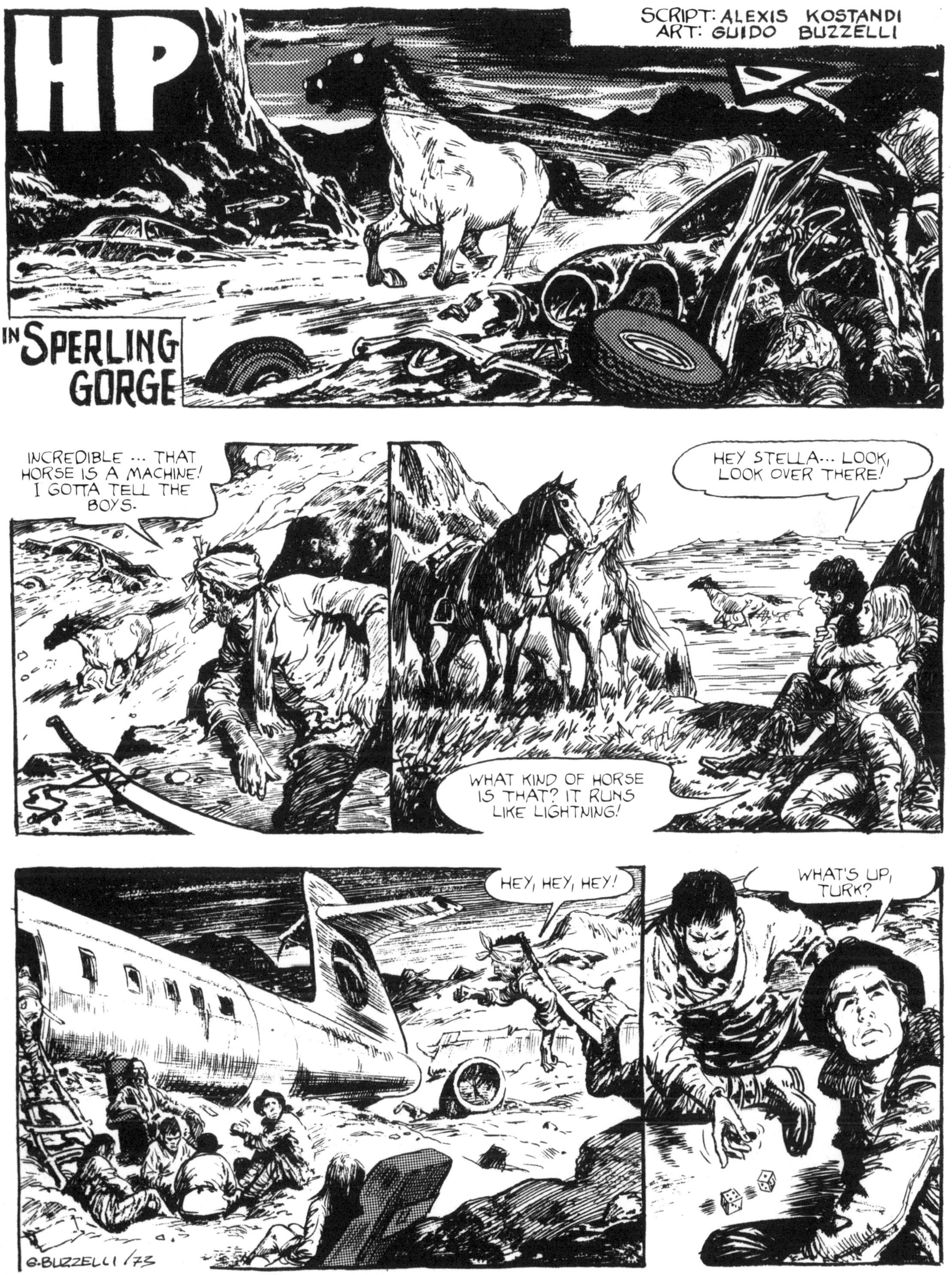
SCRIPT: ALEXIS KOSTANDI
ART: GUIDO BUZZELLI
HP
IN SPERLING GORGE
INCREDIBLE ... THAT HORSE IS A MACHINE! I GOTTA TELL THE BOYS.
HEY STELLA... LOOK, LOOK OVER THERE!
WHAT KIND OF HORSE IS THAT? IT RUNS LIKE LIGHTNING!
HEY, HEY, HEY!
G.BUZZELLI /73
WHAT'S UP, TURK?

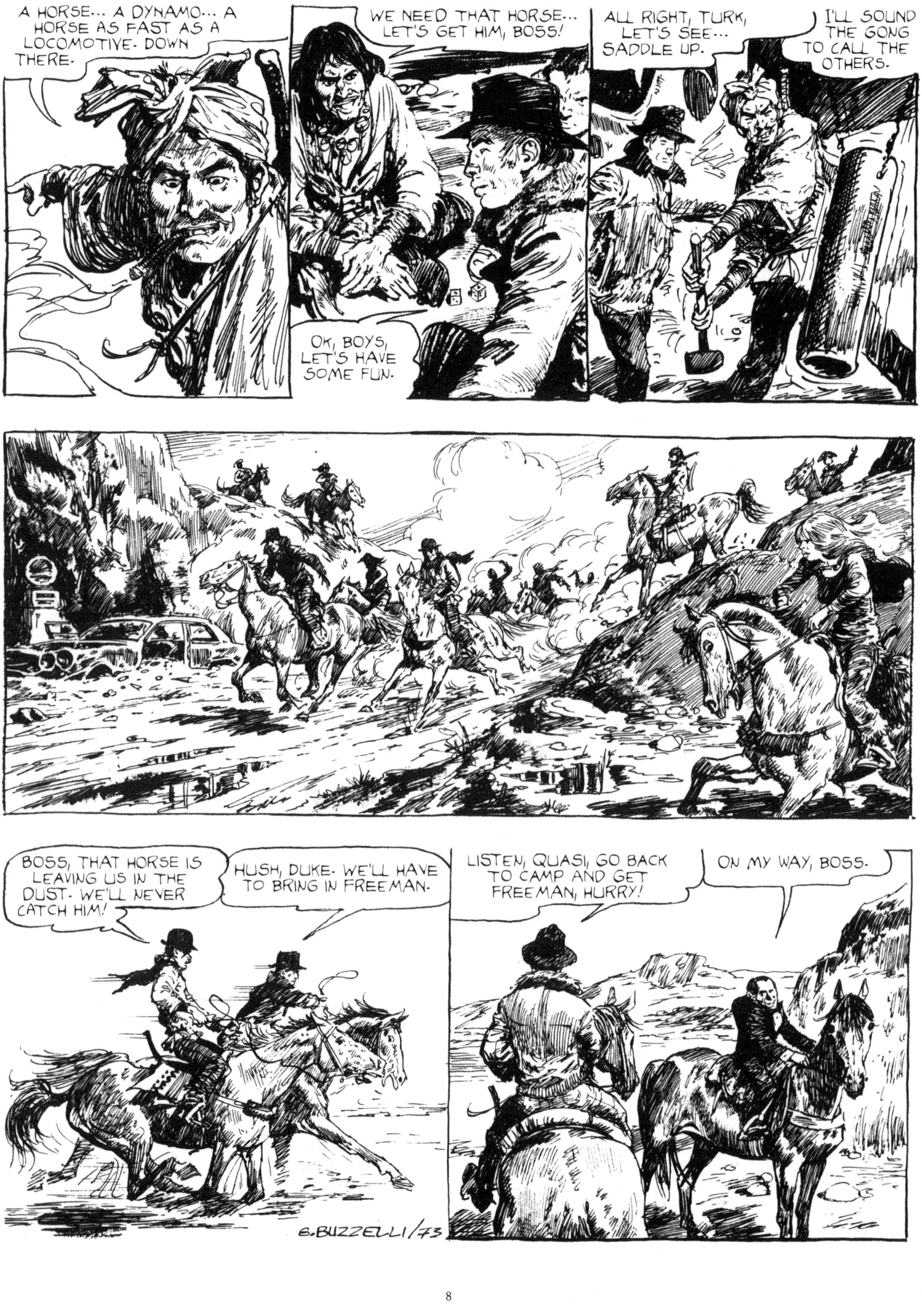
A HORSE... A DYNAMO... A HORSE AS FAST AS A LOCOMOTIVE. DOWN THERE.
WE NEED THAT HORSE... LET'S GET HIM, BOSS!
OK, BOYS, LET'S HAVE SOME FUN.
ALL RIGHT, TURK, LET'S SEE... SADDLE UP.
I'LL SOUND THE GONG TO CALL THE OTHERS.
BOSS, THAT HORSE IS LEAVING US IN THE DUST. WE'LL NEVER CATCH HIM!
HUSH, DUKE. WE'LL HAVE TO BRING IN FREEMAN.
G. BUZZELLI/73
LISTEN, QUASI, GO BACK TO CAMP AND GET FREEMAN, HURRY!
ON MY WAY, BOSS.

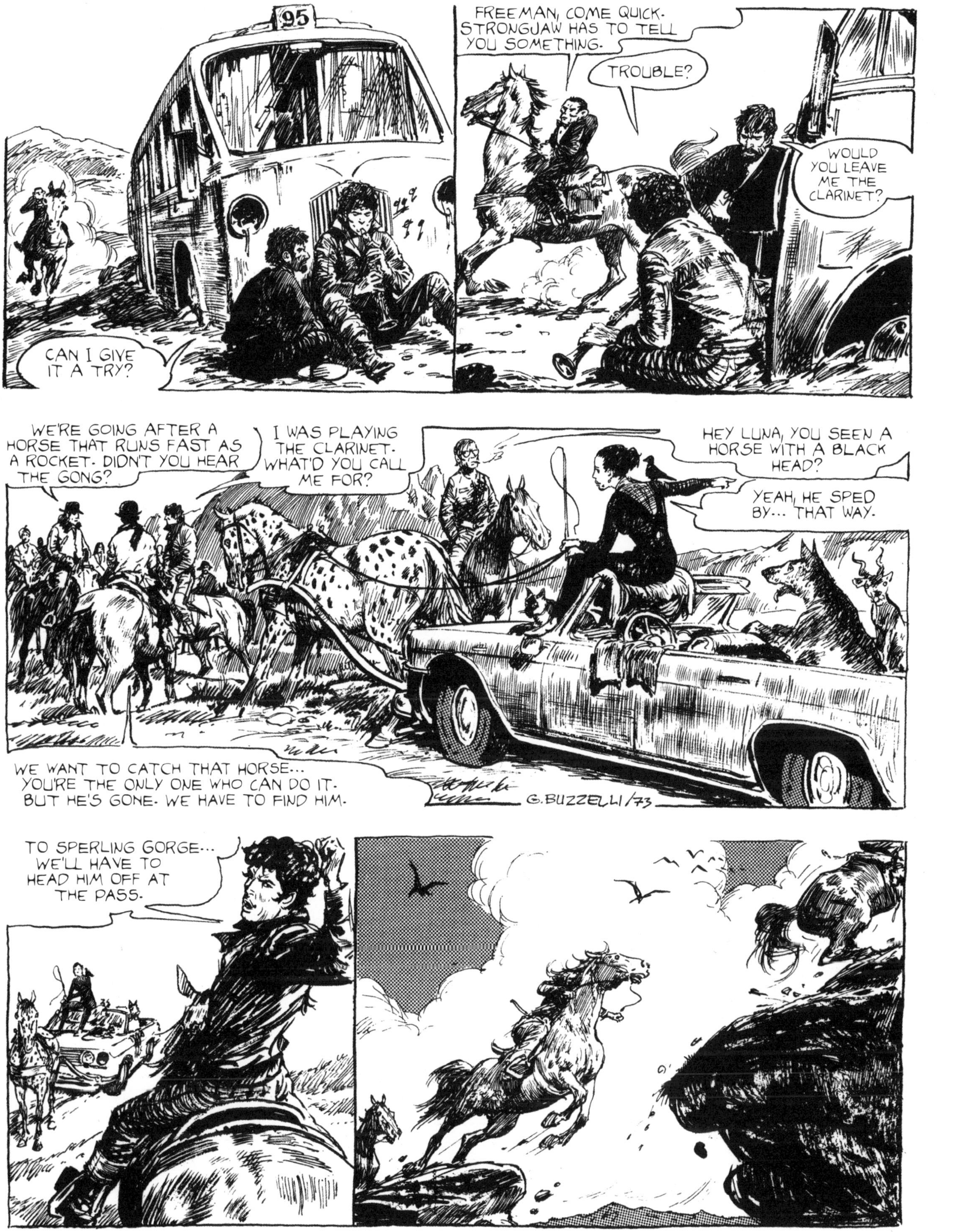
95
CAN I GIVE IT A TRY?
FREEMAN, COME QUICK. STRONGJAW HAS TO TELL YOU SOMETHING.
TROUBLE?
WOULD YOU LEAVE ME THE CLARINET?
WE'RE GOING AFTER A HORSE THAT RUNS FAST AS A ROCKET. DIDN'T YOU HEAR THE GONG?
I WAS PLAYING THE CLARINET. WHAT'D YOU CALL ME FOR?
HEY LUNA, YOU SEEN A HORSE WITH A BLACK HEAD?
YEAH, HE SPED BY... THAT WAY.
WE WANT TO CATCH THAT HORSE... YOU'RE THE ONLY ONE WHO CAN DO IT. BUT HE'S GONE. WE HAVE TO FIND HIM.
G. BUZZELLI/73
TO SPERLING GORGE... WE'LL HAVE TO HEAD HIM OFF AT THE PASS.

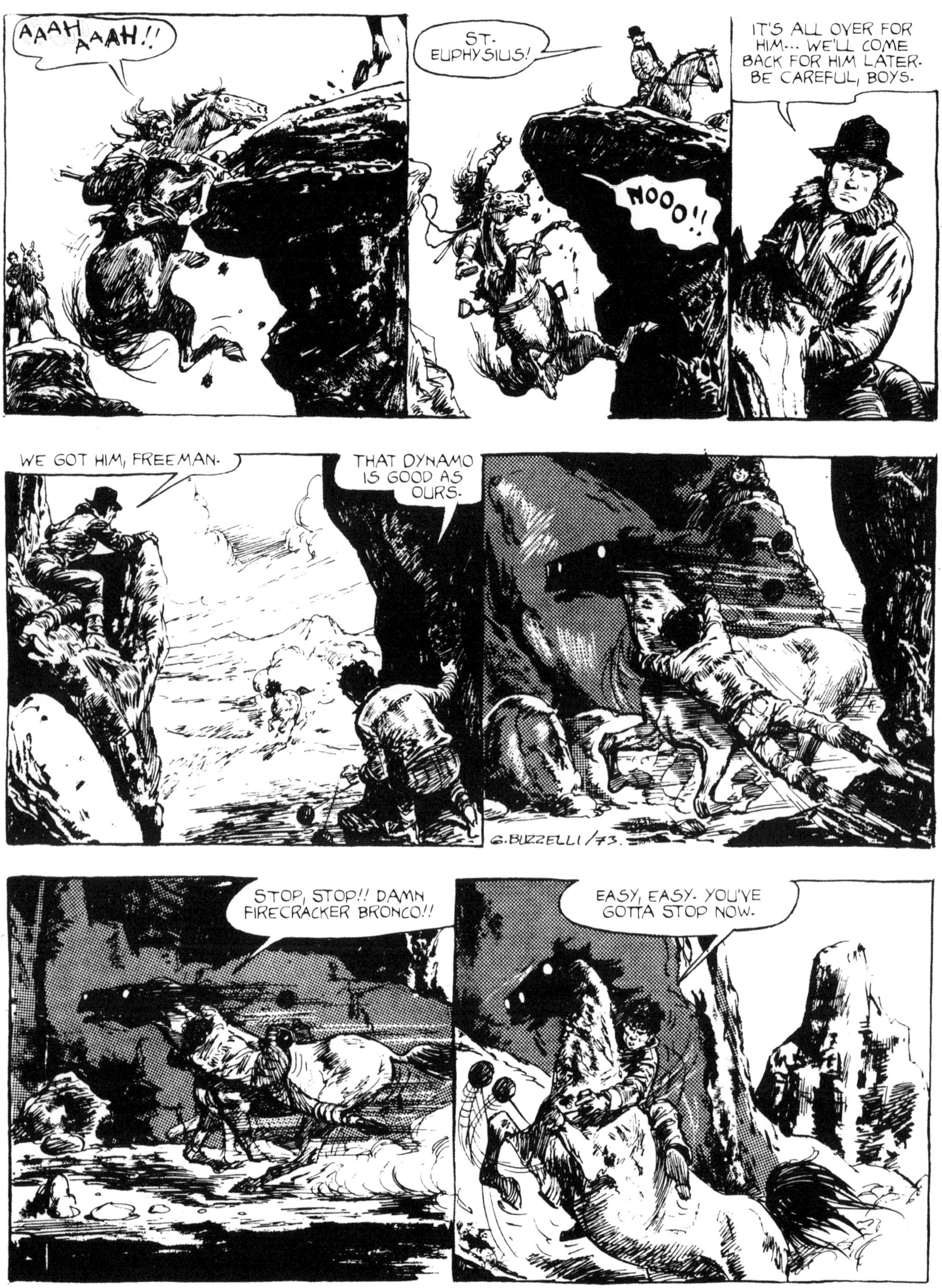
AAAH AAAH!!
ST. EUPHYSIUS!
NOOO!!
IT'S ALL OVER FOR HIM... WE'LL COME BACK FOR HIM LATER. BE CAREFUL, BOYS.
WE GOT HIM, FREEMAN.
THAT DYNAMO IS GOOD AS OURS.
G. BUZZELLI /73.
STOP, STOP!! DAMN FIRECRACKER BRONCO!!
EASY, EASY. YOU'VE GOTTA STOP NOW.

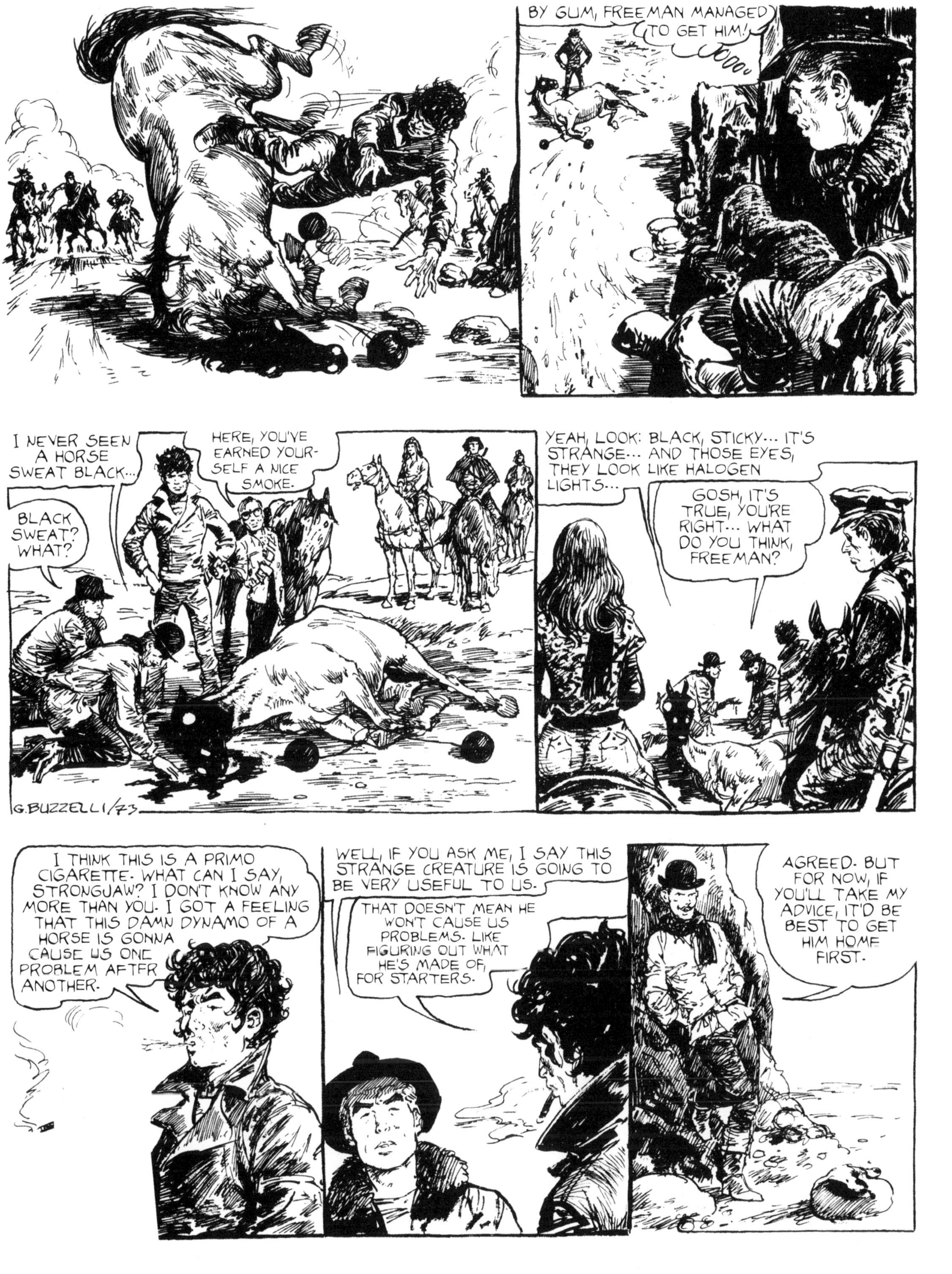

BY GUM, FREEMAN MANAGED TO GET HIM!
I NEVER SEEN A HORSE SWEAT BLACK...
BLACK SWEAT? WHAT?
HERE, YOU'VE EARNED YOURSELF A NICE SMOKE.
G.BUZZELLI/73
YEAH, LOOK: BLACK, STICKY... IT'S STRANGE... AND THOSE EYES, THEY LOOK LIKE HALOGEN LIGHTS...
GOSH, IT'S TRUE, YOU'RE RIGHT... WHAT DO YOU THINK, FREEMAN?
I THINK THIS IS A PRIMO CIGARETTE. WHAT CAN I SAY, STRONGJAW? I DON'T KNOW ANY MORE THAN YOU. I GOT A FEELING THAT THIS DAMN DYNAMO OF A HORSE IS GONNA CAUSE US ONE PROBLEM AFTER ANOTHER.
WELL, IF YOU ASK ME, I SAY THIS STRANGE CREATURE IS GOING TO BE VERY USEFUL TO US.
THAT DOESN'T MEAN HE WON'T CAUSE US PROBLEMS. LIKE FIGURING OUT WHAT HE'S MADE OF, FOR STARTERS.
AGREED. BUT FOR NOW, IF YOU'LL TAKE MY ADVICE, IT'D BE BEST TO GET HIM HOME FIRST.

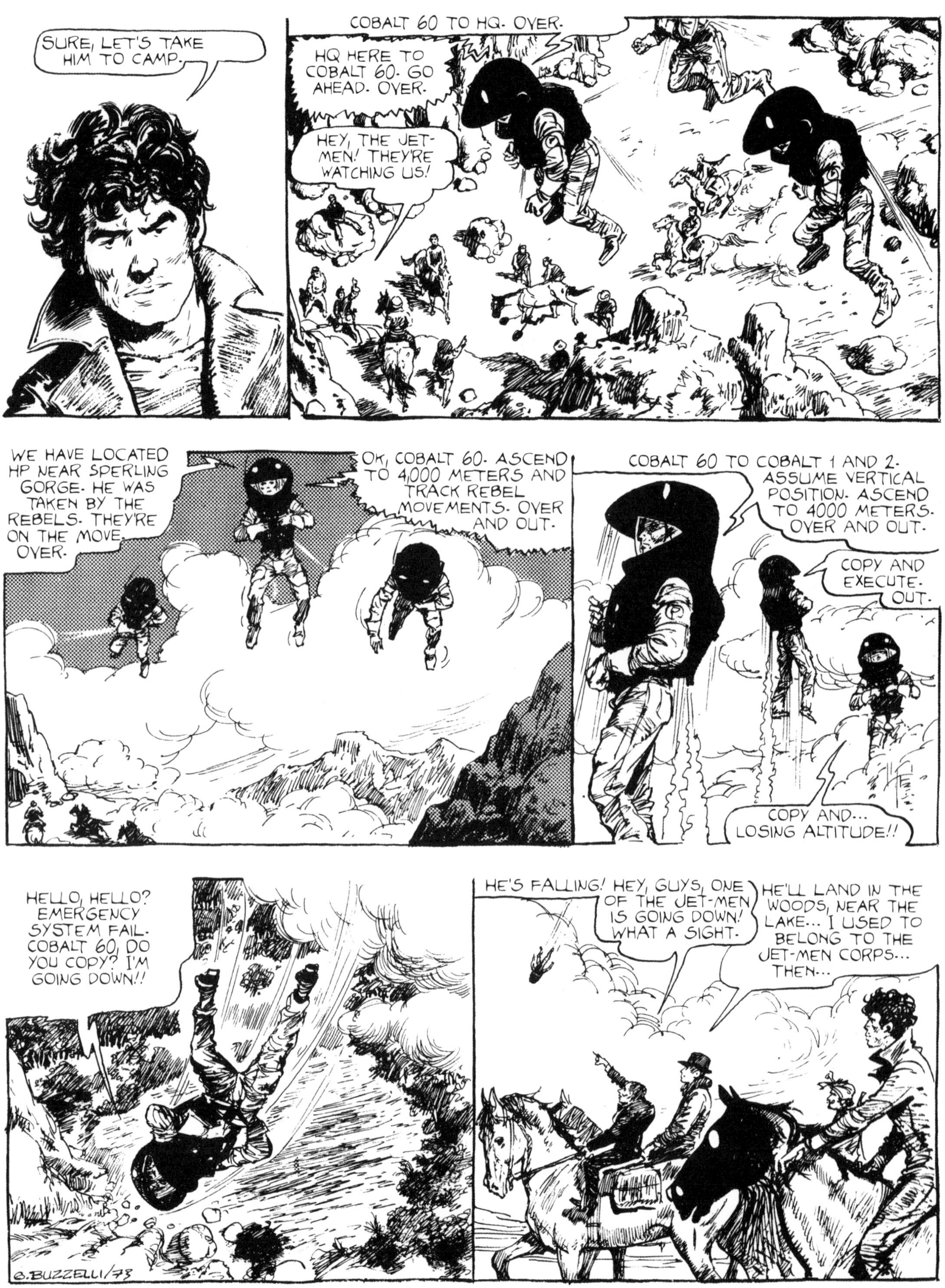
SURE, LET'S TAKE HIM TO CAMP.
COBALT 60 TO HQ. OVER.
HQ HERE TO COBALT 60. GO AHEAD. OVER.
HEY, THE JET-MEN! THEY'RE WATCHING US!
WE HAVE LOCATED HP NEAR SPERLING GORGE. HE WAS TAKEN BY THE REBELS. THEY'RE ON THE MOVE. OVER.
OK, COBALT 60. ASCEND TO 4,000 METERS AND TRACK REBEL MOVEMENTS. OVER AND OUT.
COBALT 60 TO COBALT 1 AND 2. ASSUME VERTICAL POSITION. ASCEND TO 4000 METERS. OVER AND OUT.
COPY AND EXECUTE. OUT.
COPY AND... LOSING ALTITUDE!!
HELLO, HELLO? EMERGENCY SYSTEM FAIL. COBALT 60, DO YOU COPY? I'M GOING DOWN!!
G. BUZZELLI/73
HE'S FALLING!
HEY, GUYS, ONE OF THE JET-MEN IS GOING DOWN! WHAT A SIGHT.
HE'LL LAND IN THE WOODS, NEAR THE LAKE... I USED TO BELONG TO THE JET-MEN CORPS... THEN...

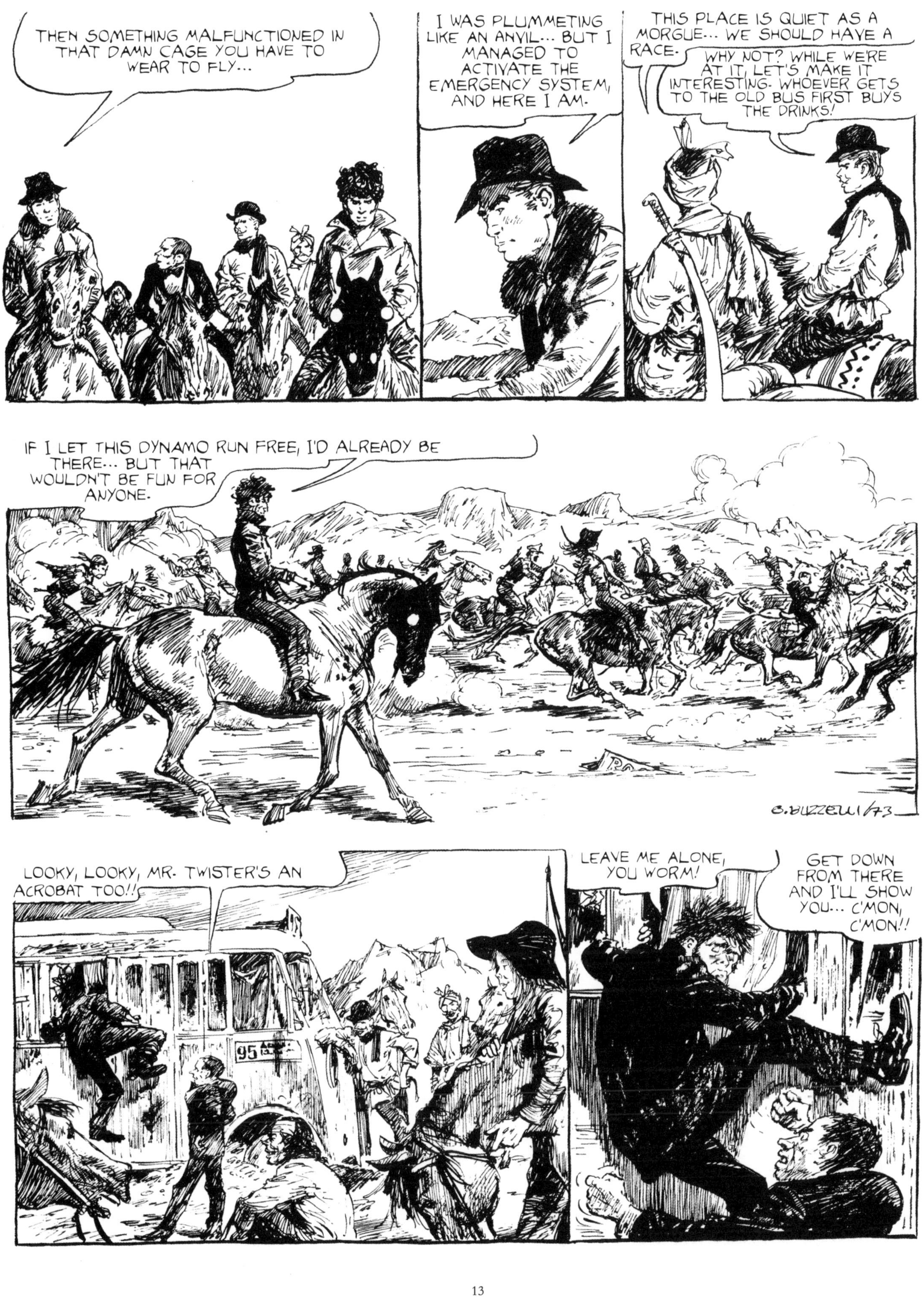
THEN SOMETHING MALFUNCTIONED IN THAT DAMN CAGE YOU HAVE TO WEAR TO FLY...
I WAS PLUMMETING LIKE AN ANVIL... BUT I MANAGED TO ACTIVATE THE EMERGENCY SYSTEM, AND HERE I AM.
THIS PLACE IS QUIET AS A MORGUE... WE SHOULD HAVE A RACE.
WHY NOT? WHILE WE'RE AT IT, LET'S MAKE IT INTERESTING. WHOEVER GETS TO THE OLD BUS FIRST BUYS THE DRINKS!
IF I LET THIS DYNAMO RUN FREE, I'D ALREADY BE THERE... BUT THAT WOULDN'T BE FUN FOR ANYONE.
G. BUZZELLI/73
LOOKY, LOOKY, MR. TWISTER'S AN ACROBAT TOO!!
95
LEAVE ME ALONE, YOU WORM!
GET DOWN FROM THERE AND I'LL SHOW YOU... C'MON, C'MON!!

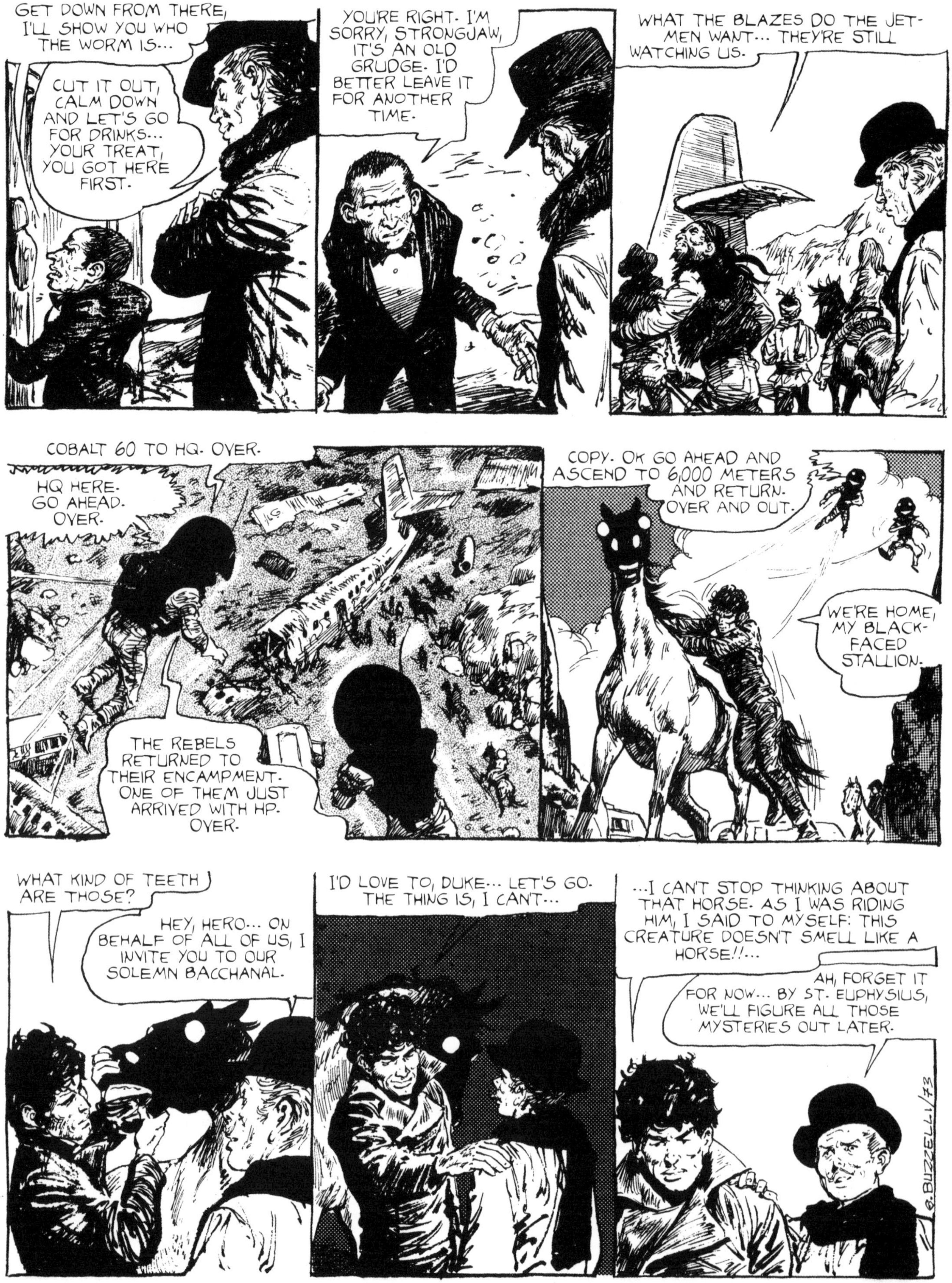
GET DOWN FROM THERE, I'LL SHOW YOU WHO THE WORM IS...
CUT IT OUT, CALM DOWN AND LET'S GO FOR DRINKS... YOUR TREAT, YOU GOT HERE FIRST.
YOU'RE RIGHT. I'M SORRY, STRONGJAW, IT'S AN OLD GRUDGE. I'D BETTER LEAVE IT FOR ANOTHER TIME.
WHAT THE BLAZES DO THE JET-MEN WANT... THEY'RE STILL WATCHING US.
COBALT 60 TO HQ. OVER.
HQ HERE. GO AHEAD. OVER.
THE REBELS RETURNED TO THEIR ENCAMPMENT. ONE OF THEM JUST ARRIVED WITH HP. OVER.
COPY. OK GO AHEAD AND ASCEND TO 6,000 METERS AND RETURN. OVER AND OUT.
WE'RE HOME, MY BLACK-FACED STALLION.
WHAT KIND OF TEETH ARE THOSE?
HEY, HERO... ON BEHALF OF ALL OF US, I INVITE YOU TO OUR SOLEMN BACCHANAL.
I'D LOVE TO, DUKE... LET'S GO. THE THING IS, I CAN'T...
...I CAN'T STOP THINKING ABOUT THAT HORSE. AS I WAS RIDING HIM, I SAID TO MYSELF: THIS CREATURE DOESN'T SMELL LIKE A HORSE!!...
AH, FORGET IT FOR NOW... BY ST. EUPHYSIUS, WE'LL FIGURE ALL THOSE MYSTERIES OUT LATER.
G. BUZZELLI /73

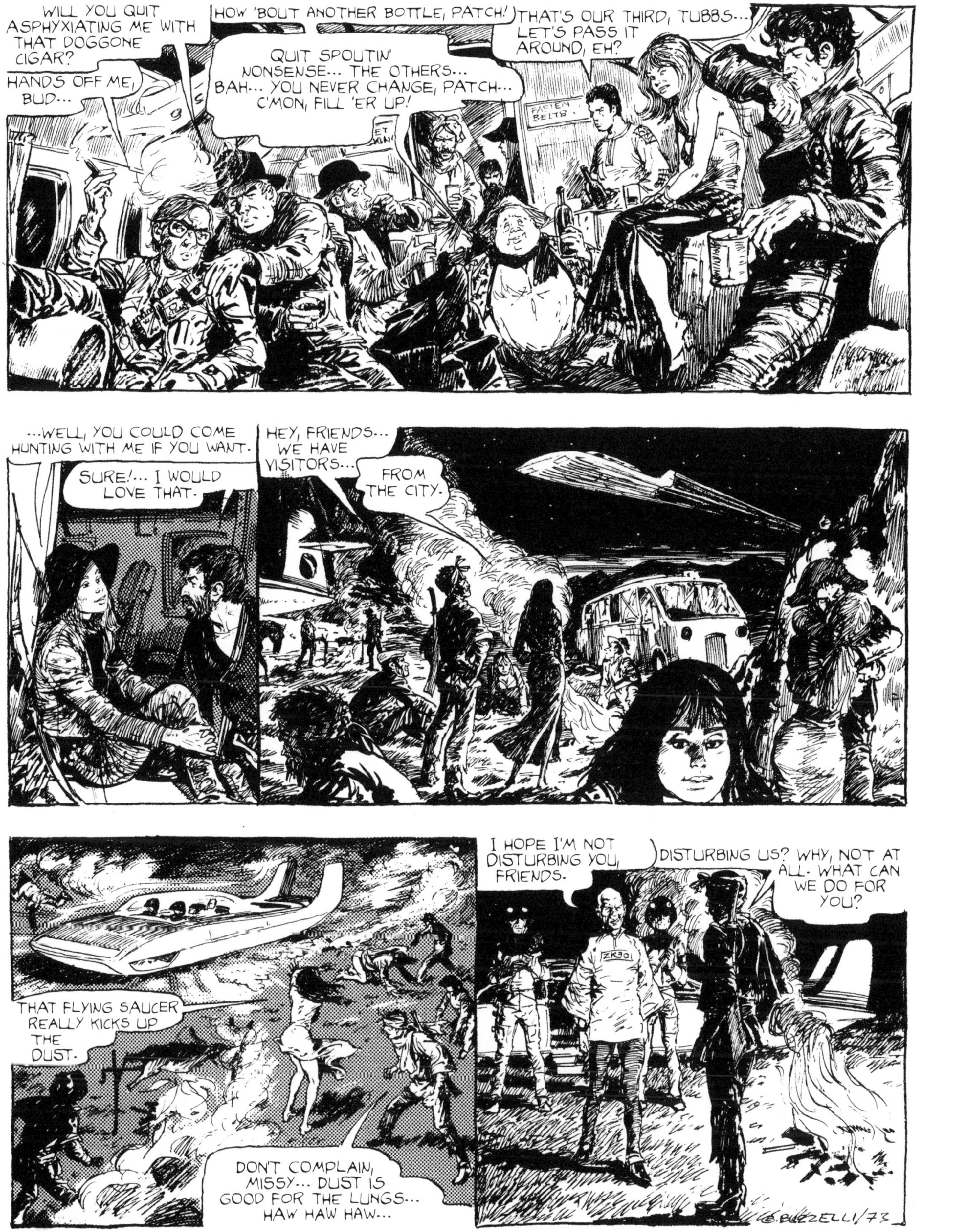
WILL YOU QUIT ASPHYXIATING ME WITH THAT DOGGONE CIGAR?
HANDS OFF ME, BUD...
HOW 'BOUT ANOTHER BOTTLE, PATCH!
QUIT SPOUTIN' NONSENSE... THE OTHERS... BAH... YOU NEVER CHANGE, PATCH... C'MON, FILL 'ER UP!
THAT'S OUR THIRD, TUBBS... LET'S PASS IT AROUND, EH?
...WELL, YOU COULD COME HUNTING WITH ME IF YOU WANT.
SURE!... I WOULD LOVE THAT.
HEY, FRIENDS... WE HAVE VISITORS...
FROM THE CITY.
THAT FLYING SAUCER REALLY KICKS UP THE DUST.
DON'T COMPLAIN, MISSY... DUST IS GOOD FOR THE LUNGS... HAW HAW HAW...
I HOPE I'M NOT DISTURBING YOU, FRIENDS.
DISTURBING US? WHY, NOT AT ALL. WHAT CAN WE DO FOR YOU?

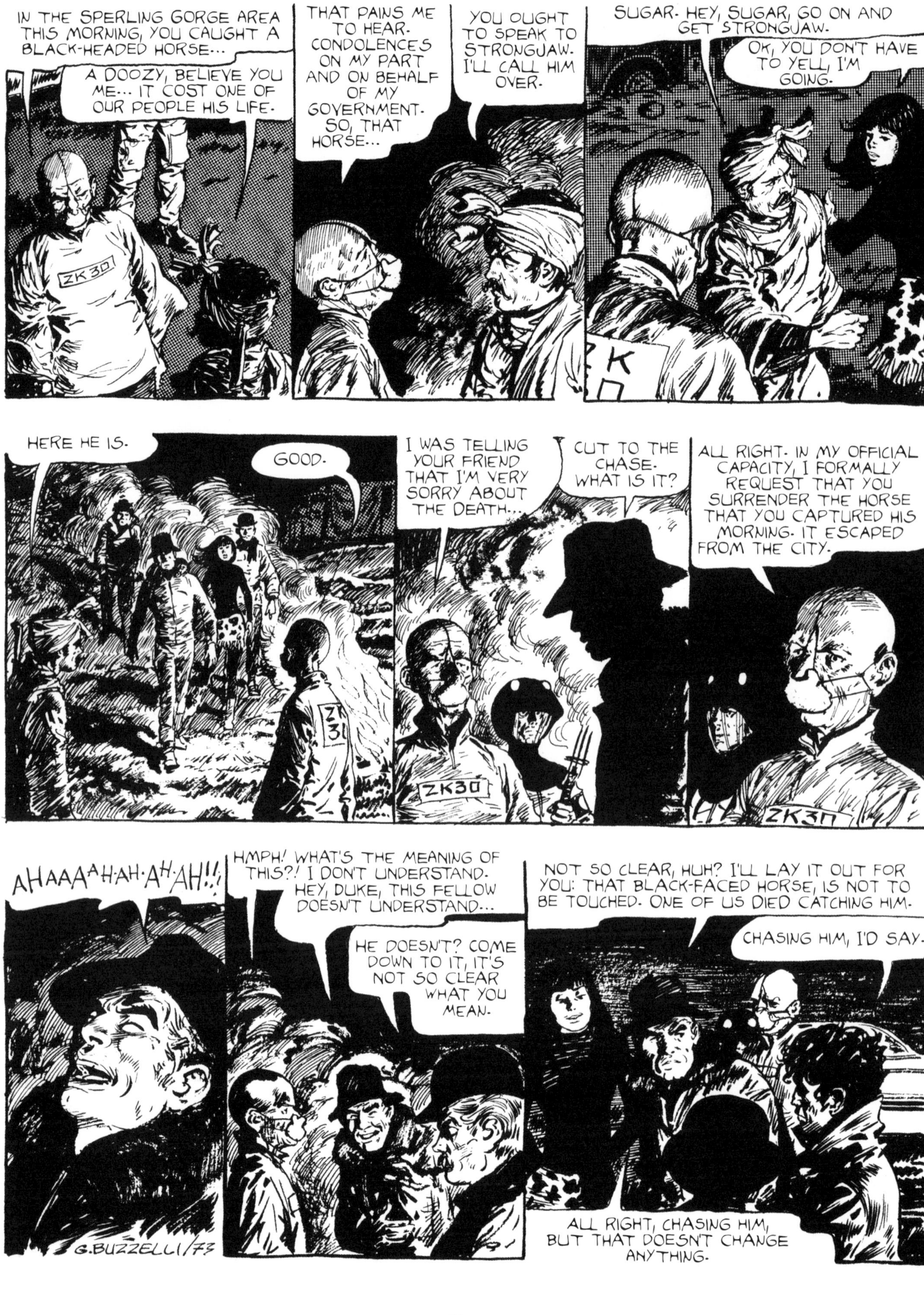
IN THE SPERLING GORGE AREA THIS MORNING, YOU CAUGHT A BLACK-HEADED HORSE...
A DOOZY, BELIEVE YOU ME... IT COST ONE OF OUR PEOPLE HIS LIFE.
ZK30
THAT PAINS ME TO HEAR. CONDOLENCES ON MY PART AND ON BEHALF OF MY GOVERNMENT. SO, THAT HORSE...
YOU OUGHT TO SPEAK TO STRONGJAW. I'LL CALL HIM OVER.
SUGAR. HEY, SUGAR, GO ON AND GET STRONGJAW.
OK, YOU DON'T HAVE TO YELL, I'M GOING.
HERE HE IS.
GOOD.
I WAS TELLING YOUR FRIEND THAT I'M VERY SORRY ABOUT THE DEATH...
CUT TO THE CHASE. WHAT IS IT?
ZK30
ALL RIGHT. IN MY OFFICIAL CAPACITY, I FORMALLY REQUEST THAT YOU SURRENDER THE HORSE THAT YOU CAPTURED HIS MORNING. IT ESCAPED FROM THE CITY.
ZK30
AHAAAAH-AH-AH-AH!!
HMPH! WHAT'S THE MEANING OF THIS?! I DON'T UNDERSTAND. HEY, DUKE, THIS FELLOW DOESN'T UNDERSTAND...
HE DOESN'T? COME DOWN TO IT, IT'S NOT SO CLEAR WHAT YOU MEAN.
G.BUZZELLI/73
NOT SO CLEAR, HUH? I'LL LAY IT OUT FOR YOU: THAT BLACK-FACED HORSE, IS NOT TO BE TOUCHED. ONE OF US DIED CATCHING HIM.
CHASING HIM, I'D SAY.
ALL RIGHT, CHASING HIM, BUT THAT DOESN'T CHANGE ANYTHING.

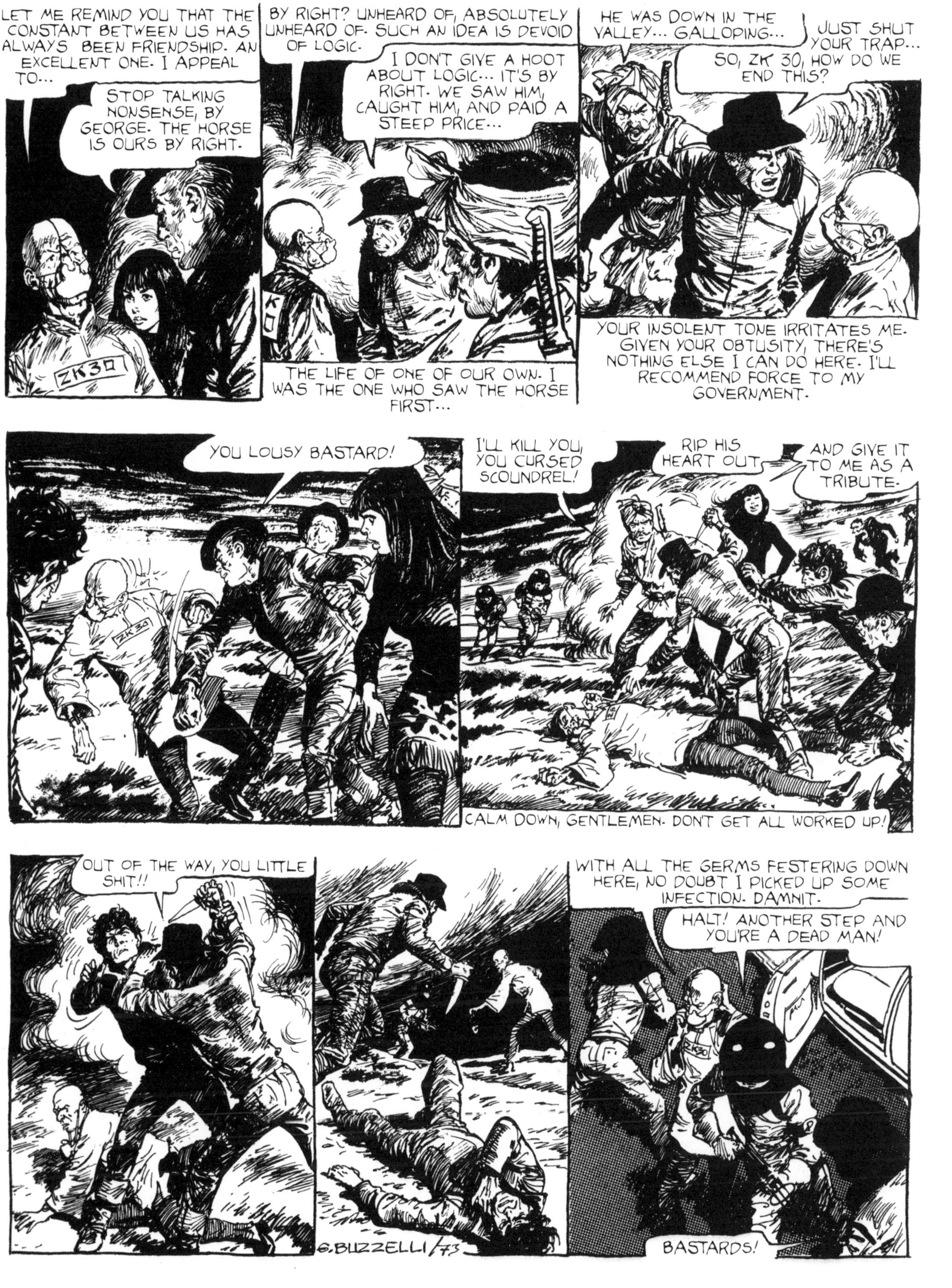
LET ME REMIND YOU THAT THE CONSTANT BETWEEN US HAS ALWAYS BEEN FRIENDSHIP. AN EXCELLENT ONE. I APPEAL TO...
STOP TALKING NONSENSE, BY GEORGE. THE HORSE IS OURS BY RIGHT.
ZK30
BY RIGHT? UNHEARD OF, ABSOLUTELY UNHEARD OF. SUCH AN IDEA IS DEVOID OF LOGIC.
I DON'T GIVE A HOOT ABOUT LOGIC... IT'S BY RIGHT. WE SAW HIM, CAUGHT HIM, AND PAID A STEEP PRICE...
THE LIFE OF ONE OF OUR OWN. I WAS THE ONE WHO SAW THE HORSE FIRST...
HE WAS DOWN IN THE VALLEY... GALLOPING...
JUST SHUT YOUR TRAP...
SO, ZK 30, HOW DO WE END THIS?
YOUR INSOLENT TONE IRRITATES ME. GIVEN YOUR OBTUSITY, THERE'S NOTHING ELSE I CAN DO HERE. I'LL RECOMMEND FORCE TO MY GOVERNMENT.
YOU LOUSY BASTARD!
I'LL KILL YOU, YOU CURSED SCOUNDREL!
RIP HIS HEART OUT
AND GIVE IT TO ME AS A TRIBUTE.
CALM DOWN, GENTLEMEN. DON'T GET ALL WORKED UP!
OUT OF THE WAY, YOU LITTLE SHIT!!
G. BUZZELLI/73
WITH ALL THE GERMS FESTERING DOWN HERE, NO DOUBT I PICKED UP SOME INFECTION. DAMNIT.
HALT! ANOTHER STEP AND YOU'RE A DEAD MAN!
BASTARDS!

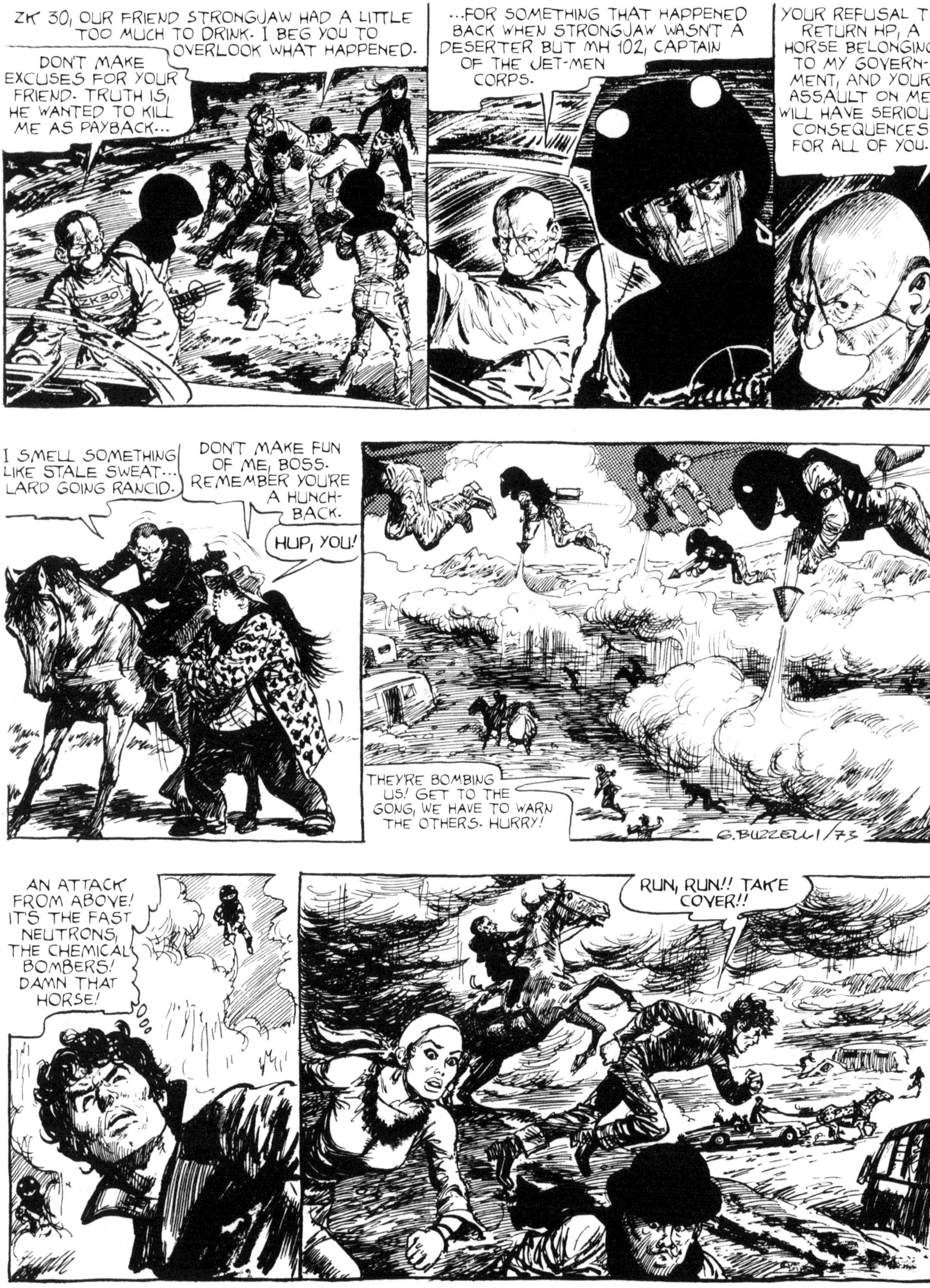
ZK 30, OUR FRIEND STRONGJAW HAD A LITTLE TOO MUCH TO DRINK. I BEG YOU TO OVERLOOK WHAT HAPPENED.
DON'T MAKE EXCUSES FOR YOUR FRIEND. TRUTH IS, HE WANTED TO KILL ME AS PAYBACK...
...FOR SOMETHING THAT HAPPENED BACK WHEN STRONGJAW WASN'T A DESERTER BUT MH 102, CAPTAIN OF THE JET-MEN CORPS.
YOUR REFUSAL TO RETURN HP, A HORSE BELONGING TO MY GOVERNMENT, AND YOUR ASSAULT ON ME WILL HAVE SERIOUS CONSEQUENCES FOR ALL OF YOU.
I SMELL SOMETHING LIKE STALE SWEAT... LARD GOING RANCID.
DON'T MAKE FUN OF ME, BOSS. REMEMBER YOU'RE A HUNCHBACK.
HUP, YOU!
THEY'RE BOMBING US! GET TO THE GONG, WE HAVE TO WARN THE OTHERS. HURRY!
G. BUZZELLI/73
AN ATTACK FROM ABOVE! IT'S THE FAST NEUTRONS, THE CHEMICAL BOMBERS! DAMN THAT HORSE!
RUN, RUN!! TAKE COVER!!

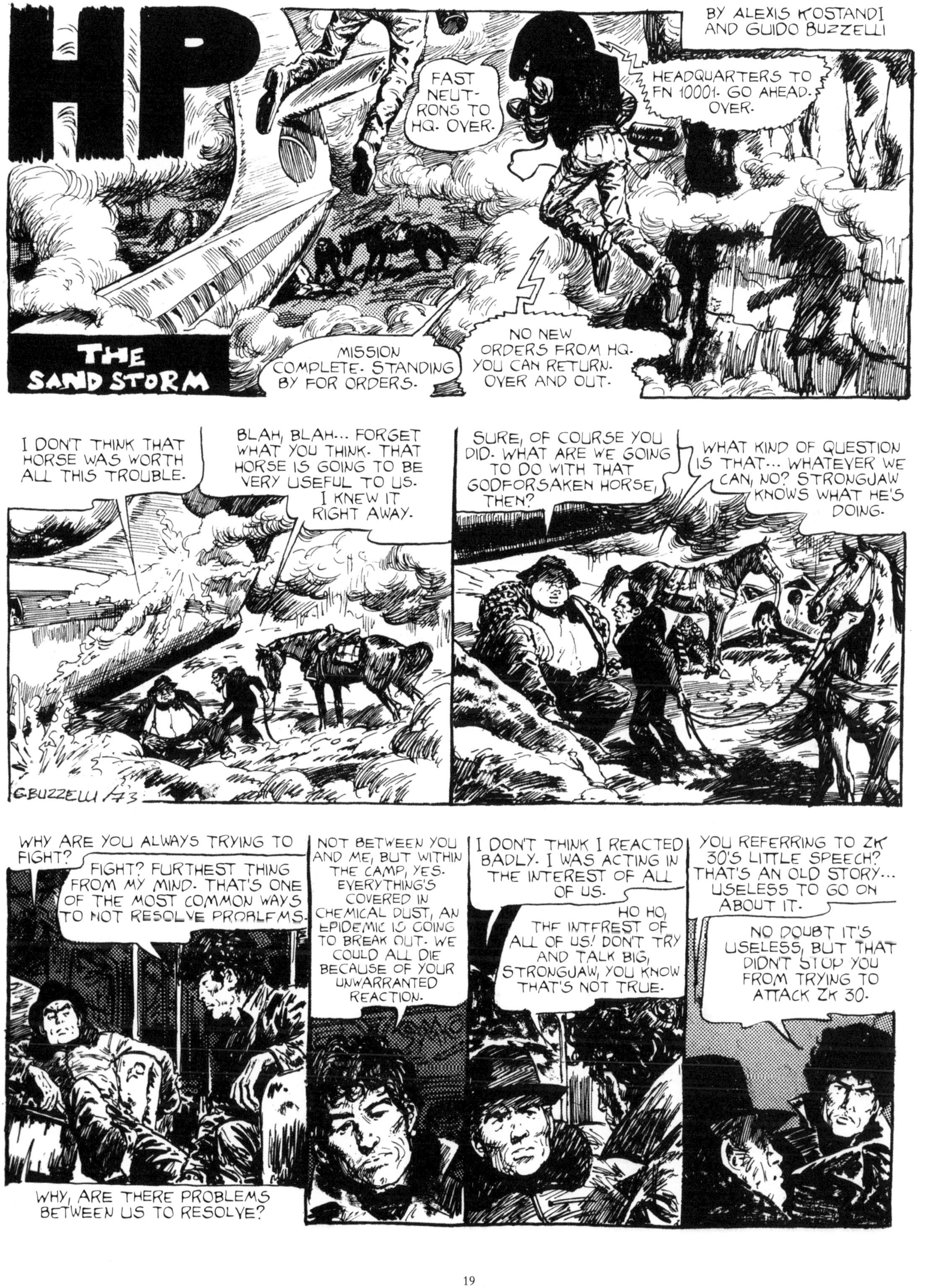
HP
THE SAND STORM
BY ALEXIS KOSTANDI AND GUIDO BUZZELLI
FAST NEUTRONS TO HQ. OVER.
HEADQUARTERS TO FN 10001. GO AHEAD. OVER.
MISSION COMPLETE. STANDING BY FOR ORDERS.
NO NEW ORDERS FROM HQ. YOU CAN RETURN. OVER AND OUT.
I DON'T THINK THAT HORSE WAS WORTH ALL THIS TROUBLE.
BLAH, BLAH... FORGET WHAT YOU THINK. THAT HORSE IS GOING TO BE VERY USEFUL TO US. I KNEW IT RIGHT AWAY.
G.BUZZELLI /73
SURE, OF COURSE YOU DID. WHAT ARE WE GOING TO DO WITH THAT GODFORSAKEN HORSE, THEN?
WHAT KIND OF QUESTION IS THAT... WHATEVER WE CAN, NO? STRONGJAW KNOWS WHAT HE'S DOING.
WHY ARE YOU ALWAYS TRYING TO FIGHT?
FIGHT? FURTHEST THING FROM MY MIND. THAT'S ONE OF THE MOST COMMON WAYS TO NOT RESOLVE PROBLEMS.
WHY, ARE THERE PROBLEMS BETWEEN US TO RESOLVE?
NOT BETWEEN YOU AND ME, BUT WITHIN THE CAMP, YES. EVERYTHING'S COVERED IN CHEMICAL DUST, AN EPIDEMIC IS GOING TO BREAK OUT. WE COULD ALL DIE BECAUSE OF YOUR UNWARRANTED REACTION.
I DON'T THINK I REACTED BADLY. I WAS ACTING IN THE INTEREST OF ALL OF US.
HO HO, THE INTEREST OF ALL OF US! DON'T TRY AND TALK BIG, STRONGJAW, YOU KNOW THAT'S NOT TRUE.
YOU REFERRING TO ZK 30'S LITTLE SPEECH? THAT'S AN OLD STORY... USELESS TO GO ON ABOUT IT.
NO DOUBT IT'S USELESS, BUT THAT DIDN'T STOP YOU FROM TRYING TO ATTACK ZK 30.

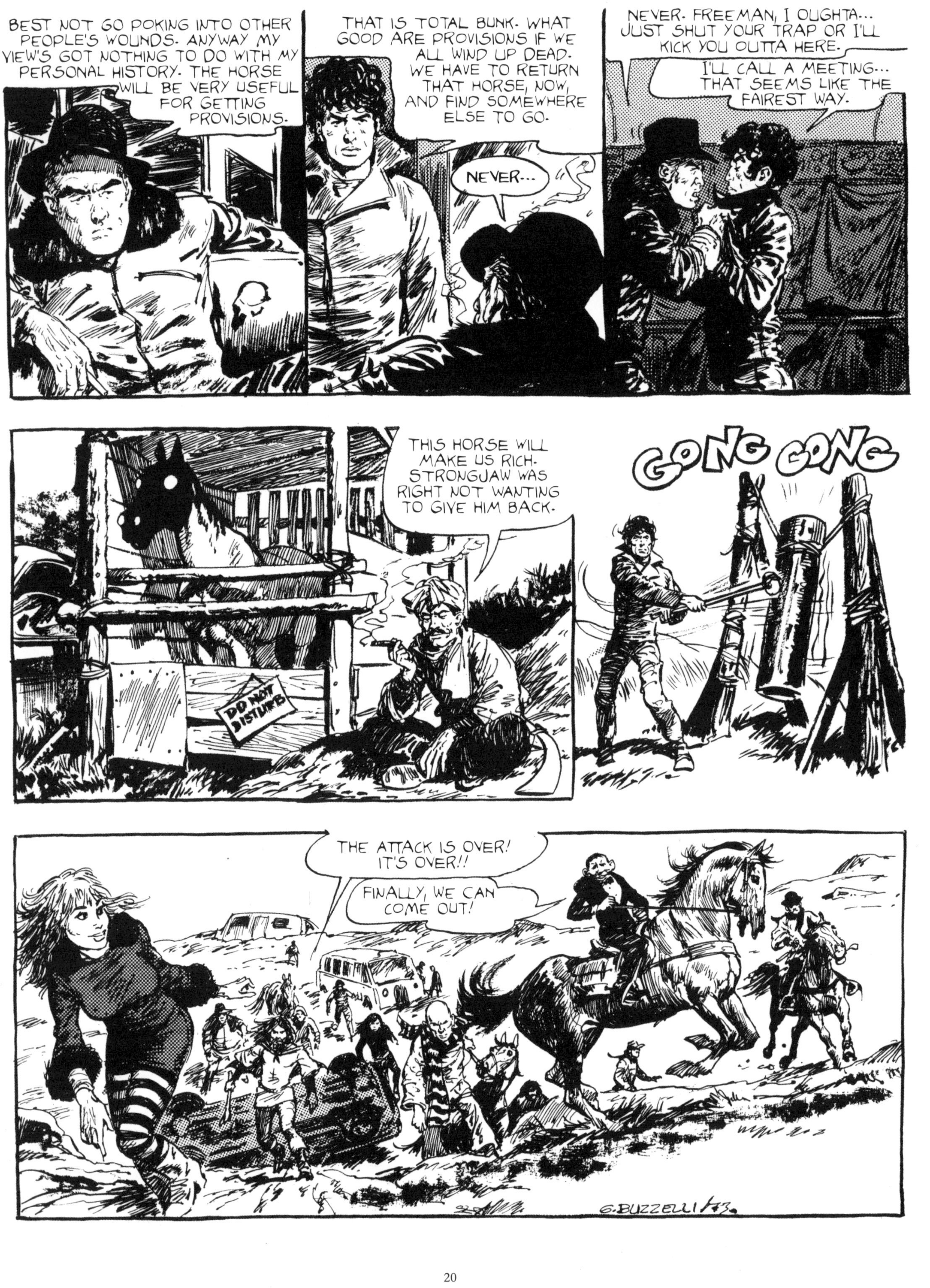
BEST NOT GO POKING INTO OTHER PEOPLE'S WOUNDS. ANYWAY MY VIEW'S GOT NOTHING TO DO WITH MY PERSONAL HISTORY. THE HORSE WILL BE VERY USEFUL FOR GETTING PROVISIONS.
THAT IS TOTAL BUNK. WHAT GOOD ARE PROVISIONS IF WE ALL WIND UP DEAD. WE HAVE TO RETURN THAT HORSE, NOW, AND FIND SOMEWHERE ELSE TO GO.
NEVER...
NEVER. FREEMAN, I OUGHTA... JUST SHUT YOUR TRAP OR I'LL KICK YOU OUTTA HERE.
I'LL CALL A MEETING... THAT SEEMS LIKE THE FAIREST WAY.
THIS HORSE WILL MAKE US RICH. STRONGJAW WAS RIGHT NOT WANTING TO GIVE HIM BACK.
DO NOT DISTURB
GONG GONG
THE ATTACK IS OVER! IT'S OVER!!
FINALLY, WE CAN COME OUT!

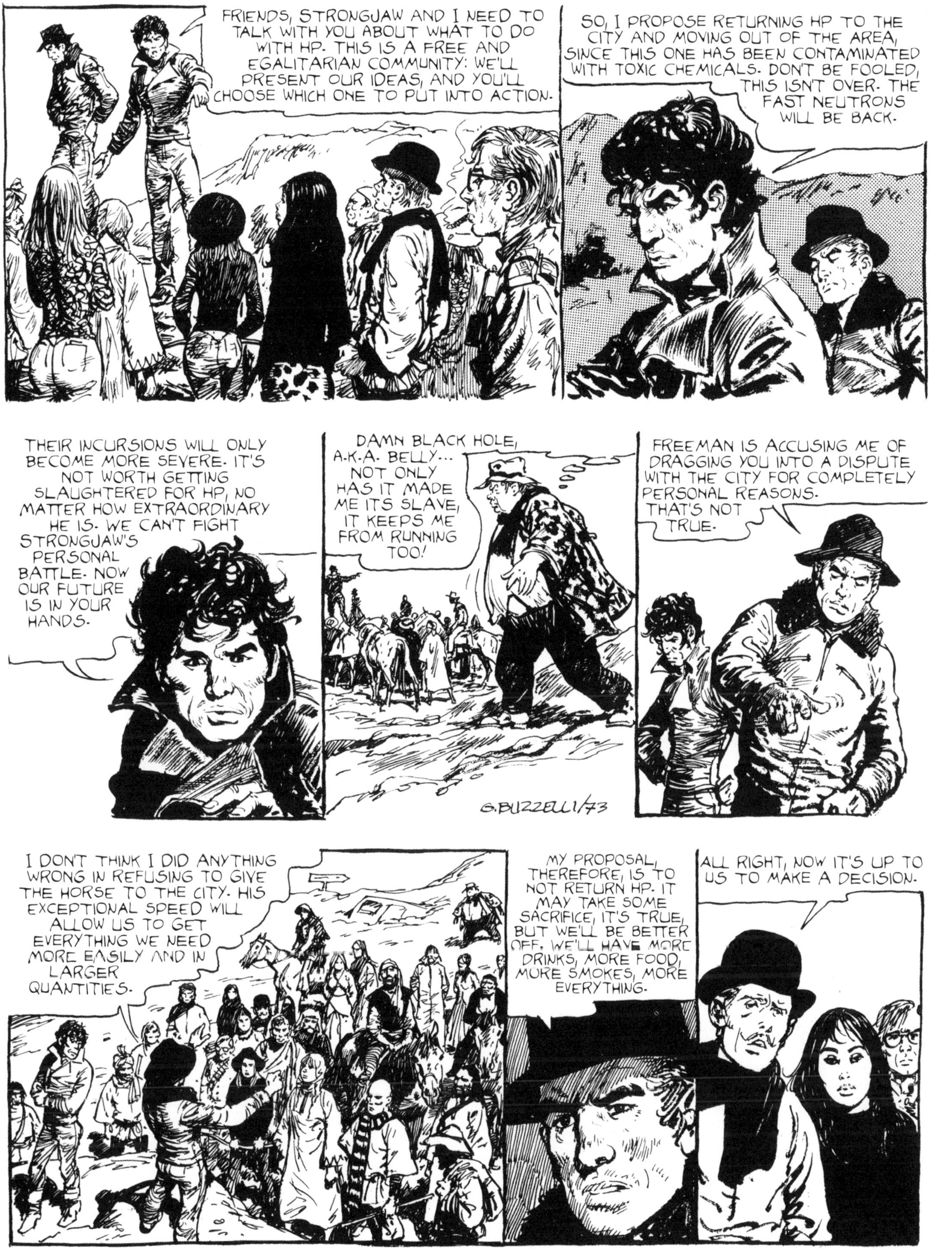
FRIENDS, STRONGJAW AND I NEED TO TALK WITH YOU ABOUT WHAT TO DO WITH HP. THIS IS A FREE AND EGALITARIAN COMMUNITY: WE'LL PRESENT OUR IDEAS, AND YOU'LL CHOOSE WHICH ONE TO PUT INTO ACTION.
SO, I PROPOSE RETURNING HP TO THE CITY AND MOVING OUT OF THE AREA, SINCE THIS ONE HAS BEEN CONTAMINATED WITH TOXIC CHEMICALS. DON'T BE FOOLED, THIS ISN'T OVER. THE FAST NEUTRONS WILL BE BACK.
THEIR INCURSIONS WILL ONLY BECOME MORE SEVERE. IT'S NOT WORTH GETTING SLAUGHTERED FOR HP, NO MATTER HOW EXTRAORDINARY HE IS. WE CAN'T FIGHT STRONGJAW'S PERSONAL BATTLE. NOW OUR FUTURE IS IN YOUR HANDS.
DAMN BLACK HOLE, A.K.A. BELLY... NOT ONLY HAS IT MADE ME ITS SLAVE, IT KEEPS ME FROM RUNNING TOO!
G. BUZZELLI/73
FREEMAN IS ACCUSING ME OF DRAGGING YOU INTO A DISPUTE WITH THE CITY FOR COMPLETELY PERSONAL REASONS. THAT'S NOT TRUE.
I DON'T THINK I DID ANYTHING WRONG IN REFUSING TO GIVE THE HORSE TO THE CITY. HIS EXCEPTIONAL SPEED WILL ALLOW US TO GET EVERYTHING WE NEED MORE EASILY AND IN LARGER QUANTITIES.
MY PROPOSAL, THEREFORE, IS TO NOT RETURN HP. IT MAY TAKE SOME SACRIFICE, IT'S TRUE, BUT WE'LL BE BETTER OFF. WE'LL HAVE MORE DRINKS, MORE FOOD, MORE SMOKES, MORE EVERYTHING.
ALL RIGHT, NOW IT'S UP TO US TO MAKE A DECISION.

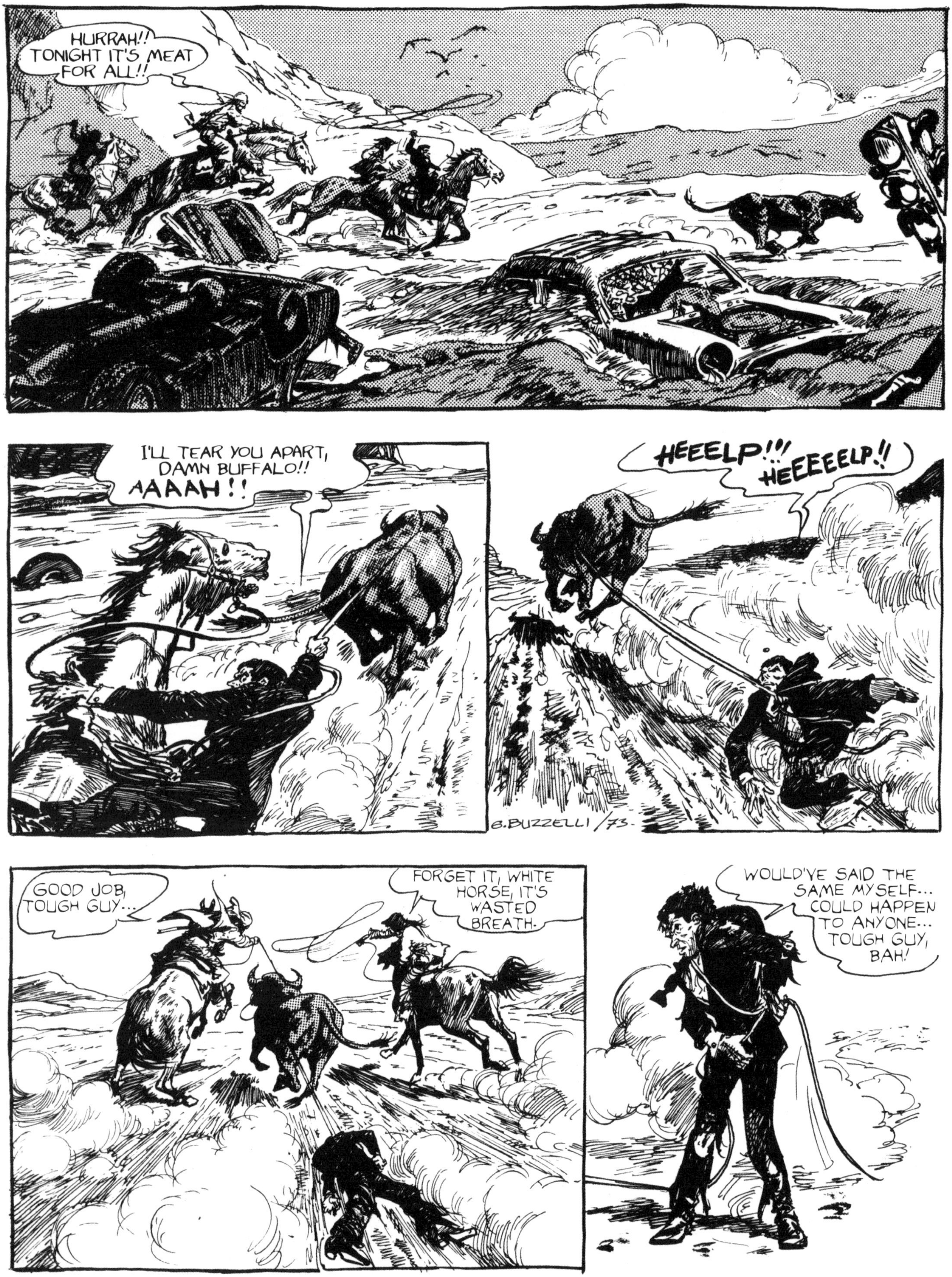
HURRAH!! TONIGHT IT'S MEAT FOR ALL!!
I'LL TEAR YOU APART, DAMN BUFFALO!! AAAAH!!
HEEELP!!! HEEEEELP!!
G. BUZZELLI /73
GOOD JOB, TOUGH GUY...
FORGET IT, WHITE HORSE, IT'S WASTED BREATH.
WOULD'VE SAID THE SAME MYSELF... COULD HAPPEN TO ANYONE... TOUGH GUY, BAH!

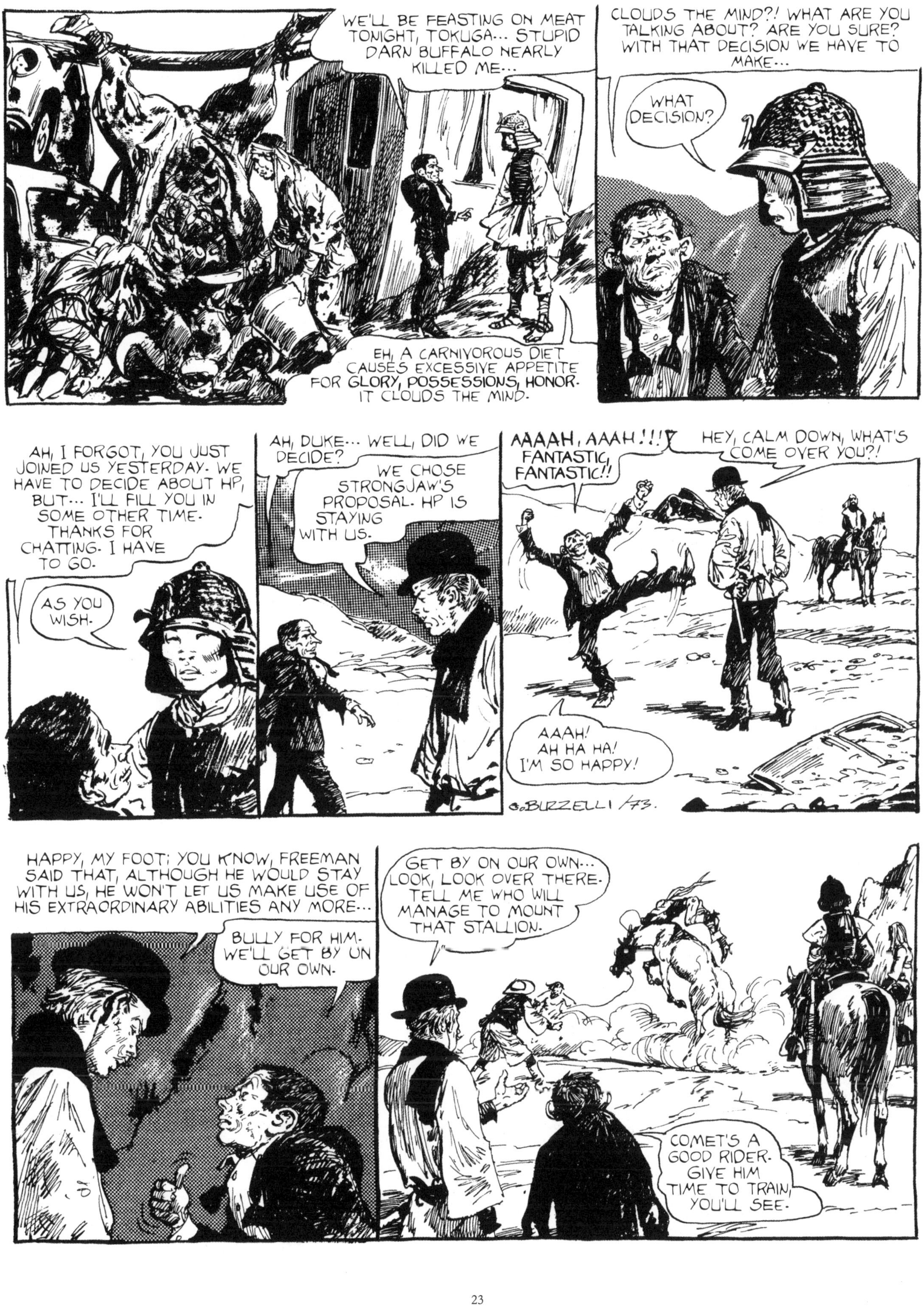
WE'LL BE FEASTING ON MEAT TONIGHT, TOKUGA... STUPID DARN BUFFALO NEARLY KILLED ME...
EH, A CARNIVOROUS DIET CAUSES EXCESSIVE APPETITE FOR GLORY, POSSESSIONS, HONOR. IT CLOUDS THE MIND.
CLOUDS THE MIND?! WHAT ARE YOU TALKING ABOUT? ARE YOU SURE? WITH THAT DECISION WE HAVE TO MAKE...
WHAT DECISION?
AH, I FORGOT, YOU JUST JOINED US YESTERDAY. WE HAVE TO DECIDE ABOUT HP, BUT... I'LL FILL YOU IN SOME OTHER TIME. THANKS FOR CHATTING. I HAVE TO GO.
AS YOU WISH.
AH, DUKE... WELL, DID WE DECIDE?
WE CHOSE STRONGJAW'S PROPOSAL. HP IS STAYING WITH US.
AAAAH, AAAH!!! FANTASTIC, FANTASTIC!!
HEY, CALM DOWN, WHAT'S COME OVER YOU?!
AAAH! AH HA HA! I'M SO HAPPY!
G. BURZELLI /73.
HAPPY, MY FOOT; YOU KNOW, FREEMAN SAID THAT, ALTHOUGH HE WOULD STAY WITH US, HE WON'T LET US MAKE USE OF HIS EXTRAORDINARY ABILITIES ANY MORE...
BULLY FOR HIM. WE'LL GET BY ON OUR OWN.
GET BY ON OUR OWN... LOOK, LOOK OVER THERE. TELL ME WHO WILL MANAGE TO MOUNT THAT STALLION.
COMET'S A GOOD RIDER. GIVE HIM TIME TO TRAIN, YOU'LL SEE.

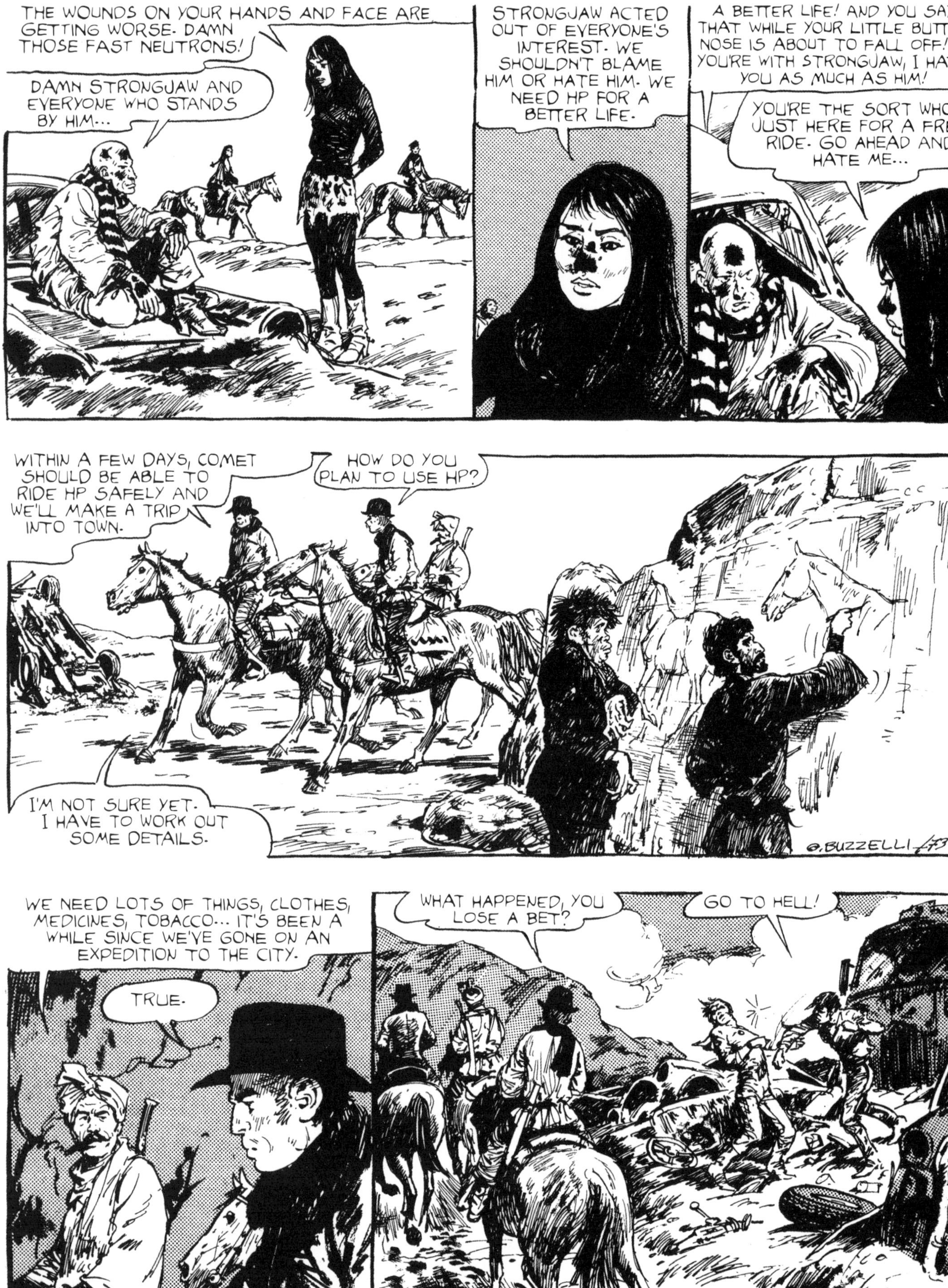
THE WOUNDS ON YOUR HANDS AND FACE ARE GETTING WORSE- DAMN THOSE FAST NEUTRONS!
DAMN STRONGJAW AND EVERYONE WHO STANDS BY HIM...
STRONGJAW ACTED OUT OF EVERYONE'S INTEREST- WE SHOULDN'T BLAME HIM OR HATE HIM- WE NEED HP FOR A BETTER LIFE-
A BETTER LIFE! AND YOU SAY THAT WHILE YOUR LITTLE BUTTON NOSE IS ABOUT TO FALL OFF! IF YOU'RE WITH STRONGJAW, I HATE YOU AS MUCH AS HIM!
YOU'RE THE SORT WHO'S JUST HERE FOR A FREE RIDE- GO AHEAD AND HATE ME...
WITHIN A FEW DAYS, COMET SHOULD BE ABLE TO RIDE HP SAFELY AND WE'LL MAKE A TRIP INTO TOWN-
HOW DO YOU PLAN TO USE HP?
I'M NOT SURE YET- I HAVE TO WORK OUT SOME DETAILS-
G. BUZZELLI 73
WE NEED LOTS OF THINGS, CLOTHES, MEDICINES, TOBACCO... IT'S BEEN A WHILE SINCE WE'VE GONE ON AN EXPEDITION TO THE CITY-
TRUE-
WHAT HAPPENED, YOU LOSE A BET?
GO TO HELL!

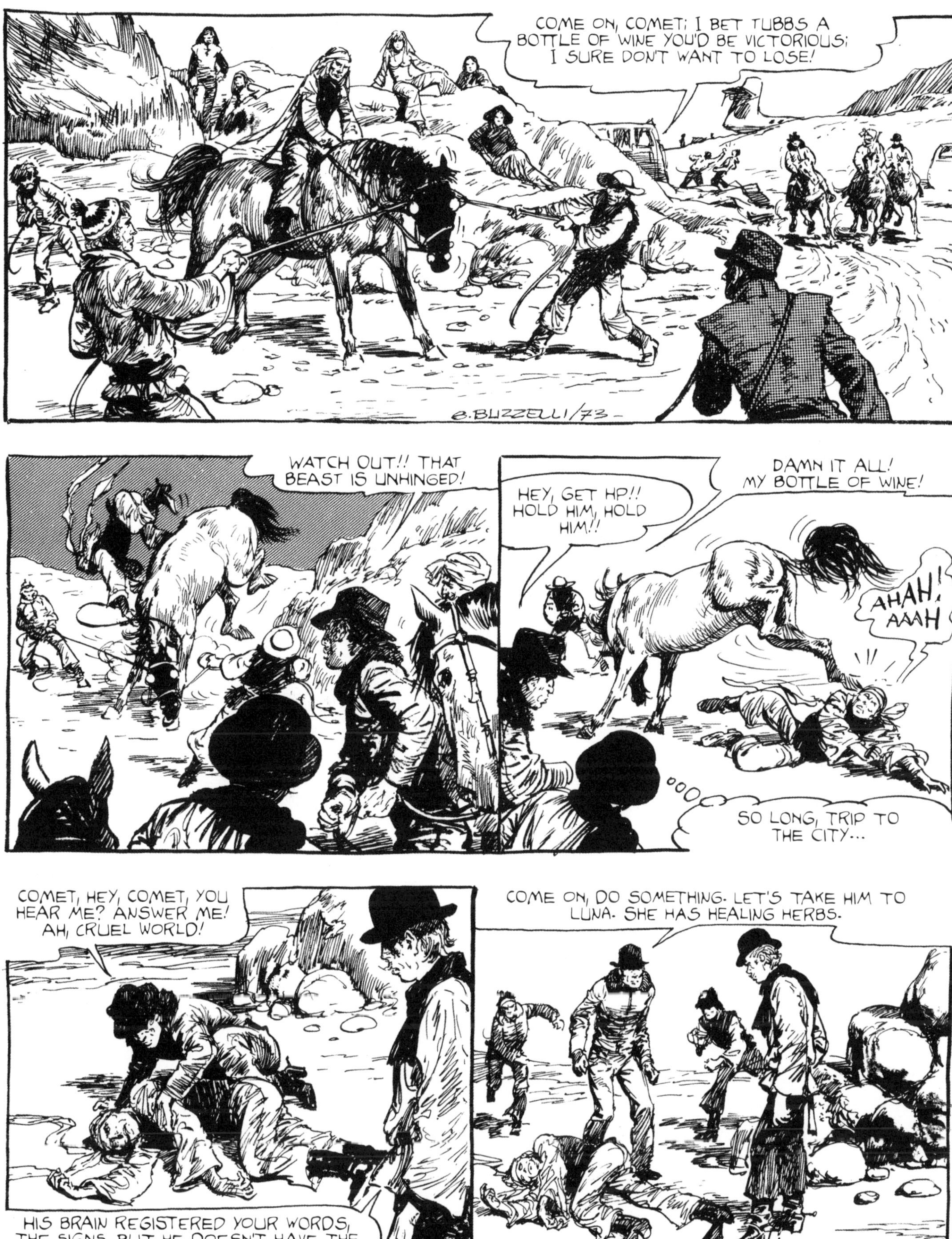

COME ON, COMET; I BET TUBBS A BOTTLE OF WINE YOU'D BE VICTORIOUS; I SURE DON'T WANT TO LOSE!
G. BUZZELLI/73
WATCH OUT!! THAT BEAST IS UNHINGED!
HEY, GET HP!! HOLD HIM, HOLD HIM!!
DAMN IT ALL! MY BOTTLE OF WINE!
AHAH! AAAH
!!!
SO LONG, TRIP TO THE CITY...
COMET, HEY, COMET, YOU HEAR ME? ANSWER ME! AH, CRUEL WORLD!
HIS BRAIN REGISTERED YOUR WORDS, THE SIGNS, BUT HE DOESN'T HAVE THE STRENGTH TO RESPOND. LOOK AT HIS EYES, HE'S GONE.
COME ON, DO SOMETHING. LET'S TAKE HIM TO LUNA. SHE HAS HEALING HERBS.
EH... IT WOULD BE FUTILE...

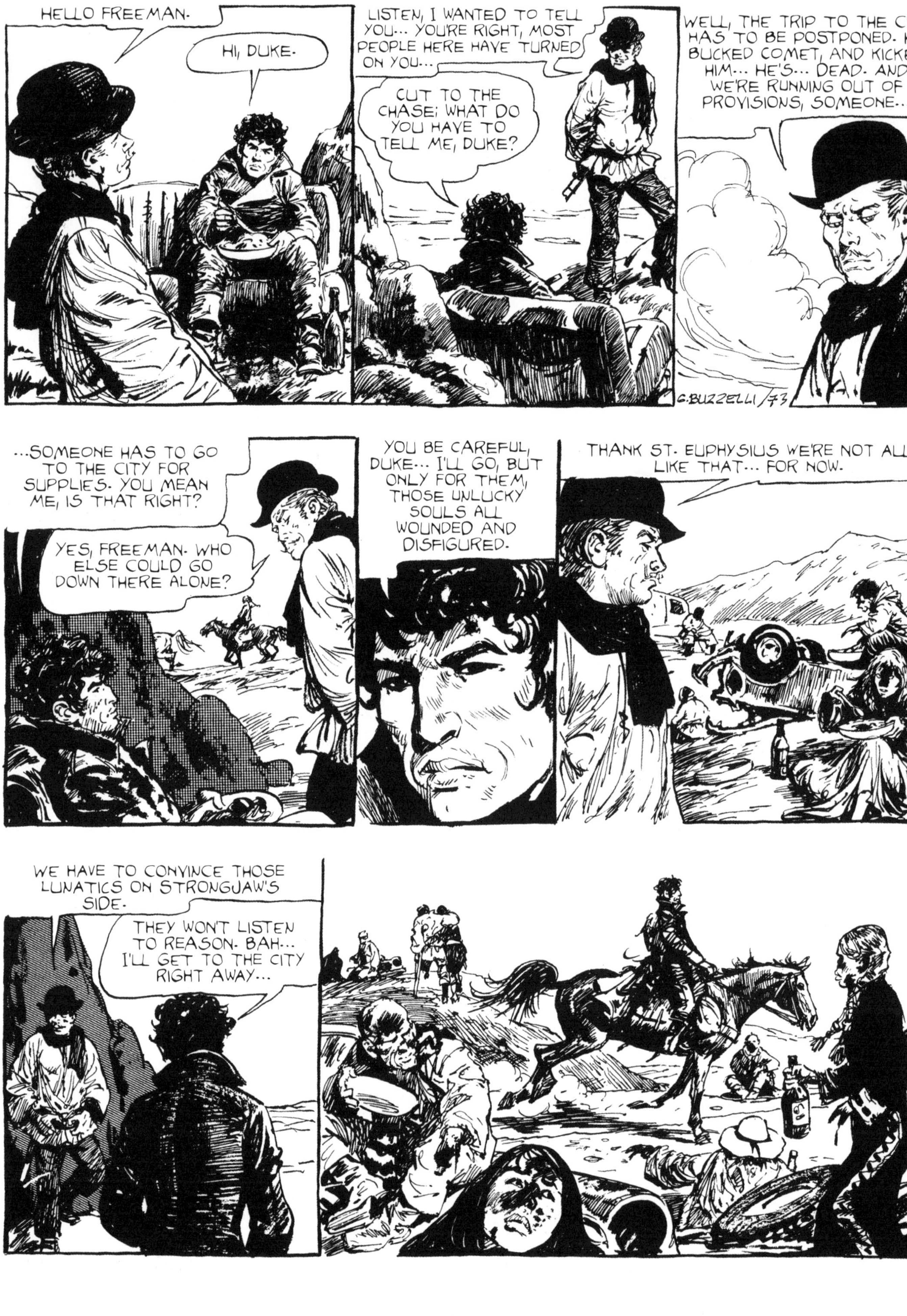
HELLO FREEMAN.
HI, DUKE.
LISTEN, I WANTED TO TELL YOU... YOU'RE RIGHT, MOST PEOPLE HERE HAVE TURNED ON YOU...
CUT TO THE CHASE; WHAT DO YOU HAVE TO TELL ME, DUKE?
WELL, THE TRIP TO THE CITY HAS TO BE POSTPONED. HP BUCKED COMET, AND KICKED HIM... HE'S... DEAD. AND WE'RE RUNNING OUT OF PROVISIONS, SOMEONE...
G. BUZZELLI/73
...SOMEONE HAS TO GO TO THE CITY FOR SUPPLIES. YOU MEAN ME, IS THAT RIGHT?
YES, FREEMAN. WHO ELSE COULD GO DOWN THERE ALONE?
YOU BE CAREFUL, DUKE... I'LL GO, BUT ONLY FOR THEM, THOSE UNLUCKY SOULS ALL WOUNDED AND DISFIGURED.
THANK ST. EUPHYSIUS WE'RE NOT ALL LIKE THAT... FOR NOW.
WE HAVE TO CONVINCE THOSE LUNATICS ON STRONGJAW'S SIDE.
THEY WON'T LISTEN TO REASON. BAH... I'LL GET TO THE CITY RIGHT AWAY...

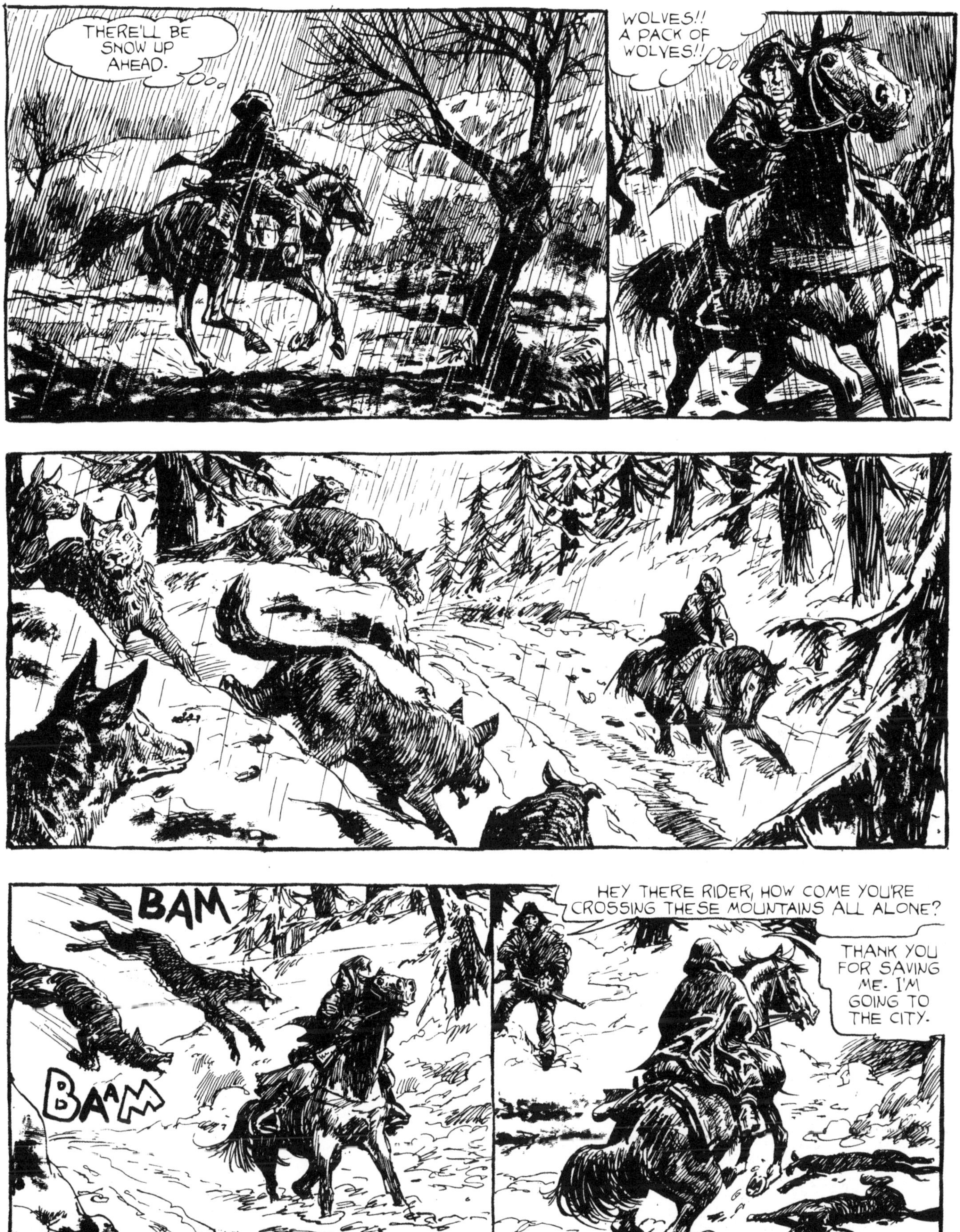
THERE'LL BE SNOW UP AHEAD.
WOLVES!! A PACK OF WOLVES!!
BAM
BAAM
HEY THERE RIDER, HOW COME YOU'RE CROSSING THESE MOUNTAINS ALL ALONE?
THANK YOU FOR SAVING ME. I'M GOING TO THE CITY.
G. BUZZELLI /73

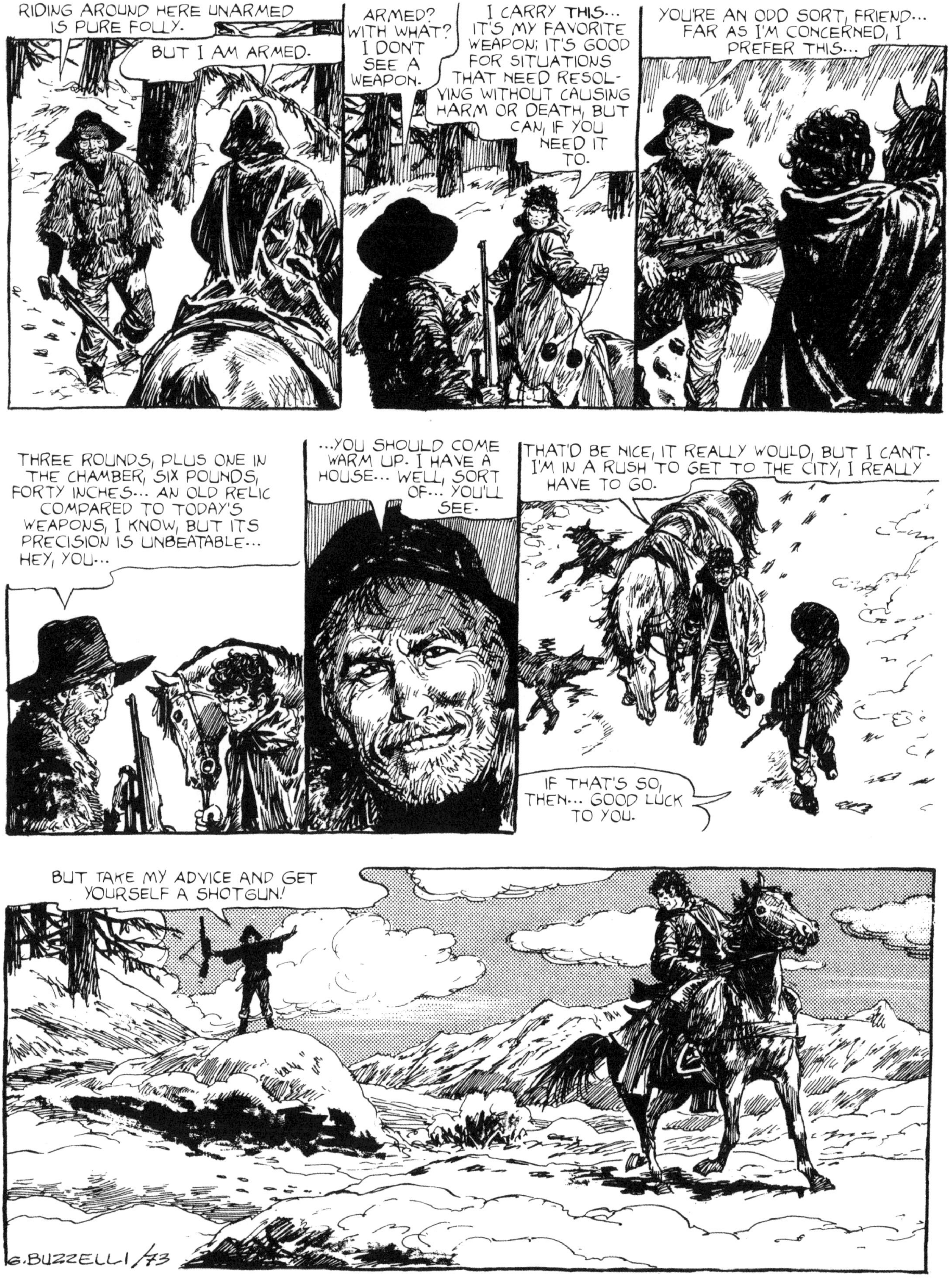
RIDING AROUND HERE UNARMED IS PURE FOLLY.
BUT I AM ARMED.
ARMED? WITH WHAT? I DON'T SEE A WEAPON.
I CARRY THIS... IT'S MY FAVORITE WEAPON; IT'S GOOD FOR SITUATIONS THAT NEED RESOLVING WITHOUT CAUSING HARM OR DEATH, BUT CAN, IF YOU NEED IT TO.
YOU'RE AN ODD SORT, FRIEND... FAR AS I'M CONCERNED, I PREFER THIS...
THREE ROUNDS, PLUS ONE IN THE CHAMBER, SIX POUNDS, FORTY INCHES... AN OLD RELIC COMPARED TO TODAY'S WEAPONS, I KNOW, BUT ITS PRECISION IS UNBEATABLE... HEY, YOU...
...YOU SHOULD COME WARM UP. I HAVE A HOUSE... WELL, SORT OF... YOU'LL SEE.
THAT'D BE NICE, IT REALLY WOULD, BUT I CAN'T. I'M IN A RUSH TO GET TO THE CITY, I REALLY HAVE TO GO.
IF THAT'S SO, THEN... GOOD LUCK TO YOU.
BUT TAKE MY ADVICE AND GET YOURSELF A SHOTGUN!
G. BUZZELLI /73

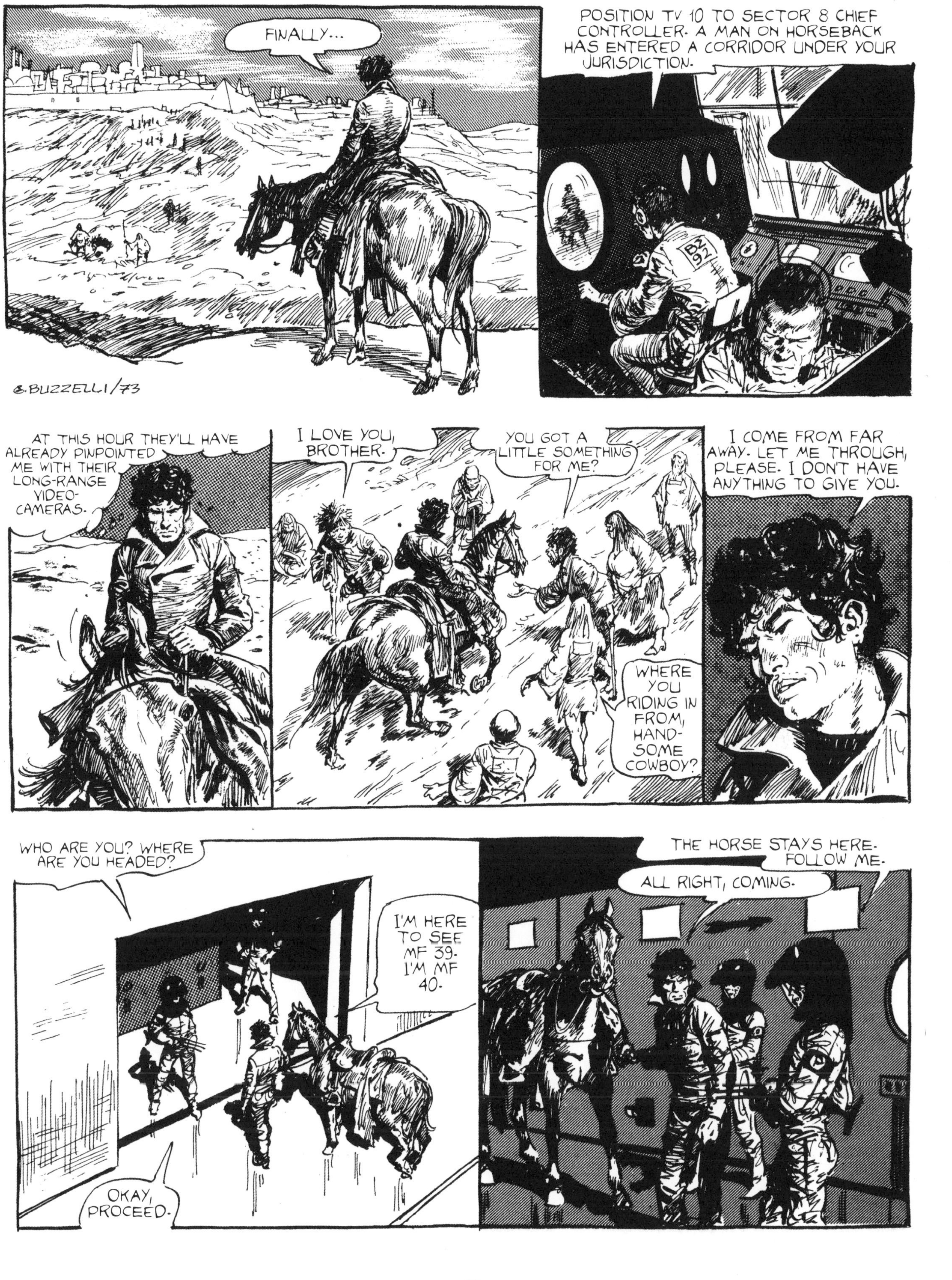
FINALLY...
G. BUZZELLI/73
POSITION TV 10 TO SECTOR 8 CHIEF CONTROLLER. A MAN ON HORSEBACK HAS ENTERED A CORRIDOR UNDER YOUR JURISDICTION.
AT THIS HOUR THEY'LL HAVE ALREADY PINPOINTED ME WITH THEIR LONG-RANGE VIDEO-CAMERAS.
I LOVE YOU, BROTHER.
YOU GOT A LITTLE SOMETHING FOR ME?
WHERE YOU RIDING IN FROM, HAND-SOME COWBOY?
I COME FROM FAR AWAY. LET ME THROUGH, PLEASE. I DON'T HAVE ANYTHING TO GIVE YOU.
WHO ARE YOU? WHERE ARE YOU HEADED?
I'M HERE TO SEE MF 39. I'M MF 40.
OKAY, PROCEED.
THE HORSE STAYS HERE. FOLLOW ME.
ALL RIGHT, COMING.

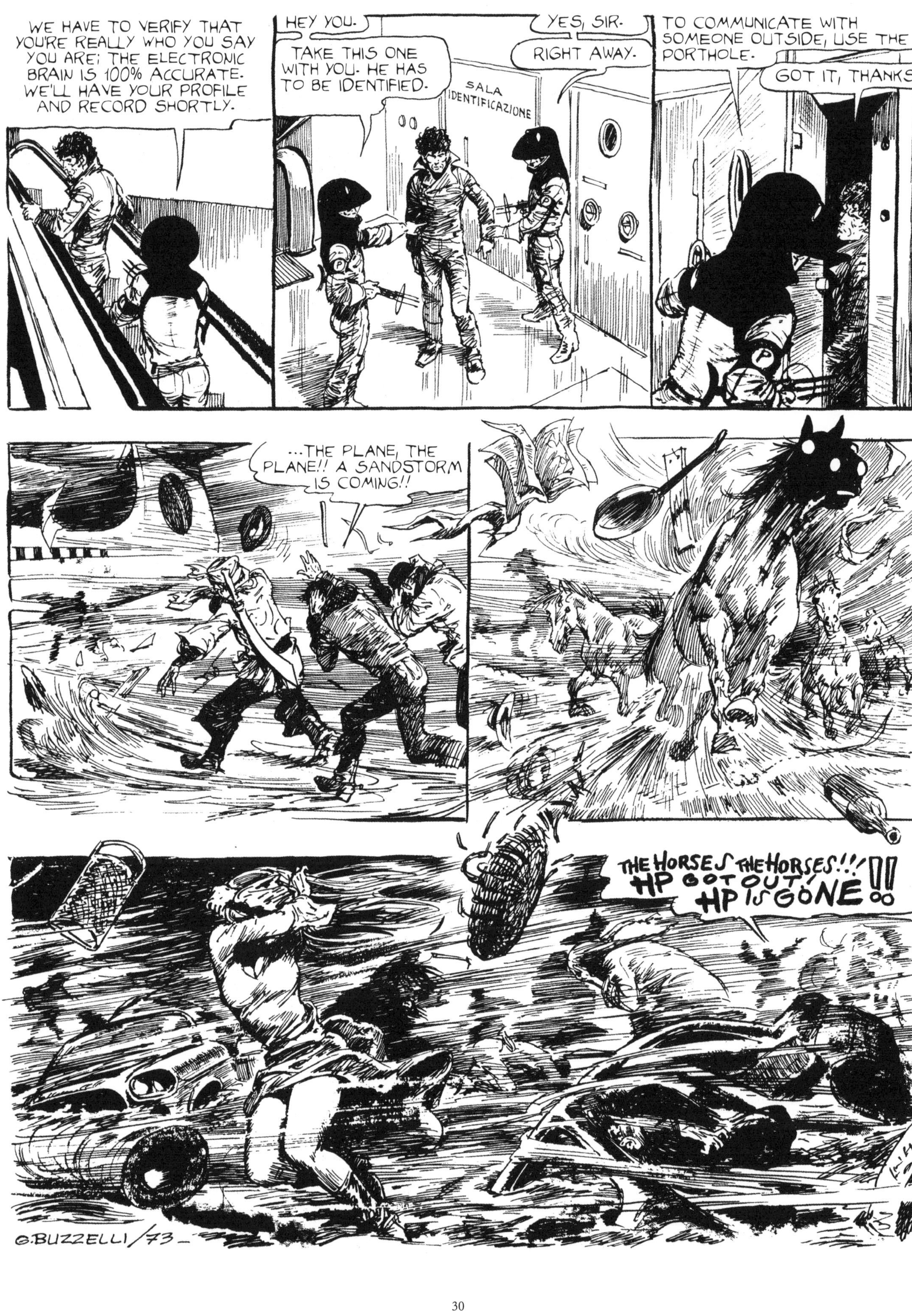
WE HAVE TO VERIFY THAT YOU'RE REALLY WHO YOU SAY YOU ARE; THE ELECTRONIC BRAIN IS 100% ACCURATE. WE'LL HAVE YOUR PROFILE AND RECORD SHORTLY.
HEY YOU.
TAKE THIS ONE WITH YOU. HE HAS TO BE IDENTIFIED.
SALA IDENTIFICAZIONE
YES, SIR.
RIGHT AWAY.
TO COMMUNICATE WITH SOMEONE OUTSIDE, USE THE PORTHOLE.
GOT IT, THANKS.
...THE PLANE, THE PLANE!! A SANDSTORM IS COMING!!
THE HORSES THE HORSES!!! HP GOT OUT! HP IS GONE!!
G.BUZZELLI/73

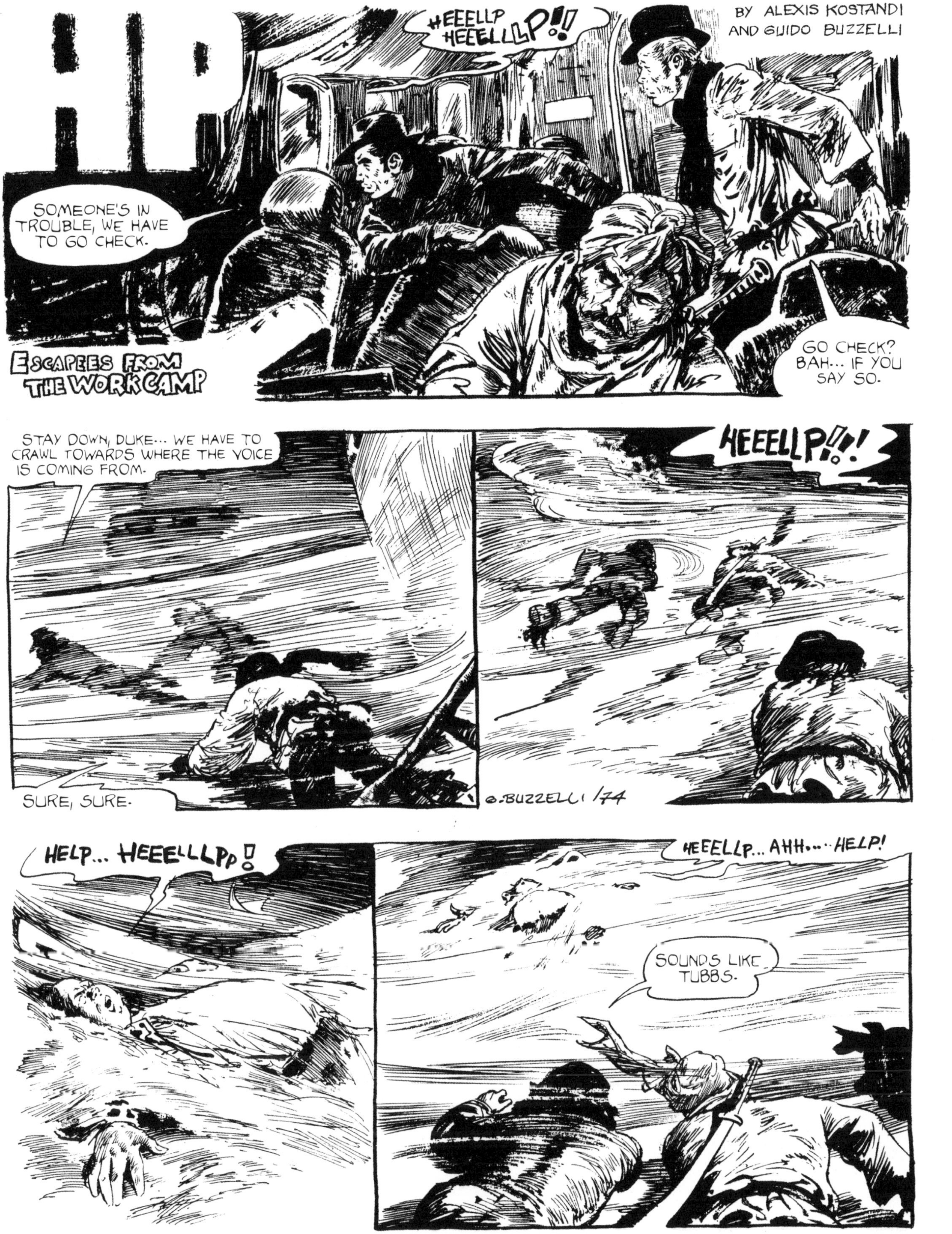
HEEELLP HEEELLLLP!!
BY ALEXIS KOSTANDI AND GUIDO BUZZELLI
SOMEONE'S IN TROUBLE, WE HAVE TO GO CHECK.
ESCAPEES FROM THE WORK CAMP
GO CHECK? BAH... IF YOU SAY SO.
STAY DOWN, DUKE... WE HAVE TO CRAWL TOWARDS WHERE THE VOICE IS COMING FROM.
SURE, SURE.
HEEELLP!!!
G. BUZZELLI /74
HELP... HEEELLLPP!
HEEELLP... AHH... HELP!
SOUNDS LIKE TUBBS.

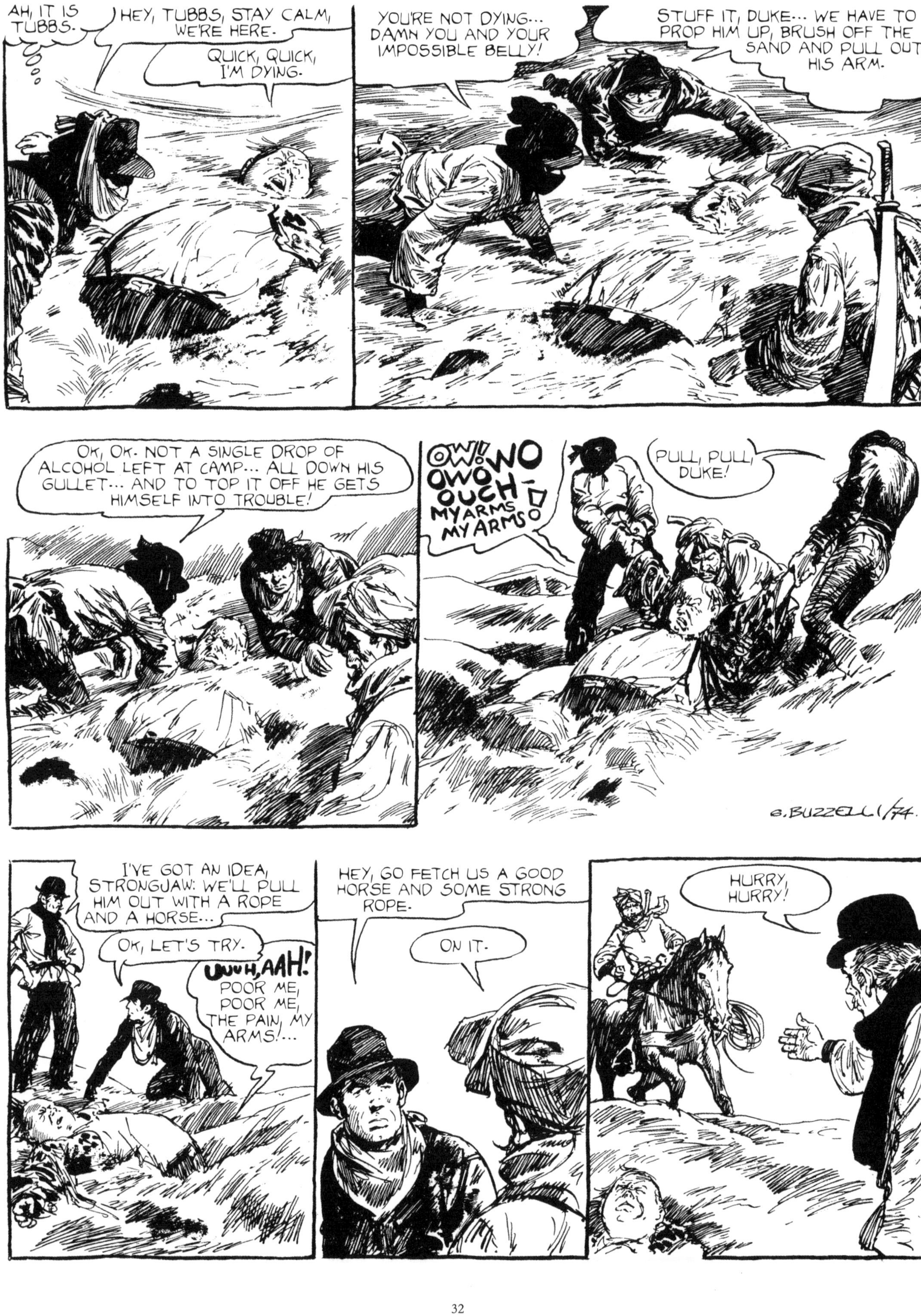
AH, IT IS TUBBS.
HEY, TUBBS, STAY CALM, WE'RE HERE.
QUICK, QUICK, I'M DYING.
YOU'RE NOT DYING... DAMN YOU AND YOUR IMPOSSIBLE BELLY!
STUFF IT, DUKE... WE HAVE TO PROP HIM UP, BRUSH OFF THE SAND AND PULL OUT HIS ARM.
OK, OK. NOT A SINGLE DROP OF ALCOHOL LEFT AT CAMP... ALL DOWN HIS GULLET... AND TO TOP IT OFF HE GETS HIMSELF INTO TROUBLE!
OW! OWO OWO OUCH MY ARMS MY ARMS
PULL, PULL, DUKE!
G. BUZZELLI/74.
I'VE GOT AN IDEA, STRONGUAW: WE'LL PULL HIM OUT WITH A ROPE AND A HORSE...
OK, LET'S TRY.
UUUH, AAH! POOR ME, POOR ME, THE PAIN, MY ARMS!...
HEY, GO FETCH US A GOOD HORSE AND SOME STRONG ROPE.
ON IT.
HURRY, HURRY!

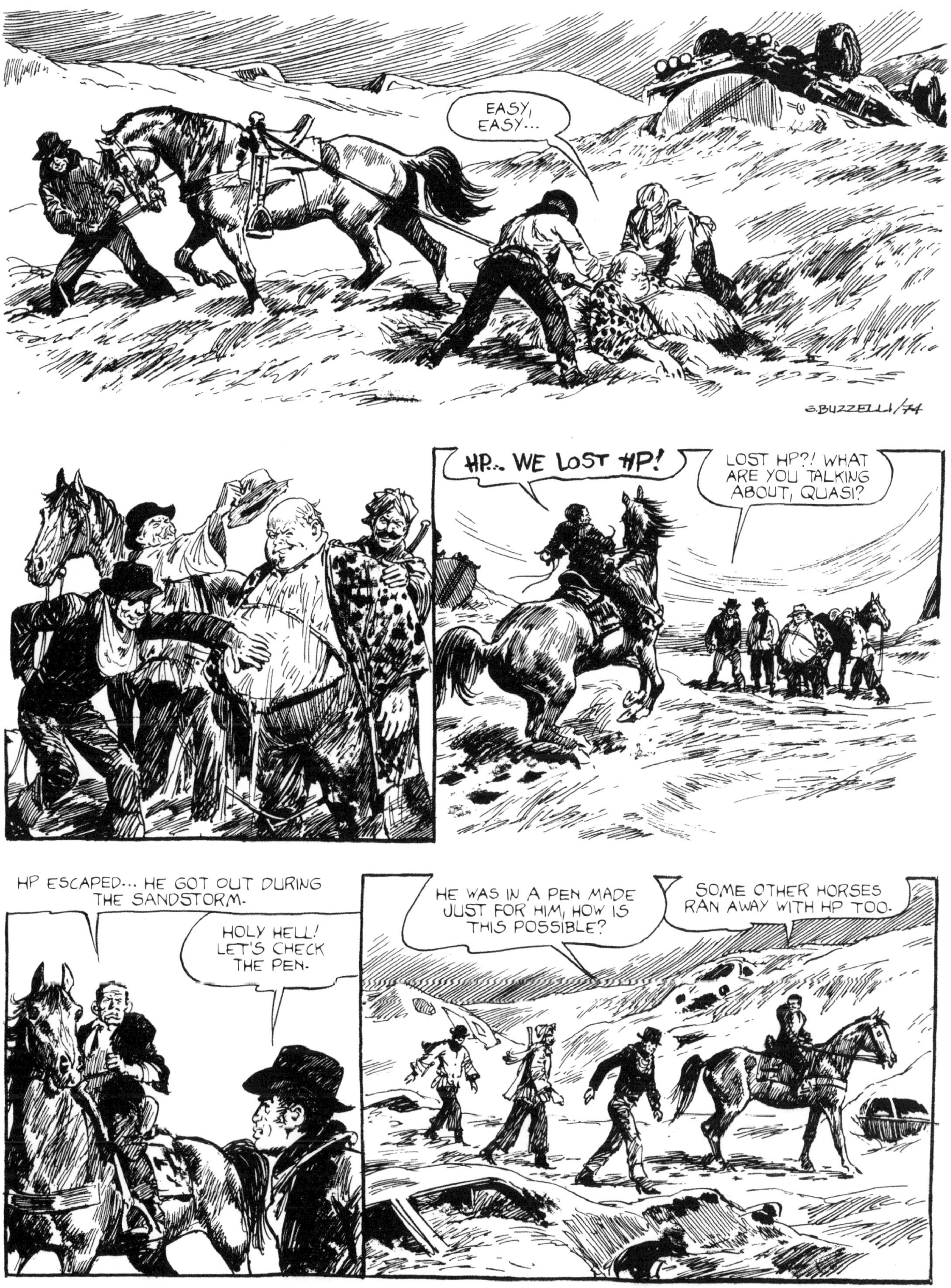
EASY, EASY...
G.BUZZELLI/74
HP... WE LOST HP!
LOST HP?! WHAT ARE YOU TALKING ABOUT, QUASI?
HP ESCAPED... HE GOT OUT DURING THE SANDSTORM.
HOLY HELL! LET'S CHECK THE PEN.
HE WAS IN A PEN MADE JUST FOR HIM, HOW IS THIS POSSIBLE?
SOME OTHER HORSES RAN AWAY WITH HP TOO.

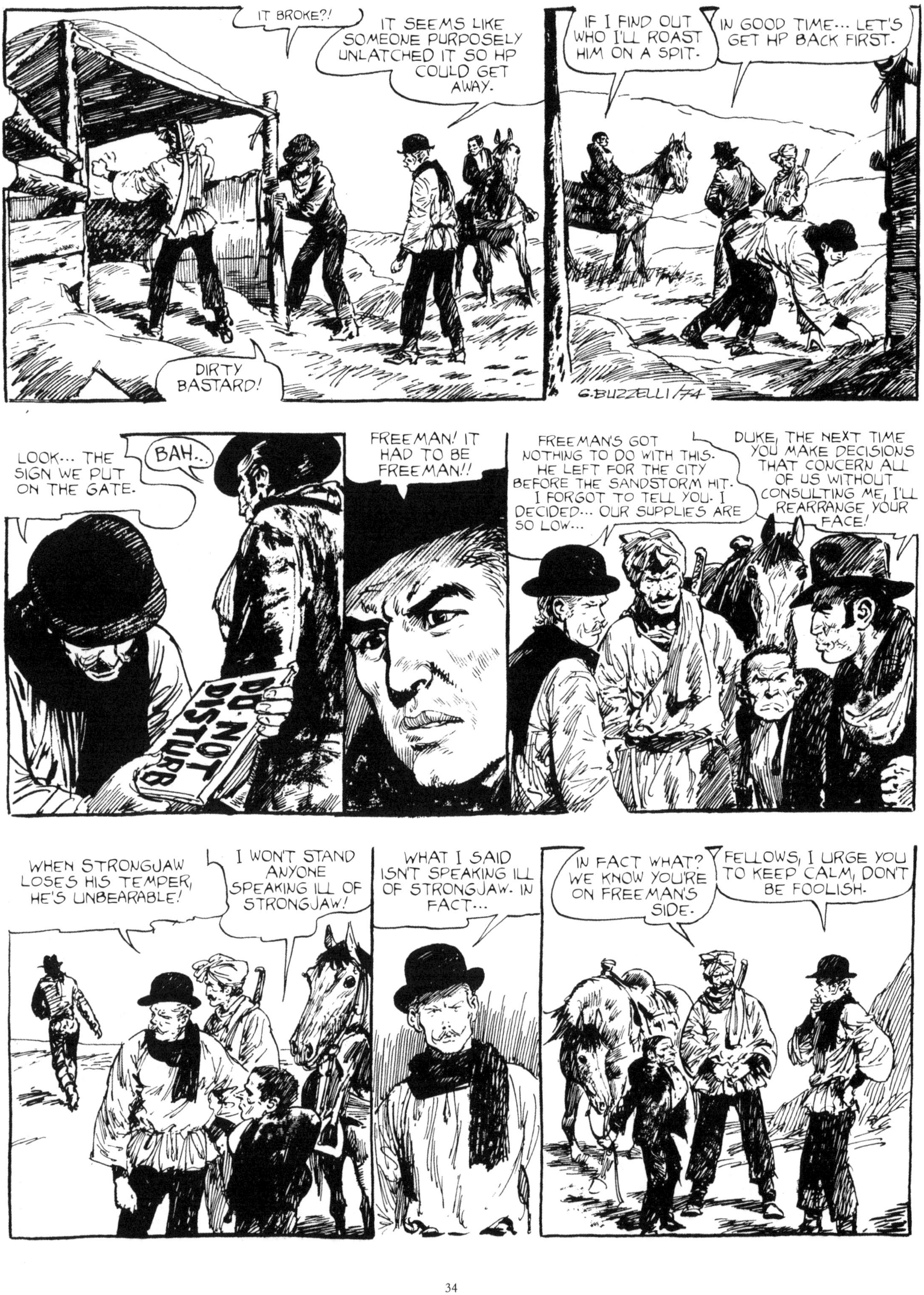
IT BROKE?!
IT SEEMS LIKE SOMEONE PURPOSELY UNLATCHED IT SO HP COULD GET AWAY.
DIRTY BASTARD!
IF I FIND OUT WHO I'LL ROAST HIM ON A SPIT.
IN GOOD TIME... LET'S GET HP BACK FIRST.
G. BUZZELLI /74
LOOK... THE SIGN WE PUT ON THE GATE.
BAH...
DO NOT DISTURB
FREEMAN! IT HAD TO BE FREEMAN!!
FREEMAN'S GOT NOTHING TO DO WITH THIS. HE LEFT FOR THE CITY BEFORE THE SANDSTORM HIT. I FORGOT TO TELL YOU. I DECIDED... OUR SUPPLIES ARE SO LOW...
DUKE, THE NEXT TIME YOU MAKE DECISIONS THAT CONCERN ALL OF US WITHOUT CONSULTING ME, I'LL REARRANGE YOUR FACE!
WHEN STRONGJAW LOSES HIS TEMPER, HE'S UNBEARABLE!
I WON'T STAND ANYONE SPEAKING ILL OF STRONGJAW!
WHAT I SAID ISN'T SPEAKING ILL OF STRONGJAW. IN FACT...
IN FACT WHAT? WE KNOW YOU'RE ON FREEMAN'S SIDE.
FELLOWS, I URGE YOU TO KEEP CALM, DON'T BE FOOLISH.

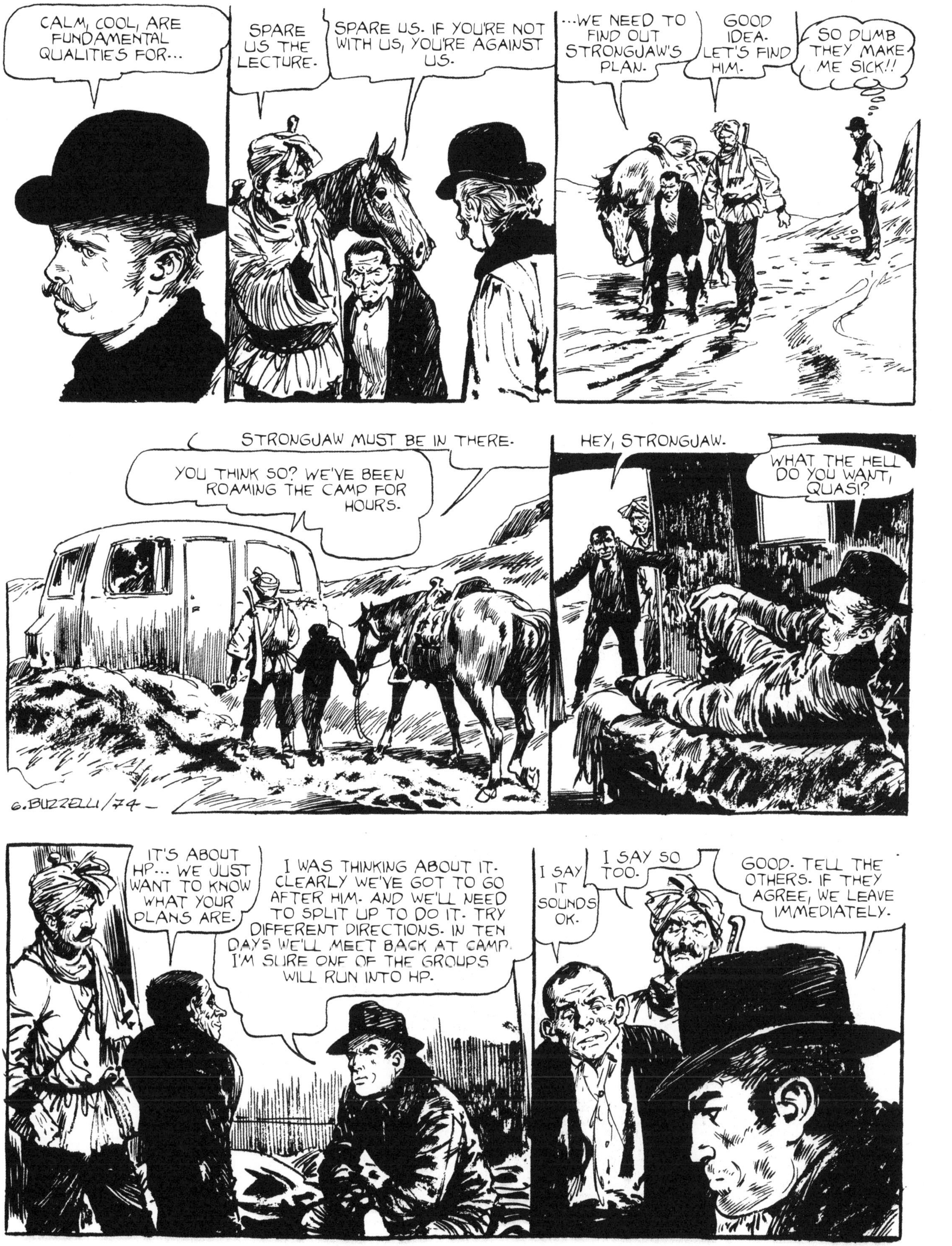
CALM, COOL, ARE FUNDAMENTAL QUALITIES FOR...
SPARE US THE LECTURE.
SPARE US. IF YOU'RE NOT WITH US, YOU'RE AGAINST US.
...WE NEED TO FIND OUT STRONGJAW'S PLAN.
GOOD IDEA. LET'S FIND HIM.
SO DUMB THEY MAKE ME SICK!!
STRONGJAW MUST BE IN THERE.
YOU THINK SO? WE'VE BEEN ROAMING THE CAMP FOR HOURS.
G. BUZZELLI/74
HEY, STRONGJAW.
WHAT THE HELL DO YOU WANT, QUASI?
IT'S ABOUT HP... WE JUST WANT TO KNOW WHAT YOUR PLANS ARE.
I WAS THINKING ABOUT IT. CLEARLY WE'VE GOT TO GO AFTER HIM. AND WE'LL NEED TO SPLIT UP TO DO IT. TRY DIFFERENT DIRECTIONS. IN TEN DAYS WE'LL MEET BACK AT CAMP. I'M SURE ONE OF THE GROUPS WILL RUN INTO HP.
I SAY IT SOUNDS OK.
I SAY SO TOO.
GOOD. TELL THE OTHERS. IF THEY AGREE, WE LEAVE IMMEDIATELY.

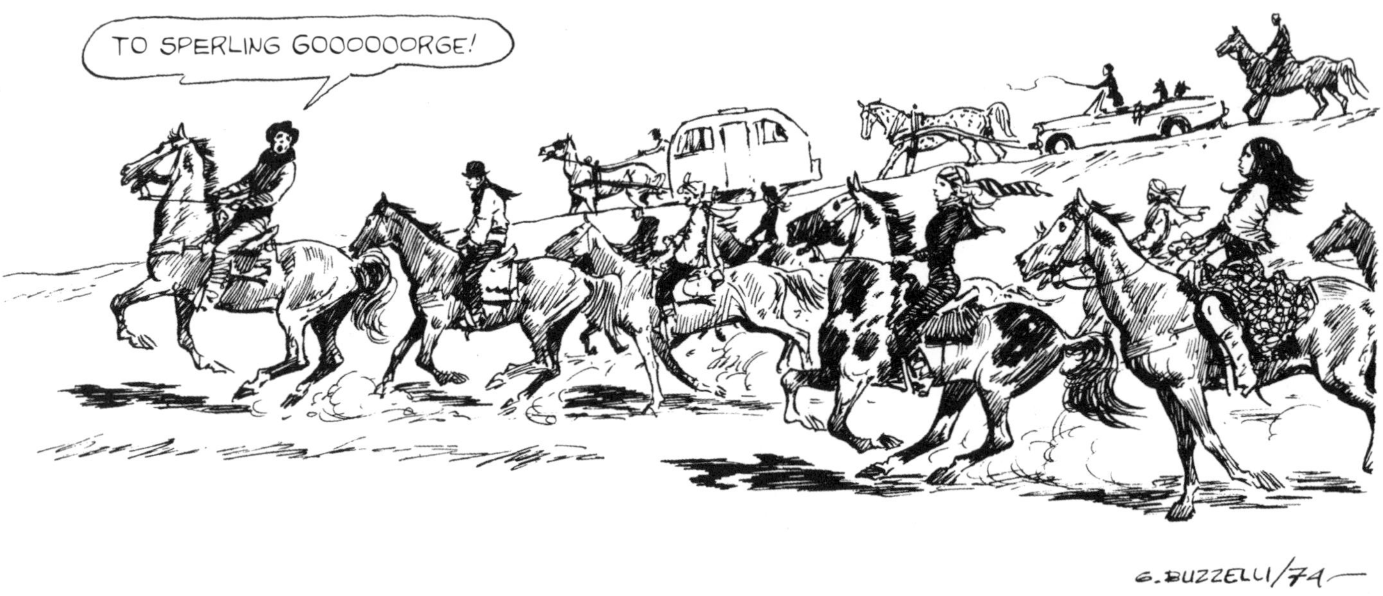
TO SPERLING GOOOOOORGE!
G. BUZZELLI/74

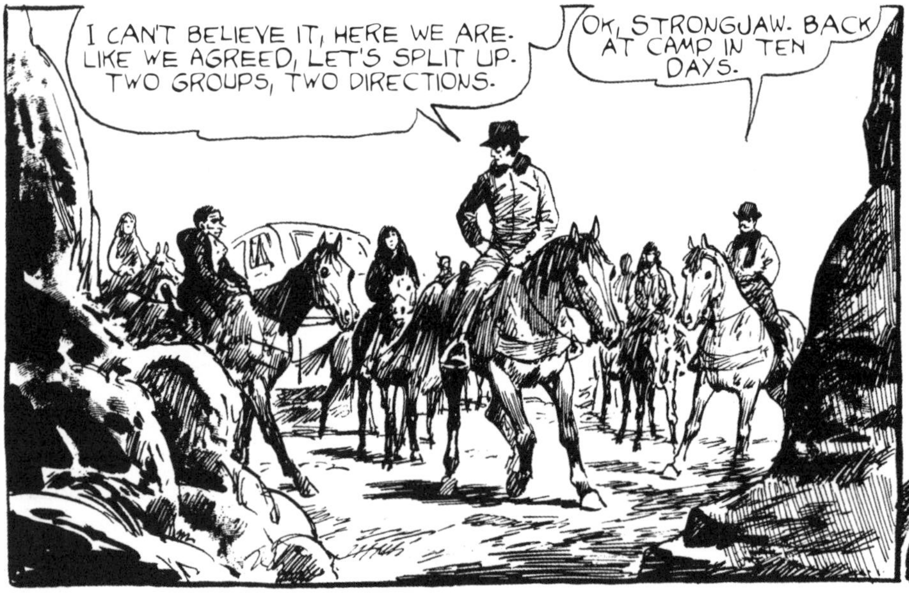
I CAN'T BELIEVE IT, HERE WE ARE. LIKE WE AGREED, LET'S SPLIT UP. TWO GROUPS, TWO DIRECTIONS.
OK, STRONGJAW. BACK AT CAMP IN TEN DAYS.

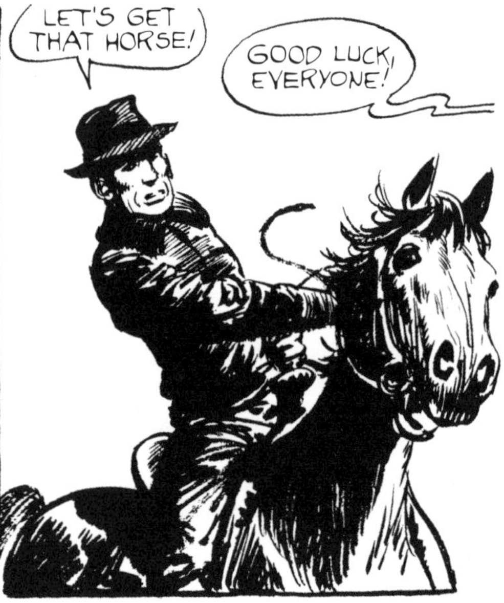
LET'S GET THAT HORSE!
GOOD LUCK, EVERYONE!

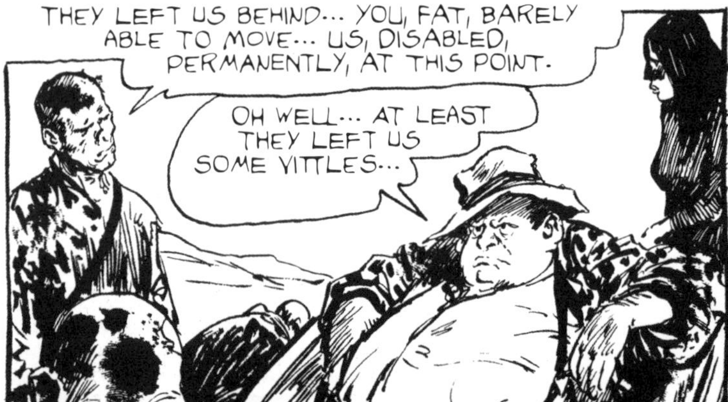
THEY LEFT US BEHIND... YOU, FAT, BARELY ABLE TO MOVE... US, DISABLED, PERMANENTLY, AT THIS POINT.
OH WELL... AT LEAST THEY LEFT US SOME VITTLES...

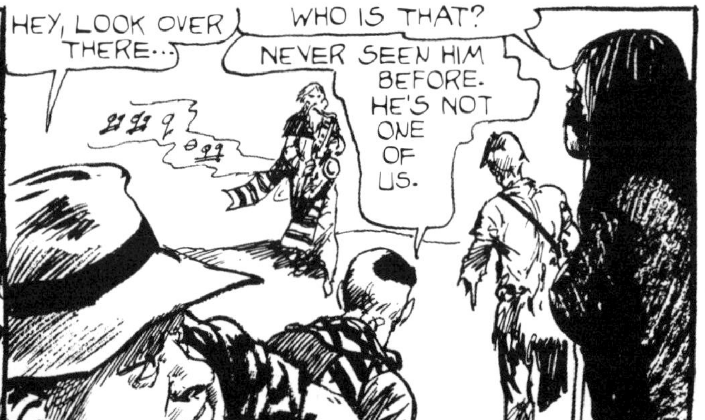
HEY, LOOK OVER THERE...
WHO IS THAT?
NEVER SEEN HIM BEFORE. HE'S NOT ONE OF US.

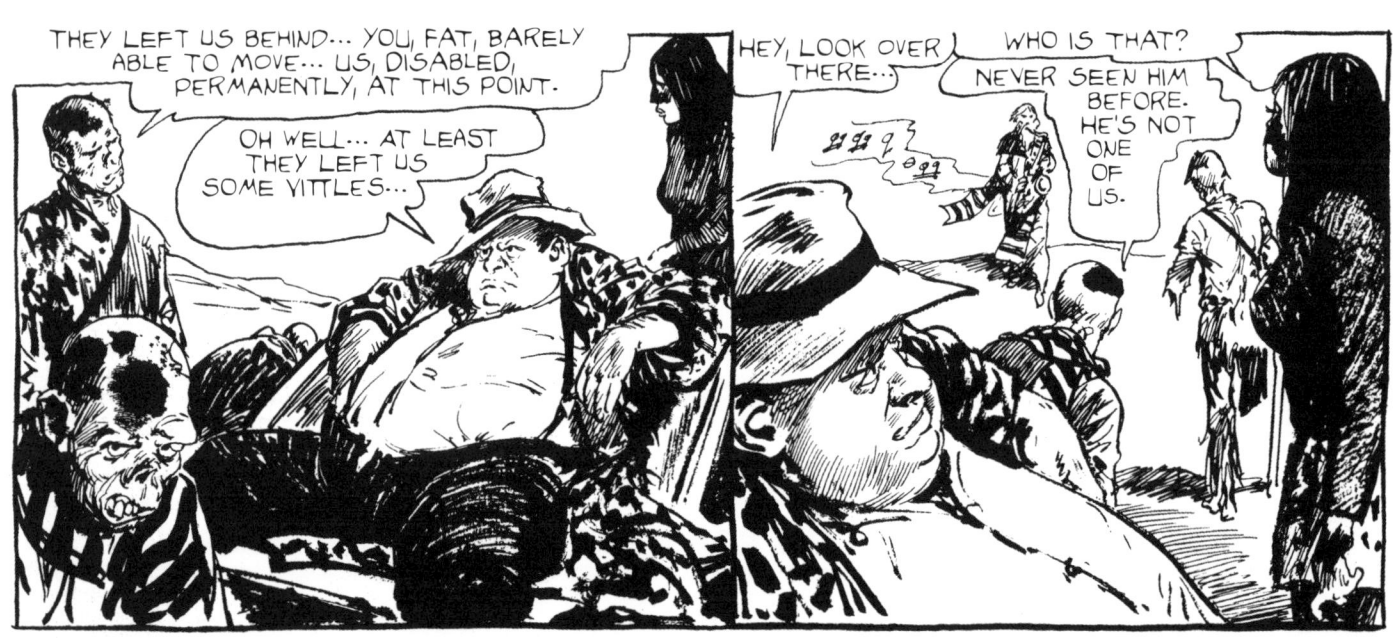

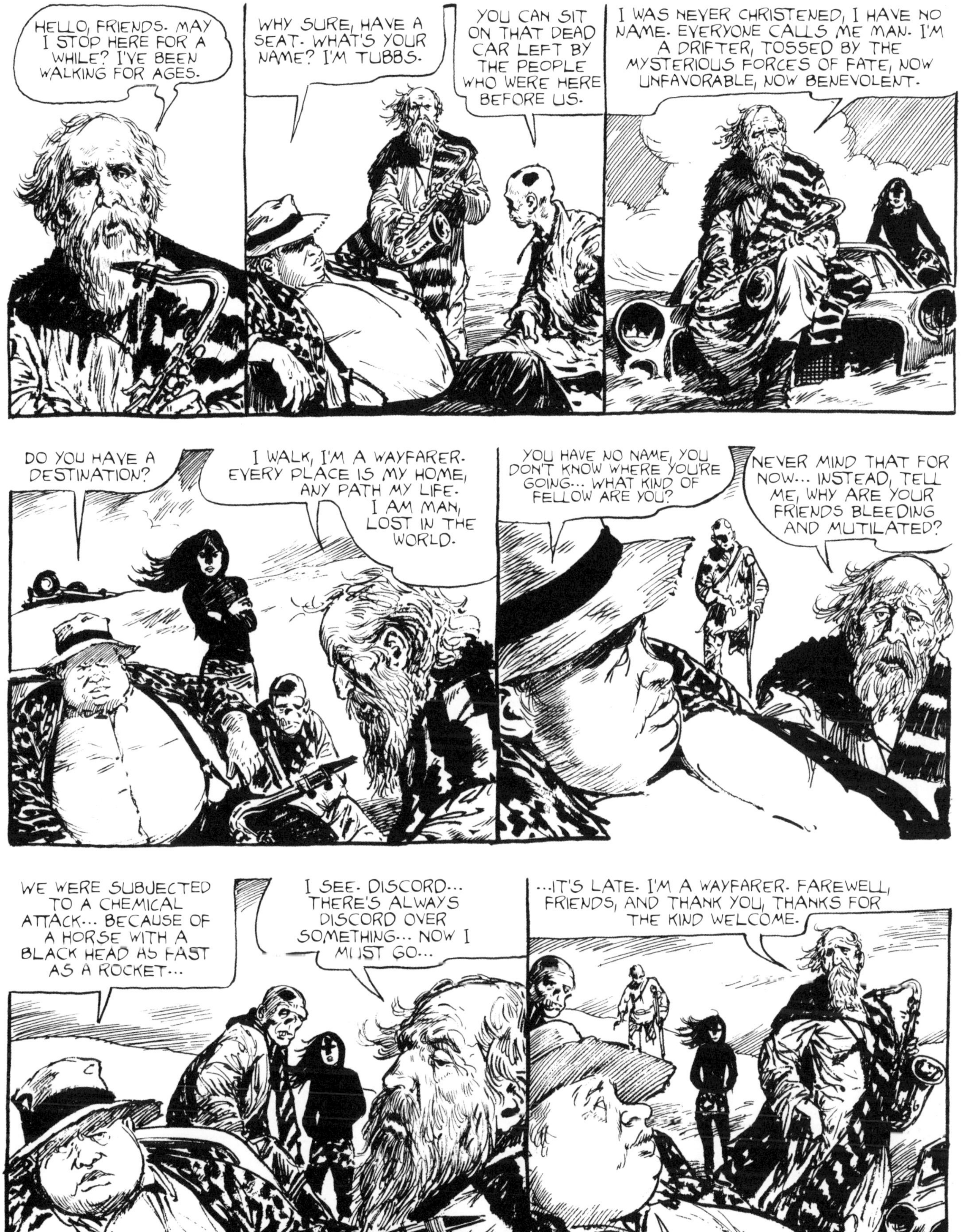
HELLO, FRIENDS. MAY I STOP HERE FOR A WHILE? I'VE BEEN WALKING FOR AGES.
WHY SURE, HAVE A SEAT. WHAT'S YOUR NAME? I'M TUBBS.
YOU CAN SIT ON THAT DEAD CAR LEFT BY THE PEOPLE WHO WERE HERE BEFORE US.
I WAS NEVER CHRISTENED, I HAVE NO NAME. EVERYONE CALLS ME MAN. I'M A DRIFTER, TOSSED BY THE MYSTERIOUS FORCES OF FATE, NOW UNFAVORABLE, NOW BENEVOLENT.
DO YOU HAVE A DESTINATION?
I WALK, I'M A WAYFARER. EVERY PLACE IS MY HOME, ANY PATH MY LIFE. I AM MAN, LOST IN THE WORLD.
YOU HAVE NO NAME, YOU DON'T KNOW WHERE YOU'RE GOING... WHAT KIND OF FELLOW ARE YOU?
NEVER MIND THAT FOR NOW... INSTEAD, TELL ME, WHY ARE YOUR FRIENDS BLEEDING AND MUTILATED?
WE WERE SUBJECTED TO A CHEMICAL ATTACK... BECAUSE OF A HORSE WITH A BLACK HEAD AS FAST AS A ROCKET...
I SEE. DISCORD... THERE'S ALWAYS DISCORD OVER SOMETHING... NOW I MUST GO...
G. BUZZELLI/74
...IT'S LATE. I'M A WAYFARER. FAREWELL, FRIENDS, AND THANK YOU, THANKS FOR THE KIND WELCOME.
SO LONG, WAYFARER.

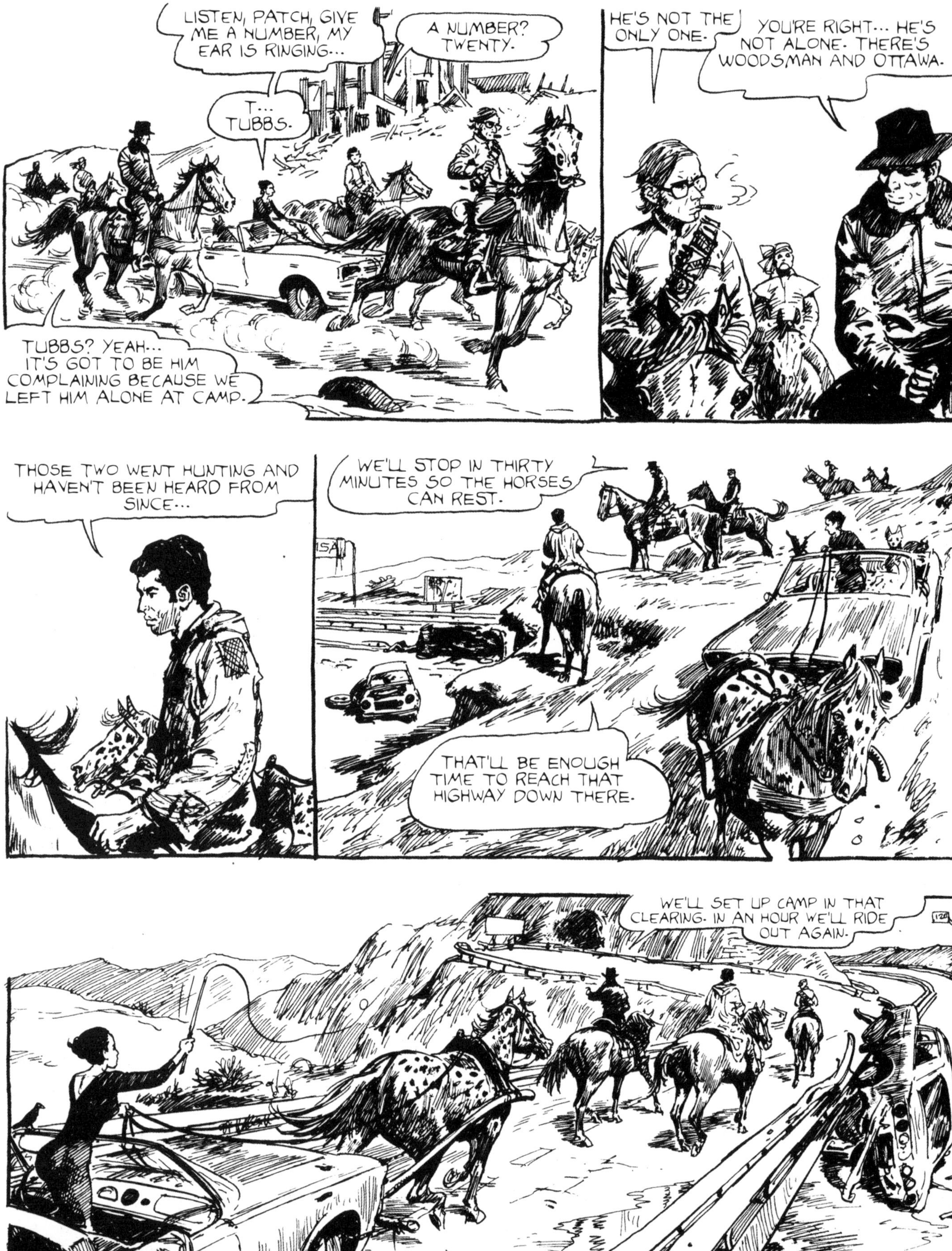

LISTEN, PATCH, GIVE ME A NUMBER, MY EAR IS RINGING...
A NUMBER? TWENTY.
T... TUBBS.
TUBBS? YEAH... IT'S GOT TO BE HIM COMPLAINING BECAUSE WE LEFT HIM ALONE AT CAMP.
HE'S NOT THE ONLY ONE.
YOU'RE RIGHT... HE'S NOT ALONE. THERE'S WOODSMAN AND OTTAWA.
THOSE TWO WENT HUNTING AND HAVEN'T BEEN HEARD FROM SINCE...
WE'LL STOP IN THIRTY MINUTES SO THE HORSES CAN REST.
THAT'LL BE ENOUGH TIME TO REACH THAT HIGHWAY DOWN THERE.
WE'LL SET UP CAMP IN THAT CLEARING. IN AN HOUR WE'LL RIDE OUT AGAIN.
G. BUZZELLI /74.

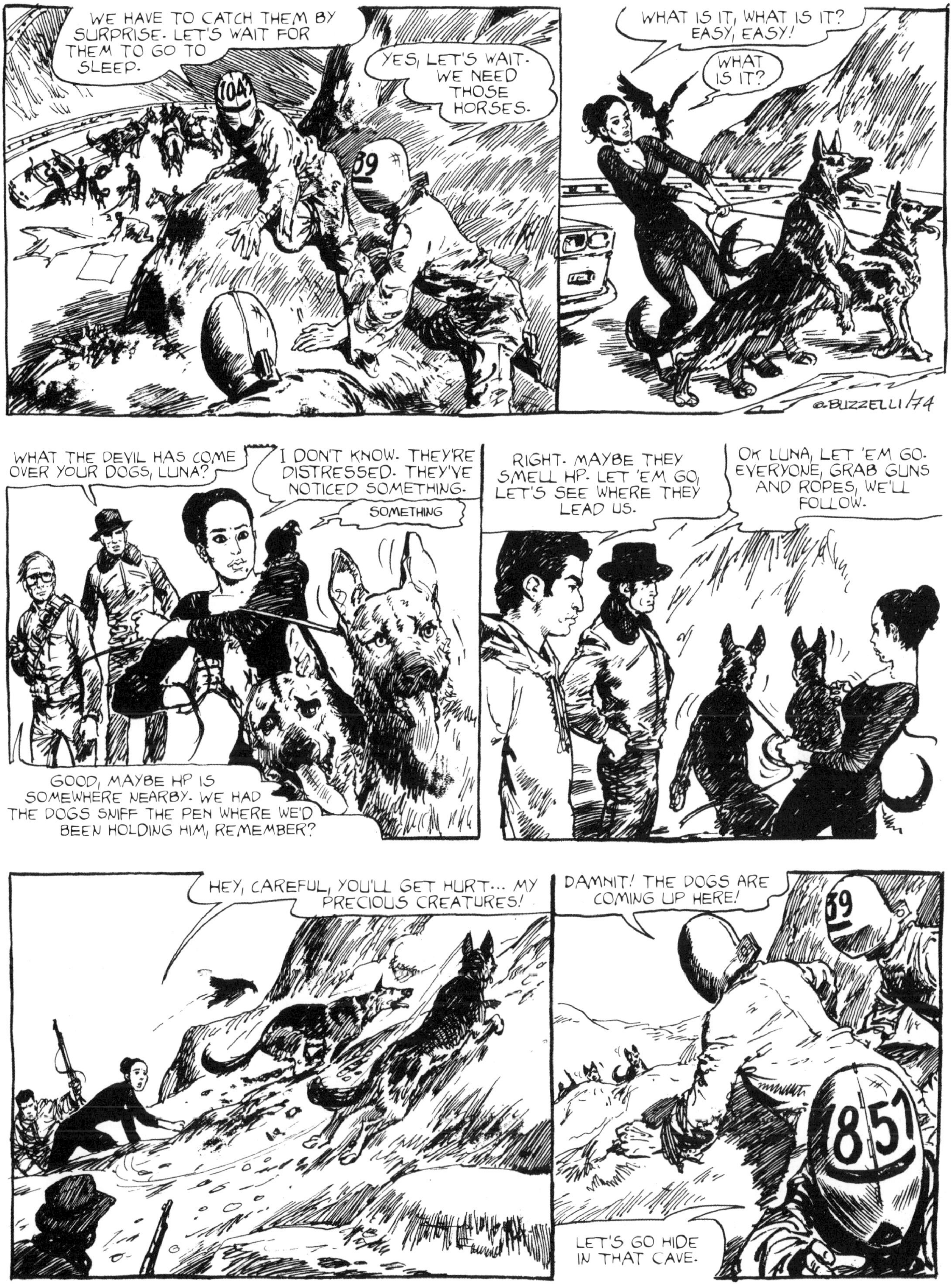
WE HAVE TO CATCH THEM BY SURPRISE. LET'S WAIT FOR THEM TO GO TO SLEEP.
YES, LET'S WAIT. WE NEED THOSE HORSES.
WHAT IS IT, WHAT IS IT? EASY, EASY!
WHAT IS IT?
©BUZZELLI/74
WHAT THE DEVIL HAS COME OVER YOUR DOGS, LUNA?
I DON'T KNOW. THEY'RE DISTRESSED. THEY'VE NOTICED SOMETHING.
SOMETHING
GOOD, MAYBE HP IS SOMEWHERE NEARBY. WE HAD THE DOGS SNIFF THE PEN WHERE WE'D BEEN HOLDING HIM, REMEMBER?
RIGHT. MAYBE THEY SMELL HP. LET 'EM GO, LET'S SEE WHERE THEY LEAD US.
OK LUNA, LET 'EM GO. EVERYONE, GRAB GUNS AND ROPES, WE'LL FOLLOW.
HEY, CAREFUL, YOU'LL GET HURT... MY PRECIOUS CREATURES!
DAMNIT! THE DOGS ARE COMING UP HERE!
LET'S GO HIDE IN THAT CAVE.

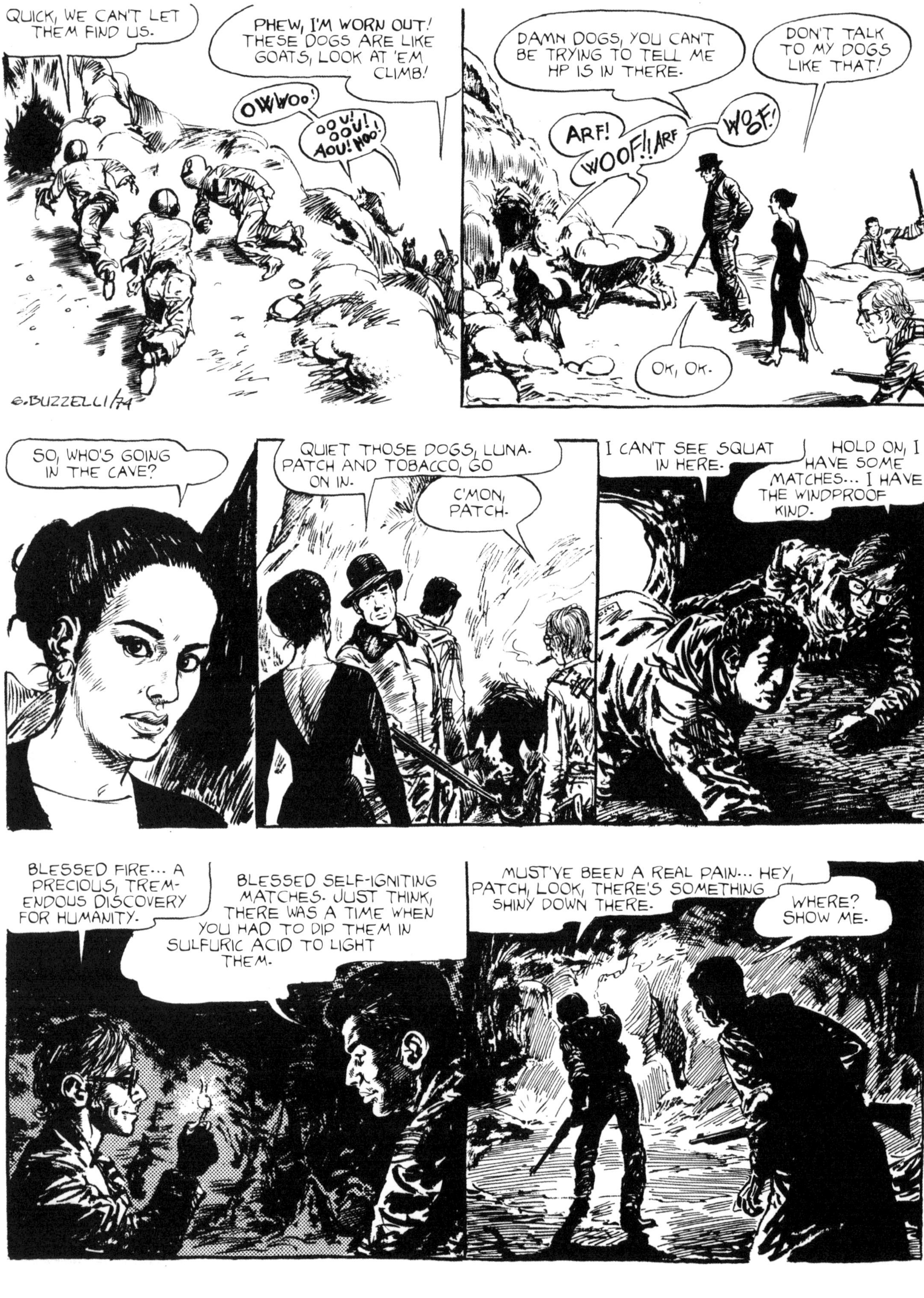
QUICK, WE CAN'T LET THEM FIND US.
PHEW, I'M WORN OUT! THESE DOGS ARE LIKE GOATS, LOOK AT 'EM CLIMB!
OWWOO!
OOU! OOU! AOU! NOO!
G. BUZZELLI /74
DAMN DOGS, YOU CAN'T BE TRYING TO TELL ME HP IS IN THERE.
DON'T TALK TO MY DOGS LIKE THAT!
ARF!
WOOF!! ARF
WOOF!
OK, OK.
SO, WHO'S GOING IN THE CAVE?
QUIET THOSE DOGS, LUNA. PATCH AND TOBACCO, GO ON IN.
C'MON, PATCH.
I CAN'T SEE SQUAT IN HERE.
HOLD ON, I HAVE SOME MATCHES... I HAVE THE WINDPROOF KIND.
BLESSED FIRE... A PRECIOUS, TREMENDOUS DISCOVERY FOR HUMANITY.
BLESSED SELF-IGNITING MATCHES. JUST THINK, THERE WAS A TIME WHEN YOU HAD TO DIP THEM IN SULFURIC ACID TO LIGHT THEM.
MUST'VE BEEN A REAL PAIN... HEY, PATCH, LOOK, THERE'S SOMETHING SHINY DOWN THERE.
WHERE? SHOW ME.

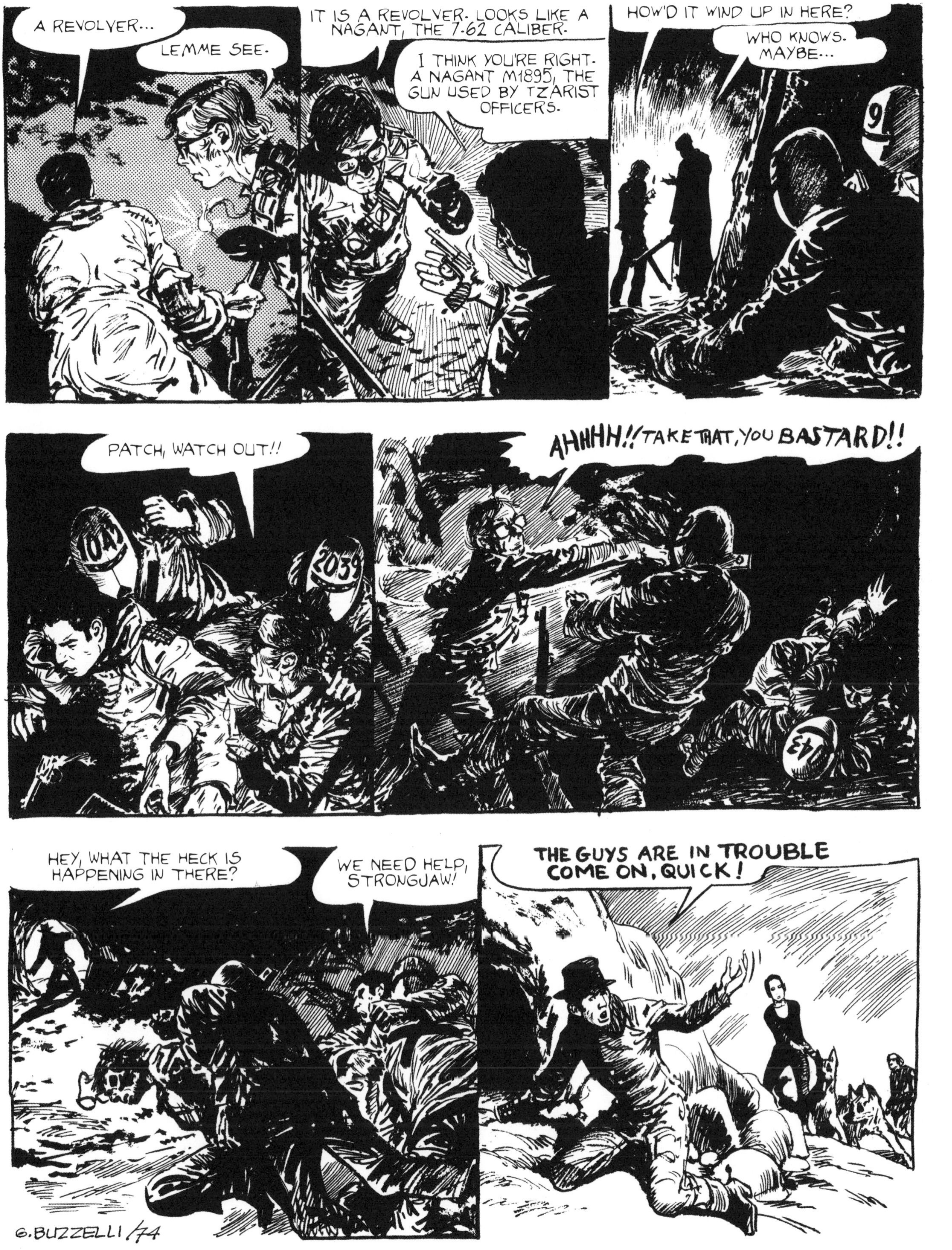
A REVOLVER...
LEMME SEE.
IT IS A REVOLVER. LOOKS LIKE A NAGANT, THE 7.62 CALIBER.
I THINK YOU'RE RIGHT. A NAGANT M1895, THE GUN USED BY TZARIST OFFICERS.
HOW'D IT WIND UP IN HERE?
WHO KNOWS. MAYBE...
9
PATCH, WATCH OUT!!
1041
2039
AHHHH!! TAKE THAT, YOU BASTARD!!
143
HEY, WHAT THE HECK IS HAPPENING IN THERE?
WE NEED HELP, STRONGJAW!
THE GUYS ARE IN TROUBLE COME ON, QUICK!
G. BUZZELLI /74

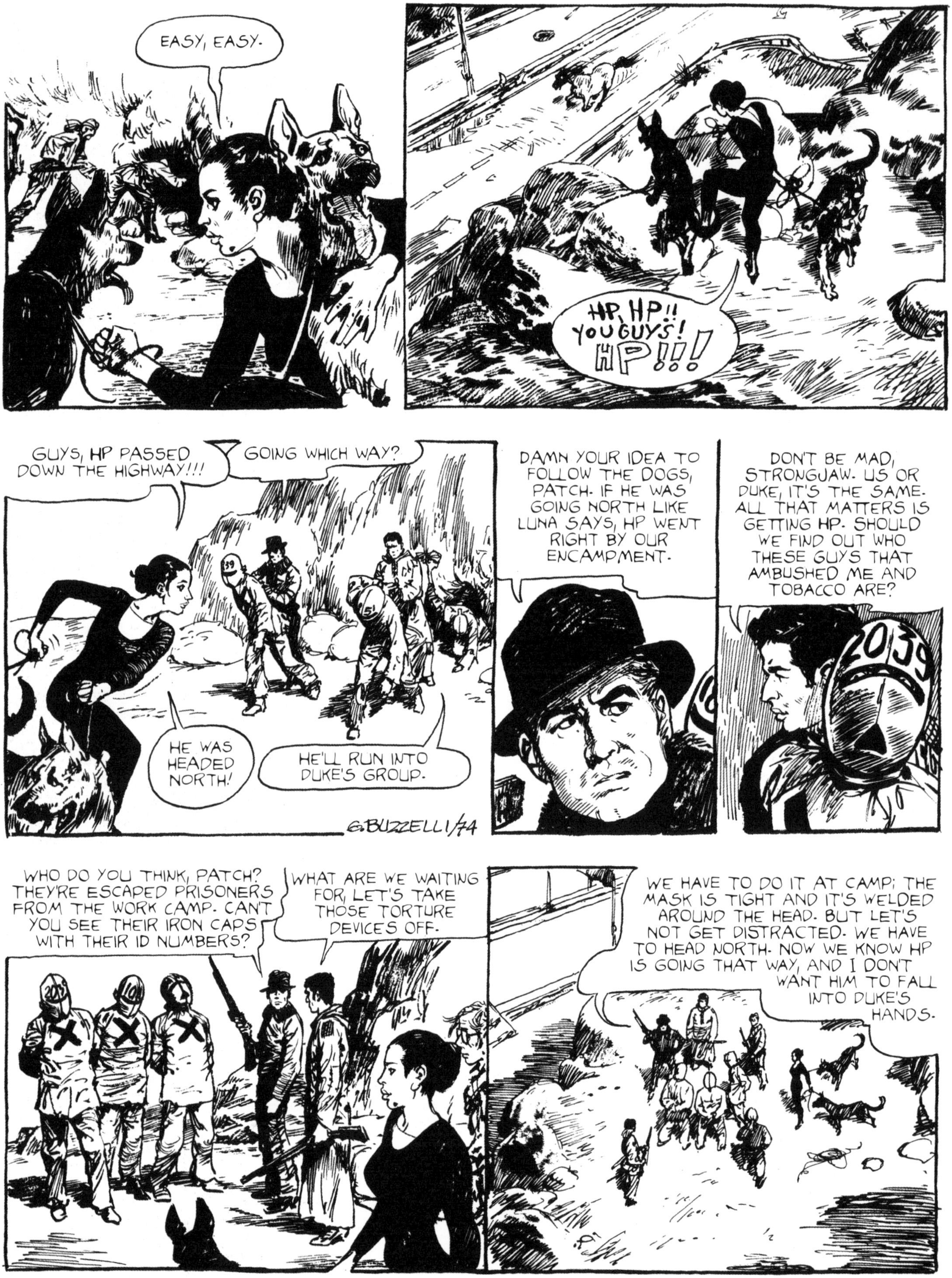
EASY, EASY.
HP, HP!! YOU GUYS! HP!!!
GUYS, HP PASSED DOWN THE HIGHWAY!!!
GOING WHICH WAY?
HE WAS HEADED NORTH!
HE'LL RUN INTO DUKE'S GROUP.
G. BUZZELLI/74
DAMN YOUR IDEA TO FOLLOW THE DOGS, PATCH. IF HE WAS GOING NORTH LIKE LUNA SAYS, HP WENT RIGHT BY OUR ENCAMPMENT.
DON'T BE MAD, STRONGJAW. US OR DUKE, IT'S THE SAME. ALL THAT MATTERS IS GETTING HP. SHOULD WE FIND OUT WHO THESE GUYS THAT AMBUSHED ME AND TOBACCO ARE?
WHO DO YOU THINK, PATCH? THEY'RE ESCAPED PRISONERS FROM THE WORK CAMP. CAN'T YOU SEE THEIR IRON CAPS WITH THEIR ID NUMBERS?
WHAT ARE WE WAITING FOR, LET'S TAKE THOSE TORTURE DEVICES OFF.
WE HAVE TO DO IT AT CAMP; THE MASK IS TIGHT AND IT'S WELDED AROUND THE HEAD. BUT LET'S NOT GET DISTRACTED. WE HAVE TO HEAD NORTH. NOW WE KNOW HP IS GOING THAT WAY, AND I DON'T WANT HIM TO FALL INTO DUKE'S HANDS.

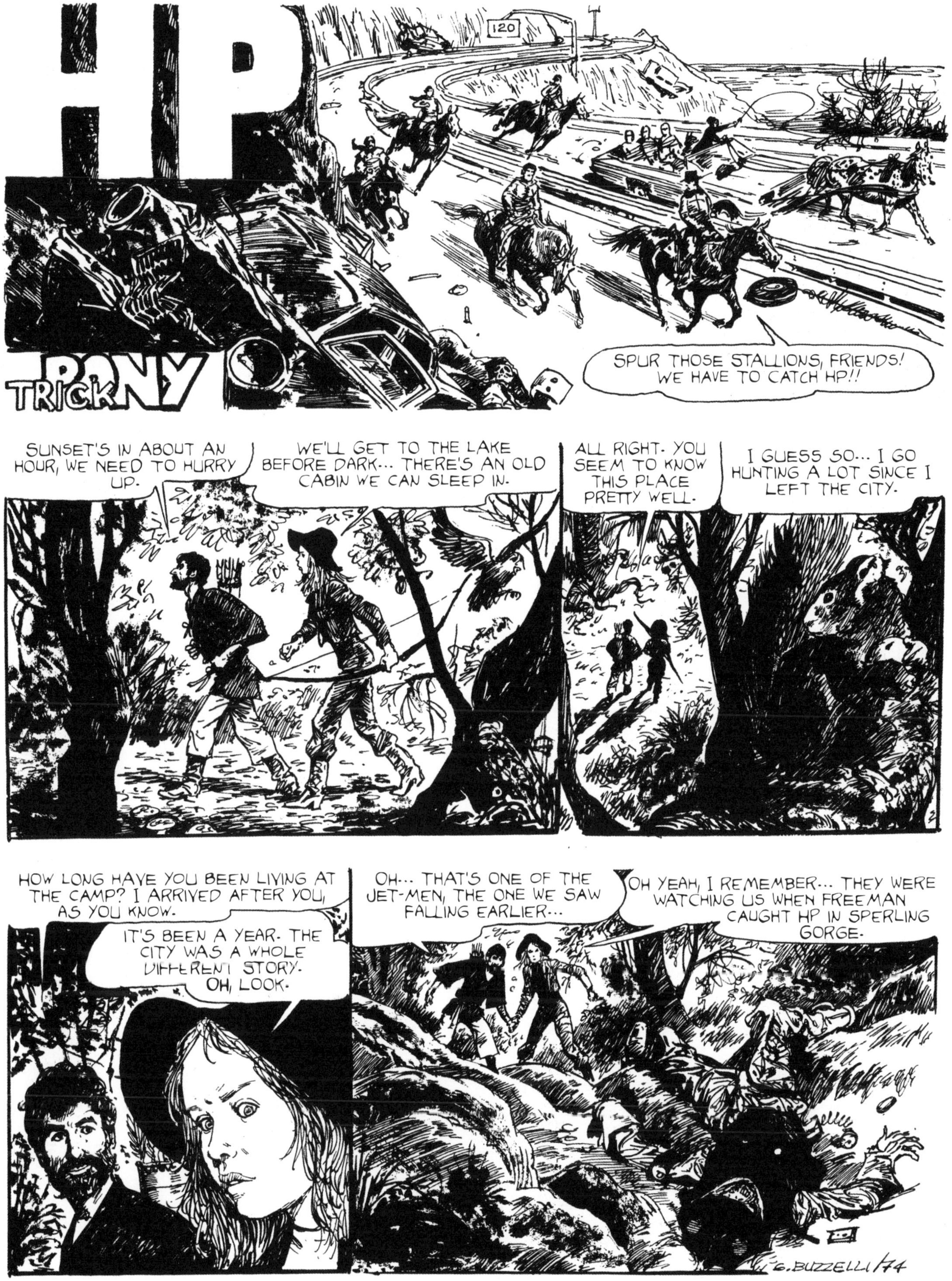
HP
TRICKY PONY
SPUR THOSE STALLIONS, FRIENDS! WE HAVE TO CATCH HP!!
SUNSET'S IN ABOUT AN HOUR, WE NEED TO HURRY UP.
WE'LL GET TO THE LAKE BEFORE DARK... THERE'S AN OLD CABIN WE CAN SLEEP IN.
ALL RIGHT. YOU SEEM TO KNOW THIS PLACE PRETTY WELL.
I GUESS SO... I GO HUNTING A LOT SINCE I LEFT THE CITY.
HOW LONG HAVE YOU BEEN LIVING AT THE CAMP? I ARRIVED AFTER YOU, AS YOU KNOW.
IT'S BEEN A YEAR. THE CITY WAS A WHOLE DIFFERENT STORY. OH, LOOK.
OH... THAT'S ONE OF THE JET-MEN, THE ONE WE SAW FALLING EARLIER...
OH YEAH, I REMEMBER... THEY WERE WATCHING US WHEN FREEMAN CAUGHT HP IN SPERLING GORGE.
G. BUZZELLI /74

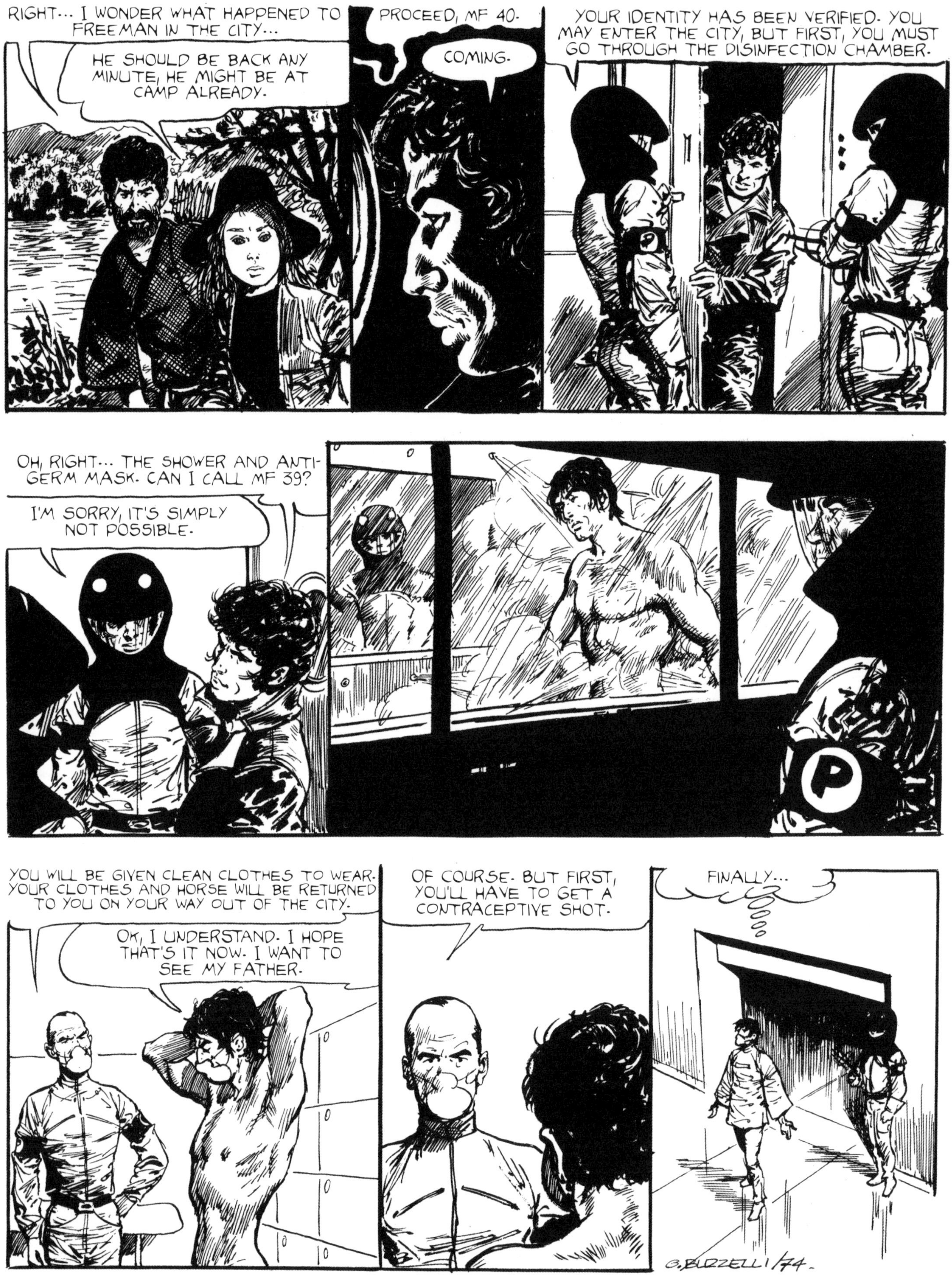
RIGHT... I WONDER WHAT HAPPENED TO FREEMAN IN THE CITY...
HE SHOULD BE BACK ANY MINUTE, HE MIGHT BE AT CAMP ALREADY.
PROCEED, MF 40.
COMING.
YOUR IDENTITY HAS BEEN VERIFIED. YOU MAY ENTER THE CITY, BUT FIRST, YOU MUST GO THROUGH THE DISINFECTION CHAMBER.
OH, RIGHT... THE SHOWER AND ANTI-GERM MASK. CAN I CALL MF 39?
I'M SORRY, IT'S SIMPLY NOT POSSIBLE.
YOU WILL BE GIVEN CLEAN CLOTHES TO WEAR. YOUR CLOTHES AND HORSE WILL BE RETURNED TO YOU ON YOUR WAY OUT OF THE CITY.
OK, I UNDERSTAND. I HOPE THAT'S IT NOW. I WANT TO SEE MY FATHER.
OF COURSE. BUT FIRST, YOU'LL HAVE TO GET A CONTRACEPTIVE SHOT.
FINALLY...
G. BUZZELLI/74.

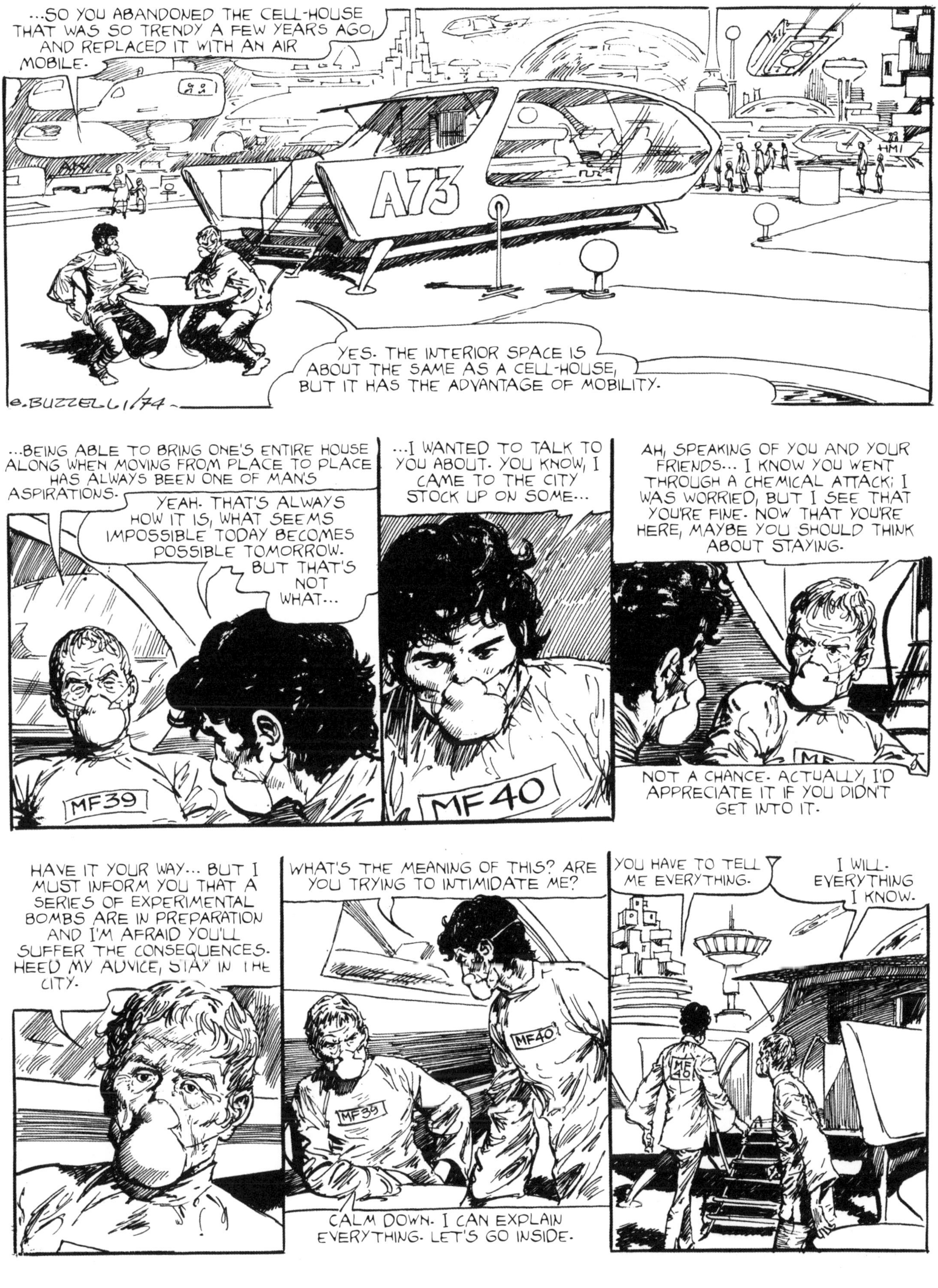

...SO YOU ABANDONED THE CELL-HOUSE THAT WAS SO TRENDY A FEW YEARS AGO, AND REPLACED IT WITH AN AIR MOBILE.
A73
HMI
YES. THE INTERIOR SPACE IS ABOUT THE SAME AS A CELL-HOUSE, BUT IT HAS THE ADVANTAGE OF MOBILITY.
G. BUZZELLI/74
...BEING ABLE TO BRING ONE'S ENTIRE HOUSE ALONG WHEN MOVING FROM PLACE TO PLACE HAS ALWAYS BEEN ONE OF MAN'S ASPIRATIONS.
YEAH. THAT'S ALWAYS HOW IT IS, WHAT SEEMS IMPOSSIBLE TODAY BECOMES POSSIBLE TOMORROW.
BUT THAT'S NOT WHAT...
MF39
...I WANTED TO TALK TO YOU ABOUT. YOU KNOW, I CAME TO THE CITY STOCK UP ON SOME...
MF40
AH, SPEAKING OF YOU AND YOUR FRIENDS... I KNOW YOU WENT THROUGH A CHEMICAL ATTACK; I WAS WORRIED, BUT I SEE THAT YOU'RE FINE. NOW THAT YOU'RE HERE, MAYBE YOU SHOULD THINK ABOUT STAYING.
NOT A CHANCE. ACTUALLY, I'D APPRECIATE IT IF YOU DIDN'T GET INTO IT.
HAVE IT YOUR WAY... BUT I MUST INFORM YOU THAT A SERIES OF EXPERIMENTAL BOMBS ARE IN PREPARATION AND I'M AFRAID YOU'LL SUFFER THE CONSEQUENCES. HEED MY ADVICE, STAY IN THE CITY.
WHAT'S THE MEANING OF THIS? ARE YOU TRYING TO INTIMIDATE ME?
MF40
MF39
CALM DOWN. I CAN EXPLAIN EVERYTHING. LET'S GO INSIDE.
YOU HAVE TO TELL ME EVERYTHING.
I WILL. EVERYTHING I KNOW.
MF 40

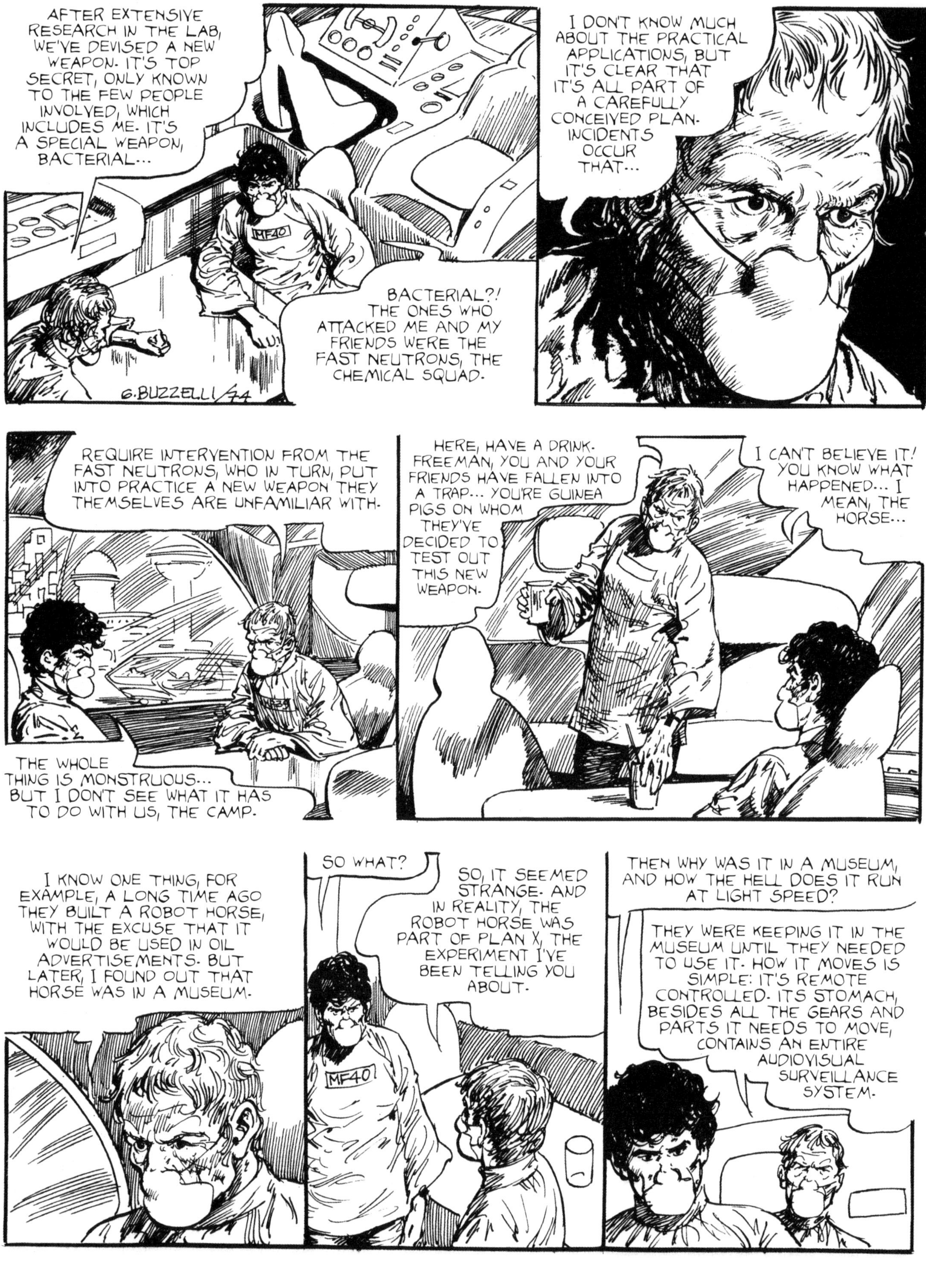

AFTER EXTENSIVE RESEARCH IN THE LAB, WE'VE DEVISED A NEW WEAPON. IT'S TOP SECRET, ONLY KNOWN TO THE FEW PEOPLE INVOLVED, WHICH INCLUDES ME. IT'S A SPECIAL WEAPON, BACTERIAL...
MF40
BACTERIAL?! THE ONES WHO ATTACKED ME AND MY FRIENDS WERE THE FAST NEUTRONS, THE CHEMICAL SQUAD.
G. BUZZELLI/74
I DON'T KNOW MUCH ABOUT THE PRACTICAL APPLICATIONS, BUT IT'S CLEAR THAT IT'S ALL PART OF A CAREFULLY CONCEIVED PLAN. INCIDENTS OCCUR THAT...
REQUIRE INTERVENTION FROM THE FAST NEUTRONS, WHO IN TURN, PUT INTO PRACTICE A NEW WEAPON THEY THEMSELVES ARE UNFAMILIAR WITH.
THE WHOLE THING IS MONSTRUOUS... BUT I DON'T SEE WHAT IT HAS TO DO WITH US, THE CAMP.
HERE, HAVE A DRINK. FREEMAN, YOU AND YOUR FRIENDS HAVE FALLEN INTO A TRAP... YOU'RE GUINEA PIGS ON WHOM THEY'VE DECIDED TO TEST OUT THIS NEW WEAPON.
I CAN'T BELIEVE IT! YOU KNOW WHAT HAPPENED... I MEAN, THE HORSE...
I KNOW ONE THING, FOR EXAMPLE, A LONG TIME AGO THEY BUILT A ROBOT HORSE, WITH THE EXCUSE THAT IT WOULD BE USED IN OIL ADVERTISEMENTS. BUT LATER, I FOUND OUT THAT HORSE WAS IN A MUSEUM.
SO WHAT?
SO, IT SEEMED STRANGE. AND IN REALITY, THE ROBOT HORSE WAS PART OF PLAN X, THE EXPERIMENT I'VE BEEN TELLING YOU ABOUT.
MF40
THEN WHY WAS IT IN A MUSEUM, AND HOW THE HELL DOES IT RUN AT LIGHT SPEED?
THEY WERE KEEPING IT IN THE MUSEUM UNTIL THEY NEEDED TO USE IT. HOW IT MOVES IS SIMPLE: IT'S REMOTE CONTROLLED. ITS STOMACH, BESIDES ALL THE GEARS AND PARTS IT NEEDS TO MOVE, CONTAINS AN ENTIRE AUDIOVISUAL SURVEILLANCE SYSTEM.

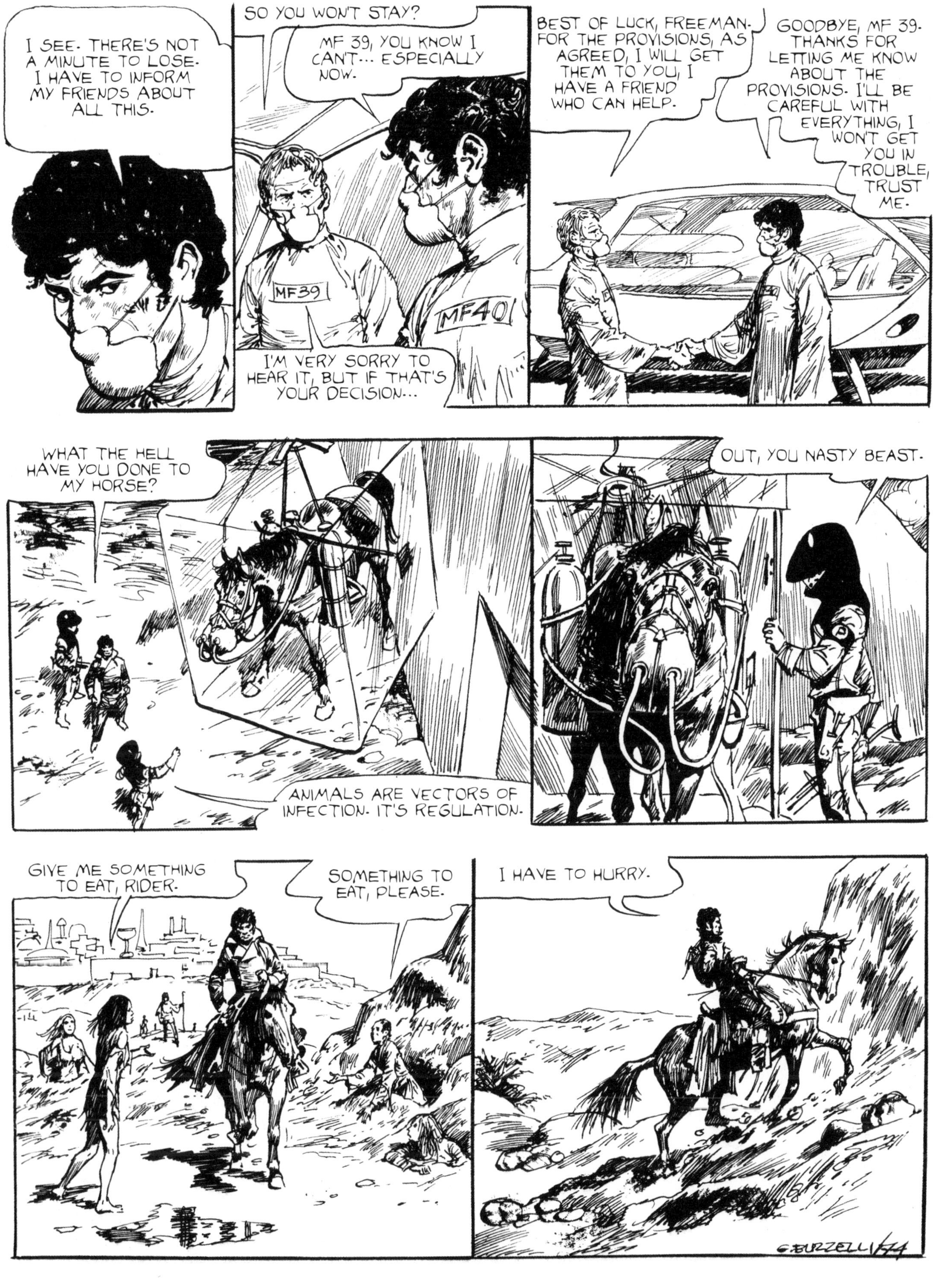
I SEE. THERE'S NOT A MINUTE TO LOSE. I HAVE TO INFORM MY FRIENDS ABOUT ALL THIS.
SO YOU WON'T STAY?
MF 39, YOU KNOW I CAN'T... ESPECIALLY NOW.
MF39
MF40
I'M VERY SORRY TO HEAR IT, BUT IF THAT'S YOUR DECISION...
BEST OF LUCK, FREEMAN. FOR THE PROVISIONS, AS AGREED, I WILL GET THEM TO YOU, I HAVE A FRIEND WHO CAN HELP.
GOODBYE, MF 39. THANKS FOR LETTING ME KNOW ABOUT THE PROVISIONS. I'LL BE CAREFUL WITH EVERYTHING, I WON'T GET YOU IN TROUBLE, TRUST ME.
WHAT THE HELL HAVE YOU DONE TO MY HORSE?
OUT, YOU NASTY BEAST.
ANIMALS ARE VECTORS OF INFECTION. IT'S REGULATION.
GIVE ME SOMETHING TO EAT, RIDER.
SOMETHING TO EAT, PLEASE.
I HAVE TO HURRY.
G.BURZELLI/84

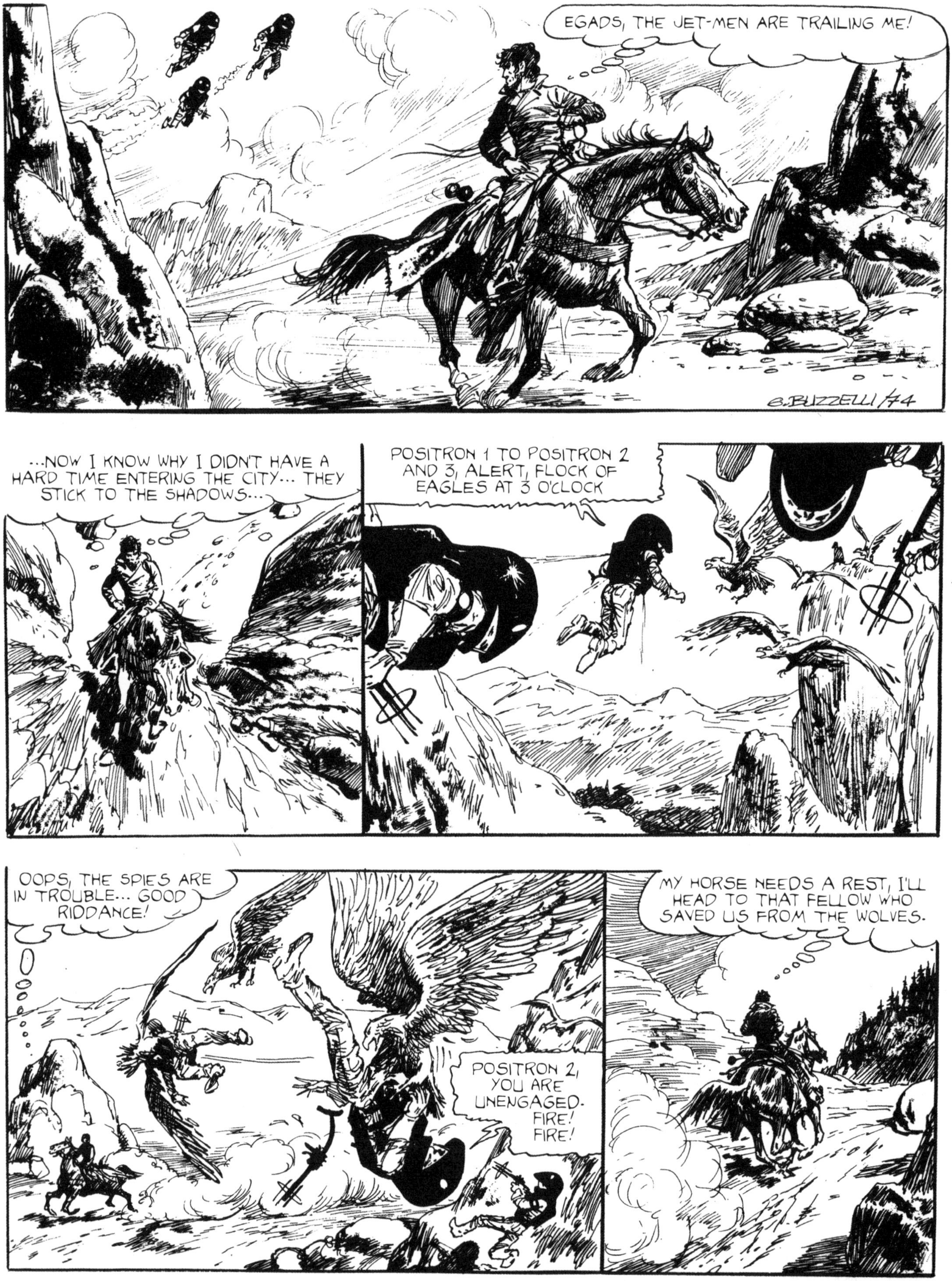

EGADS, THE JET-MEN ARE TRAILING ME!
B. BUZZELLI /74
...NOW I KNOW WHY I DIDN'T HAVE A HARD TIME ENTERING THE CITY... THEY STICK TO THE SHADOWS...
POSITRON 1 TO POSITRON 2 AND 3, ALERT, FLOCK OF EAGLES AT 3 O'CLOCK
OOPS, THE SPIES ARE IN TROUBLE... GOOD RIDDANCE!
POSITRON 2, YOU ARE UNENGAGED- FIRE! FIRE!
MY HORSE NEEDS A REST, I'LL HEAD TO THAT FELLOW WHO SAVED US FROM THE WOLVES.

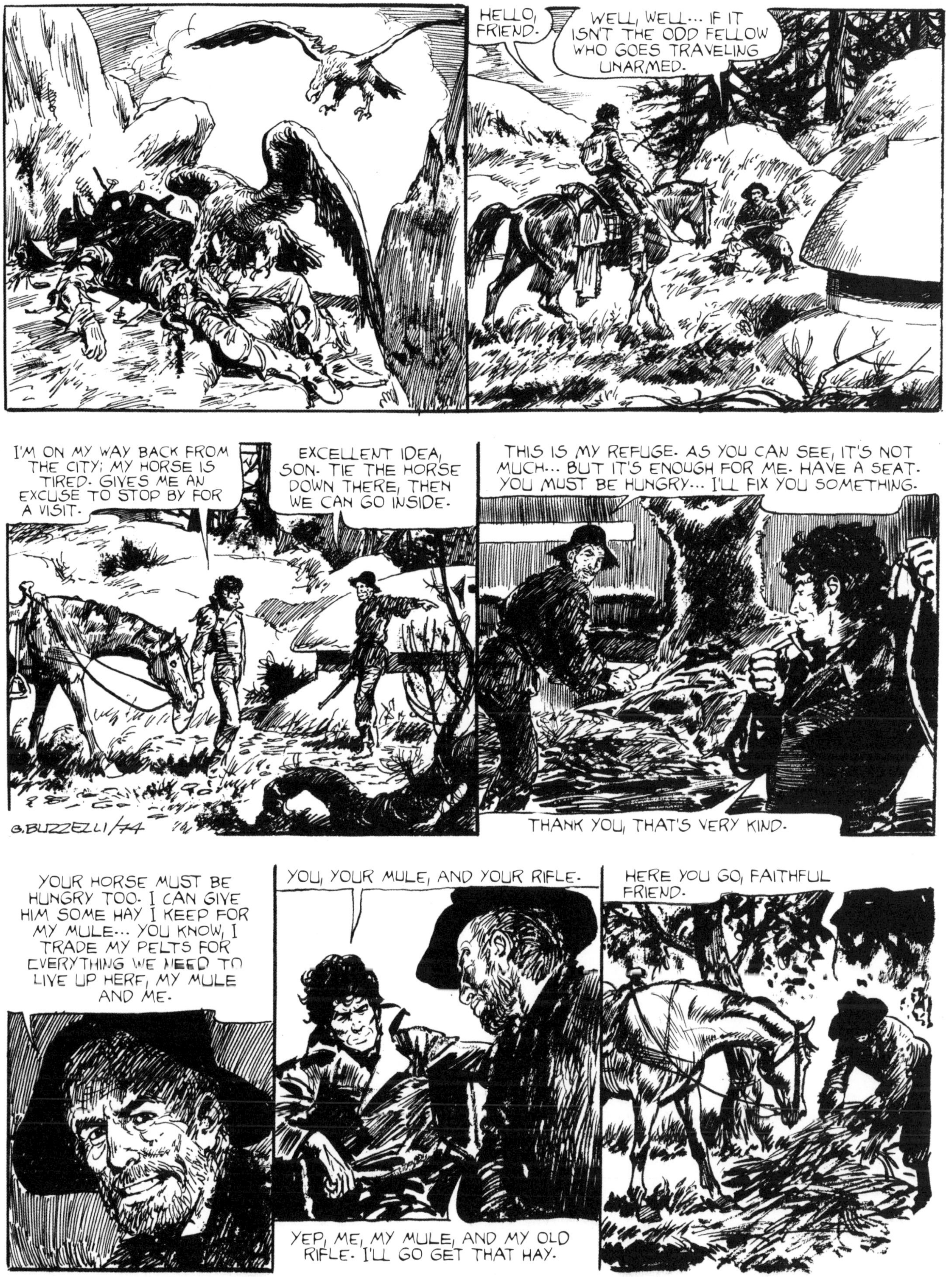
HELLO, FRIEND.
WELL, WELL... IF IT ISN'T THE ODD FELLOW WHO GOES TRAVELING UNARMED.
I'M ON MY WAY BACK FROM THE CITY; MY HORSE IS TIRED. GIVES ME AN EXCUSE TO STOP BY FOR A VISIT.
EXCELLENT IDEA, SON. TIE THE HORSE DOWN THERE, THEN WE CAN GO INSIDE.
G. BUZZELLI/74
THIS IS MY REFUGE. AS YOU CAN SEE, IT'S NOT MUCH... BUT IT'S ENOUGH FOR ME. HAVE A SEAT. YOU MUST BE HUNGRY... I'LL FIX YOU SOMETHING.
THANK YOU, THAT'S VERY KIND.
YOUR HORSE MUST BE HUNGRY TOO. I CAN GIVE HIM SOME HAY I KEEP FOR MY MULE... YOU KNOW, I TRADE MY PELTS FOR EVERYTHING WE NEED TO LIVE UP HERE, MY MULE AND ME.
YOU, YOUR MULE, AND YOUR RIFLE.
YEP, ME, MY MULE, AND MY OLD RIFLE. I'LL GO GET THAT HAY.
HERE YOU GO, FAITHFUL FRIEND.

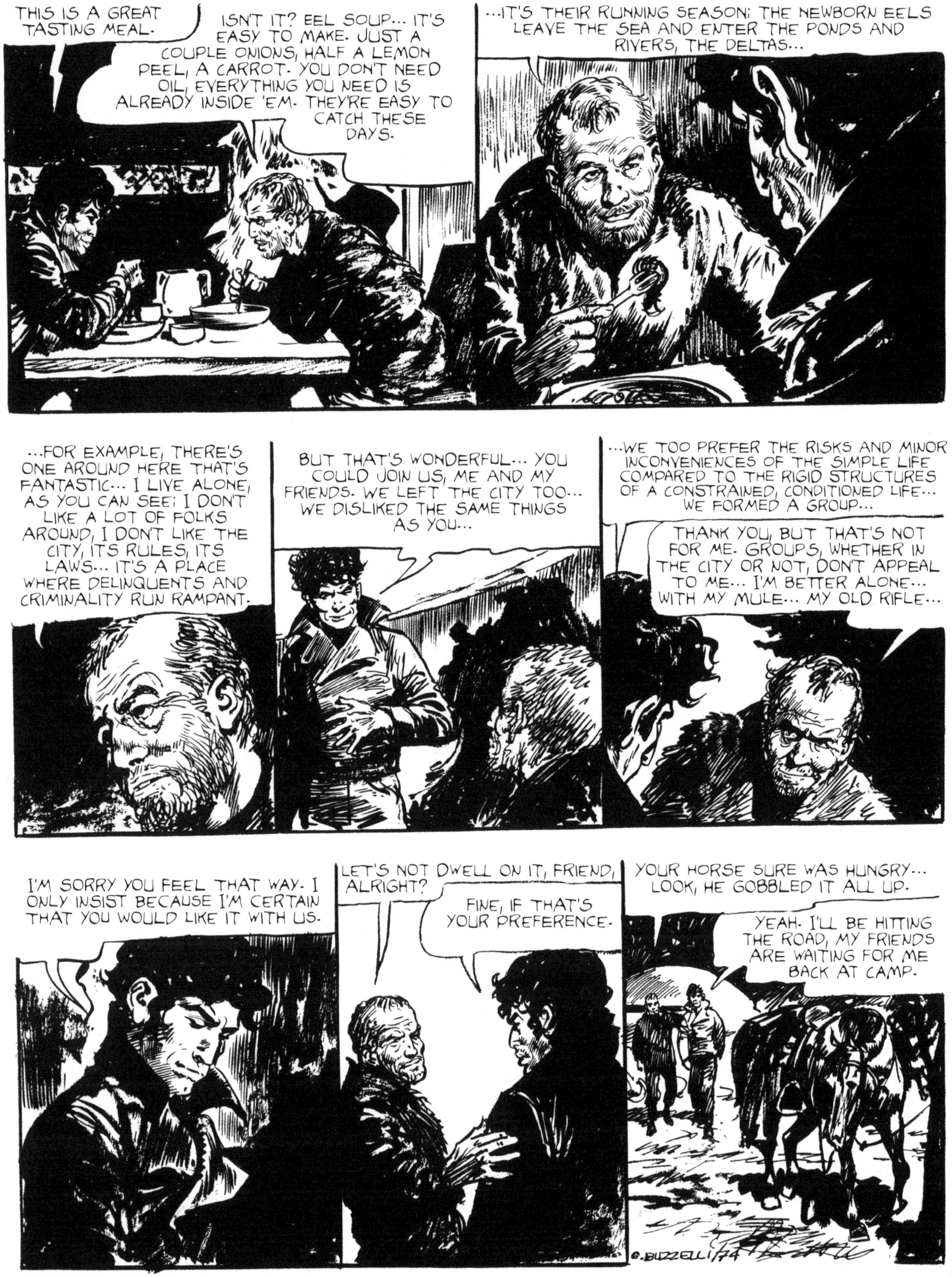
THIS IS A GREAT TASTING MEAL.
ISN'T IT? EEL SOUP... IT'S EASY TO MAKE. JUST A COUPLE ONIONS, HALF A LEMON PEEL, A CARROT. YOU DON'T NEED OIL, EVERYTHING YOU NEED IS ALREADY INSIDE 'EM. THEY'RE EASY TO CATCH THESE DAYS.
...IT'S THEIR RUNNING SEASON; THE NEWBORN EELS LEAVE THE SEA AND ENTER THE PONDS AND RIVERS, THE DELTAS...
...FOR EXAMPLE, THERE'S ONE AROUND HERE THAT'S FANTASTIC... I LIVE ALONE, AS YOU CAN SEE; I DON'T LIKE A LOT OF FOLKS AROUND, I DON'T LIKE THE CITY, ITS RULES, ITS LAWS... IT'S A PLACE WHERE DELINQUENTS AND CRIMINALITY RUN RAMPANT.
BUT THAT'S WONDERFUL... YOU COULD JOIN US, ME AND MY FRIENDS. WE LEFT THE CITY TOO... WE DISLIKED THE SAME THINGS AS YOU...
...WE TOO PREFER THE RISKS AND MINOR INCONVENIENCES OF THE SIMPLE LIFE COMPARED TO THE RIGID STRUCTURES OF A CONSTRAINED, CONDITIONED LIFE... WE FORMED A GROUP...
THANK YOU, BUT THAT'S NOT FOR ME. GROUPS, WHETHER IN THE CITY OR NOT, DON'T APPEAL TO ME... I'M BETTER ALONE... WITH MY MULE... MY OLD RIFLE...
I'M SORRY YOU FEEL THAT WAY. I ONLY INSIST BECAUSE I'M CERTAIN THAT YOU WOULD LIKE IT WITH US.
LET'S NOT DWELL ON IT, FRIEND, ALRIGHT?
FINE, IF THAT'S YOUR PREFERENCE.
YOUR HORSE SURE WAS HUNGRY... LOOK, HE GOBBLED IT ALL UP.
YEAH. I'LL BE HITTING THE ROAD, MY FRIENDS ARE WAITING FOR ME BACK AT CAMP.
G. BUZZELLI/74

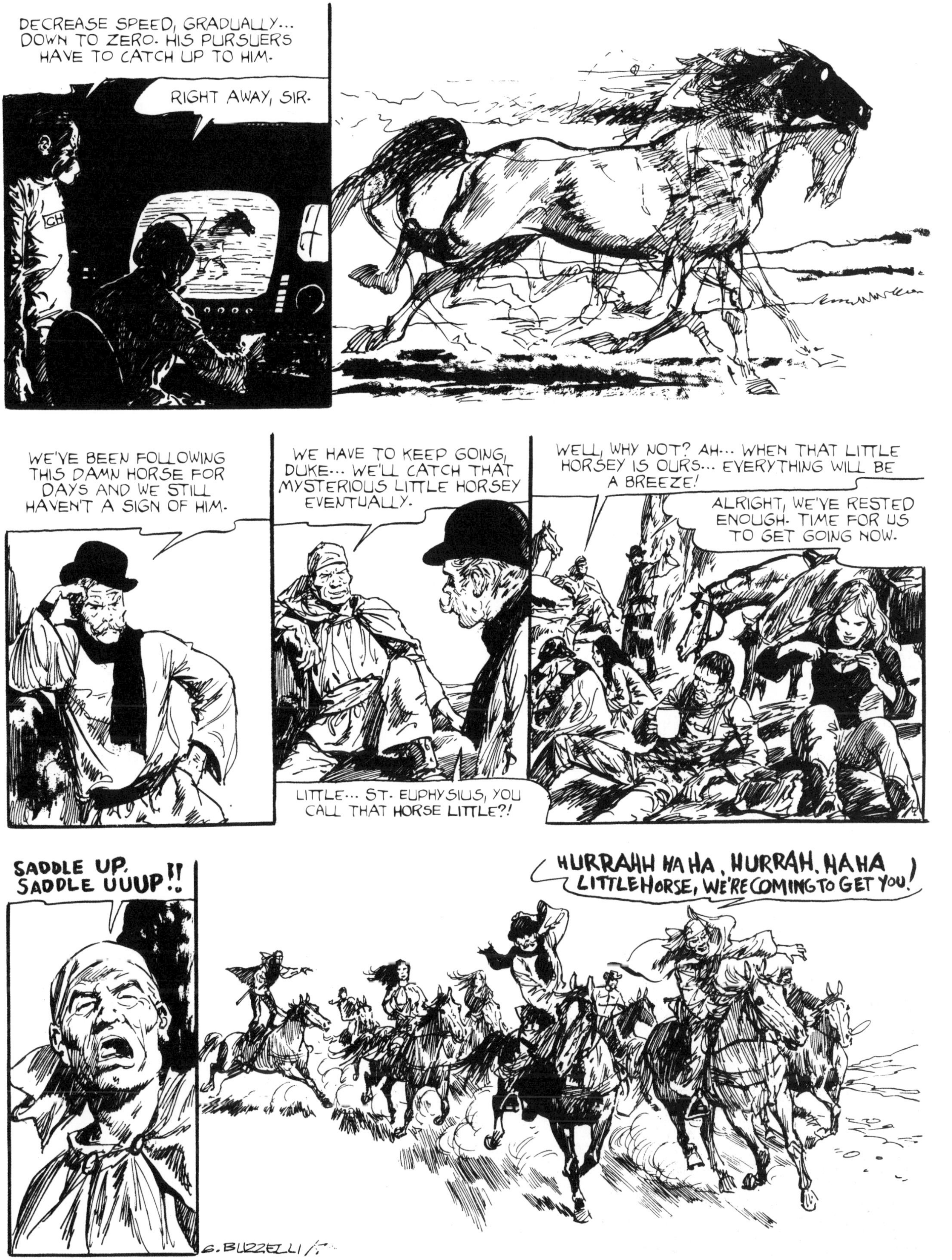

DECREASE SPEED, GRADUALLY... DOWN TO ZERO. HIS PURSUERS HAVE TO CATCH UP TO HIM.
RIGHT AWAY, SIR.
WE'VE BEEN FOLLOWING THIS DAMN HORSE FOR DAYS AND WE STILL HAVEN'T A SIGN OF HIM.
WE HAVE TO KEEP GOING, DUKE... WE'LL CATCH THAT MYSTERIOUS LITTLE HORSEY EVENTUALLY.
LITTLE... ST. EUPHYSIUS, YOU CALL THAT HORSE LITTLE?!
WELL, WHY NOT? AH... WHEN THAT LITTLE HORSEY IS OURS... EVERYTHING WILL BE A BREEZE!
ALRIGHT, WE'VE RESTED ENOUGH. TIME FOR US TO GET GOING NOW.
SADDLE UP, SADDLE UUUP!!
HURRAHH HA HA, HURRAH, HA HA LITTLEHORSE, WE'RE COMING TO GET YOU!
G. BUZZELLI

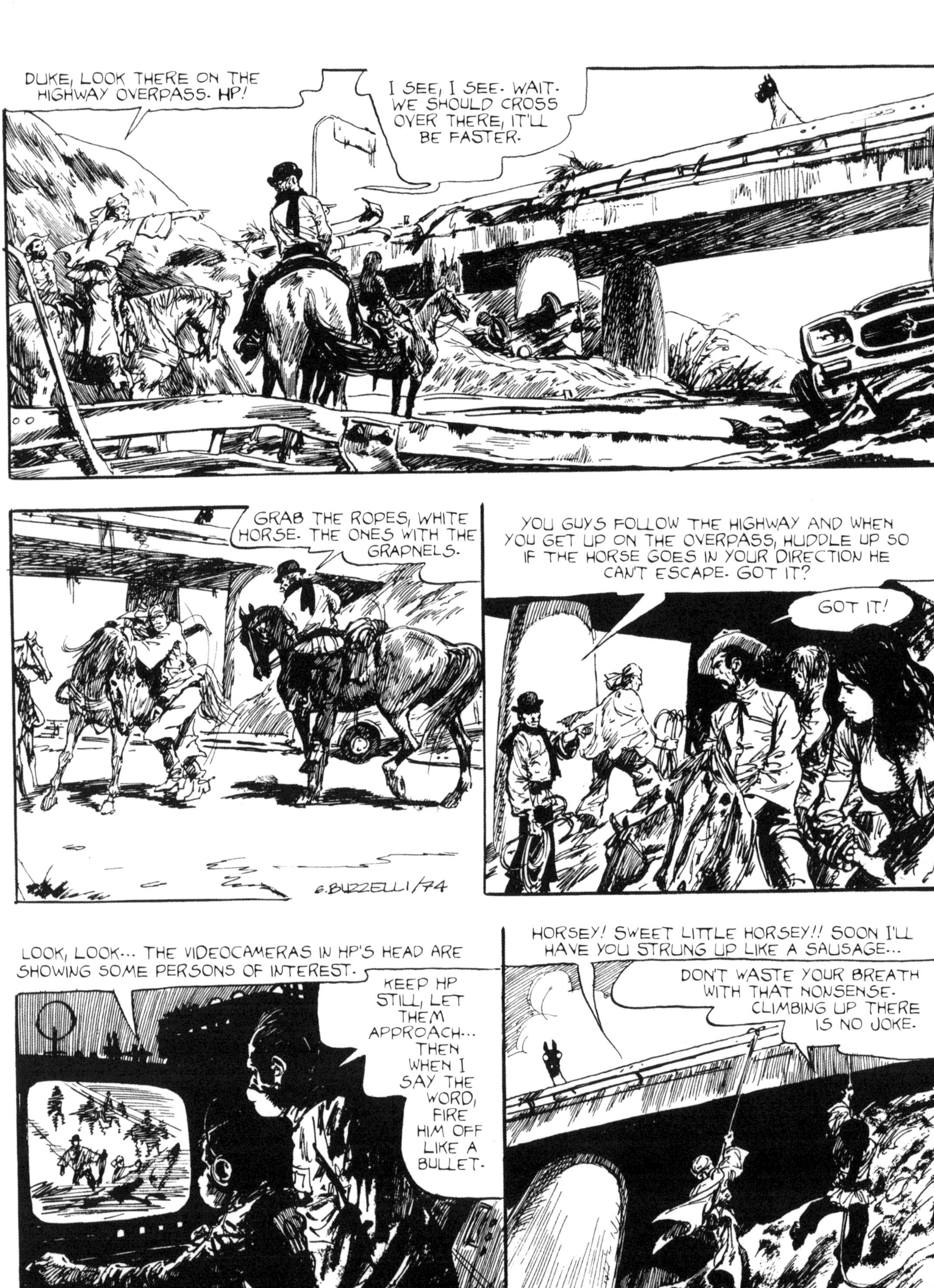

DUKE, LOOK THERE ON THE HIGHWAY OVERPASS. HP!
I SEE, I SEE. WAIT. WE SHOULD CROSS OVER THERE, IT'LL BE FASTER.
GRAB THE ROPES, WHITE HORSE. THE ONES WITH THE GRAPNELS.
G. BUZZELLI/74
YOU GUYS FOLLOW THE HIGHWAY AND WHEN YOU GET UP ON THE OVERPASS, HUDDLE UP SO IF THE HORSE GOES IN YOUR DIRECTION HE CAN'T ESCAPE. GOT IT?
GOT IT!
LOOK, LOOK... THE VIDEOCAMERAS IN HP'S HEAD ARE SHOWING SOME PERSONS OF INTEREST.
KEEP HP STILL, LET THEM APPROACH... THEN WHEN I SAY THE WORD, FIRE HIM OFF LIKE A BULLET.
HORSEY! SWEET LITTLE HORSEY!! SOON I'LL HAVE YOU STRUNG UP LIKE A SAUSAGE...
DON'T WASTE YOUR BREATH WITH THAT NONSENSE. CLIMBING UP THERE IS NO JOKE.

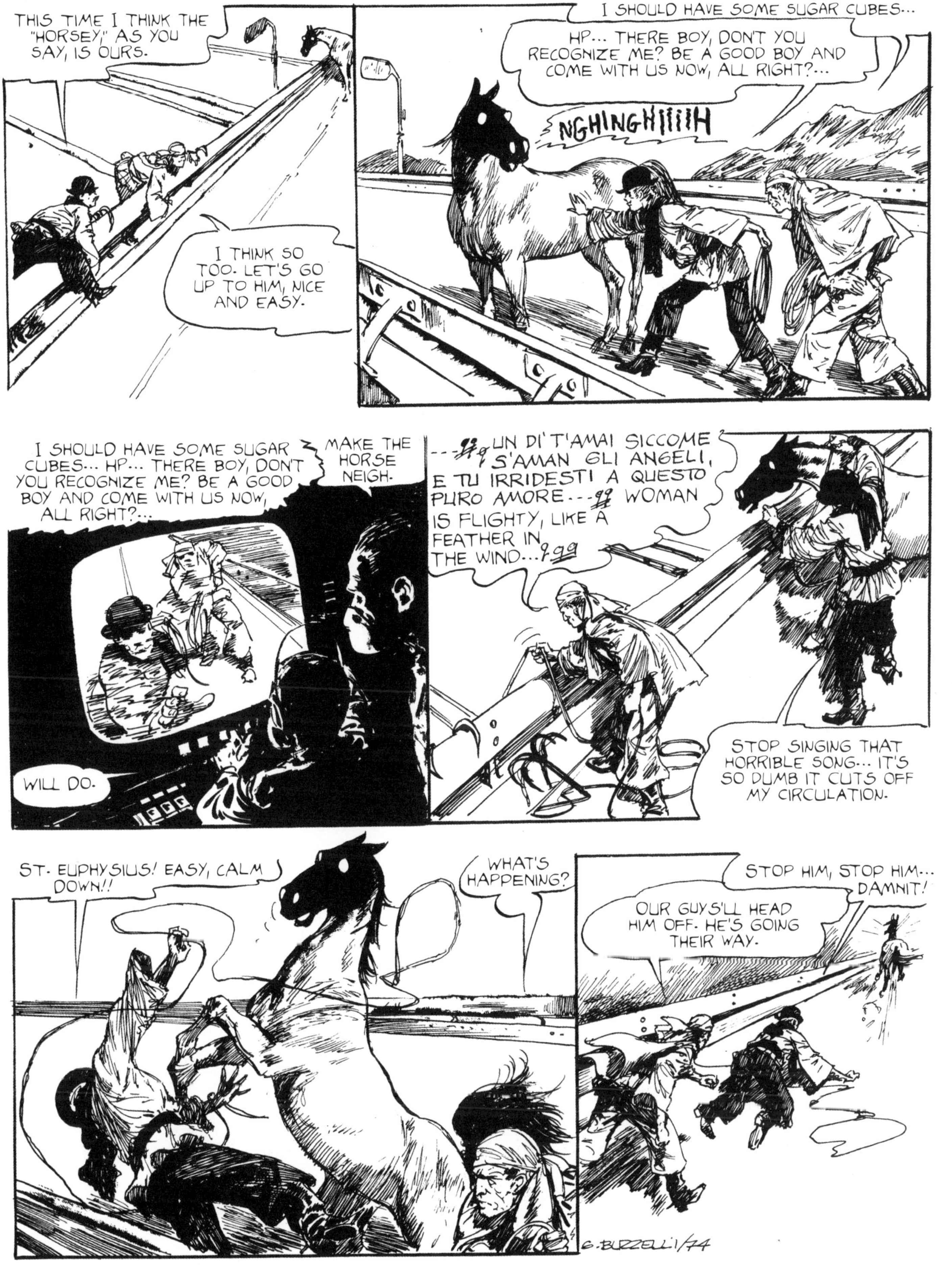
THIS TIME I THINK THE "HORSEY," AS YOU SAY, IS OURS.
I THINK SO TOO. LET'S GO UP TO HIM, NICE AND EASY.
I SHOULD HAVE SOME SUGAR CUBES...
HP... THERE BOY, DON'T YOU RECOGNIZE ME? BE A GOOD BOY AND COME WITH US NOW, ALL RIGHT?...
NGHINGHIIIIIH
I SHOULD HAVE SOME SUGAR CUBES... HP... THERE BOY, DON'T YOU RECOGNIZE ME? BE A GOOD BOY AND COME WITH US NOW, ALL RIGHT?...
MAKE THE HORSE NEIGH.
WILL DO.
...UN DI' T'AMAI SICCOME S'AMAN GLI ANGELI, E TU IRRIDESTI A QUESTO PURO AMORE... WOMAN IS FLIGHTY, LIKE A FEATHER IN THE WIND...
STOP SINGING THAT HORRIBLE SONG... IT'S SO DUMB IT CUTS OFF MY CIRCULATION.
ST. EUPHYSIUS! EASY, CALM DOWN!!
WHAT'S HAPPENING?
STOP HIM, STOP HIM... DAMNIT!
OUR GUYS'LL HEAD HIM OFF. HE'S GOING THEIR WAY.
G. BUZZELLI 1/74

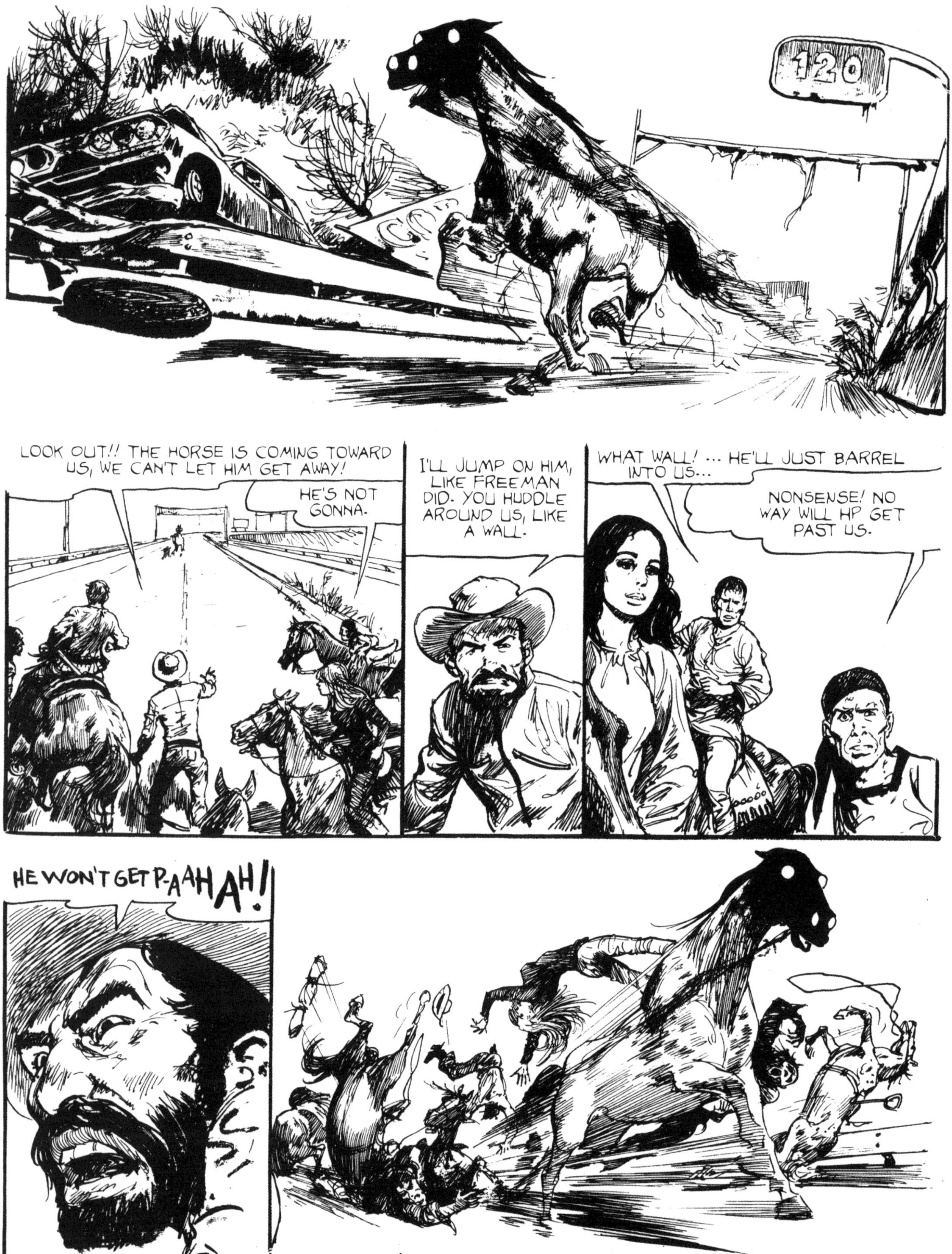
120
LOOK OUT!! THE HORSE IS COMING TOWARD US, WE CAN'T LET HIM GET AWAY!
HE'S NOT GONNA.
I'LL JUMP ON HIM, LIKE FREEMAN DID- YOU HUDDLE AROUND US, LIKE A WALL.
WHAT WALL! ... HE'LL JUST BARREL INTO US...
NONSENSE! NO WAY WILL HP GET PAST US.
HE WON'T GET P-AAHAH!
G. BUZZELLI/74

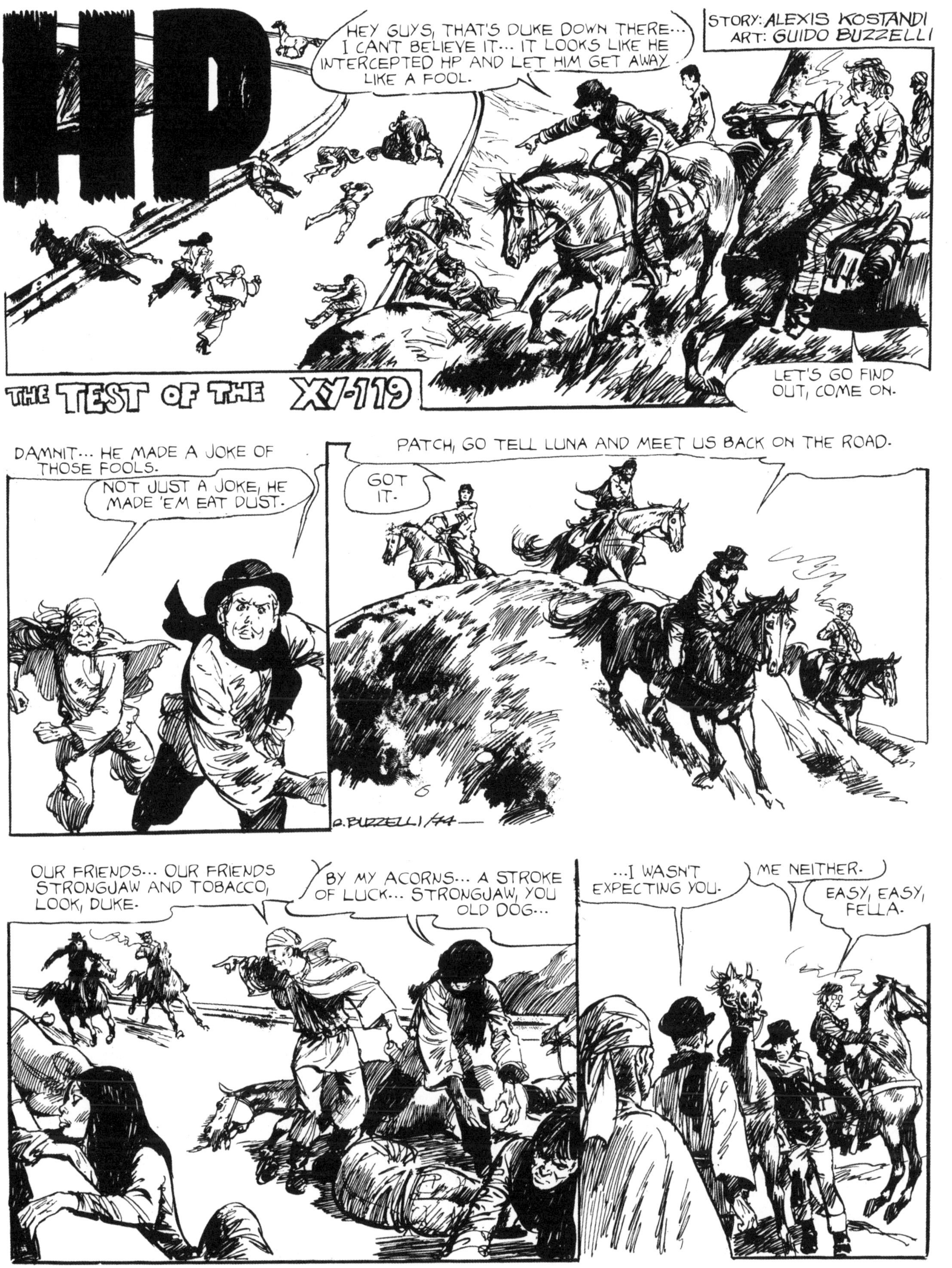
HP
STORY: ALEXIS KOSTANDI
ART: GUIDO BUZZELLI
HEY GUYS, THAT'S DUKE DOWN THERE... I CAN'T BELIEVE IT... IT LOOKS LIKE HE INTERCEPTED HP AND LET HIM GET AWAY LIKE A FOOL.
THE TEST OF THE XY-119
LET'S GO FIND OUT, COME ON.
DAMNIT... HE MADE A JOKE OF THOSE FOOLS.
NOT JUST A JOKE, HE MADE 'EM EAT DUST.
PATCH, GO TELL LUNA AND MEET US BACK ON THE ROAD.
GOT IT.
G. BUZZELLI/74
OUR FRIENDS... OUR FRIENDS STRONGJAW AND TOBACCO, LOOK, DUKE.
BY MY ACORNS... A STROKE OF LUCK... STRONGJAW, YOU OLD DOG...
...I WASN'T EXPECTING YOU.
ME NEITHER.
EASY, EASY, FELLA.

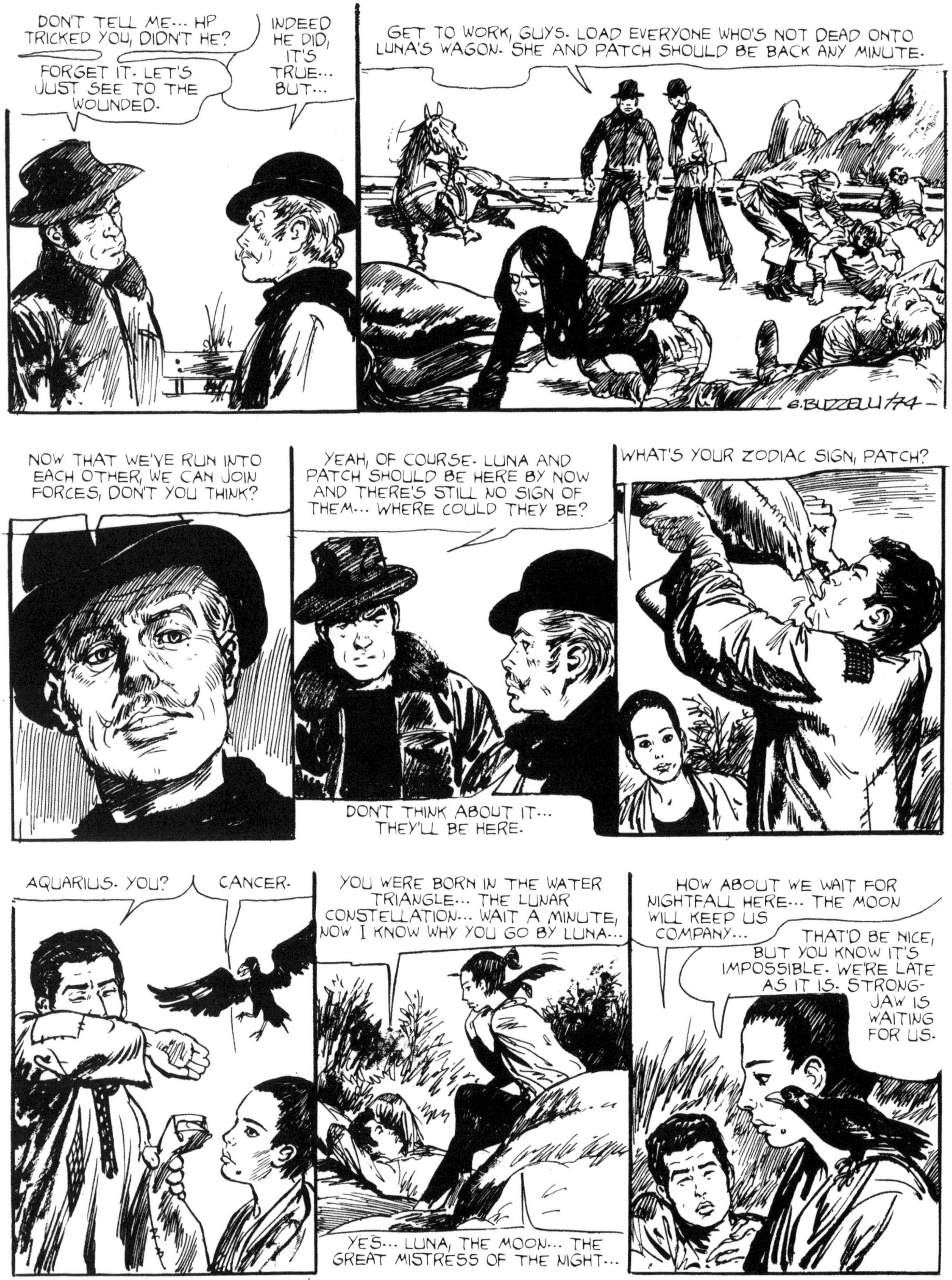
DON'T TELL ME... HP TRICKED YOU, DIDN'T HE?
INDEED HE DID, IT'S TRUE... BUT...
FORGET IT. LET'S JUST SEE TO THE WOUNDED.
GET TO WORK, GUYS. LOAD EVERYONE WHO'S NOT DEAD ONTO LUNA'S WAGON. SHE AND PATCH SHOULD BE BACK ANY MINUTE.
G. BUZZELLI 74
NOW THAT WE'VE RUN INTO EACH OTHER, WE CAN JOIN FORCES, DON'T YOU THINK?
YEAH, OF COURSE. LUNA AND PATCH SHOULD BE HERE BY NOW AND THERE'S STILL NO SIGN OF THEM... WHERE COULD THEY BE?
DON'T THINK ABOUT IT... THEY'LL BE HERE.
WHAT'S YOUR ZODIAC SIGN, PATCH?
AQUARIUS. YOU?
CANCER.
YOU WERE BORN IN THE WATER TRIANGLE... THE LUNAR CONSTELLATION... WAIT A MINUTE, NOW I KNOW WHY YOU GO BY LUNA...
YES... LUNA, THE MOON... THE GREAT MISTRESS OF THE NIGHT...
HOW ABOUT WE WAIT FOR NIGHTFALL HERE... THE MOON WILL KEEP US COMPANY...
THAT'D BE NICE, BUT YOU KNOW IT'S IMPOSSIBLE. WE'RE LATE AS IT IS. STRONG-JAW IS WAITING FOR US.

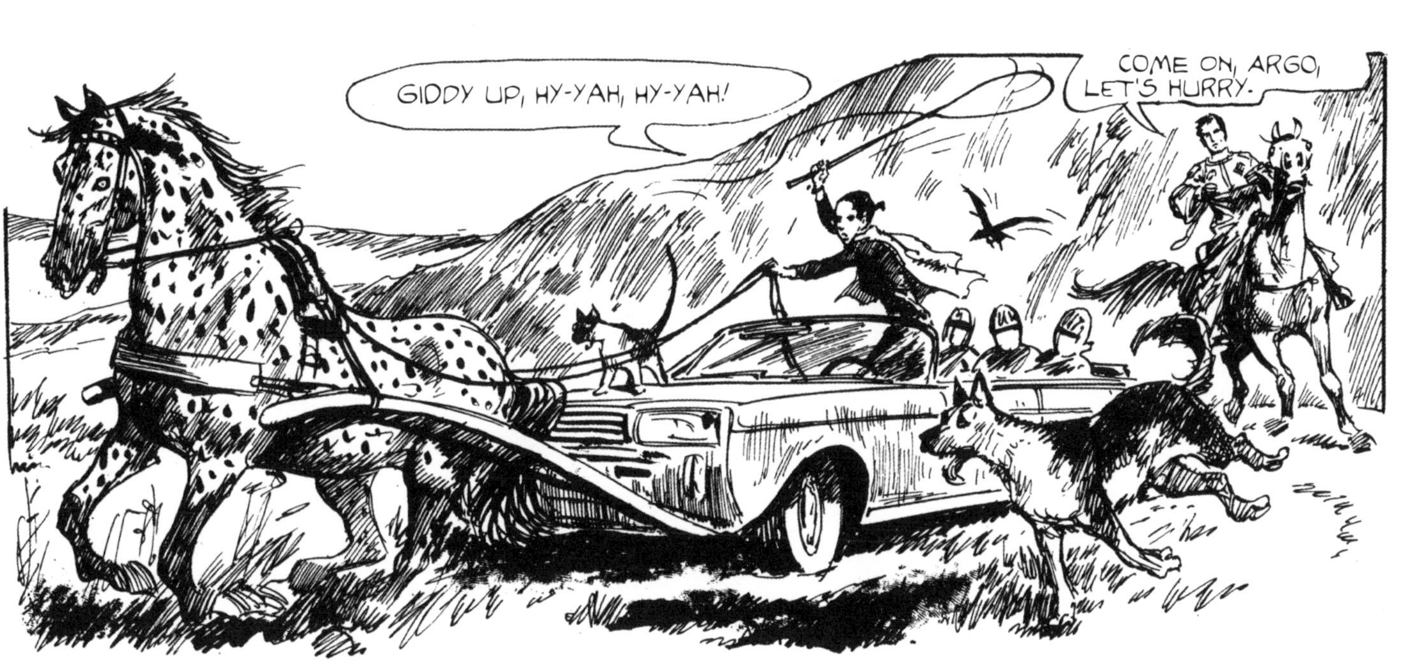
GIDDY UP, HY-YAH, HY-YAH!
COME ON, ARGO, LET'S HURRY.

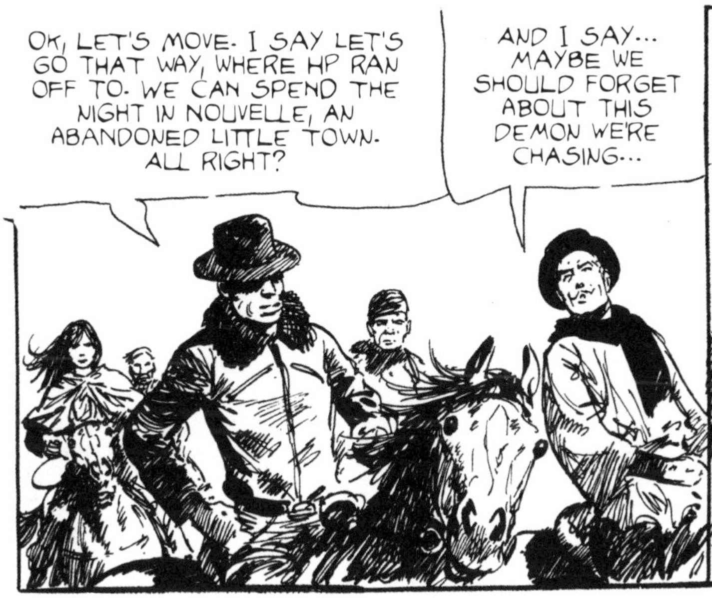
OK, LET'S MOVE. I SAY LET'S GO THAT WAY, WHERE HP RAN OFF TO. WE CAN SPEND THE NIGHT IN NOUVELLE, AN ABANDONED LITTLE TOWN. ALL RIGHT?
AND I SAY... MAYBE WE SHOULD FORGET ABOUT THIS DEMON WE'RE CHASING...

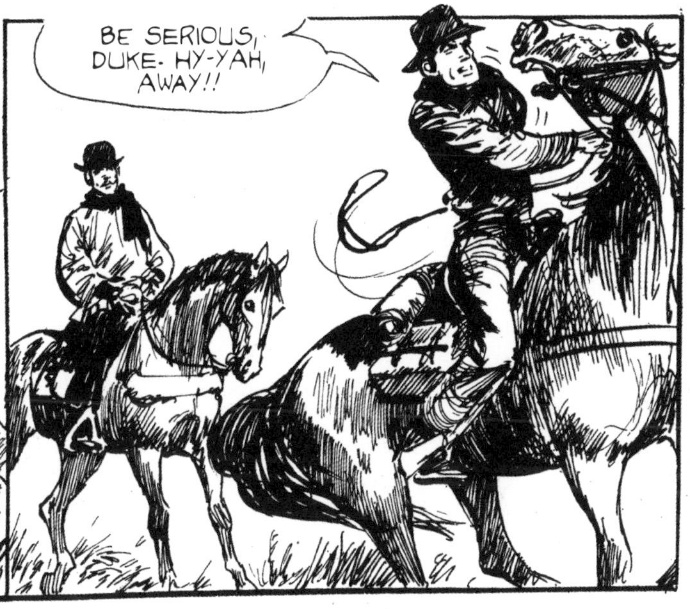
BE SERIOUS, DUKE. HY-YAH, AWAY!!

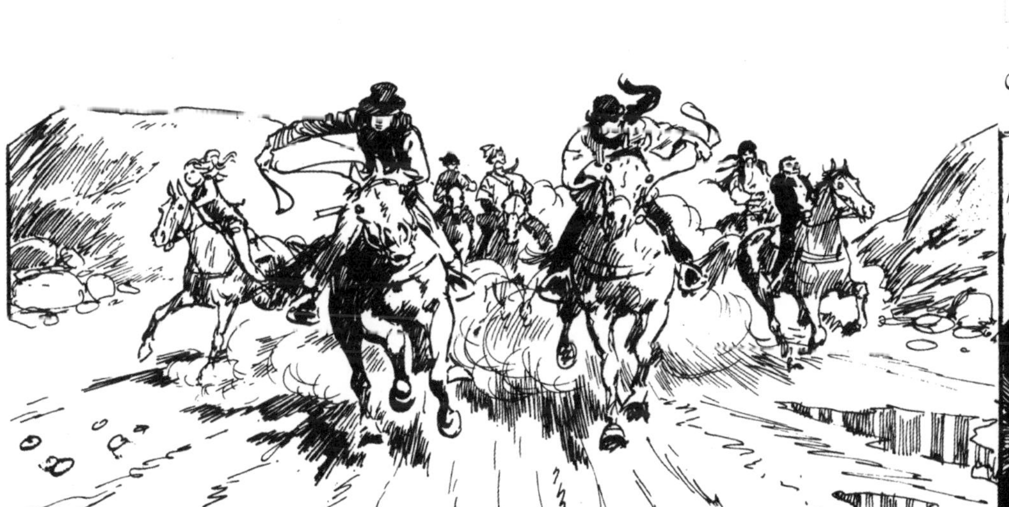
G.BUZZELLI/74

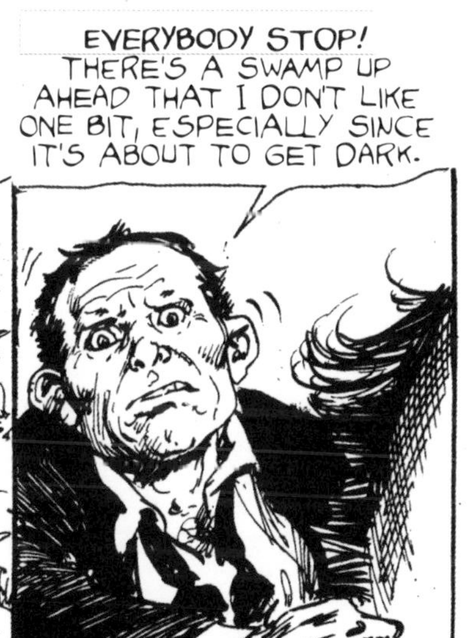
EVERYBODY STOP! THERE'S A SWAMP UP AHEAD THAT I DON'T LIKE ONE BIT, ESPECIALLY SINCE IT'S ABOUT TO GET DARK.

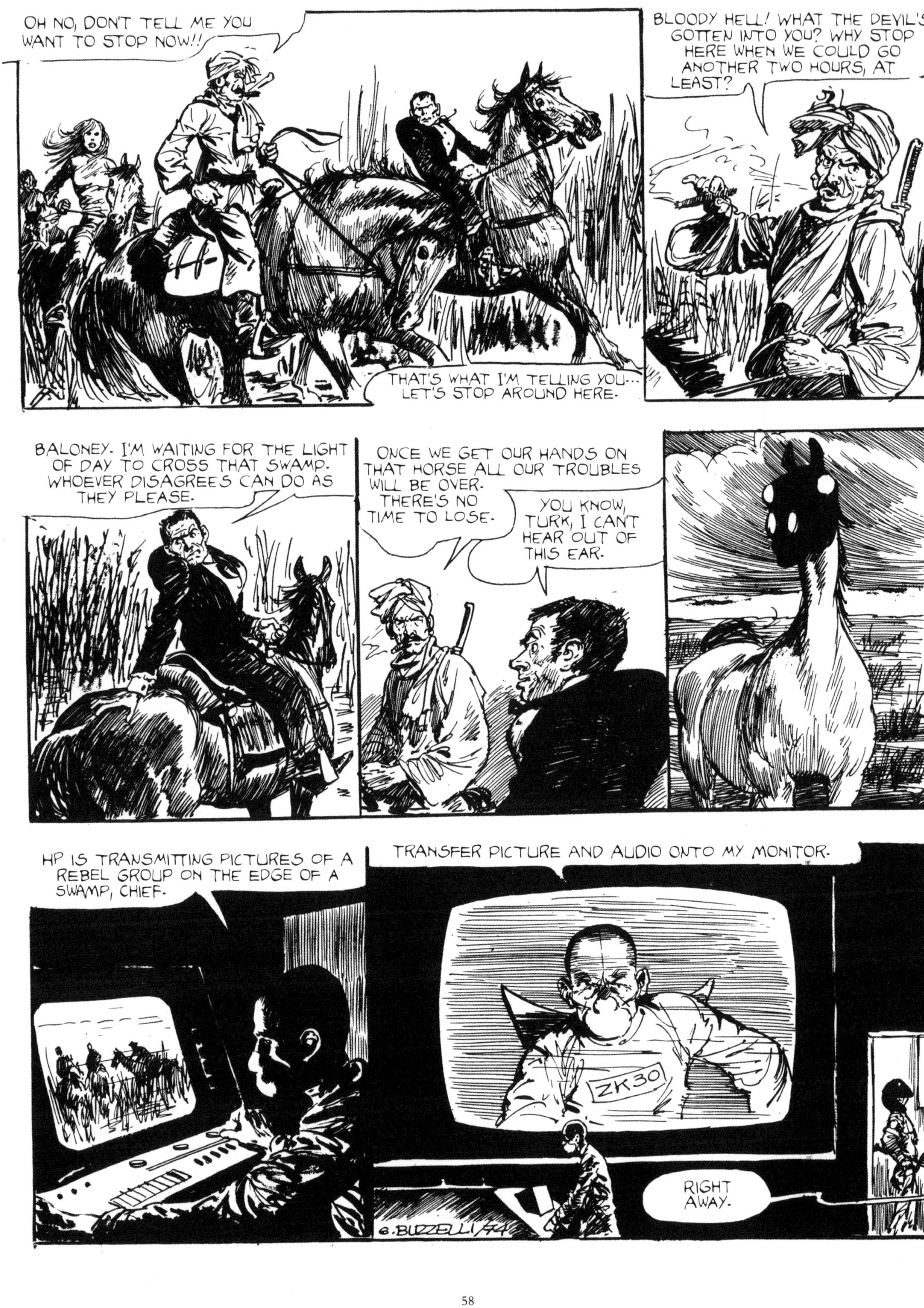
OH NO, DON'T TELL ME YOU WANT TO STOP NOW!!
THAT'S WHAT I'M TELLING YOU... LET'S STOP AROUND HERE.
BLOODY HELL! WHAT THE DEVIL'S GOTTEN INTO YOU? WHY STOP HERE WHEN WE COULD GO ANOTHER TWO HOURS, AT LEAST?
BALONEY. I'M WAITING FOR THE LIGHT OF DAY TO CROSS THAT SWAMP. WHOEVER DISAGREES CAN DO AS THEY PLEASE.
ONCE WE GET OUR HANDS ON THAT HORSE ALL OUR TROUBLES WILL BE OVER. THERE'S NO TIME TO LOSE.
YOU KNOW, TURK, I CAN'T HEAR OUT OF THIS EAR.
HP IS TRANSMITTING PICTURES OF A REBEL GROUP ON THE EDGE OF A SWAMP, CHIEF.
TRANSFER PICTURE AND AUDIO ONTO MY MONITOR.
ZK30
RIGHT AWAY.
G. BUZZELLI/74

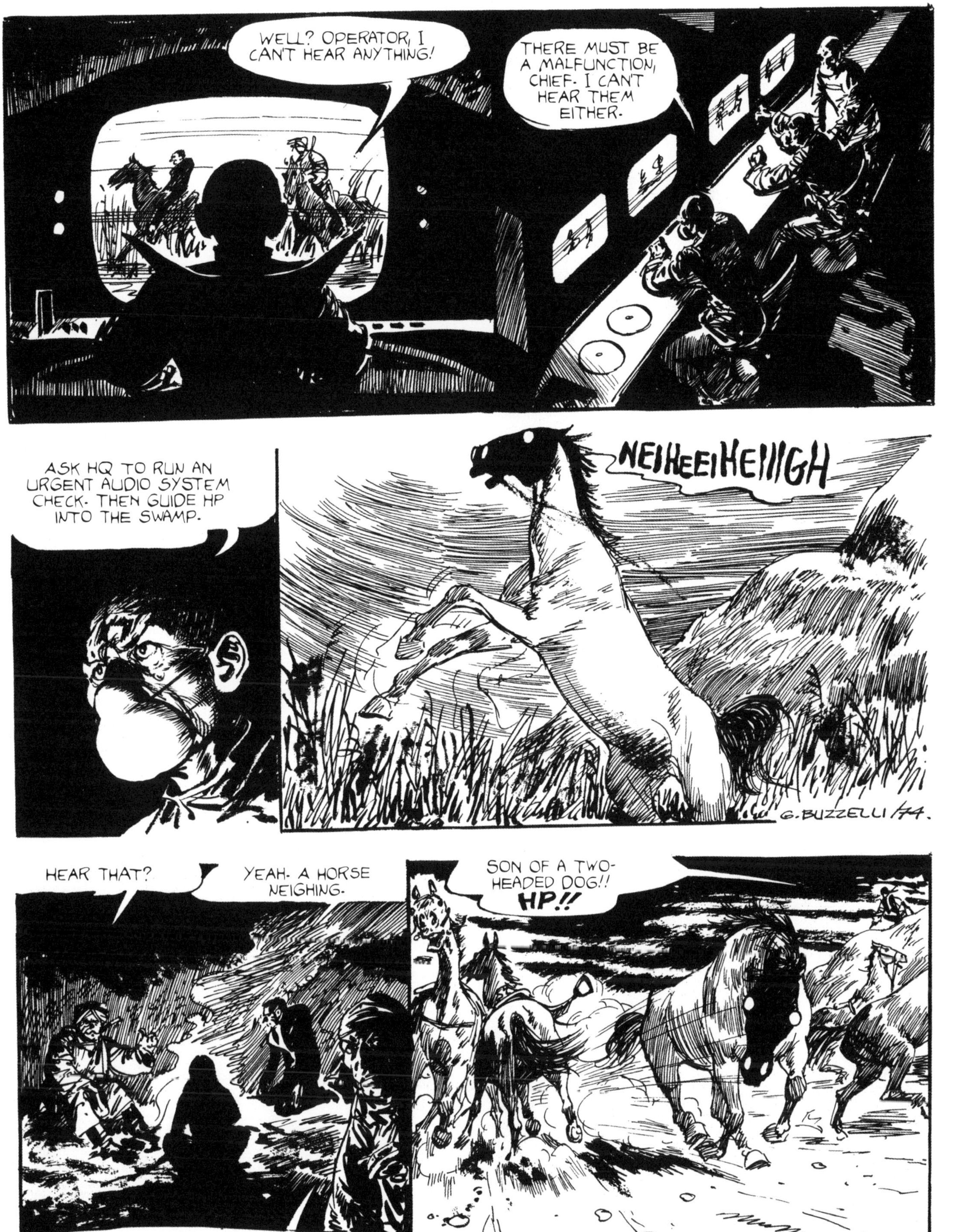

WELL? OPERATOR, I CAN'T HEAR ANYTHING!
THERE MUST BE A MALFUNCTION, CHIEF. I CAN'T HEAR THEM EITHER.
ASK HQ TO RUN AN URGENT AUDIO SYSTEM CHECK. THEN GUIDE HP INTO THE SWAMP.
NEIHEEIHEIIIGH
G. BUZZELLI/74.
HEAR THAT?
YEAH. A HORSE NEIGHING.
AND OUR HORSES ARE SPOOKED.
SON OF A TWO-HEADED DOG!! HP!!

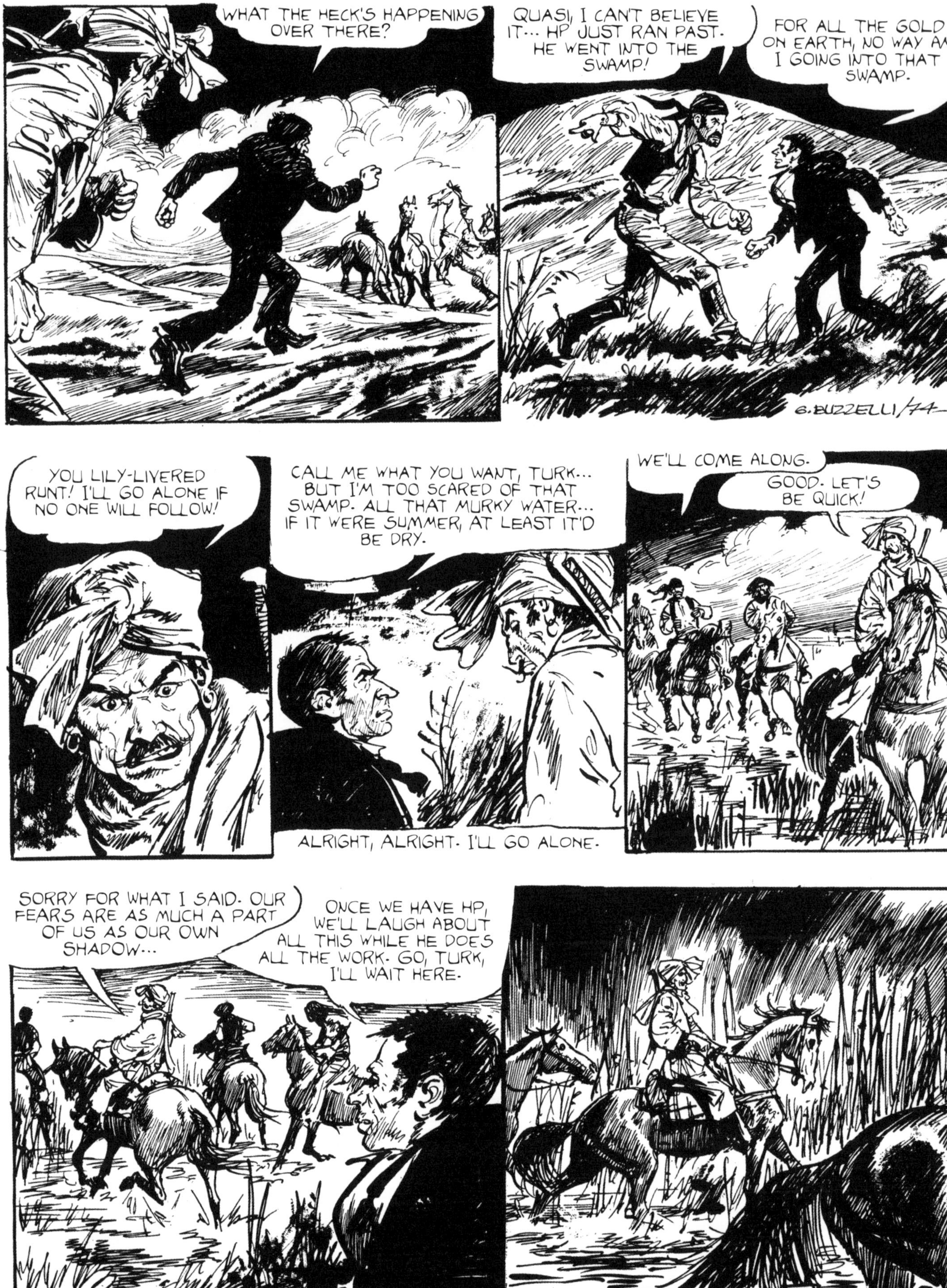
WHAT THE HECK'S HAPPENING OVER THERE?
QUASI, I CAN'T BELIEVE IT... HP JUST RAN PAST. HE WENT INTO THE SWAMP!
FOR ALL THE GOLD ON EARTH, NO WAY AM I GOING INTO THAT SWAMP.
G. BUZZELLI/74
YOU LILY-LIVERED RUNT! I'LL GO ALONE IF NO ONE WILL FOLLOW!
CALL ME WHAT YOU WANT, TURK... BUT I'M TOO SCARED OF THAT SWAMP. ALL THAT MURKY WATER... IF IT WERE SUMMER, AT LEAST IT'D BE DRY.
ALRIGHT, ALRIGHT. I'LL GO ALONE.
WE'LL COME ALONG.
GOOD. LET'S BE QUICK!
SORRY FOR WHAT I SAID. OUR FEARS ARE AS MUCH A PART OF US AS OUR OWN SHADOW...
ONCE WE HAVE HP, WE'LL LAUGH ABOUT ALL THIS WHILE HE DOES ALL THE WORK. GO, TURK, I'LL WAIT HERE.

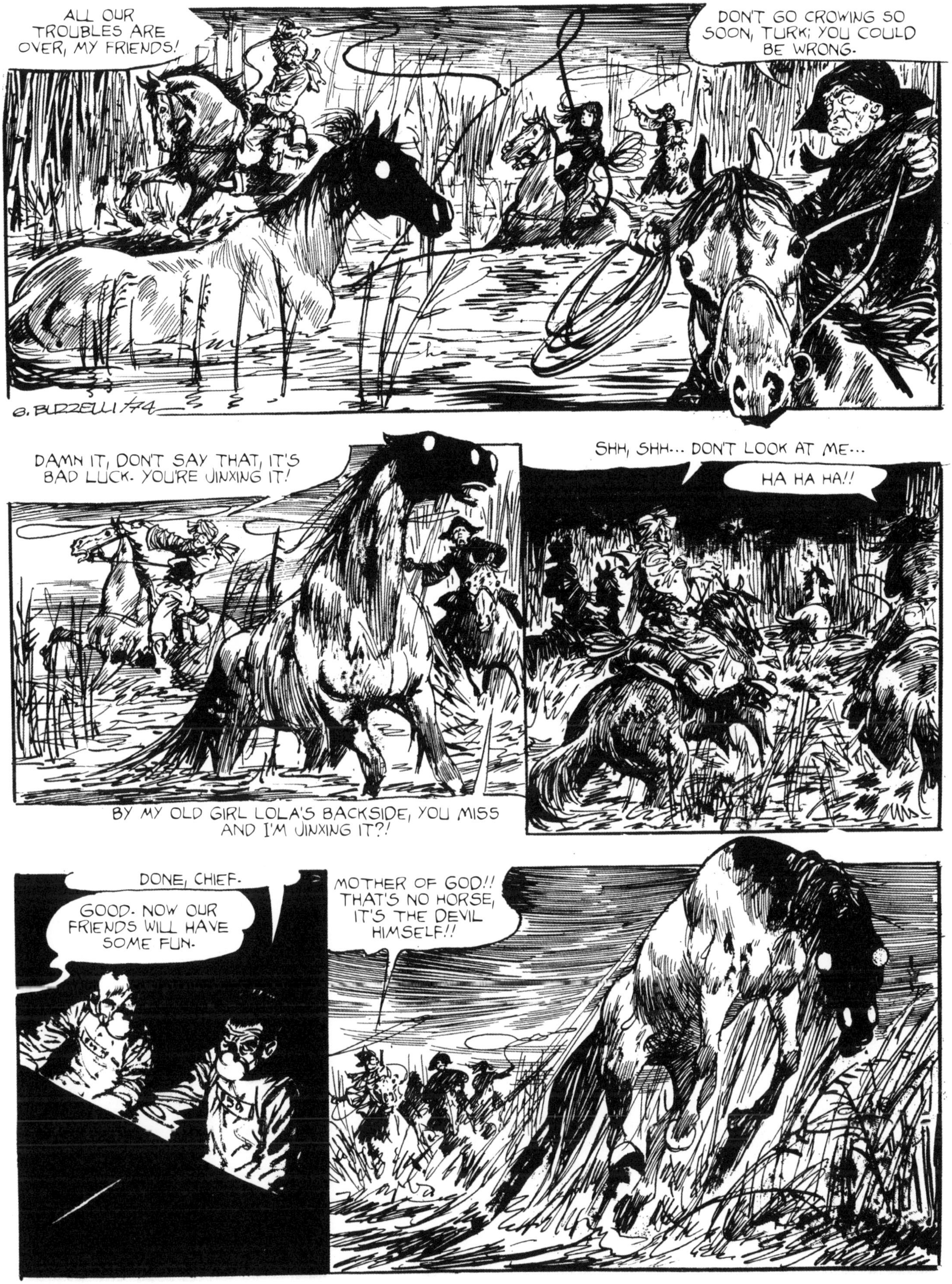
ALL OUR TROUBLES ARE OVER, MY FRIENDS!
DON'T GO CROWING SO SOON, TURK; YOU COULD BE WRONG.
G. BUZZELLI /74
DAMN IT, DON'T SAY THAT, IT'S BAD LUCK. YOU'RE JINXING IT!
BY MY OLD GIRL LOLA'S BACKSIDE, YOU MISS AND I'M JINXING IT?!
SHH, SHH... DON'T LOOK AT ME...
HA HA HA!!
DONE, CHIEF.
GOOD. NOW OUR FRIENDS WILL HAVE SOME FUN.
MOTHER OF GOD!! THAT'S NO HORSE, IT'S THE DEVIL HIMSELF!!

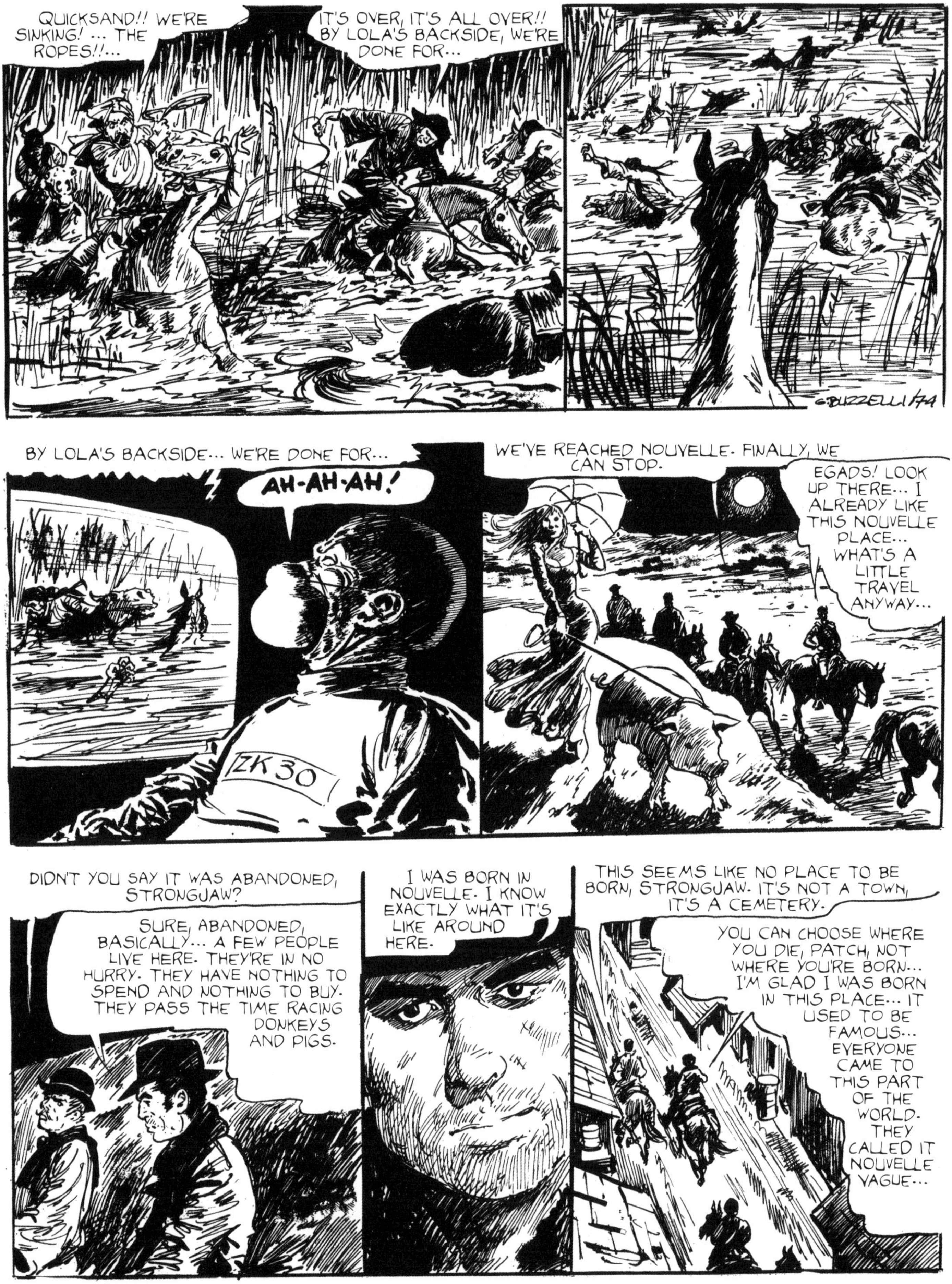
QUICKSAND!! WE'RE SINKING! ... THE ROPES!!...
IT'S OVER, IT'S ALL OVER!! BY LOLA'S BACKSIDE, WE'RE DONE FOR...
G.BUZZELLI/74
BY LOLA'S BACKSIDE... WE'RE DONE FOR...
AH-AH-AH!
ZK30
WE'VE REACHED NOUVELLE. FINALLY, WE CAN STOP.
EGADS! LOOK UP THERE... I ALREADY LIKE THIS NOUVELLE PLACE... WHAT'S A LITTLE TRAVEL ANYWAY...
DIDN'T YOU SAY IT WAS ABANDONED, STRONGJAW?
SURE, ABANDONED, BASICALLY... A FEW PEOPLE LIVE HERE. THEY'RE IN NO HURRY. THEY HAVE NOTHING TO SPEND AND NOTHING TO BUY. THEY PASS THE TIME RACING DONKEYS AND PIGS.
I WAS BORN IN NOUVELLE. I KNOW EXACTLY WHAT IT'S LIKE AROUND HERE.
THIS SEEMS LIKE NO PLACE TO BE BORN, STRONGJAW. IT'S NOT A TOWN, IT'S A CEMETERY.
YOU CAN CHOOSE WHERE YOU DIE, PATCH, NOT WHERE YOU'RE BORN... I'M GLAD I WAS BORN IN THIS PLACE... IT USED TO BE FAMOUS... EVERYONE CAME TO THIS PART OF THE WORLD. THEY CALLED IT NOUVELLE VAGUE...

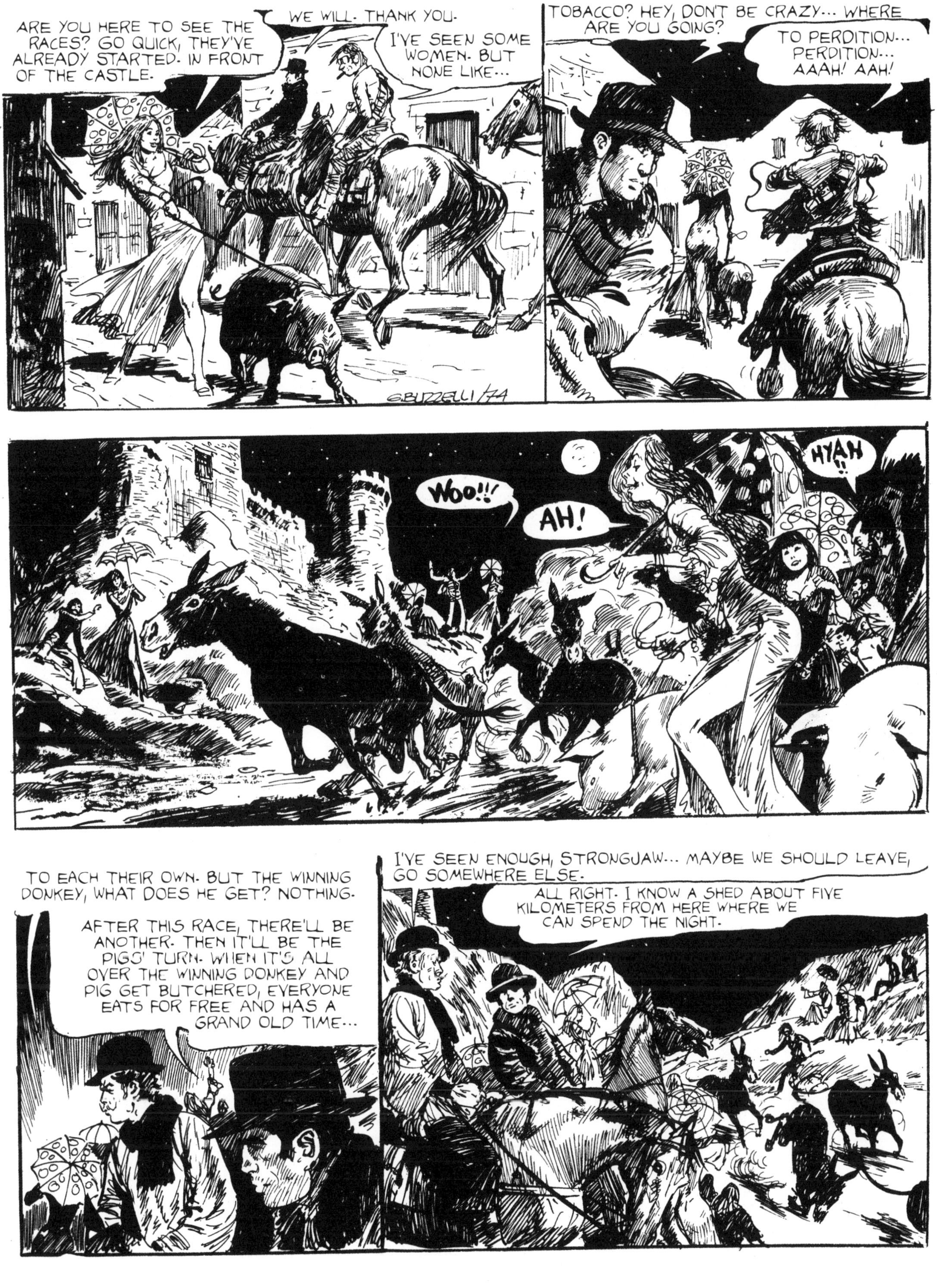
ARE YOU HERE TO SEE THE RACES? GO QUICK, THEY'VE ALREADY STARTED. IN FRONT OF THE CASTLE.
WE WILL. THANK YOU.
I'VE SEEN SOME WOMEN. BUT NONE LIKE...
GBUZZELLI/74
TOBACCO? HEY, DON'T BE CRAZY... WHERE ARE YOU GOING?
TO PERDITION... PERDITION... AAAH! AAH!
WOO!!!
AH!
HYAH!!
TO EACH THEIR OWN. BUT THE WINNING DONKEY, WHAT DOES HE GET? NOTHING.
AFTER THIS RACE, THERE'LL BE ANOTHER. THEN IT'LL BE THE PIGS' TURN. WHEN IT'S ALL OVER THE WINNING DONKEY AND PIG GET BUTCHERED, EVERYONE EATS FOR FREE AND HAS A GRAND OLD TIME...
I'VE SEEN ENOUGH, STRONGJAW... MAYBE WE SHOULD LEAVE, GO SOMEWHERE ELSE.
ALL RIGHT. I KNOW A SHED ABOUT FIVE KILOMETERS FROM HERE WHERE WE CAN SPEND THE NIGHT.

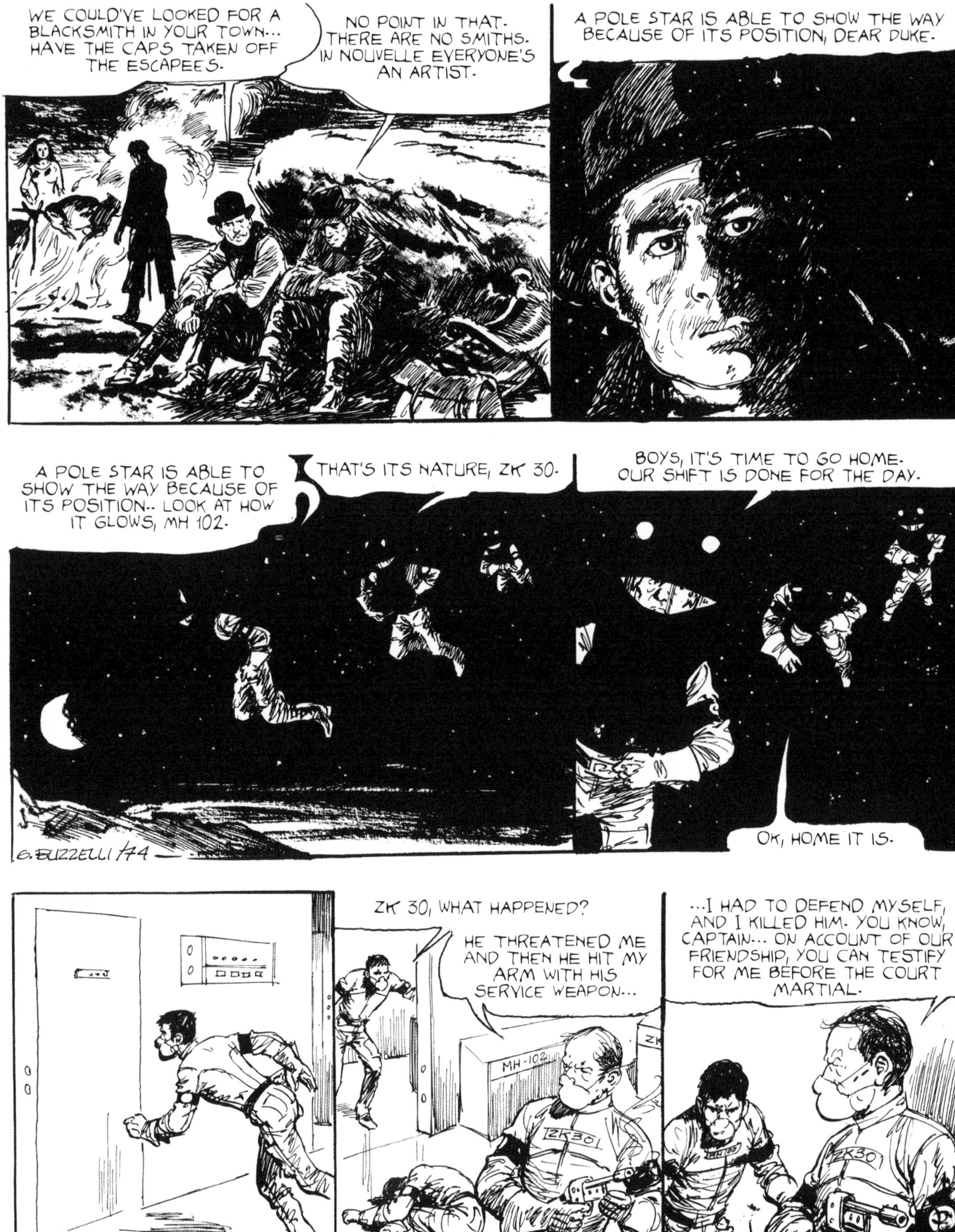
WE COULD'VE LOOKED FOR A BLACKSMITH IN YOUR TOWN... HAVE THE CAPS TAKEN OFF THE ESCAPEES.
NO POINT IN THAT. THERE ARE NO SMITHS. IN NOUVELLE EVERYONE'S AN ARTIST.
A POLE STAR IS ABLE TO SHOW THE WAY BECAUSE OF ITS POSITION, DEAR DUKE.
A POLE STAR IS ABLE TO SHOW THE WAY BECAUSE OF ITS POSITION.. LOOK AT HOW IT GLOWS, MH 102.
THAT'S ITS NATURE, ZK 30.
BOYS, IT'S TIME TO GO HOME. OUR SHIFT IS DONE FOR THE DAY.
OK, HOME IT IS.
G. BUZZELLI /74
ZK 30, WHAT HAPPENED?
HE THREATENED ME AND THEN HE HIT MY ARM WITH HIS SERVICE WEAPON...
MH-102
ZK30
...I HAD TO DEFEND MYSELF, AND I KILLED HIM. YOU KNOW, CAPTAIN... ON ACCOUNT OF OUR FRIENDSHIP, YOU CAN TESTIFY FOR ME BEFORE THE COURT MARTIAL.
ZK30
BUT... BUT... THAT'S...

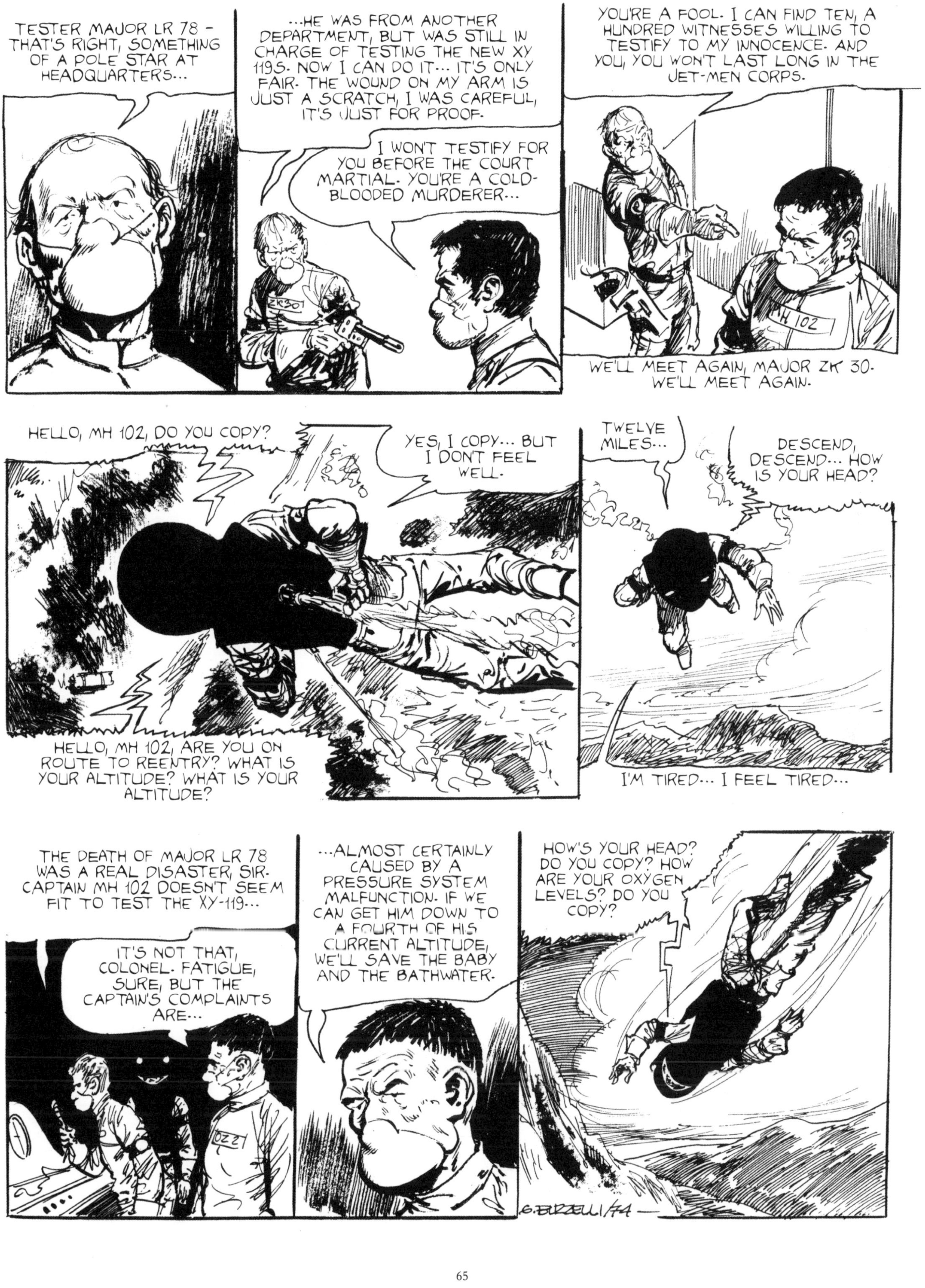
TESTER MAJOR LR 78 – THAT'S RIGHT, SOMETHING OF A POLE STAR AT HEADQUARTERS...
...HE WAS FROM ANOTHER DEPARTMENT, BUT WAS STILL IN CHARGE OF TESTING THE NEW XY 119S. NOW I CAN DO IT... IT'S ONLY FAIR. THE WOUND ON MY ARM IS JUST A SCRATCH, I WAS CAREFUL, IT'S JUST FOR PROOF.
I WON'T TESTIFY FOR YOU BEFORE THE COURT MARTIAL. YOU'RE A COLD-BLOODED MURDERER...
ZK 30
YOU'RE A FOOL. I CAN FIND TEN, A HUNDRED WITNESSES WILLING TO TESTIFY TO MY INNOCENCE. AND YOU, YOU WON'T LAST LONG IN THE JET-MEN CORPS.
MH 102
WE'LL MEET AGAIN, MAJOR ZK 30. WE'LL MEET AGAIN.
HELLO, MH 102, DO YOU COPY?
YES, I COPY... BUT I DON'T FEEL WELL.
HELLO, MH 102, ARE YOU ON ROUTE TO REENTRY? WHAT IS YOUR ALTITUDE? WHAT IS YOUR ALTITUDE?
TWELVE MILES...
DESCEND, DESCEND... HOW IS YOUR HEAD?
I'M TIRED... I FEEL TIRED...
THE DEATH OF MAJOR LR 78 WAS A REAL DISASTER, SIR. CAPTAIN MH 102 DOESN'T SEEM FIT TO TEST THE XY-119...
IT'S NOT THAT, COLONEL. FATIGUE, SURE, BUT THE CAPTAIN'S COMPLAINTS ARE...
OZ 2
...ALMOST CERTAINLY CAUSED BY A PRESSURE SYSTEM MALFUNCTION. IF WE CAN GET HIM DOWN TO A FOURTH OF HIS CURRENT ALTITUDE, WE'LL SAVE THE BABY AND THE BATHWATER.
HOW'S YOUR HEAD? DO YOU COPY? HOW ARE YOUR OXYGEN LEVELS? DO YOU COPY?
G. BUZZELLI/74

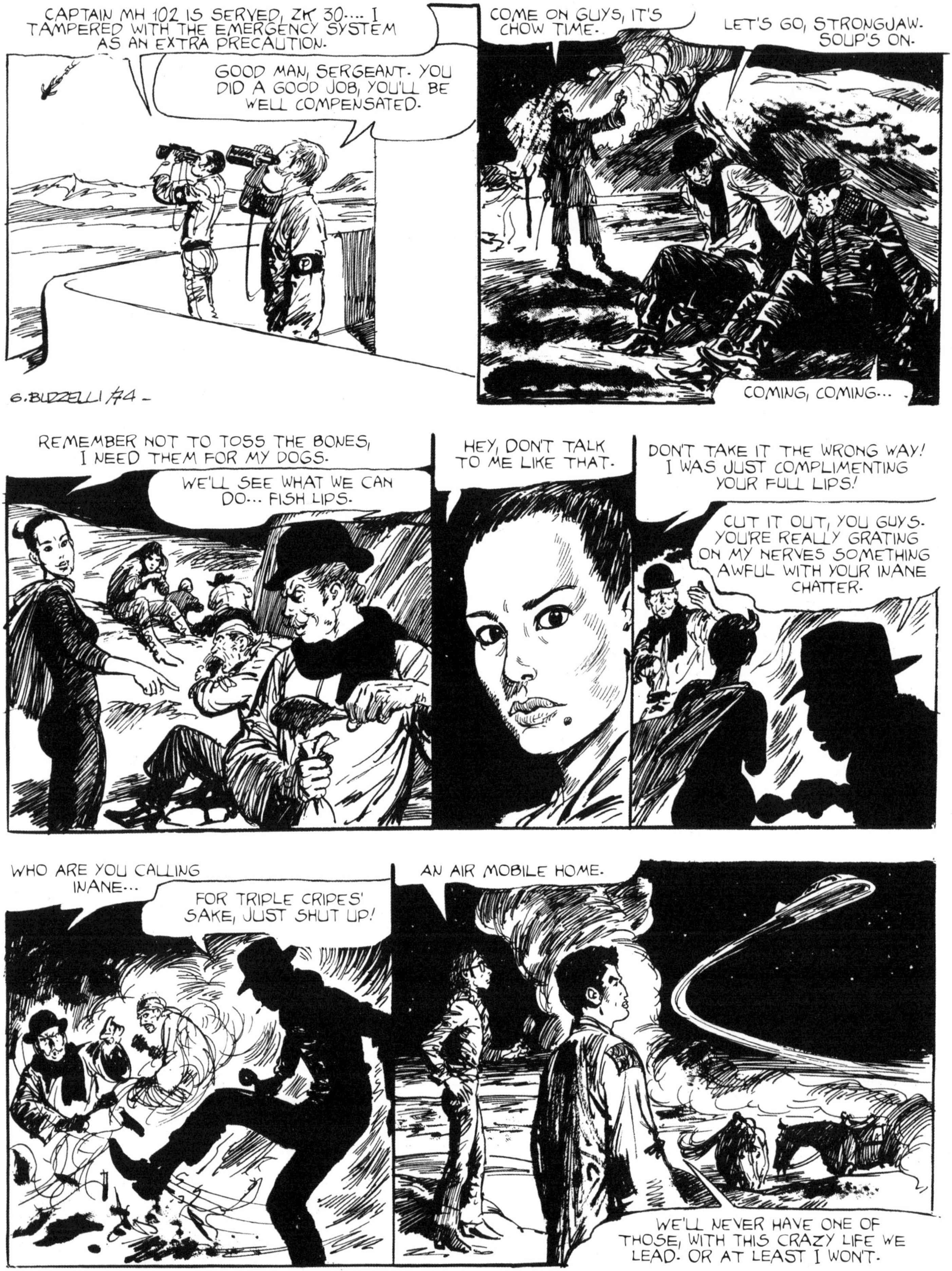
CAPTAIN MH 102 IS SERVED, ZK 30.... I TAMPERED WITH THE EMERGENCY SYSTEM AS AN EXTRA PRECAUTION.
GOOD MAN, SERGEANT. YOU DID A GOOD JOB, YOU'LL BE WELL COMPENSATED.
G. BUZZELLI 74 -
COME ON GUYS, IT'S CHOW TIME.
LET'S GO, STRONGJAW. SOUP'S ON.
COMING, COMING...
REMEMBER NOT TO TOSS THE BONES, I NEED THEM FOR MY DOGS.
WE'LL SEE WHAT WE CAN DO... FISH LIPS.
HEY, DON'T TALK TO ME LIKE THAT.
DON'T TAKE IT THE WRONG WAY! I WAS JUST COMPLIMENTING YOUR FULL LIPS!
CUT IT OUT, YOU GUYS. YOU'RE REALLY GRATING ON MY NERVES SOMETHING AWFUL WITH YOUR INANE CHATTER.
WHO ARE YOU CALLING INANE...
FOR TRIPLE CRIPES' SAKE, JUST SHUT UP!
AN AIR MOBILE HOME.
WE'LL NEVER HAVE ONE OF THOSE, WITH THIS CRAZY LIFE WE LEAD. OR AT LEAST I WON'T.

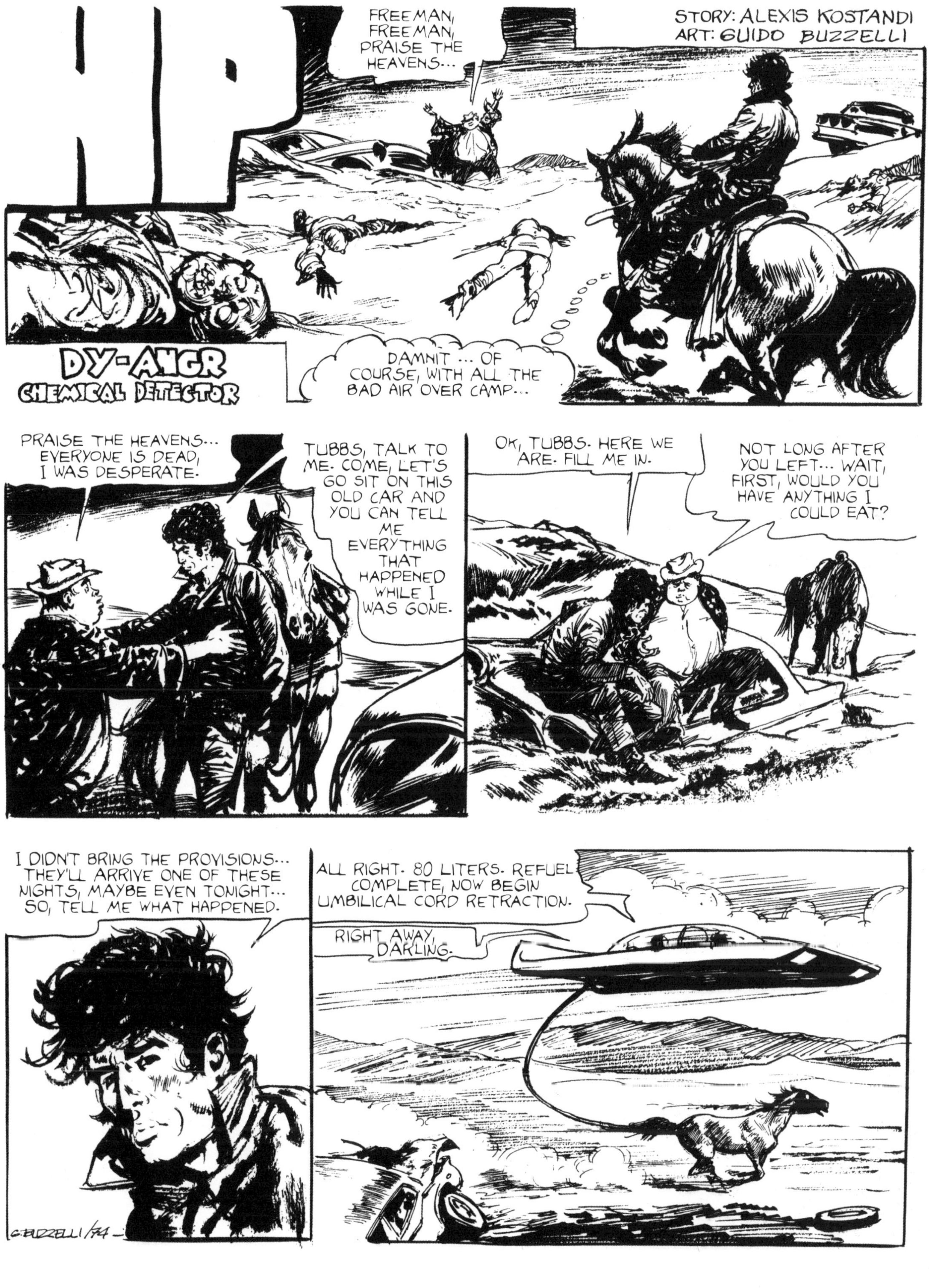
STORY: ALEXIS KOSTANDI
ART: GUIDO BUZZELLI
FREEMAN, FREEMAN, PRAISE THE HEAVENS...
DY-ANGR
CHEMICAL DETECTOR
DAMNIT ... OF COURSE, WITH ALL THE BAD AIR OVER CAMP...
PRAISE THE HEAVENS... EVERYONE IS DEAD, I WAS DESPERATE.
TUBBS, TALK TO ME. COME, LET'S GO SIT ON THIS OLD CAR AND YOU CAN TELL ME EVERYTHING THAT HAPPENED WHILE I WAS GONE.
OK, TUBBS. HERE WE ARE. FILL ME IN.
NOT LONG AFTER YOU LEFT... WAIT, FIRST, WOULD YOU HAVE ANYTHING I COULD EAT?
I DIDN'T BRING THE PROVISIONS... THEY'LL ARRIVE ONE OF THESE NIGHTS, MAYBE EVEN TONIGHT... SO, TELL ME WHAT HAPPENED.
G. BUZZELLI /74
ALL RIGHT. 80 LITERS. REFUEL COMPLETE, NOW BEGIN UMBILICAL CORD RETRACTION.
RIGHT AWAY, DARLING.

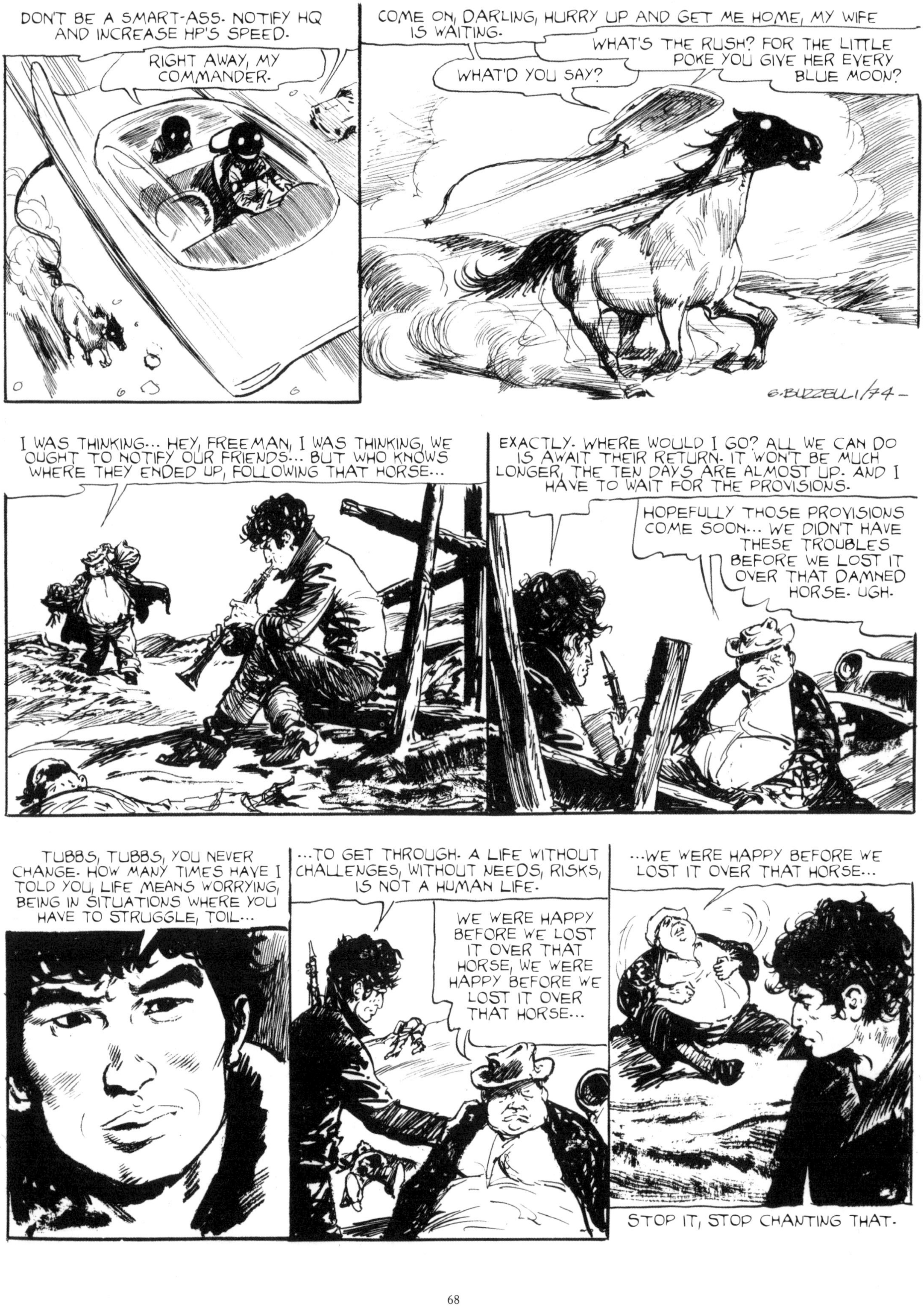
DON'T BE A SMART-ASS. NOTIFY HQ AND INCREASE HP'S SPEED.
RIGHT AWAY, MY COMMANDER.
COME ON, DARLING, HURRY UP AND GET ME HOME, MY WIFE IS WAITING.
WHAT'D YOU SAY?
WHAT'S THE RUSH? FOR THE LITTLE POKE YOU GIVE HER EVERY BLUE MOON?
G. BUZZELLI/74
I WAS THINKING... HEY, FREEMAN, I WAS THINKING, WE OUGHT TO NOTIFY OUR FRIENDS... BUT WHO KNOWS WHERE THEY ENDED UP, FOLLOWING THAT HORSE...
EXACTLY. WHERE WOULD I GO? ALL WE CAN DO IS AWAIT THEIR RETURN. IT WON'T BE MUCH LONGER, THE TEN DAYS ARE ALMOST UP. AND I HAVE TO WAIT FOR THE PROVISIONS.
HOPEFULLY THOSE PROVISIONS COME SOON... WE DIDN'T HAVE THESE TROUBLES BEFORE WE LOST IT OVER THAT DAMNED HORSE. UGH.
TUBBS, TUBBS, YOU NEVER CHANGE. HOW MANY TIMES HAVE I TOLD YOU, LIFE MEANS WORRYING, BEING IN SITUATIONS WHERE YOU HAVE TO STRUGGLE, TOIL...
...TO GET THROUGH. A LIFE WITHOUT CHALLENGES, WITHOUT NEEDS, RISKS, IS NOT A HUMAN LIFE.
WE WERE HAPPY BEFORE WE LOST IT OVER THAT HORSE, WE WERE HAPPY BEFORE WE LOST IT OVER THAT HORSE...
...WE WERE HAPPY BEFORE WE LOST IT OVER THAT HORSE...
STOP IT, STOP CHANTING THAT.

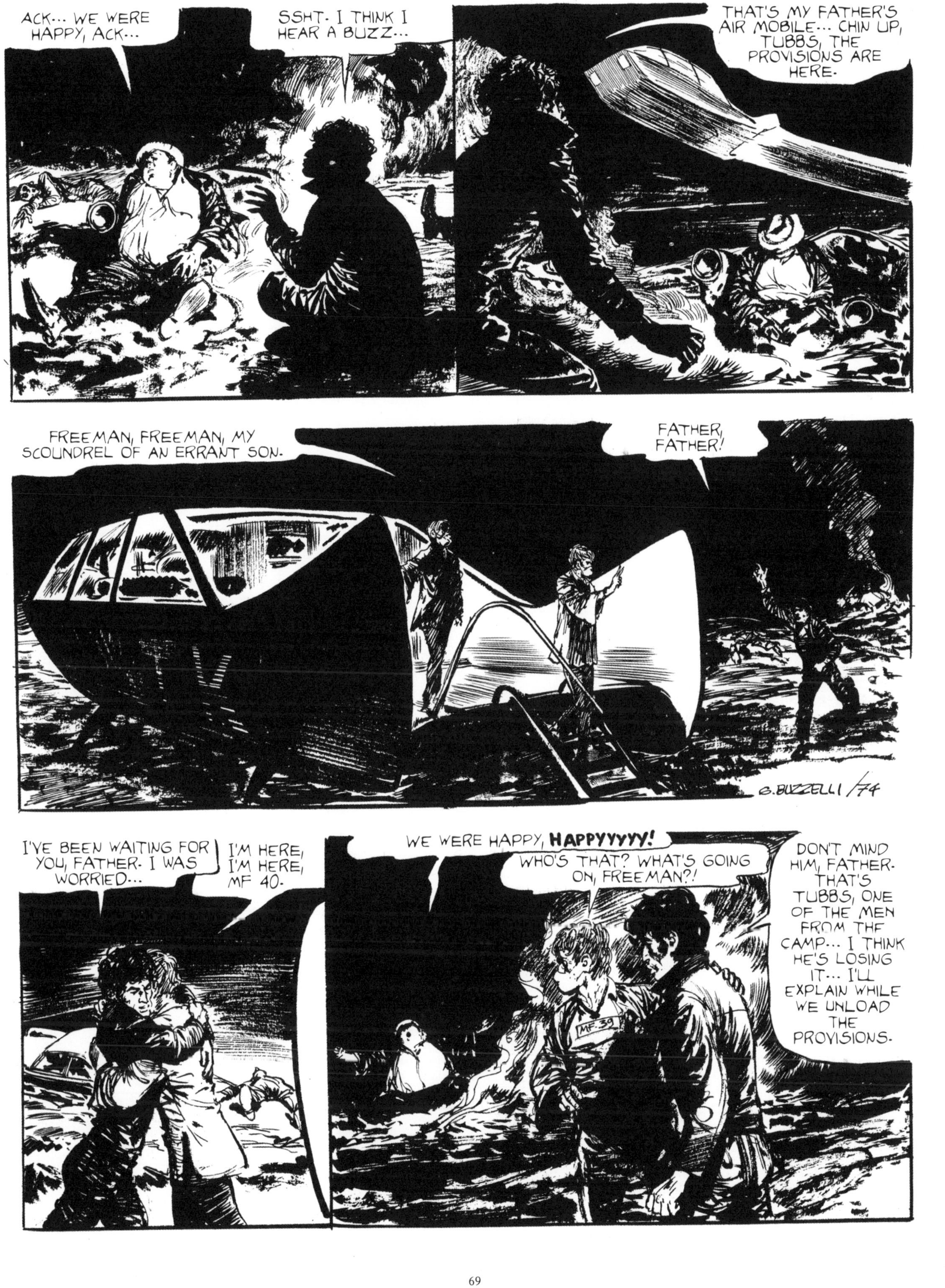
ACK··· WE WERE HAPPY, ACK···
SSHT· I THINK I HEAR A BUZZ···
THAT'S MY FATHER'S AIR MOBILE··· CHIN UP, TUBBS, THE PROVISIONS ARE HERE·
FREEMAN, FREEMAN, MY SCOUNDREL OF AN ERRANT SON·
FATHER, FATHER!
G.BUZZELLI /74
I'VE BEEN WAITING FOR YOU, FATHER· I WAS WORRIED···
I'M HERE, I'M HERE, MF 40·
WE WERE HAPPY, HAPPYYYYY!
WHO'S THAT? WHAT'S GOING ON, FREEMAN?!
DON'T MIND HIM, FATHER· THAT'S TUBBS, ONE OF THE MEN FROM THE CAMP··· I THINK HE'S LOSING IT··· I'LL EXPLAIN WHILE WE UNLOAD THE PROVISIONS·

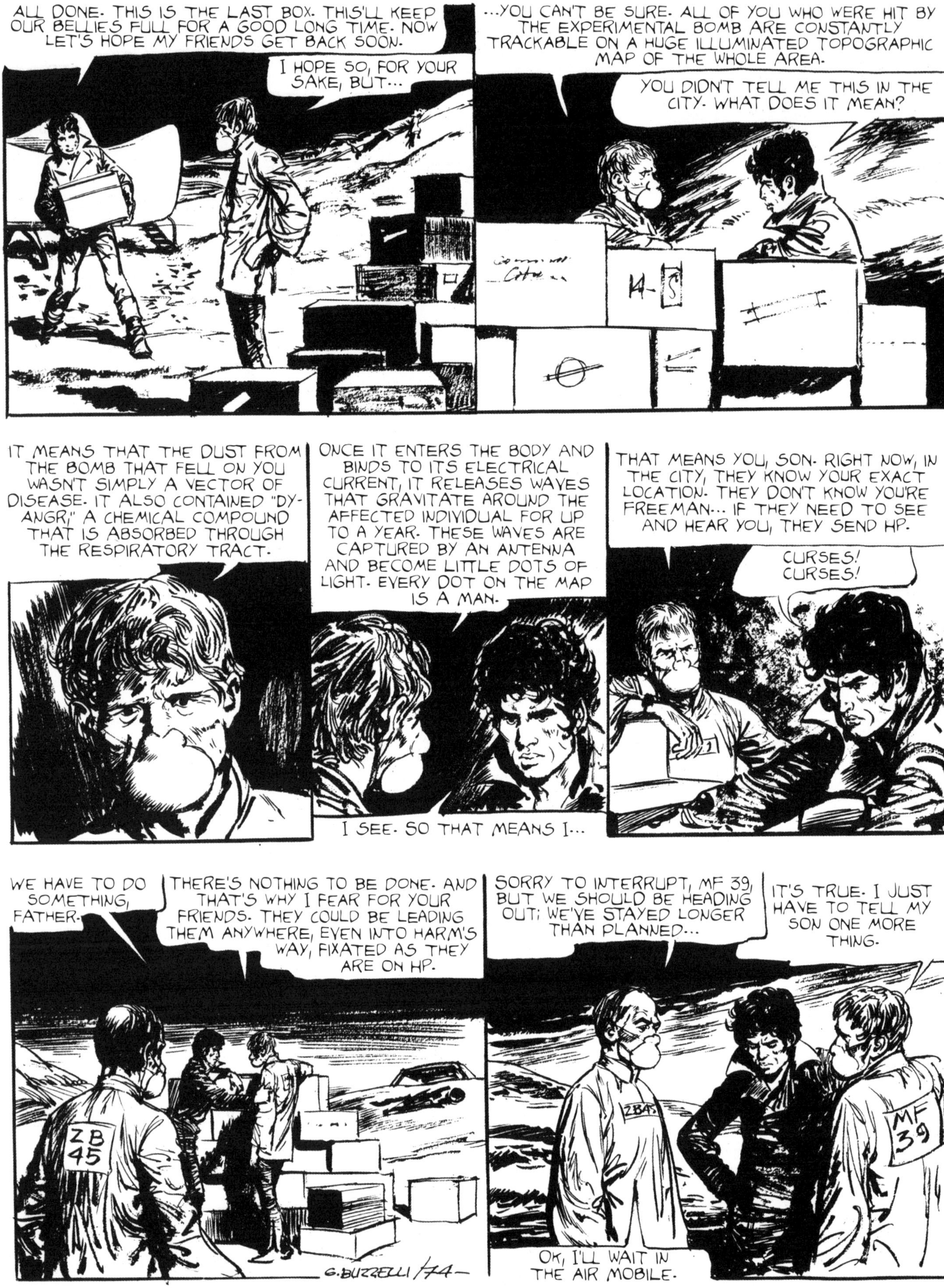
ALL DONE. THIS IS THE LAST BOX. THIS'LL KEEP OUR BELLIES FULL FOR A GOOD LONG TIME. NOW LET'S HOPE MY FRIENDS GET BACK SOON.
I HOPE SO, FOR YOUR SAKE, BUT...
...YOU CAN'T BE SURE. ALL OF YOU WHO WERE HIT BY THE EXPERIMENTAL BOMB ARE CONSTANTLY TRACKABLE ON A HUGE ILLUMINATED TOPOGRAPHIC MAP OF THE WHOLE AREA.
YOU DIDN'T TELL ME THIS IN THE CITY. WHAT DOES IT MEAN?
IT MEANS THAT THE DUST FROM THE BOMB THAT FELL ON YOU WASN'T SIMPLY A VECTOR OF DISEASE. IT ALSO CONTAINED "DY-ANGR," A CHEMICAL COMPOUND THAT IS ABSORBED THROUGH THE RESPIRATORY TRACT.
ONCE IT ENTERS THE BODY AND BINDS TO ITS ELECTRICAL CURRENT, IT RELEASES WAVES THAT GRAVITATE AROUND THE AFFECTED INDIVIDUAL FOR UP TO A YEAR. THESE WAVES ARE CAPTURED BY AN ANTENNA AND BECOME LITTLE DOTS OF LIGHT. EVERY DOT ON THE MAP IS A MAN.
I SEE. SO THAT MEANS I...
THAT MEANS YOU, SON. RIGHT NOW, IN THE CITY, THEY KNOW YOUR EXACT LOCATION. THEY DON'T KNOW YOU'RE FREEMAN... IF THEY NEED TO SEE AND HEAR YOU, THEY SEND HP.
CURSES! CURSES!
WE HAVE TO DO SOMETHING, FATHER.
THERE'S NOTHING TO BE DONE. AND THAT'S WHY I FEAR FOR YOUR FRIENDS. THEY COULD BE LEADING THEM ANYWHERE, EVEN INTO HARM'S WAY, FIXATED AS THEY ARE ON HP.
ZB 45
G. BUZZELLI /74
SORRY TO INTERRUPT, MF 39, BUT WE SHOULD BE HEADING OUT: WE'VE STAYED LONGER THAN PLANNED...
IT'S TRUE. I JUST HAVE TO TELL MY SON ONE MORE THING.
ZB45
MF 39
OK, I'LL WAIT IN THE AIR MOBILE.

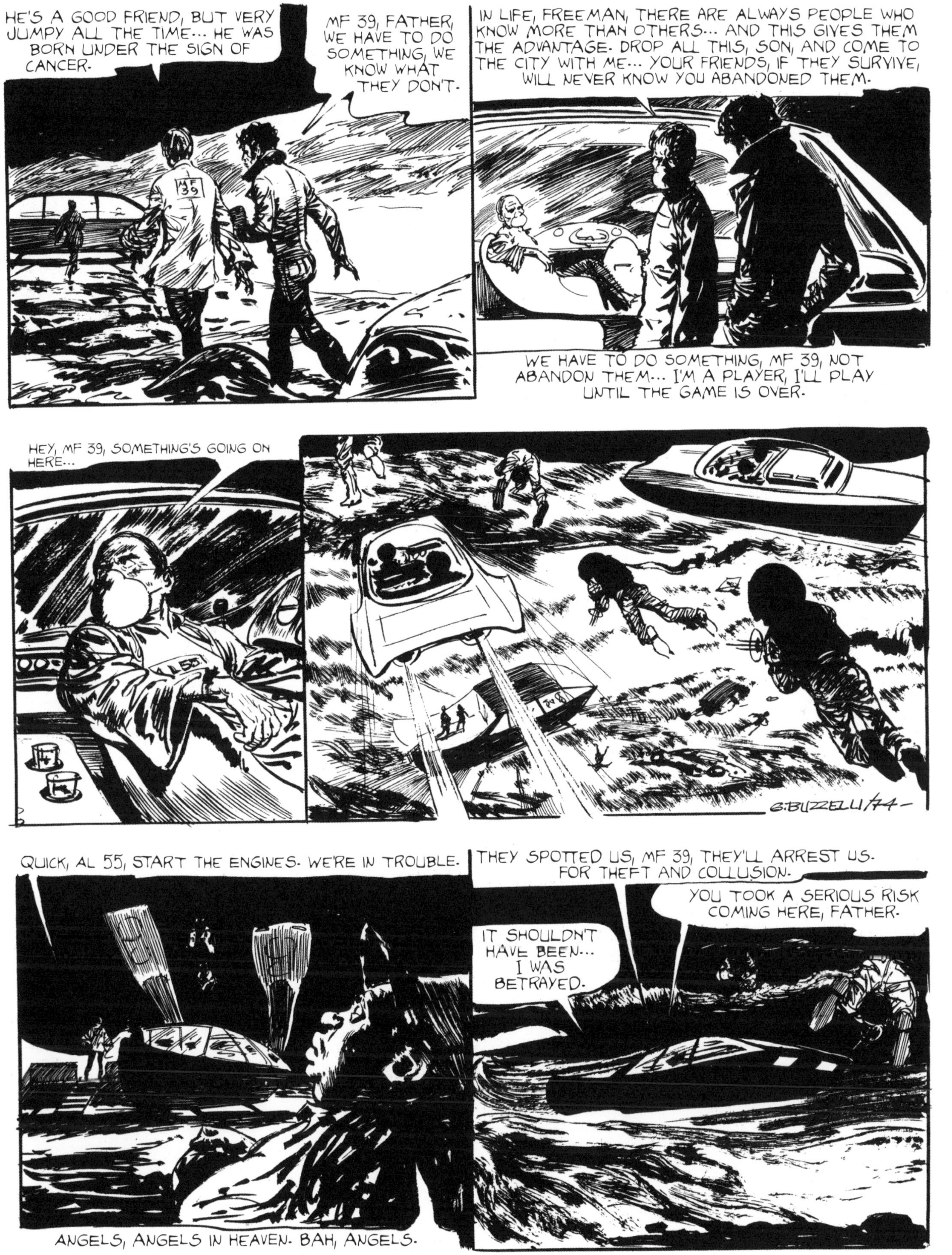
HE'S A GOOD FRIEND, BUT VERY JUMPY ALL THE TIME... HE WAS BORN UNDER THE SIGN OF CANCER.
MF 39, FATHER, WE HAVE TO DO SOMETHING, WE KNOW WHAT THEY DON'T.
MF 39
IN LIFE, FREEMAN, THERE ARE ALWAYS PEOPLE WHO KNOW MORE THAN OTHERS... AND THIS GIVES THEM THE ADVANTAGE. DROP ALL THIS, SON, AND COME TO THE CITY WITH ME... YOUR FRIENDS, IF THEY SURVIVE, WILL NEVER KNOW YOU ABANDONED THEM.
WE HAVE TO DO SOMETHING, MF 39, NOT ABANDON THEM... I'M A PLAYER, I'LL PLAY UNTIL THE GAME IS OVER.
HEY, MF 39, SOMETHING'S GOING ON HERE...
AL 55
G. BUZZELLI/74
QUICK, AL 55, START THE ENGINES. WE'RE IN TROUBLE.
ANGELS, ANGELS IN HEAVEN. BAH, ANGELS.
THEY SPOTTED US, MF 39, THEY'LL ARREST US. FOR THEFT AND COLLUSION.
YOU TOOK A SERIOUS RISK COMING HERE, FATHER.
IT SHOULDN'T HAVE BEEN... I WAS BETRAYED.

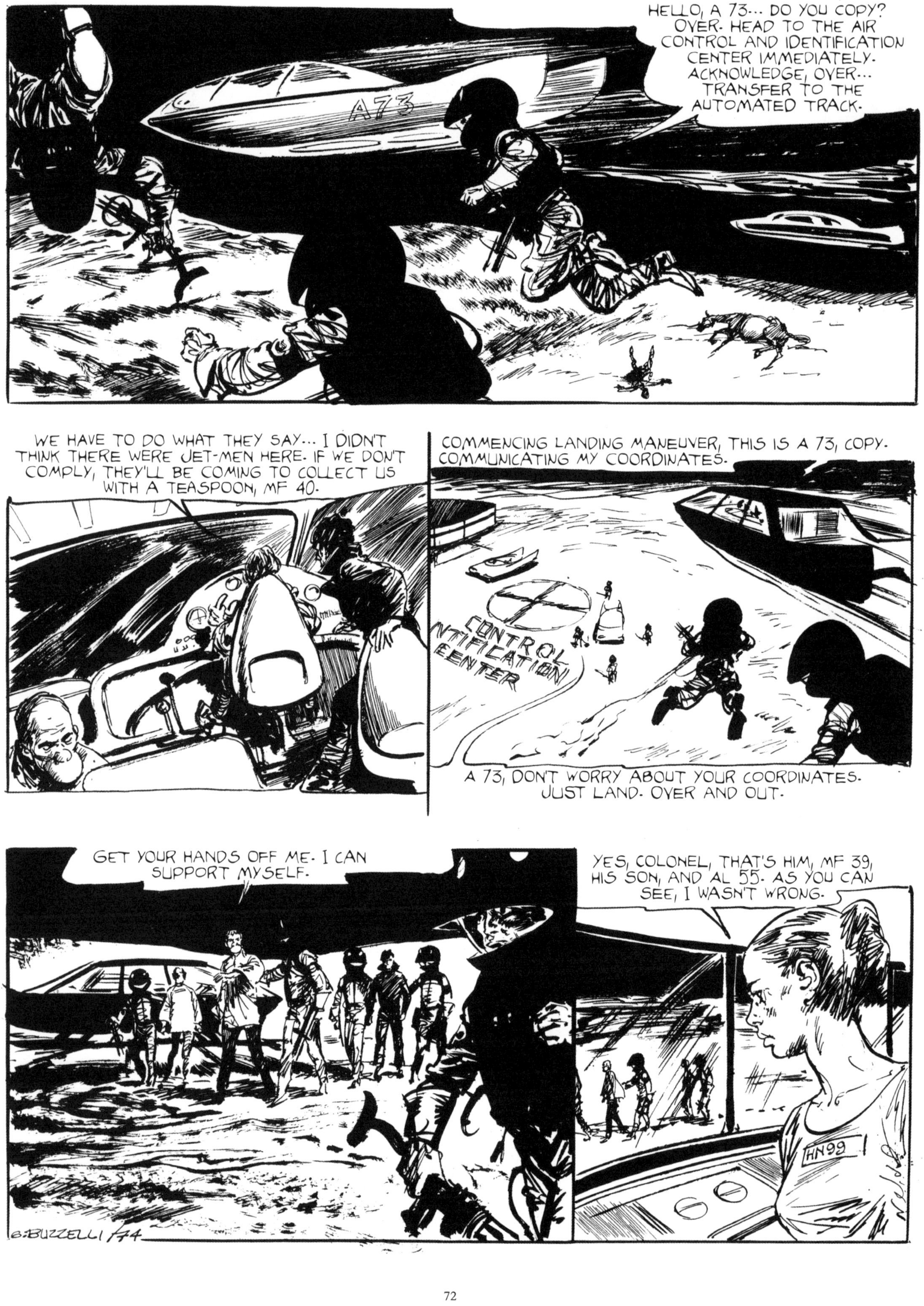
HELLO, A 73... DO YOU COPY? OVER. HEAD TO THE AIR CONTROL AND IDENTIFICATION CENTER IMMEDIATELY. ACKNOWLEDGE, OVER... TRANSFER TO THE AUTOMATED TRACK.
A73
WE HAVE TO DO WHAT THEY SAY... I DIDN'T THINK THERE WERE JET-MEN HERE. IF WE DON'T COMPLY, THEY'LL BE COMING TO COLLECT US WITH A TEASPOON, MF 40.
COMMENCING LANDING MANEUVER, THIS IS A 73, COPY. COMMUNICATING MY COORDINATES.
CONTROL
NTIFICATION
CENTER
A 73, DON'T WORRY ABOUT YOUR COORDINATES. JUST LAND. OVER AND OUT.
GET YOUR HANDS OFF ME. I CAN SUPPORT MYSELF.
G. BUZZELLI /74
YES, COLONEL, THAT'S HIM, MF 39, HIS SON, AND AL 55. AS YOU CAN SEE, I WASN'T WRONG.
HN99

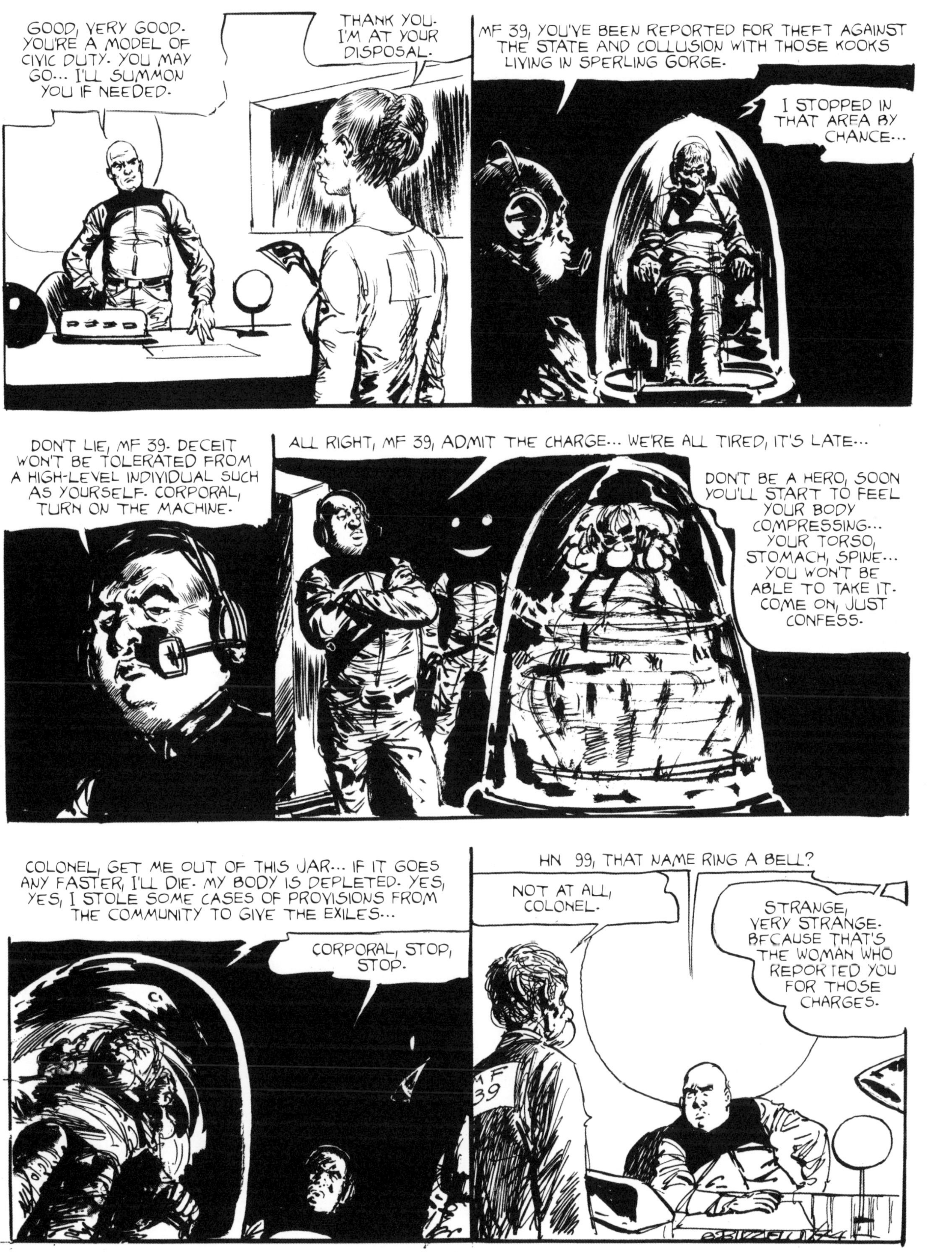
GOOD, VERY GOOD. YOU'RE A MODEL OF CIVIC DUTY. YOU MAY GO... I'LL SUMMON YOU IF NEEDED.
THANK YOU. I'M AT YOUR DISPOSAL.
MF 39, YOU'VE BEEN REPORTED FOR THEFT AGAINST THE STATE AND COLLUSION WITH THOSE KOOKS LIVING IN SPERLING GORGE.
I STOPPED IN THAT AREA BY CHANCE...
DON'T LIE, MF 39. DECEIT WON'T BE TOLERATED FROM A HIGH-LEVEL INDIVIDUAL SUCH AS YOURSELF. CORPORAL, TURN ON THE MACHINE.
ALL RIGHT, MF 39, ADMIT THE CHARGE... WE'RE ALL TIRED, IT'S LATE...
DON'T BE A HERO, SOON YOU'LL START TO FEEL YOUR BODY COMPRESSING... YOUR TORSO, STOMACH, SPINE... YOU WON'T BE ABLE TO TAKE IT. COME ON, JUST CONFESS.
COLONEL, GET ME OUT OF THIS JAR... IF IT GOES ANY FASTER, I'LL DIE. MY BODY IS DEPLETED. YES, YES, I STOLE SOME CASES OF PROVISIONS FROM THE COMMUNITY TO GIVE THE EXILES...
CORPORAL, STOP, STOP.
HN 99, THAT NAME RING A BELL?
NOT AT ALL, COLONEL.
STRANGE, VERY STRANGE. BECAUSE THAT'S THE WOMAN WHO REPORTED YOU FOR THOSE CHARGES.
MF 39

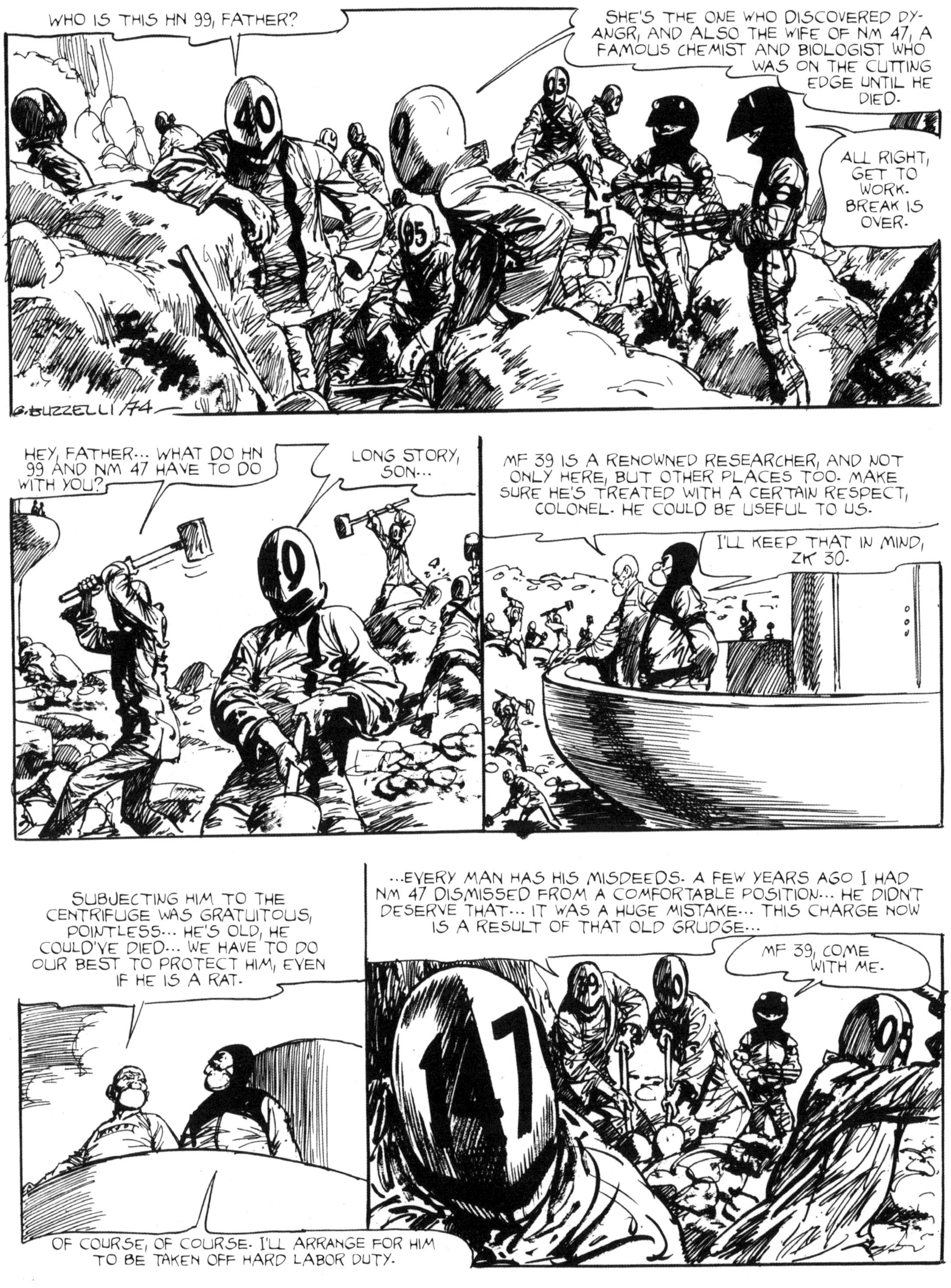
WHO IS THIS HN 99, FATHER?
SHE'S THE ONE WHO DISCOVERED DY-ANGR, AND ALSO THE WIFE OF NM 47, A FAMOUS CHEMIST AND BIOLOGIST WHO WAS ON THE CUTTING EDGE UNTIL HE DIED.
ALL RIGHT, GET TO WORK. BREAK IS OVER.
G. BUZZELLI /74
HEY, FATHER... WHAT DO HN 99 AND NM 47 HAVE TO DO WITH YOU?
LONG STORY, SON...
MF 39 IS A RENOWNED RESEARCHER, AND NOT ONLY HERE, BUT OTHER PLACES TOO. MAKE SURE HE'S TREATED WITH A CERTAIN RESPECT, COLONEL. HE COULD BE USEFUL TO US.
I'LL KEEP THAT IN MIND, ZK 30.
SUBJECTING HIM TO THE CENTRIFUGE WAS GRATUITOUS, POINTLESS... HE'S OLD, HE COULD'VE DIED... WE HAVE TO DO OUR BEST TO PROTECT HIM, EVEN IF HE IS A RAT.
OF COURSE, OF COURSE. I'LL ARRANGE FOR HIM TO BE TAKEN OFF HARD LABOR DUTY.
...EVERY MAN HAS HIS MISDEEDS. A FEW YEARS AGO I HAD NM 47 DISMISSED FROM A COMFORTABLE POSITION... HE DIDN'T DESERVE THAT... IT WAS A HUGE MISTAKE... THIS CHARGE NOW IS A RESULT OF THAT OLD GRUDGE...
MF 39, COME WITH ME.

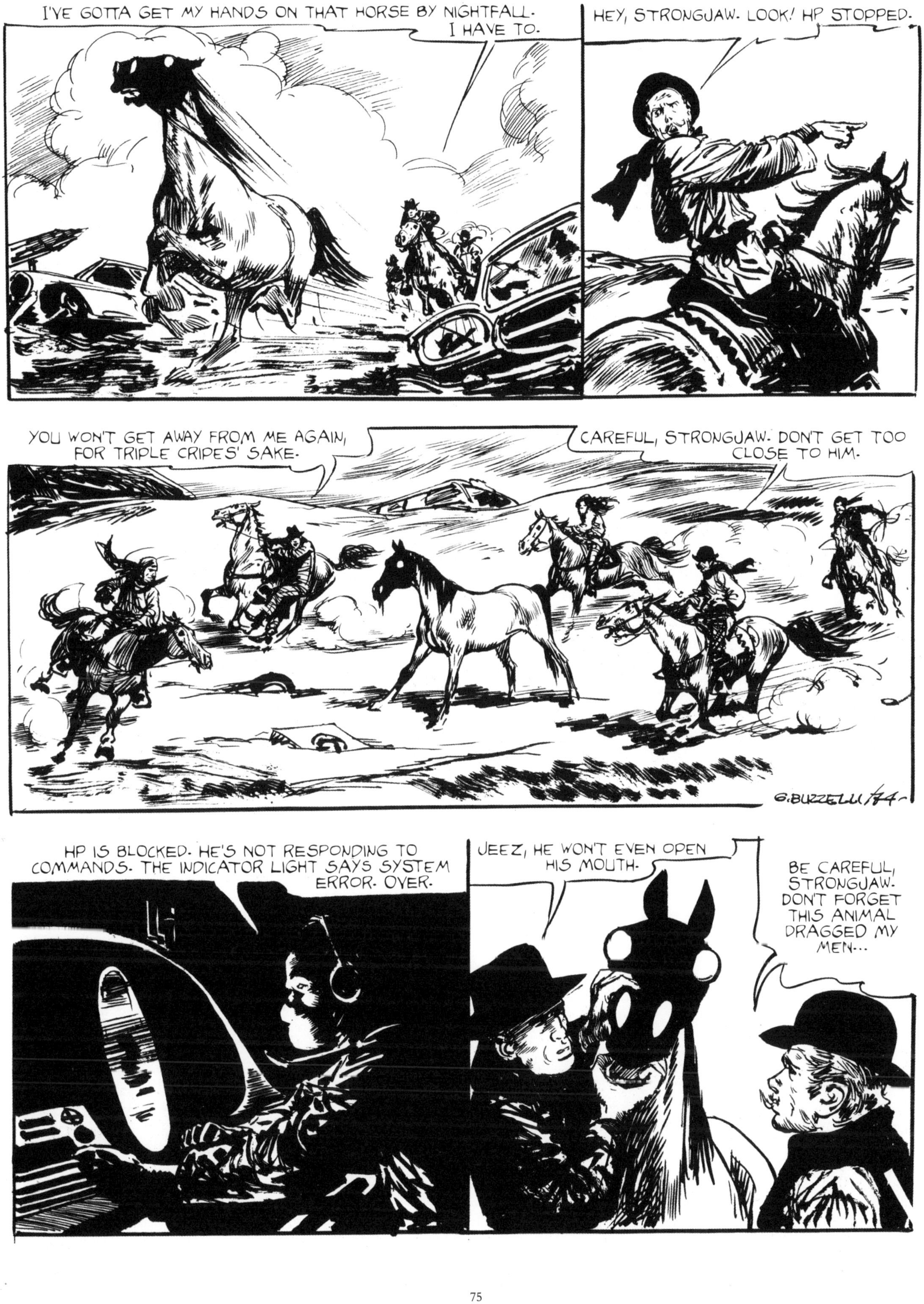
I'VE GOTTA GET MY HANDS ON THAT HORSE BY NIGHTFALL. I HAVE TO.
HEY, STRONGJAW. LOOK! HP STOPPED.
YOU WON'T GET AWAY FROM ME AGAIN, FOR TRIPLE CRIPES' SAKE.
CAREFUL, STRONGJAW. DON'T GET TOO CLOSE TO HIM.
G.BUZZELLI/74
HP IS BLOCKED. HE'S NOT RESPONDING TO COMMANDS. THE INDICATOR LIGHT SAYS SYSTEM ERROR. OVER.
JEEZ, HE WON'T EVEN OPEN HIS MOUTH.
BE CAREFUL, STRONGJAW. DON'T FORGET THIS ANIMAL DRAGGED MY MEN...

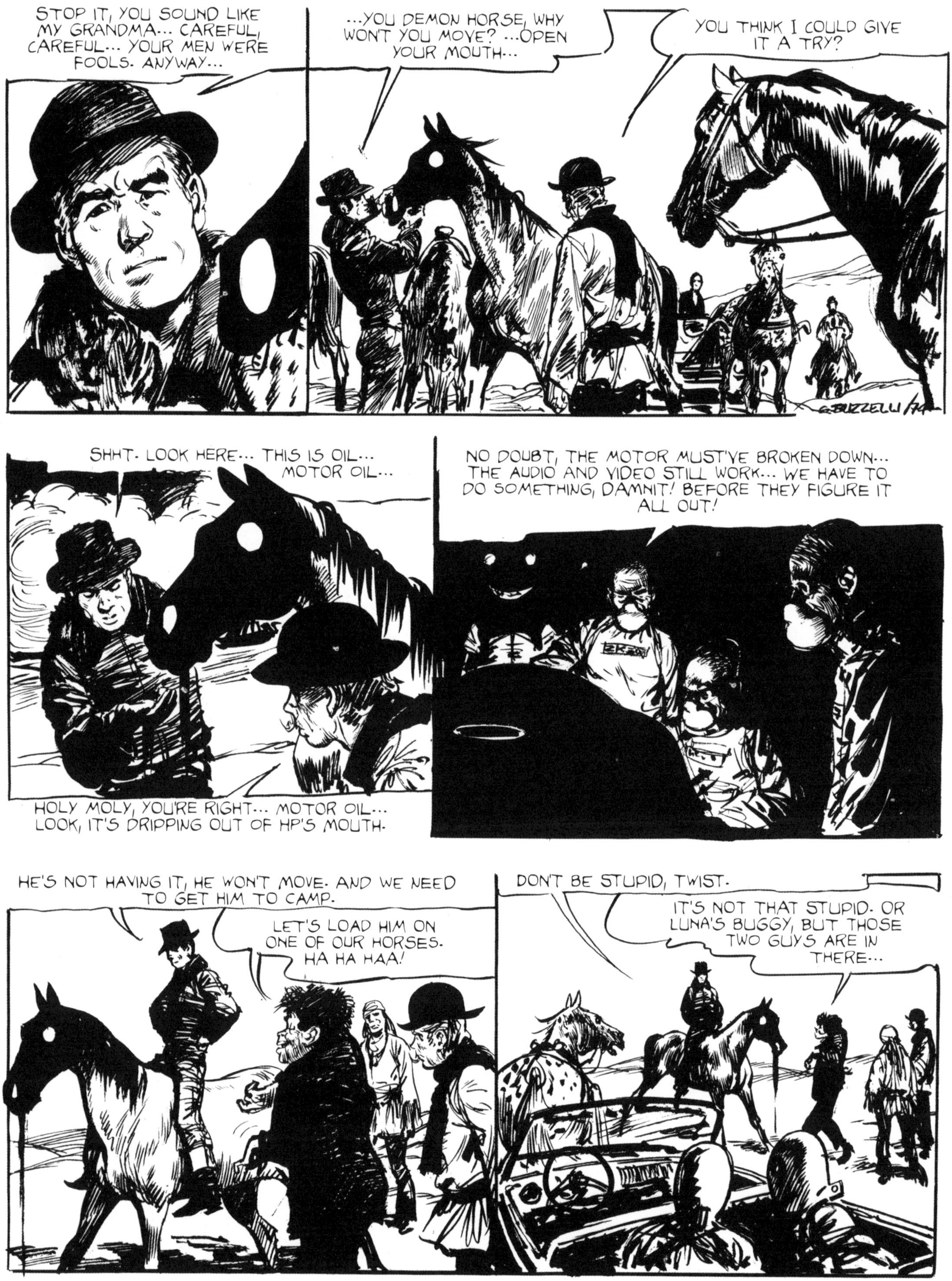

STOP IT, YOU SOUND LIKE MY GRANDMA... CAREFUL, CAREFUL... YOUR MEN WERE FOOLS. ANYWAY...
...YOU DEMON HORSE, WHY WON'T YOU MOVE? ...OPEN YOUR MOUTH...
YOU THINK I COULD GIVE IT A TRY?
G. BUZZELLI /74
SHHT. LOOK HERE... THIS IS OIL... MOTOR OIL...
HOLY MOLY, YOU'RE RIGHT... MOTOR OIL... LOOK, IT'S DRIPPING OUT OF HP'S MOUTH.
NO DOUBT, THE MOTOR MUST'VE BROKEN DOWN... THE AUDIO AND VIDEO STILL WORK... WE HAVE TO DO SOMETHING, DAMNIT! BEFORE THEY FIGURE IT ALL OUT!
HE'S NOT HAVING IT, HE WON'T MOVE. AND WE NEED TO GET HIM TO CAMP.
LET'S LOAD HIM ON ONE OF OUR HORSES. HA HA HAA!
DON'T BE STUPID, TWIST.
IT'S NOT THAT STUPID. OR LUNA'S BUGGY, BUT THOSE TWO GUYS ARE IN THERE...

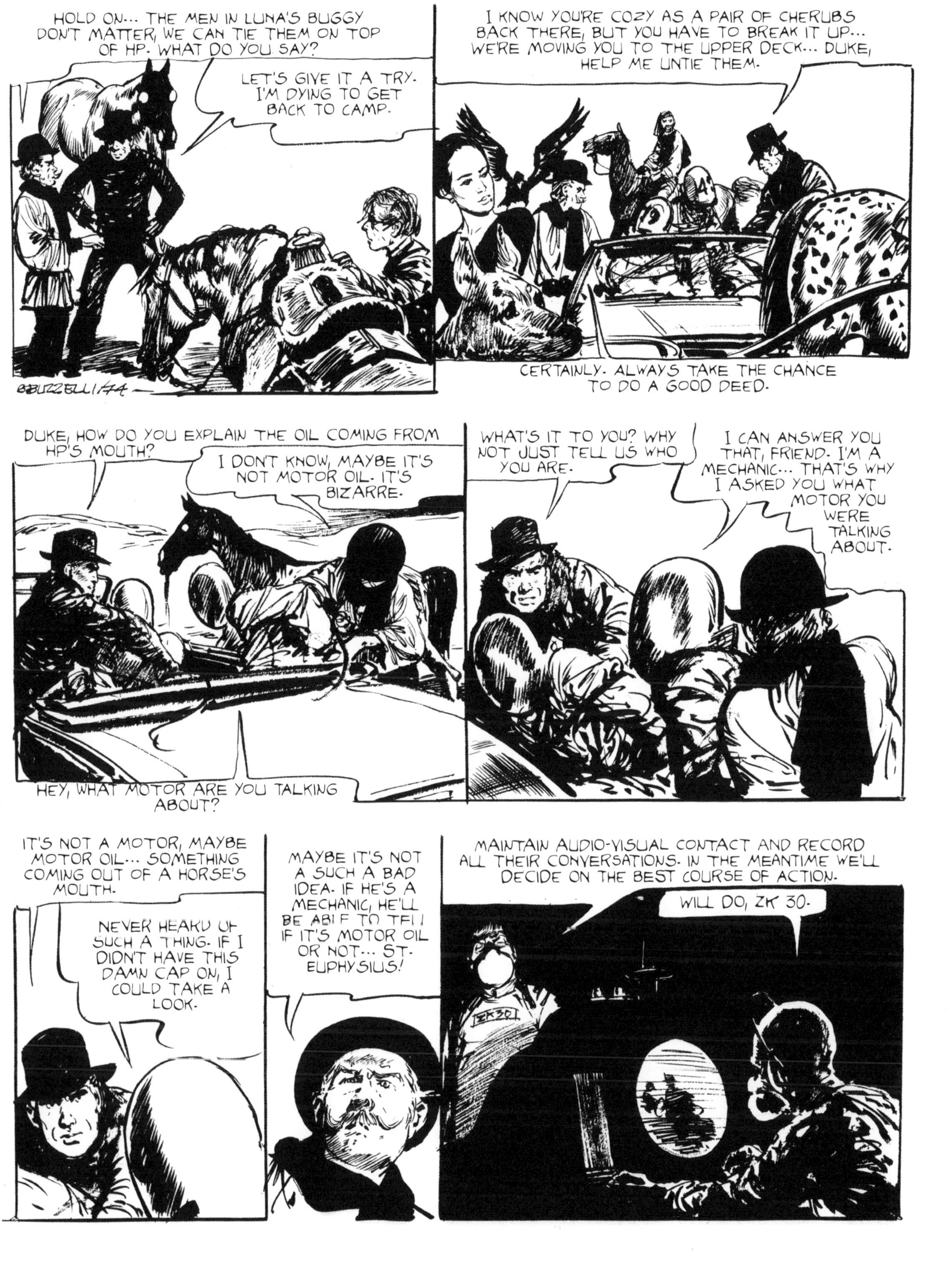
HOLD ON... THE MEN IN LUNA'S BUGGY DON'T MATTER, WE CAN TIE THEM ON TOP OF HP. WHAT DO YOU SAY?
LET'S GIVE IT A TRY. I'M DYING TO GET BACK TO CAMP.
BBUZZELLI/74
I KNOW YOU'RE COZY AS A PAIR OF CHERUBS BACK THERE, BUT YOU HAVE TO BREAK IT UP... WE'RE MOVING YOU TO THE UPPER DECK... DUKE, HELP ME UNTIE THEM.
CERTAINLY. ALWAYS TAKE THE CHANCE TO DO A GOOD DEED.
DUKE, HOW DO YOU EXPLAIN THE OIL COMING FROM HP'S MOUTH?
I DON'T KNOW, MAYBE IT'S NOT MOTOR OIL. IT'S BIZARRE.
HEY, WHAT MOTOR ARE YOU TALKING ABOUT?
WHAT'S IT TO YOU? WHY NOT JUST TELL US WHO YOU ARE.
I CAN ANSWER YOU THAT, FRIEND. I'M A MECHANIC... THAT'S WHY I ASKED YOU WHAT MOTOR YOU WERE TALKING ABOUT.
IT'S NOT A MOTOR, MAYBE MOTOR OIL... SOMETHING COMING OUT OF A HORSE'S MOUTH.
NEVER HEARD OF SUCH A THING. IF I DIDN'T HAVE THIS DAMN CAP ON, I COULD TAKE A LOOK.
MAYBE IT'S NOT A SUCH A BAD IDEA. IF HE'S A MECHANIC, HE'LL BE ABLE TO TELL IF IT'S MOTOR OIL OR NOT... ST. EUPHYSIUS!
MAINTAIN AUDIO-VISUAL CONTACT AND RECORD ALL THEIR CONVERSATIONS. IN THE MEANTIME WE'LL DECIDE ON THE BEST COURSE OF ACTION.
WILL DO, ZK 30.
ZK 30

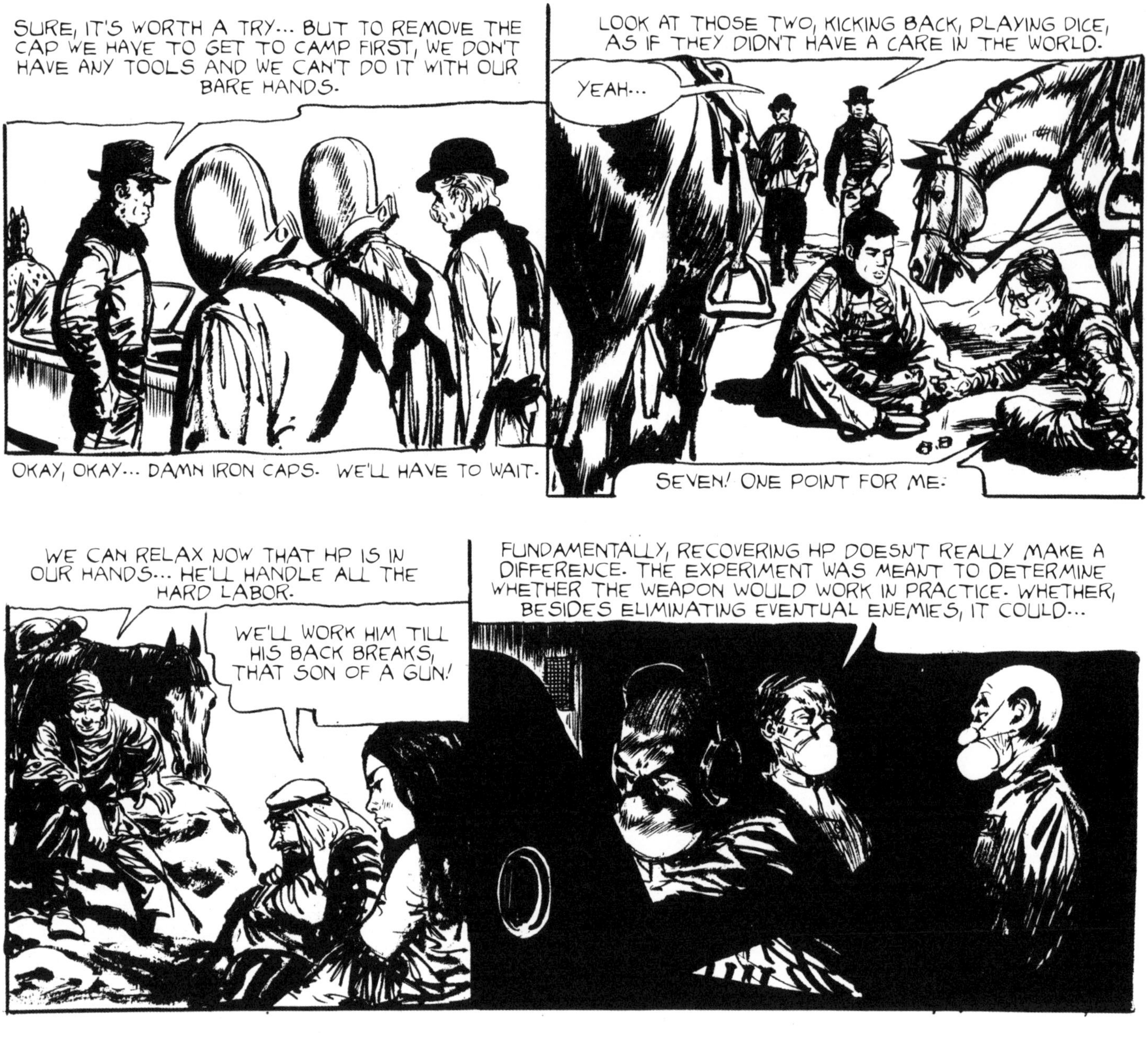
SURE, IT'S WORTH A TRY... BUT TO REMOVE THE CAP WE HAVE TO GET TO CAMP FIRST, WE DON'T HAVE ANY TOOLS AND WE CAN'T DO IT WITH OUR BARE HANDS.
OKAY, OKAY... DAMN IRON CAPS. WE'LL HAVE TO WAIT.
LOOK AT THOSE TWO, KICKING BACK, PLAYING DICE, AS IF THEY DIDN'T HAVE A CARE IN THE WORLD.
YEAH...
SEVEN! ONE POINT FOR ME.
WE CAN RELAX NOW THAT HP IS IN OUR HANDS... HE'LL HANDLE ALL THE HARD LABOR.
WE'LL WORK HIM TILL HIS BACK BREAKS, THAT SON OF A GUN!
FUNDAMENTALLY, RECOVERING HP DOESN'T REALLY MAKE A DIFFERENCE. THE EXPERIMENT WAS MEANT TO DETERMINE WHETHER THE WEAPON WOULD WORK IN PRACTICE. WHETHER, BESIDES ELIMINATING EVENTUAL ENEMIES, IT COULD...
...CONSTANTLY MONITOR THEIR PRESENCE, IF THEY SURVIVED. SEEMS TO ME DY-ANGR WORKS PERFECTLY, ZK 30...
AGREED, BUT THAT DOESN'T MEAN WE DON'T NEED HP BACK. IT CAN'T REMAIN IN THE HANDS OF OUR GUINEA PIGS... THEY MUSTN'T KNOW...
PZ 16
THEIR IGNORANCE IS OUR ADVANTAGE. SO WE NEED TO ACT QUICKLY.
ZK30
G. BUZZELLI /74
COME ON, YOU DAMN VAGABONDS! GET TO WORK... HP NEEDS US!
GONG
GONG
GONG

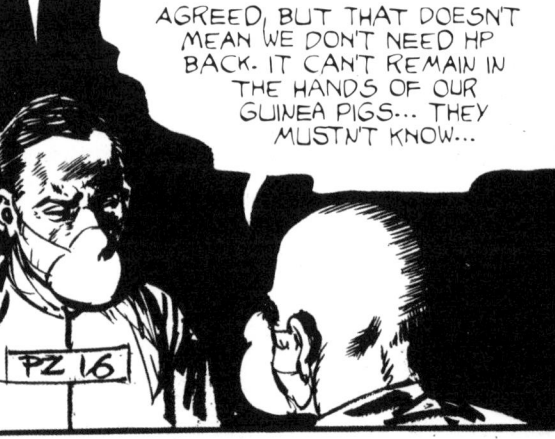

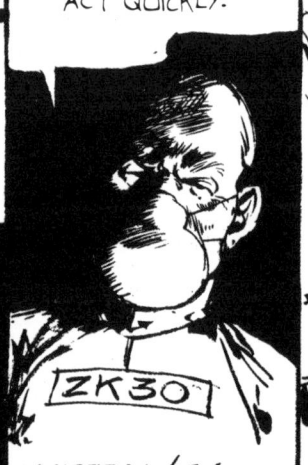

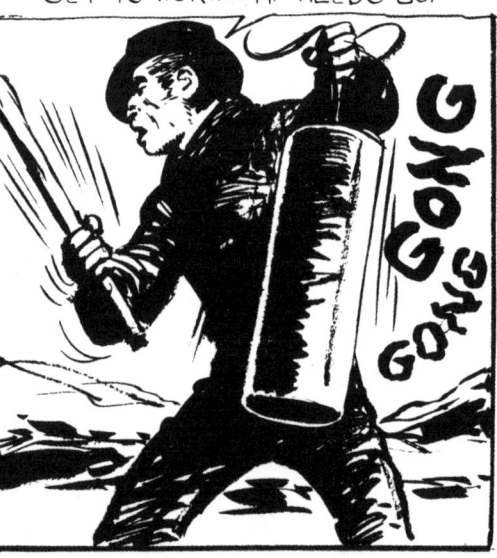

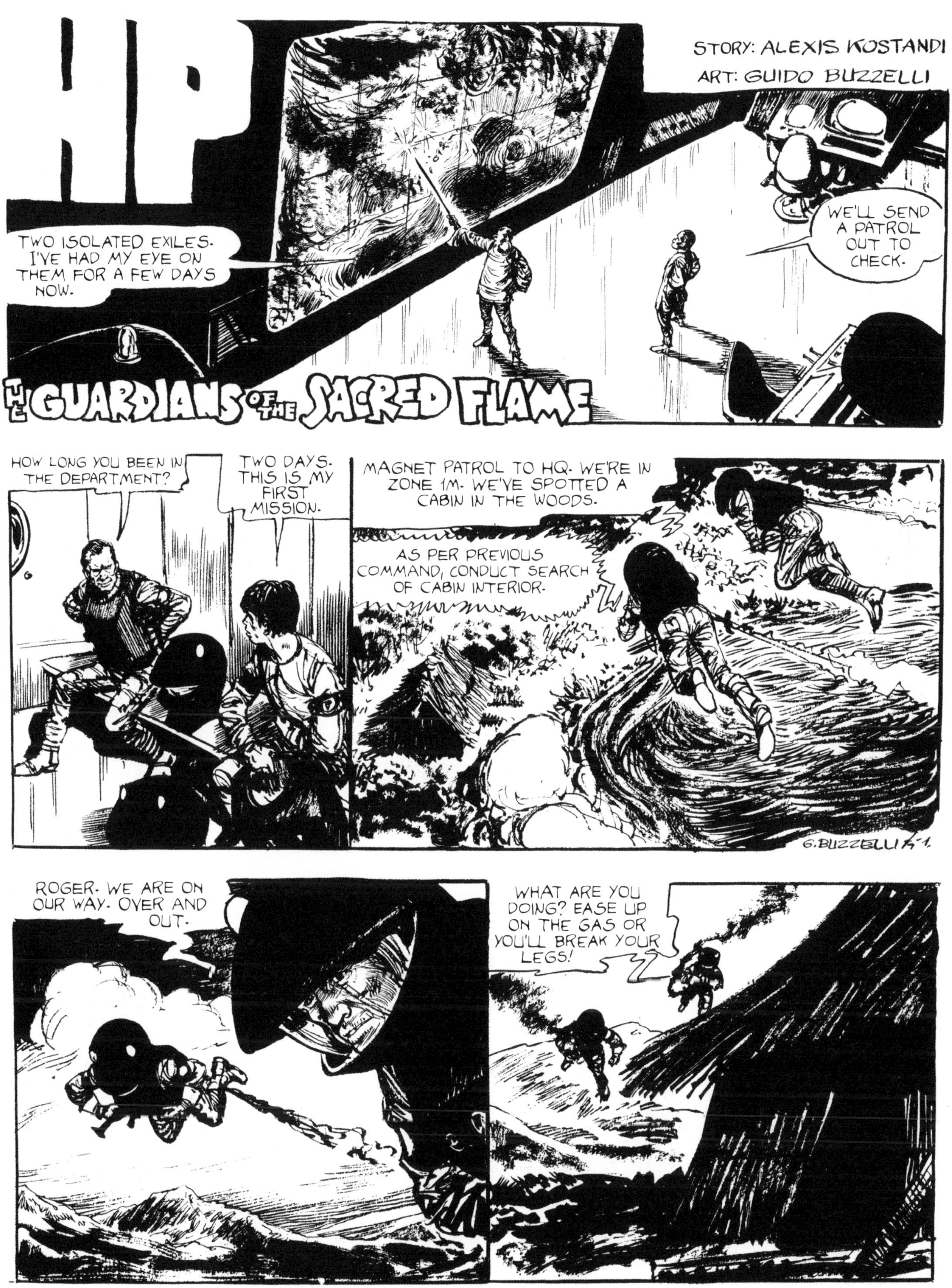
HP
STORY: ALEXIS KOSTANDI
ART: GUIDO BUZZELLI
TWO ISOLATED EXILES. I'VE HAD MY EYE ON THEM FOR A FEW DAYS NOW.
WE'LL SEND A PATROL OUT TO CHECK.
THE GUARDIANS OF THE SACRED FLAME
HOW LONG YOU BEEN IN THE DEPARTMENT?
TWO DAYS. THIS IS MY FIRST MISSION.
MAGNET PATROL TO HQ. WE'RE IN ZONE 1M. WE'VE SPOTTED A CABIN IN THE WOODS.
AS PER PREVIOUS COMMAND, CONDUCT SEARCH OF CABIN INTERIOR.
G. BUZZELLI
ROGER. WE ARE ON OUR WAY. OVER AND OUT.
WHAT ARE YOU DOING? EASE UP ON THE GAS OR YOU'LL BREAK YOUR LEGS!

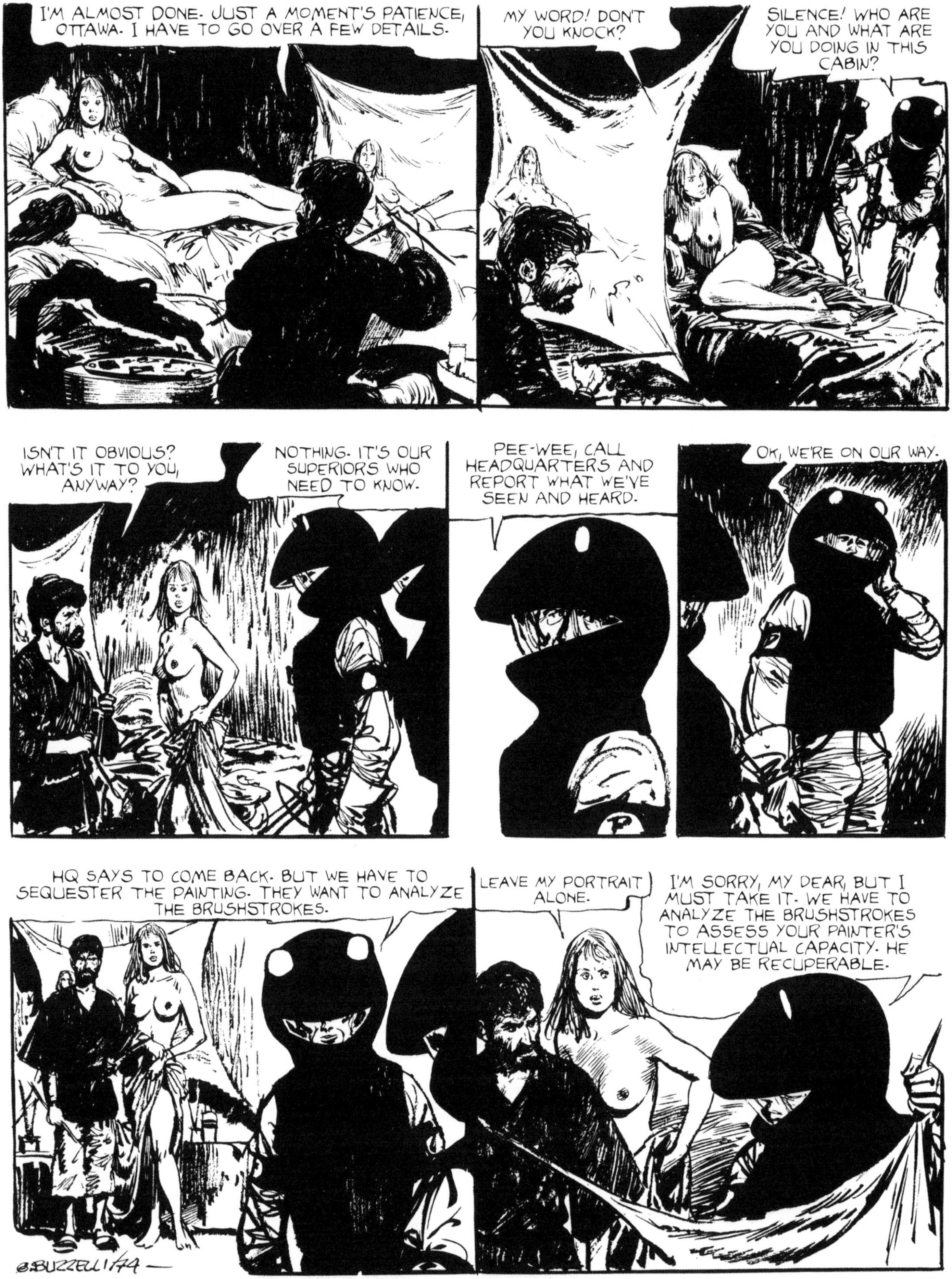
I'M ALMOST DONE. JUST A MOMENT'S PATIENCE, OTTAWA. I HAVE TO GO OVER A FEW DETAILS.
MY WORD! DON'T YOU KNOCK?
SILENCE! WHO ARE YOU AND WHAT ARE YOU DOING IN THIS CABIN?
ISN'T IT OBVIOUS? WHAT'S IT TO YOU, ANYWAY?
NOTHING. IT'S OUR SUPERIORS WHO NEED TO KNOW.
PEE-WEE, CALL HEADQUARTERS AND REPORT WHAT WE'VE SEEN AND HEARD.
OK, WE'RE ON OUR WAY.
HQ SAYS TO COME BACK. BUT WE HAVE TO SEQUESTER THE PAINTING. THEY WANT TO ANALYZE THE BRUSHSTROKES.
LEAVE MY PORTRAIT ALONE.
I'M SORRY, MY DEAR, BUT I MUST TAKE IT. WE HAVE TO ANALYZE THE BRUSHSTROKES TO ASSESS YOUR PAINTER'S INTELLECTUAL CAPACITY. HE MAY BE RECUPERABLE.
© BUZZELLI /74

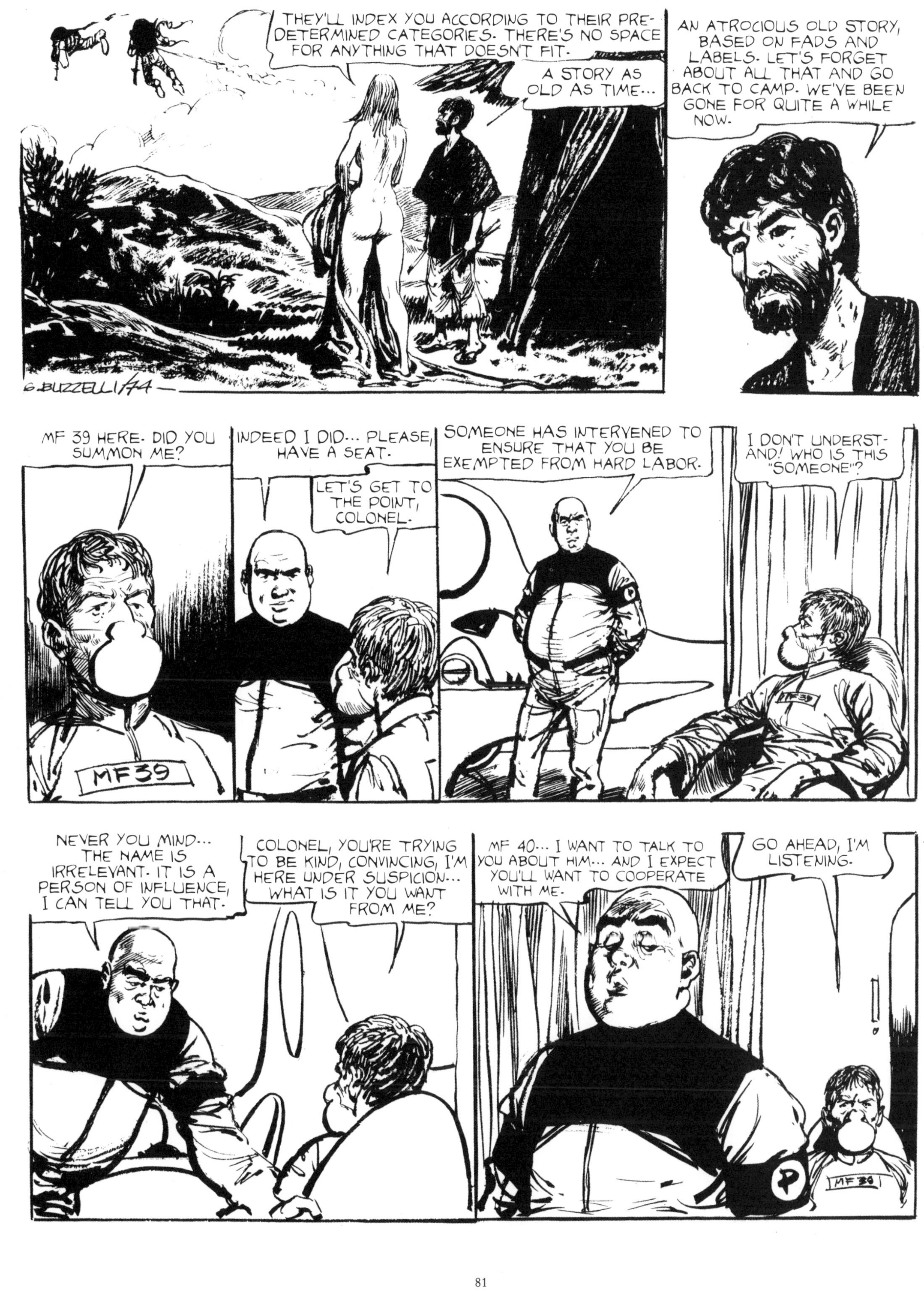
THEY'LL INDEX YOU ACCORDING TO THEIR PRE-DETERMINED CATEGORIES. THERE'S NO SPACE FOR ANYTHING THAT DOESN'T FIT.
A STORY AS OLD AS TIME...
G. BUZZELLI/74
AN ATROCIOUS OLD STORY, BASED ON FADS AND LABELS. LET'S FORGET ABOUT ALL THAT AND GO BACK TO CAMP. WE'VE BEEN GONE FOR QUITE A WHILE NOW.
MF 39 HERE. DID YOU SUMMON ME?
MF39
INDEED I DID... PLEASE, HAVE A SEAT.
LET'S GET TO THE POINT, COLONEL.
SOMEONE HAS INTERVENED TO ENSURE THAT YOU BE EXEMPTED FROM HARD LABOR.
I DON'T UNDERST-AND! WHO IS THIS "SOMEONE"?
NEVER YOU MIND... THE NAME IS IRRELEVANT. IT IS A PERSON OF INFLUENCE, I CAN TELL YOU THAT.
COLONEL, YOU'RE TRYING TO BE KIND, CONVINCING, I'M HERE UNDER SUSPICION... WHAT IS IT YOU WANT FROM ME?
MF 40... I WANT TO TALK TO YOU ABOUT HIM... AND I EXPECT YOU'LL WANT TO COOPERATE WITH ME.
GO AHEAD, I'M LISTENING.

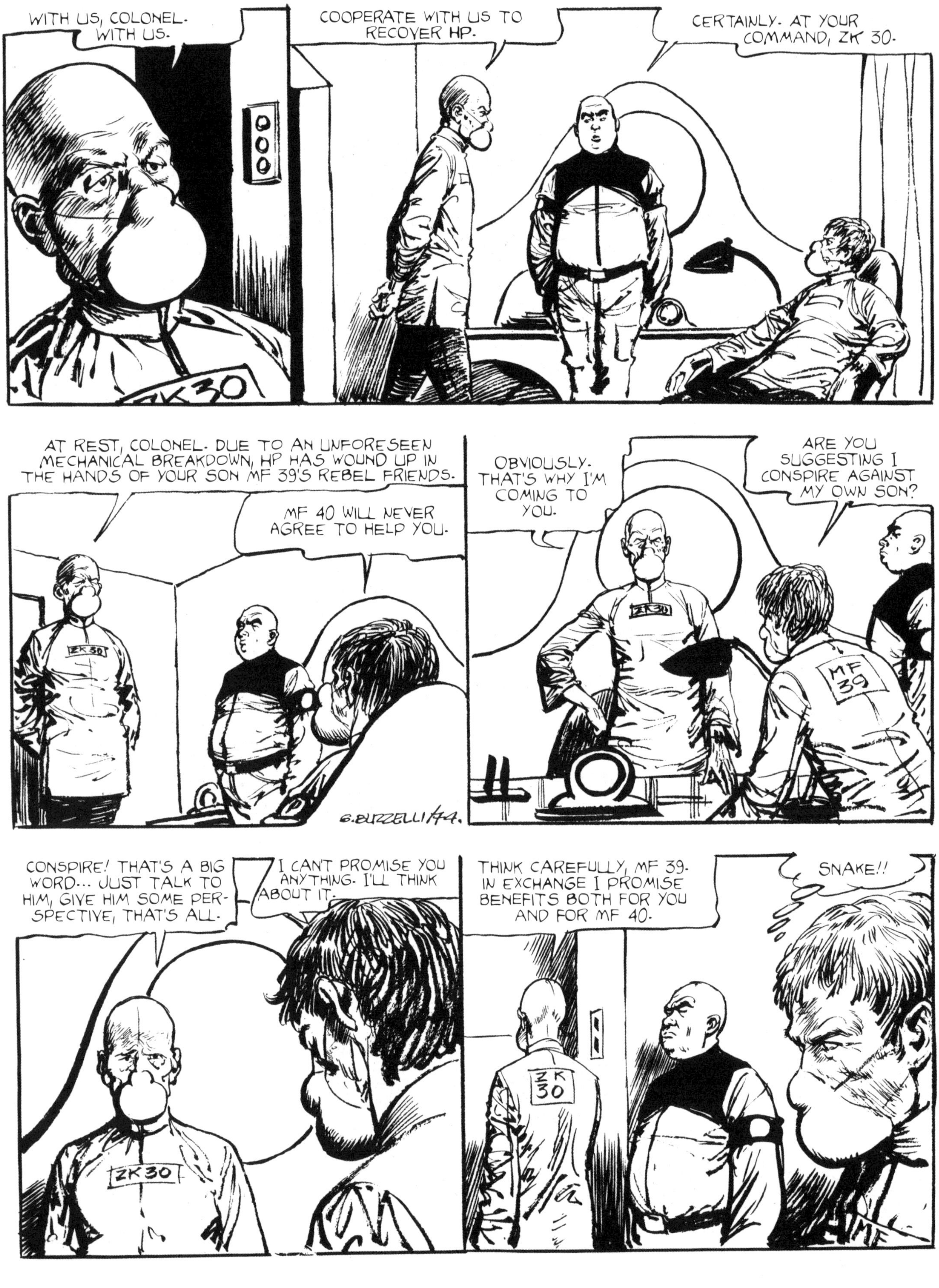
WITH US, COLONEL. WITH US.
COOPERATE WITH US TO RECOVER HP.
CERTAINLY. AT YOUR COMMAND, ZK 30.
ZK30
AT REST, COLONEL. DUE TO AN UNFORESEEN MECHANICAL BREAKDOWN, HP HAS WOUND UP IN THE HANDS OF YOUR SON MF 39'S REBEL FRIENDS.
MF 40 WILL NEVER AGREE TO HELP YOU.
ZK 30
G. BUZZELLI 74.
OBVIOUSLY. THAT'S WHY I'M COMING TO YOU.
ARE YOU SUGGESTING I CONSPIRE AGAINST MY OWN SON?
ZK 30
MF 39
CONSPIRE! THAT'S A BIG WORD... JUST TALK TO HIM, GIVE HIM SOME PERSPECTIVE, THAT'S ALL.
I CAN'T PROMISE YOU ANYTHING. I'LL THINK ABOUT IT.
ZK 30
THINK CAREFULLY, MF 39. IN EXCHANGE I PROMISE BENEFITS BOTH FOR YOU AND FOR MF 40.
SNAKE!!
ZK 30

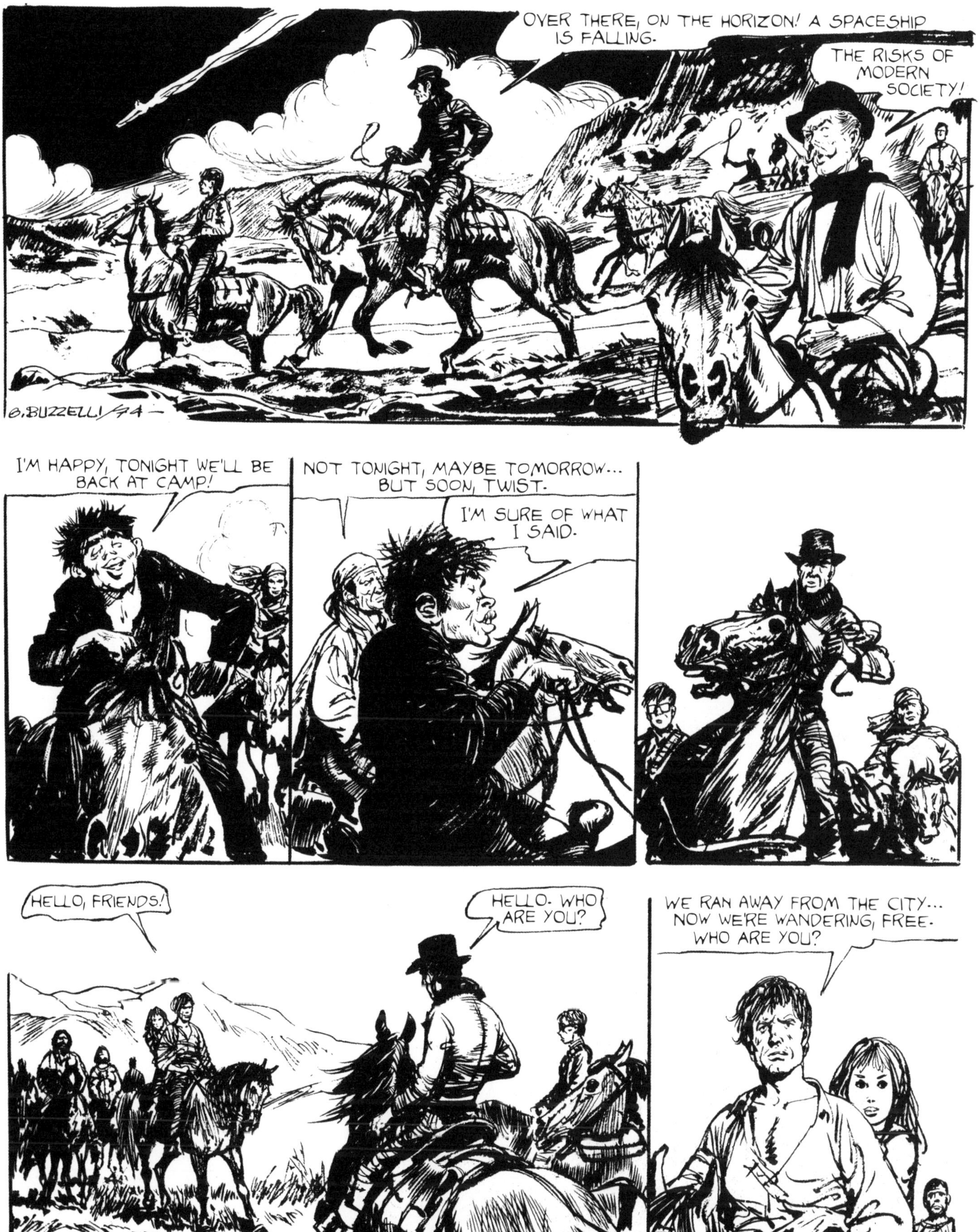
OVER THERE, ON THE HORIZON! A SPACESHIP IS FALLING.
THE RISKS OF MODERN SOCIETY!
G. BUZZELLI /74 -
I'M HAPPY, TONIGHT WE'LL BE BACK AT CAMP!
NOT TONIGHT, MAYBE TOMORROW... BUT SOON, TWIST.
I'M SURE OF WHAT I SAID.
HELLO, FRIENDS!
HELLO. WHO ARE YOU?
WE RAN AWAY FROM THE CITY... NOW WE'RE WANDERING, FREE. WHO ARE YOU?

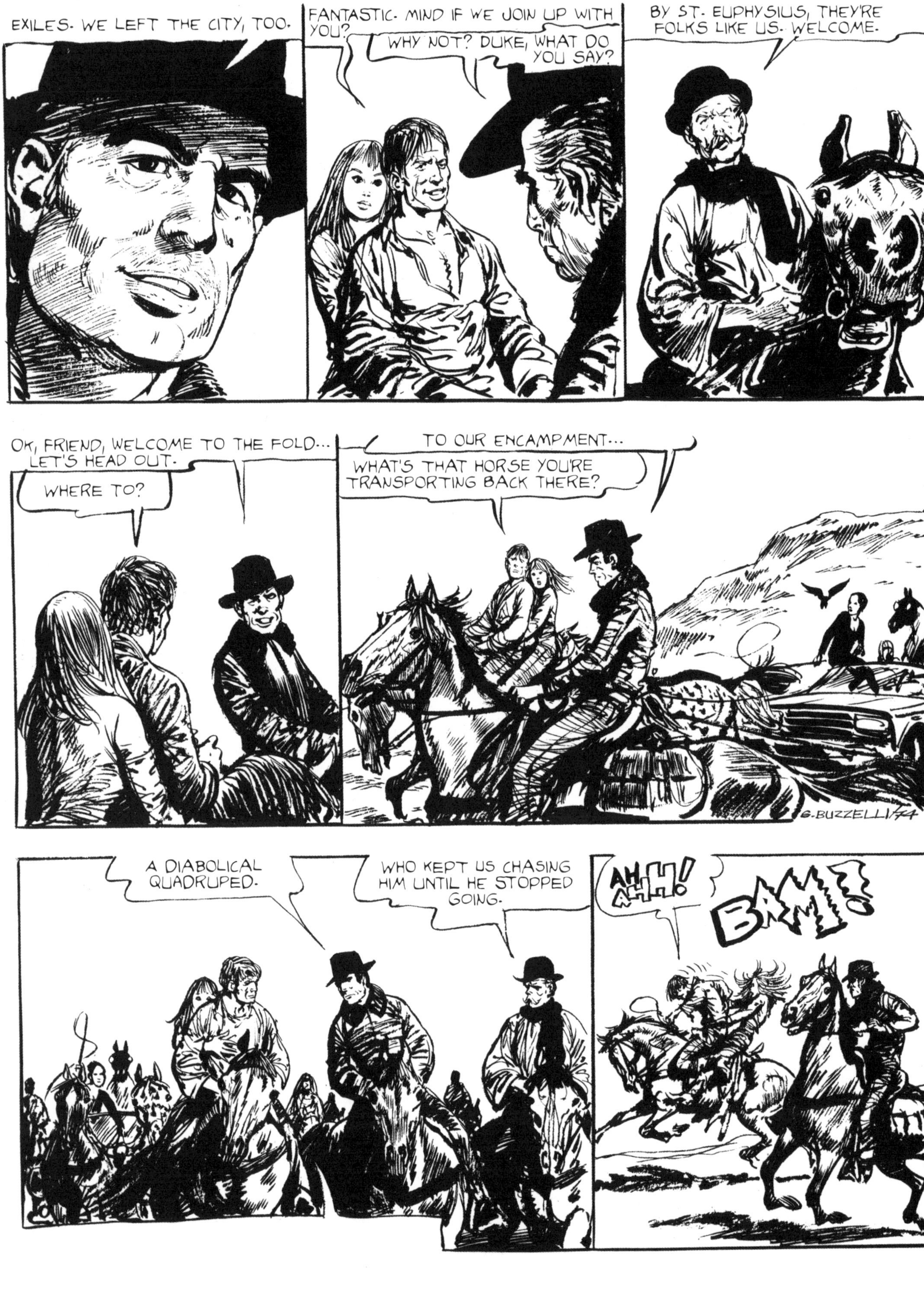
EXILES. WE LEFT THE CITY, TOO.
FANTASTIC. MIND IF WE JOIN UP WITH YOU?
WHY NOT? DUKE, WHAT DO YOU SAY?
BY ST. EUPHYSIUS, THEY'RE FOLKS LIKE US. WELCOME.
OK, FRIEND, WELCOME TO THE FOLD... LET'S HEAD OUT.
WHERE TO?
TO OUR ENCAMPMENT...
WHAT'S THAT HORSE YOU'RE TRANSPORTING BACK THERE?
G. BUZZELLI/74
A DIABOLICAL QUADRUPED.
WHO KEPT US CHASING HIM UNTIL HE STOPPED GOING.
AHHH! AHHH!
BAM!

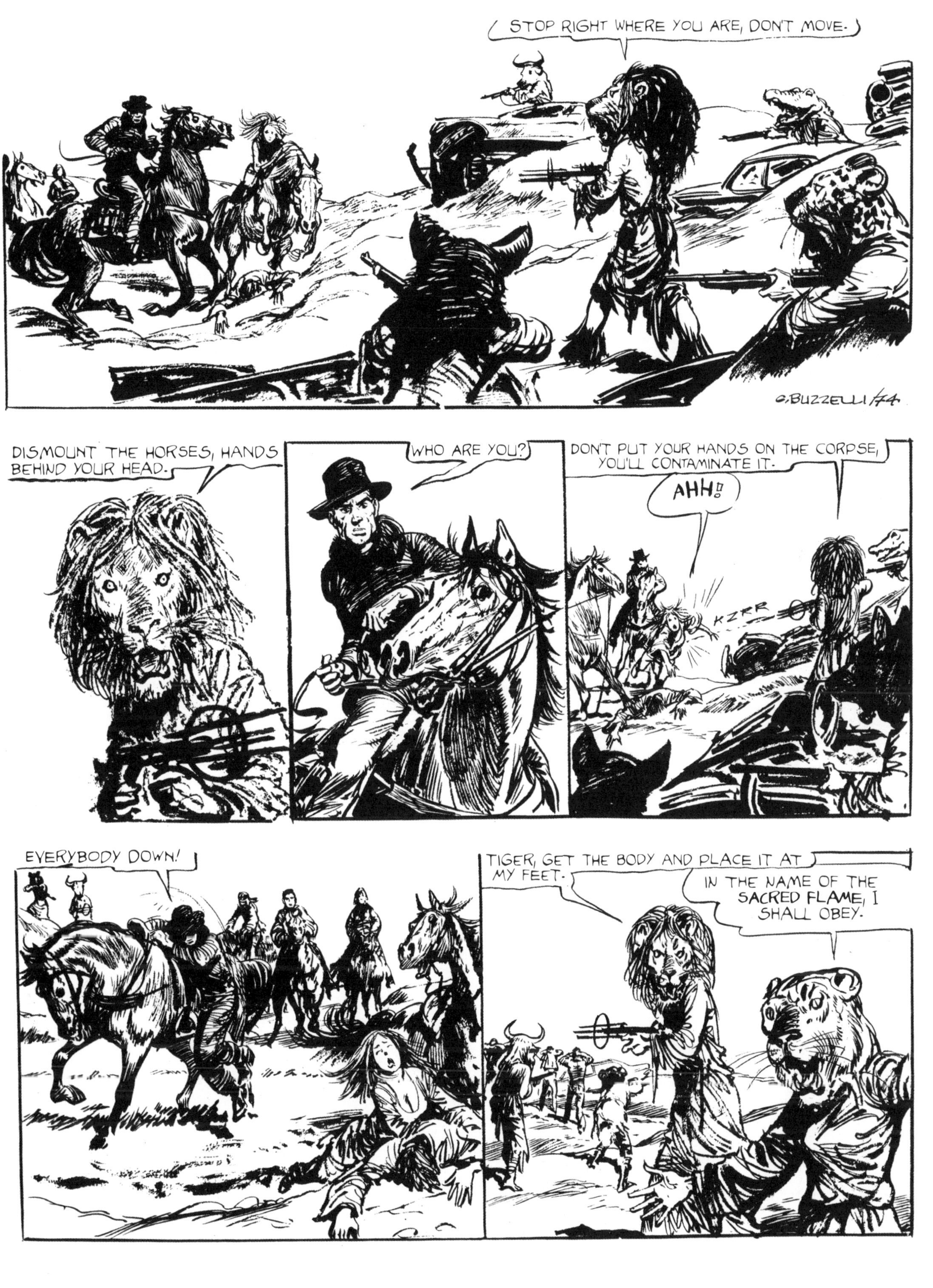
STOP RIGHT WHERE YOU ARE, DON'T MOVE.
G. BUZZELLI /74
DISMOUNT THE HORSES, HANDS BEHIND YOUR HEAD.
WHO ARE YOU?
DON'T PUT YOUR HANDS ON THE CORPSE, YOU'LL CONTAMINATE IT.
AHH!!
KZRR
EVERYBODY DOWN!
TIGER, GET THE BODY AND PLACE IT AT MY FEET.
IN THE NAME OF THE SACRED FLAME, I SHALL OBEY.

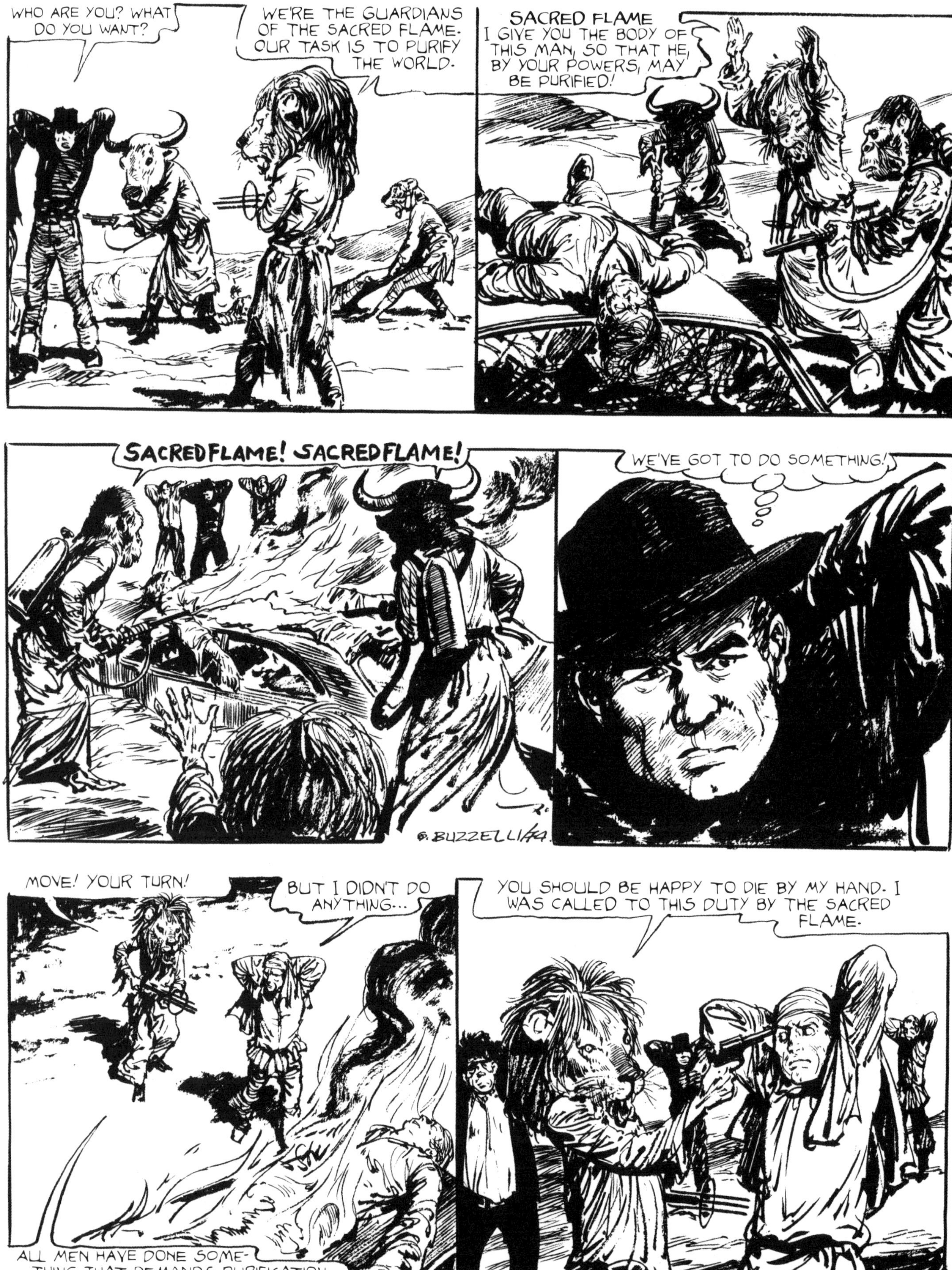
WHO ARE YOU? WHAT DO YOU WANT?
WE'RE THE GUARDIANS OF THE SACRED FLAME. OUR TASK IS TO PURIFY THE WORLD.
SACRED FLAME I GIVE YOU THE BODY OF THIS MAN, SO THAT HE, BY YOUR POWERS, MAY BE PURIFIED!
SACREDFLAME! SACREDFLAME!
G. BUZZELLI
WE'VE GOT TO DO SOMETHING!
MOVE! YOUR TURN!
BUT I DIDN'T DO ANYTHING...
ALL MEN HAVE DONE SOMETHING THAT DEMANDS PURIFICATION.
YOU SHOULD BE HAPPY TO DIE BY MY HAND. I WAS CALLED TO THIS DUTY BY THE SACRED FLAME.

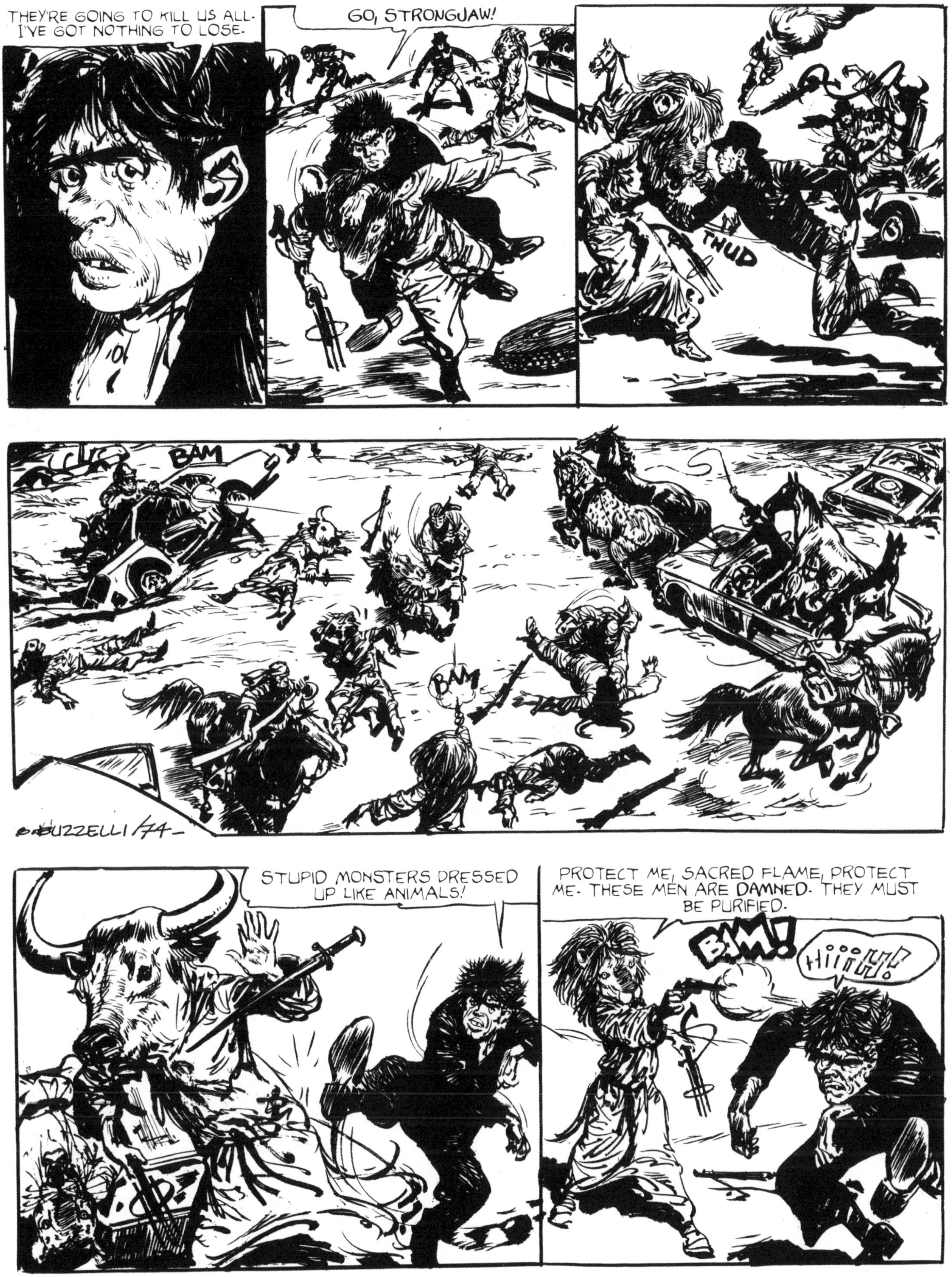
THEY'RE GOING TO KILL US ALL. I'VE GOT NOTHING TO LOSE.
GO, STRONGJAW!
THUD
BAM
BAM
BUZZELLI /74
STUPID MONSTERS DRESSED UP LIKE ANIMALS!
PROTECT ME, SACRED FLAME, PROTECT ME. THESE MEN ARE **DAMNED**. THEY MUST BE PURIFIED.
BAM!

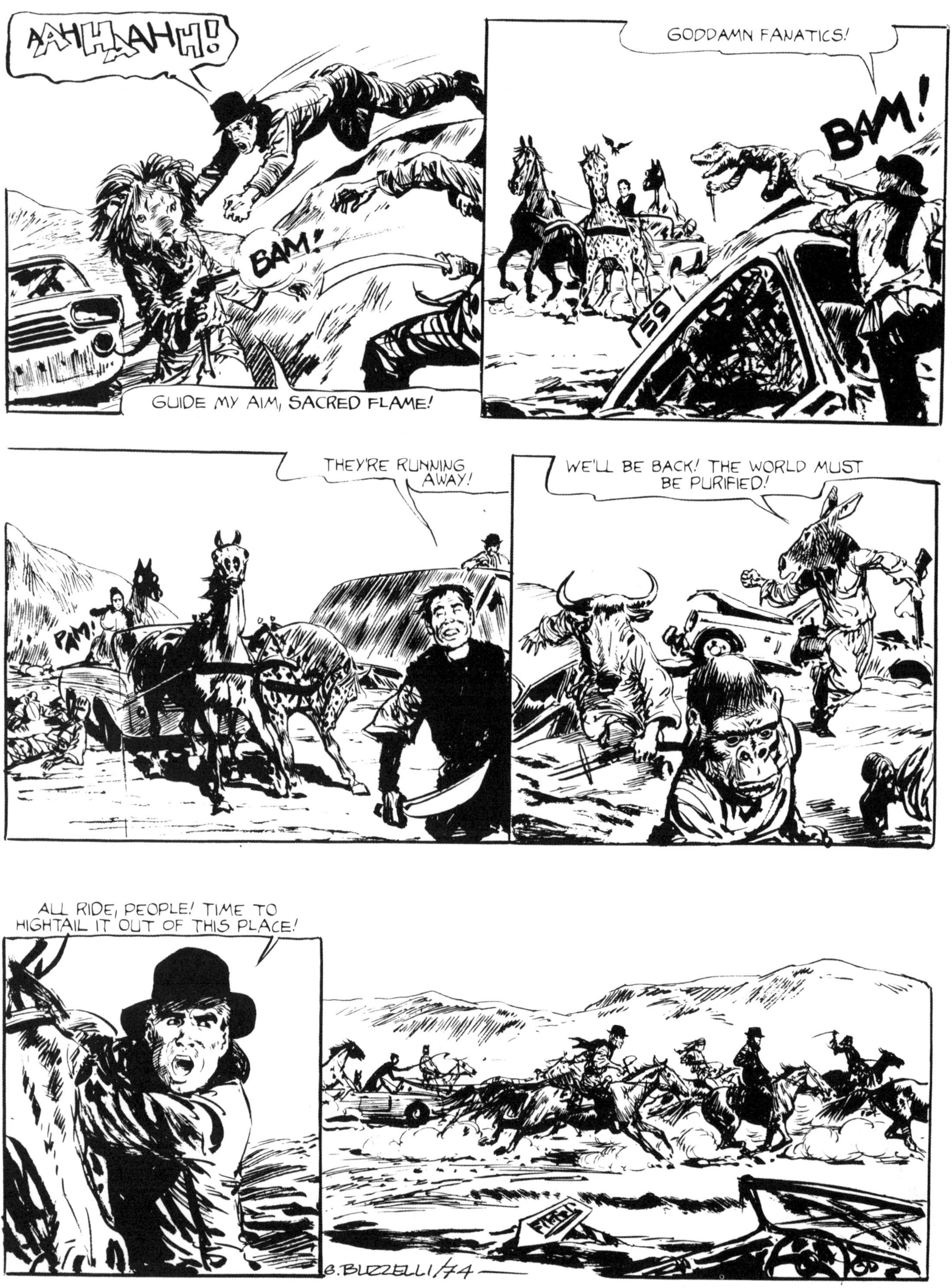
AAHHAAHH!
BAM!
GUIDE MY AIM, SACRED FLAME!
GODDAMN FANATICS!
BAM!
THEY'RE RUNNING AWAY!
PAM!
WE'LL BE BACK! THE WORLD MUST BE PURIFIED!
ALL RIDE, PEOPLE! TIME TO HIGHTAIL IT OUT OF THIS PLACE!
G. BUZZELLI/74

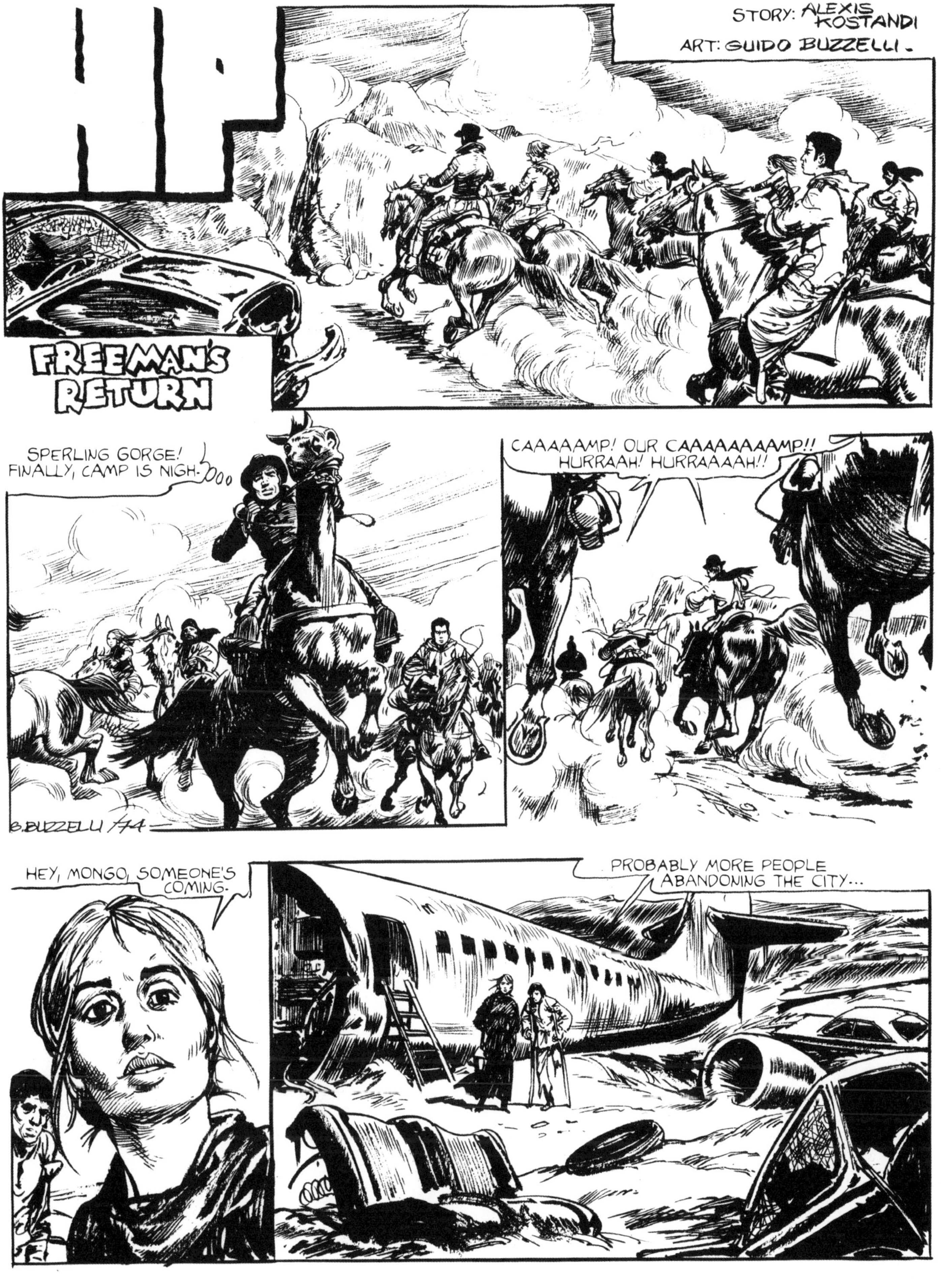
STORY: ALEXIS KOSTANDI
ART: GUIDO BUZZELLI
FREEMAN'S RETURN
SPERLING GORGE! FINALLY, CAMP IS NIGH.
G. BUZZELLI 74
CAAAAAAMP! OUR CAAAAAAAAAMP!! HURRAAH! HURRAAAAH!!
HEY, MONGO, SOMEONE'S COMING.
PROBABLY MORE PEOPLE ABANDONING THE CITY...

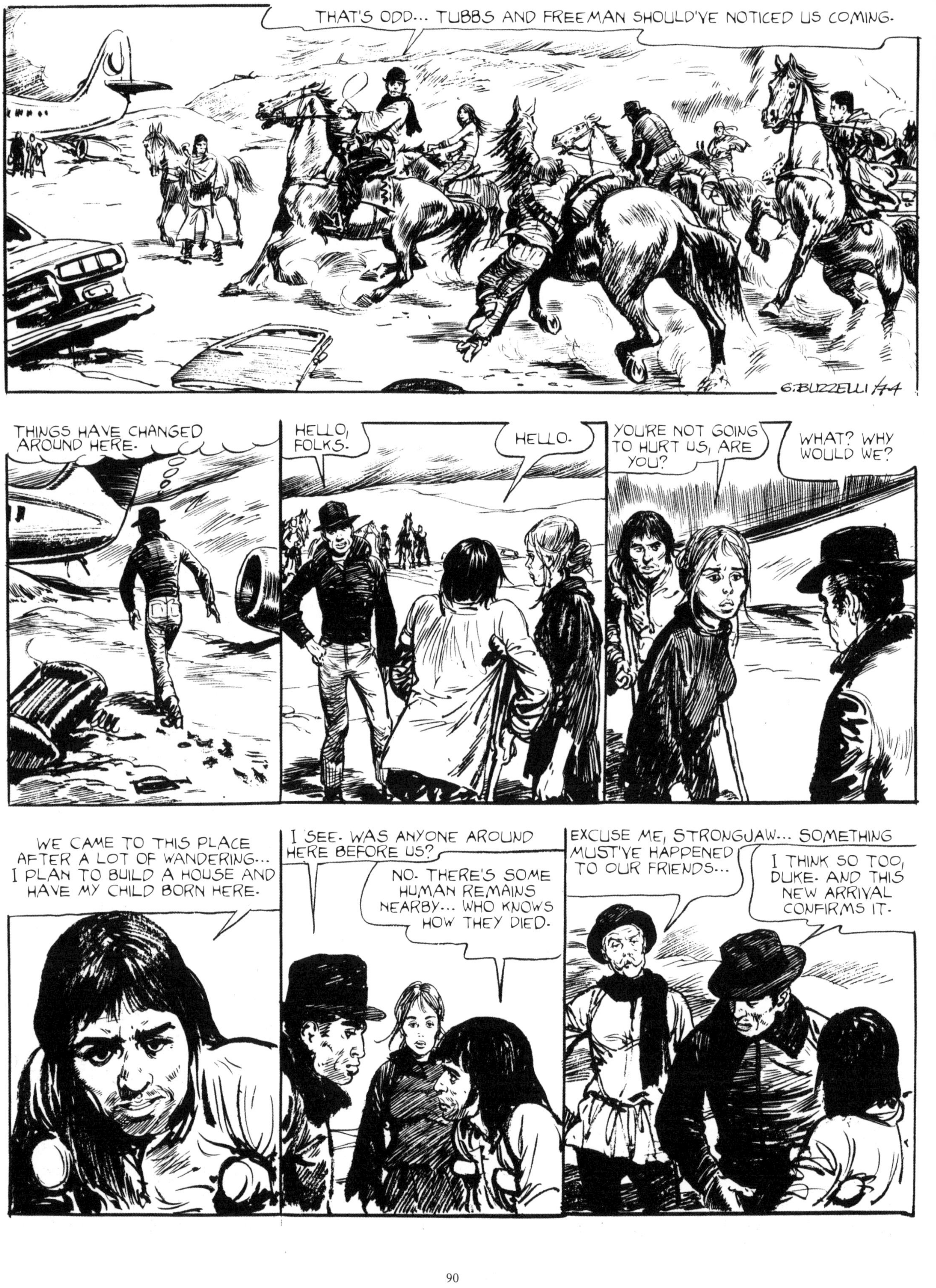
THAT'S ODD... TUBBS AND FREEMAN SHOULD'VE NOTICED US COMING.
G. BUZZELLI 74
THINGS HAVE CHANGED AROUND HERE.
HELLO, FOLKS.
HELLO.
YOU'RE NOT GOING TO HURT US, ARE YOU?
WHAT? WHY WOULD WE?
WE CAME TO THIS PLACE AFTER A LOT OF WANDERING... I PLAN TO BUILD A HOUSE AND HAVE MY CHILD BORN HERE.
I SEE. WAS ANYONE AROUND HERE BEFORE US?
NO. THERE'S SOME HUMAN REMAINS NEARBY... WHO KNOWS HOW THEY DIED.
EXCUSE ME, STRONGJAW... SOMETHING MUST'VE HAPPENED TO OUR FRIENDS...
I THINK SO TOO, DUKE. AND THIS NEW ARRIVAL CONFIRMS IT.

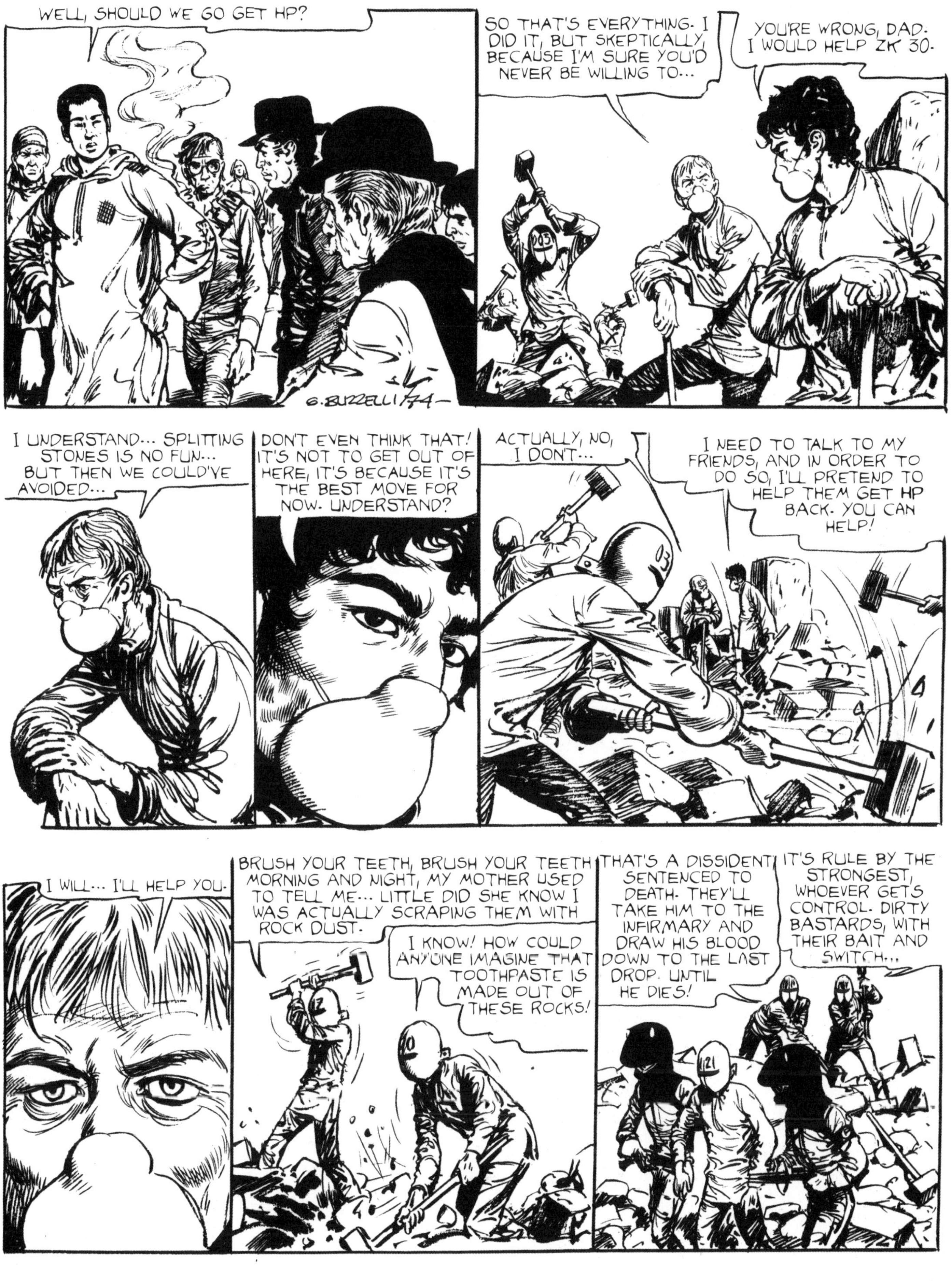
WELL, SHOULD WE GO GET HP?
G. BUZZELLI '74
SO THAT'S EVERYTHING. I DID IT, BUT SKEPTICALLY, BECAUSE I'M SURE YOU'D NEVER BE WILLING TO...
YOU'RE WRONG, DAD. I WOULD HELP ZK 30.
I UNDERSTAND... SPLITTING STONES IS NO FUN... BUT THEN WE COULD'VE AVOIDED...
DON'T EVEN THINK THAT! IT'S NOT TO GET OUT OF HERE, IT'S BECAUSE IT'S THE BEST MOVE FOR NOW. UNDERSTAND?
ACTUALLY, NO, I DON'T...
I NEED TO TALK TO MY FRIENDS, AND IN ORDER TO DO SO, I'LL PRETEND TO HELP THEM GET HP BACK. YOU CAN HELP!
I WILL... I'LL HELP YOU.
BRUSH YOUR TEETH, BRUSH YOUR TEETH MORNING AND NIGHT, MY MOTHER USED TO TELL ME... LITTLE DID SHE KNOW I WAS ACTUALLY SCRAPING THEM WITH ROCK DUST.
I KNOW! HOW COULD ANYONE IMAGINE THAT TOOTHPASTE IS MADE OUT OF THESE ROCKS!
THAT'S A DISSIDENT! SENTENCED TO DEATH. THEY'LL TAKE HIM TO THE INFIRMARY AND DRAW HIS BLOOD DOWN TO THE LAST DROP. UNTIL HE DIES!
IT'S RULE BY THE STRONGEST, WHOEVER GETS CONTROL. DIRTY BASTARDS, WITH THEIR BAIT AND SWITCH...

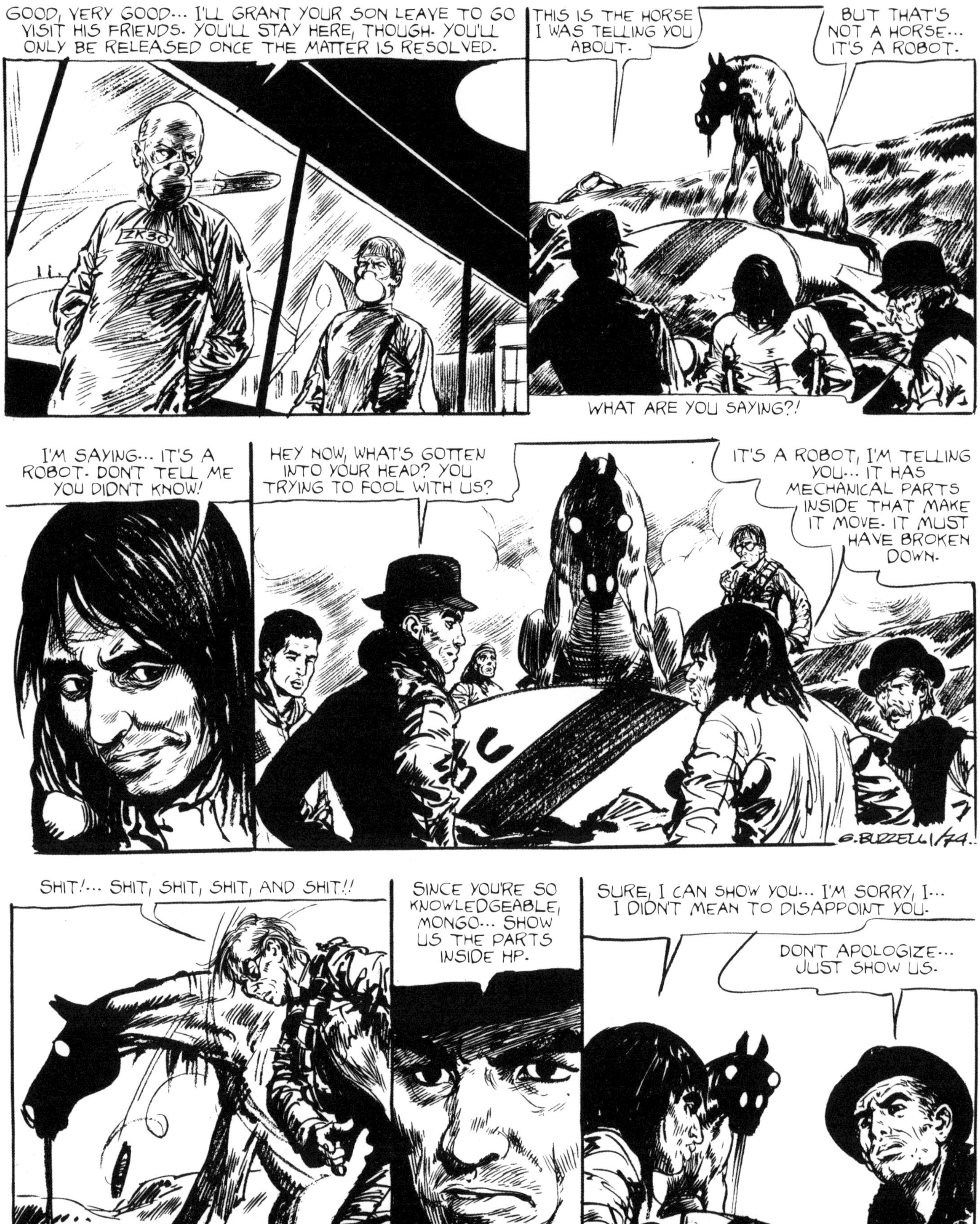

GOOD, VERY GOOD... I'LL GRANT YOUR SON LEAVE TO GO VISIT HIS FRIENDS. YOU'LL STAY HERE, THOUGH. YOU'LL ONLY BE RELEASED ONCE THE MATTER IS RESOLVED.
ZK3C
THIS IS THE HORSE I WAS TELLING YOU ABOUT.
BUT THAT'S NOT A HORSE... IT'S A ROBOT.
WHAT ARE YOU SAYING?!
I'M SAYING... IT'S A ROBOT. DON'T TELL ME YOU DIDN'T KNOW!
HEY NOW, WHAT'S GOTTEN INTO YOUR HEAD? YOU TRYING TO FOOL WITH US?
IT'S A ROBOT, I'M TELLING YOU... IT HAS MECHANICAL PARTS INSIDE THAT MAKE IT MOVE. IT MUST HAVE BROKEN DOWN.
G. BUZZELLI/74.
SHIT!... SHIT, SHIT, SHIT, AND SHIT!!
SINCE YOU'RE SO KNOWLEDGEABLE, MONGO... SHOW US THE PARTS INSIDE HP.
SURE, I CAN SHOW YOU... I'M SORRY, I... I DIDN'T MEAN TO DISAPPOINT YOU.
DON'T APOLOGIZE... JUST SHOW US.

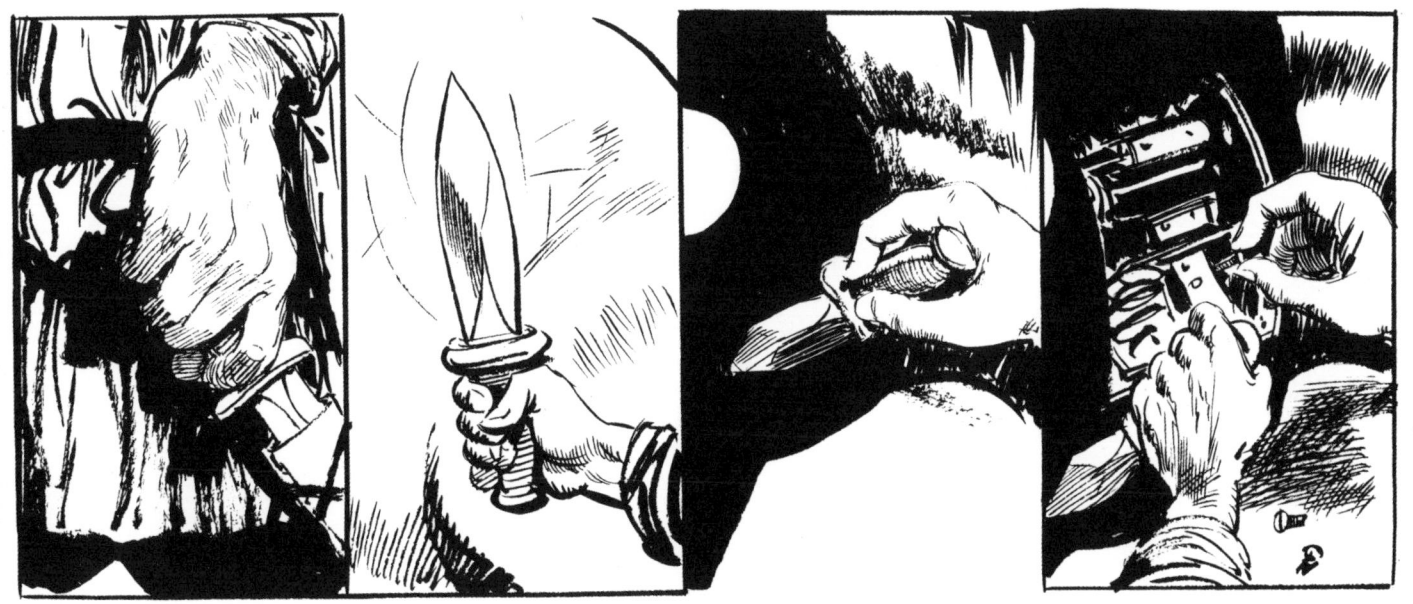

SEE, HERE IS A VIDEOCAMERA SYSTEM DESIGNED TO LOOK LIKE HIS EYES.

I'M REALIZING THAT WE'RE NOT SO UP-TO-DATE ON THE LATEST TECHNOLOGY.

I WAS A TECHNICIAN, AND I WAS PROUD OF MY PROFESSION, BECAUSE I HAD A PART IN THESE ALMOST MAGICAL PROJECTS.

BUT?

THE RESULTS WERE ANYTHING BUT MAGICAL... I DIDN'T WANT TO BE HELPING OUT THE CITY OR ITS GOVERNMENT ANYMORE, SO I LEFT... THERE'S A MASS EXODUS TAKING PLACE, YOU KNOW?

YOU MEAN THE CITY IS EMPTYING OUT?

MOST PEOPLE THERE ARE CHOOSING TO LEAVE; SOME BECAUSE IT'S A TREND, OTHERS FOR ETHICAL REASONS. EITHER WAY, THE CITY IS EMPTYING OUT, YES.

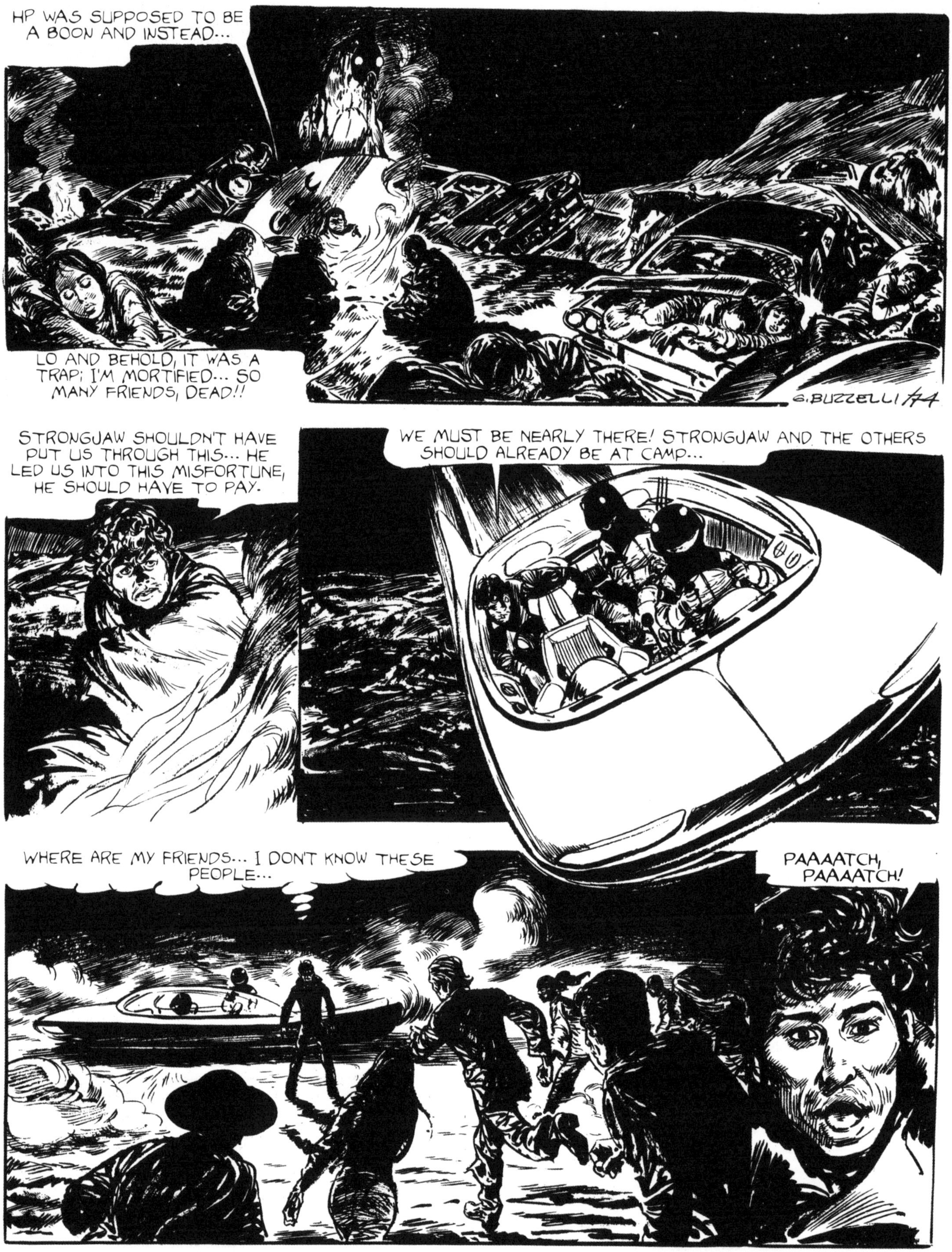
HP WAS SUPPOSED TO BE A BOON AND INSTEAD...
LO AND BEHOLD, IT WAS A TRAP; I'M MORTIFIED... SO MANY FRIENDS, DEAD!!
G. BUZZELLI 74
STRONGJAW SHOULDN'T HAVE PUT US THROUGH THIS... HE LED US INTO THIS MISFORTUNE, HE SHOULD HAVE TO PAY.
WE MUST BE NEARLY THERE! STRONGJAW AND THE OTHERS SHOULD ALREADY BE AT CAMP...
WHERE ARE MY FRIENDS... I DON'T KNOW THESE PEOPLE...
PAAAATCH, PAAAATCH!

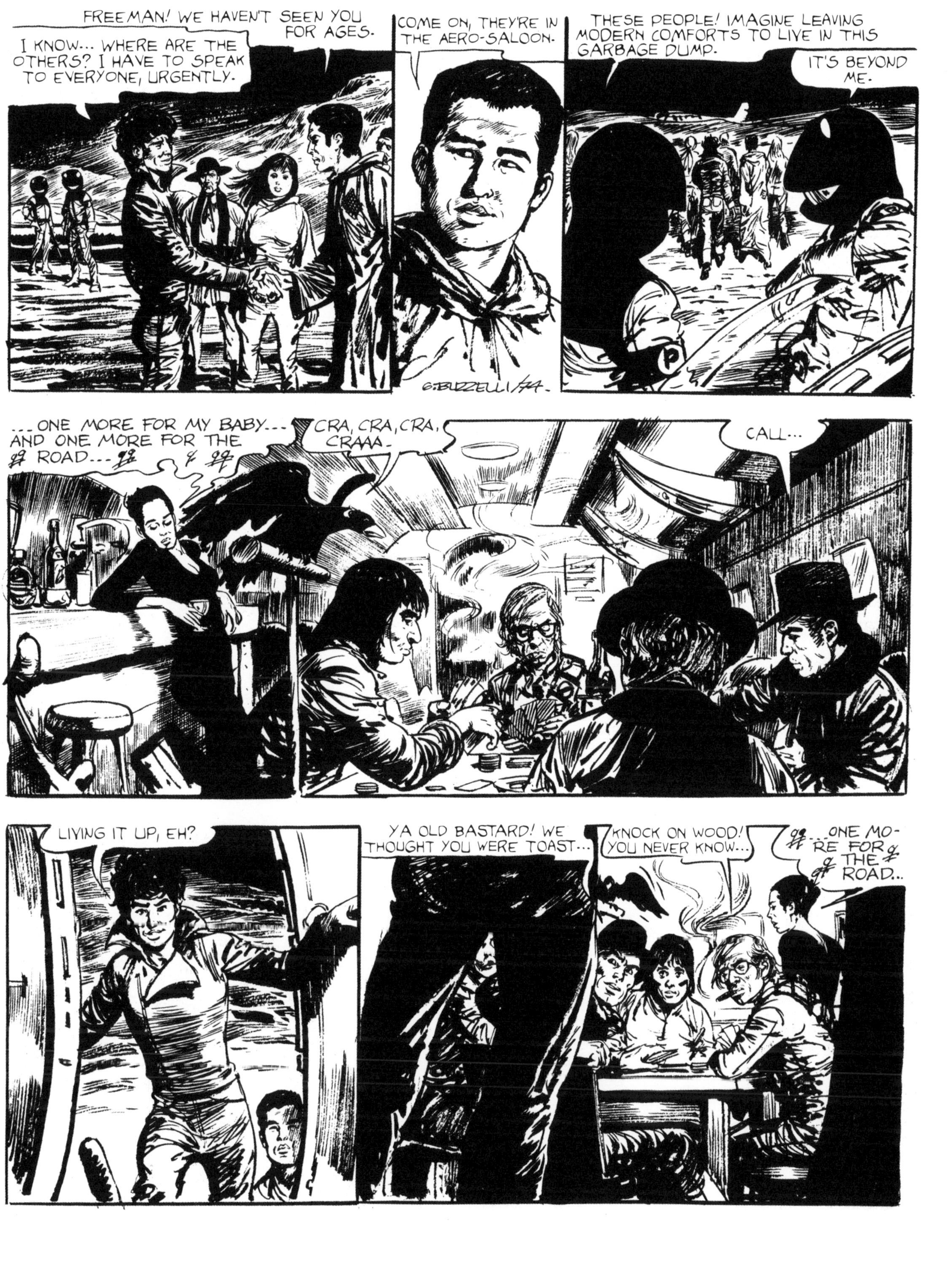

FREEMAN! WE HAVEN'T SEEN YOU FOR AGES.
I KNOW... WHERE ARE THE OTHERS? I HAVE TO SPEAK TO EVERYONE, URGENTLY.
COME ON, THEY'RE IN THE AERO-SALOON.
G. BUZZELLI/74
THESE PEOPLE! IMAGINE LEAVING MODERN COMFORTS TO LIVE IN THIS GARBAGE DUMP.
IT'S BEYOND ME.
...ONE MORE FOR MY BABY... AND ONE MORE FOR THE ROAD...
CRA, CRA, CRA, CRAAA.
CALL...
LIVING IT UP, EH?
YA OLD BASTARD! WE THOUGHT YOU WERE TOAST...
KNOCK ON WOOD! YOU NEVER KNOW...
...ONE MORE FOR THE ROAD...

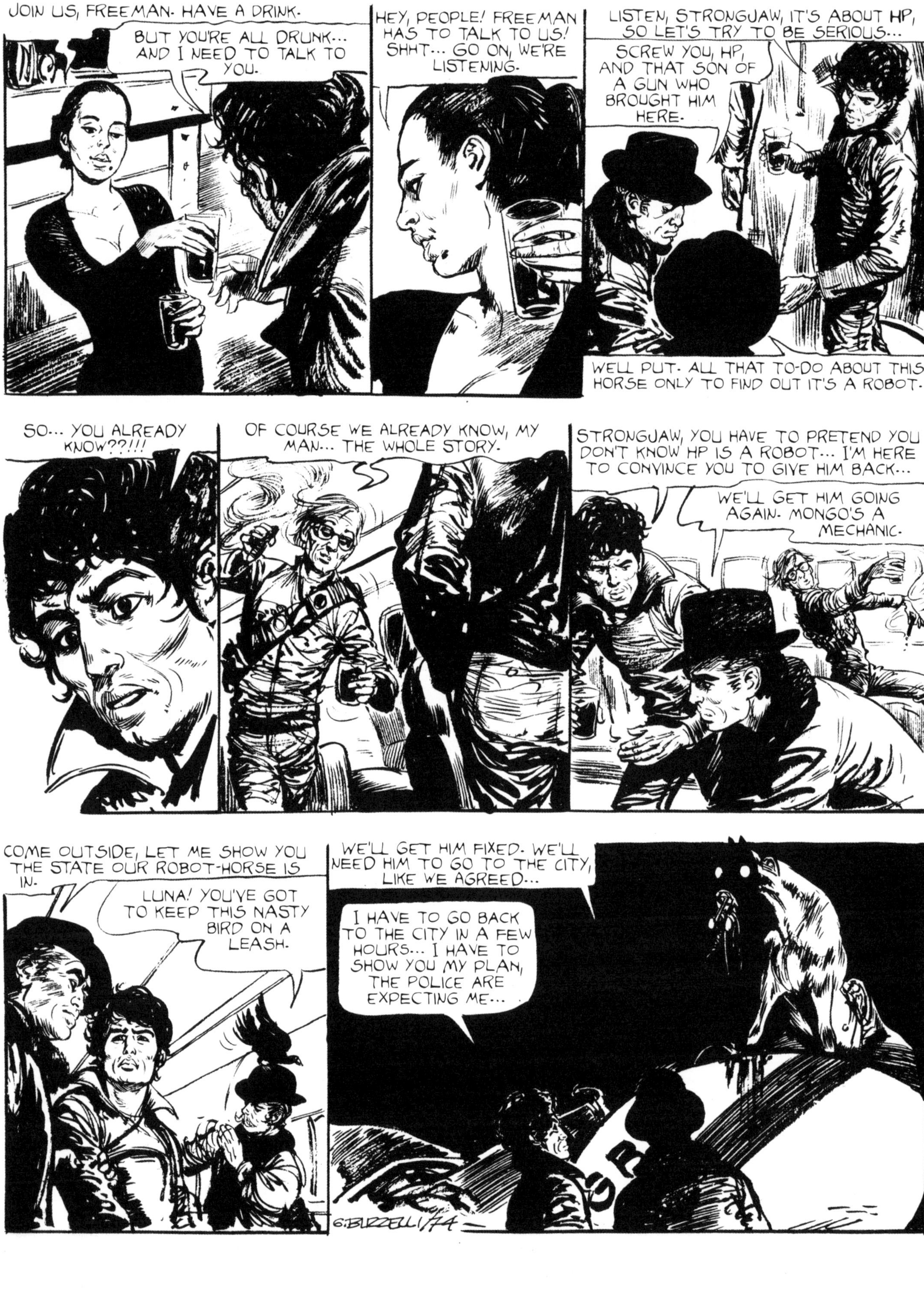

JOIN US, FREEMAN. HAVE A DRINK.
BUT YOU'RE ALL DRUNK... AND I NEED TO TALK TO YOU.
HEY, PEOPLE! FREEMAN HAS TO TALK TO US! SHHT... GO ON, WE'RE LISTENING.
LISTEN, STRONGJAW, IT'S ABOUT HP, SO LET'S TRY TO BE SERIOUS...
SCREW YOU, HP, AND THAT SON OF A GUN WHO BROUGHT HIM HERE.
WELL PUT. ALL THAT TO-DO ABOUT THIS HORSE ONLY TO FIND OUT IT'S A ROBOT.
SO... YOU ALREADY KNOW??!!!
OF COURSE WE ALREADY KNOW, MY MAN... THE WHOLE STORY.
STRONGJAW, YOU HAVE TO PRETEND YOU DON'T KNOW HP IS A ROBOT... I'M HERE TO CONVINCE YOU TO GIVE HIM BACK...
WE'LL GET HIM GOING AGAIN. MONGO'S A MECHANIC.
COME OUTSIDE, LET ME SHOW YOU THE STATE OUR ROBOT-HORSE IS IN.
LUNA! YOU'VE GOT TO KEEP THIS NASTY BIRD ON A LEASH.
WE'LL GET HIM FIXED. WE'LL NEED HIM TO GO TO THE CITY, LIKE WE AGREED...
I HAVE TO GO BACK TO THE CITY IN A FEW HOURS... I HAVE TO SHOW YOU MY PLAN, THE POLICE ARE EXPECTING ME...
G. BUZZELLI/74

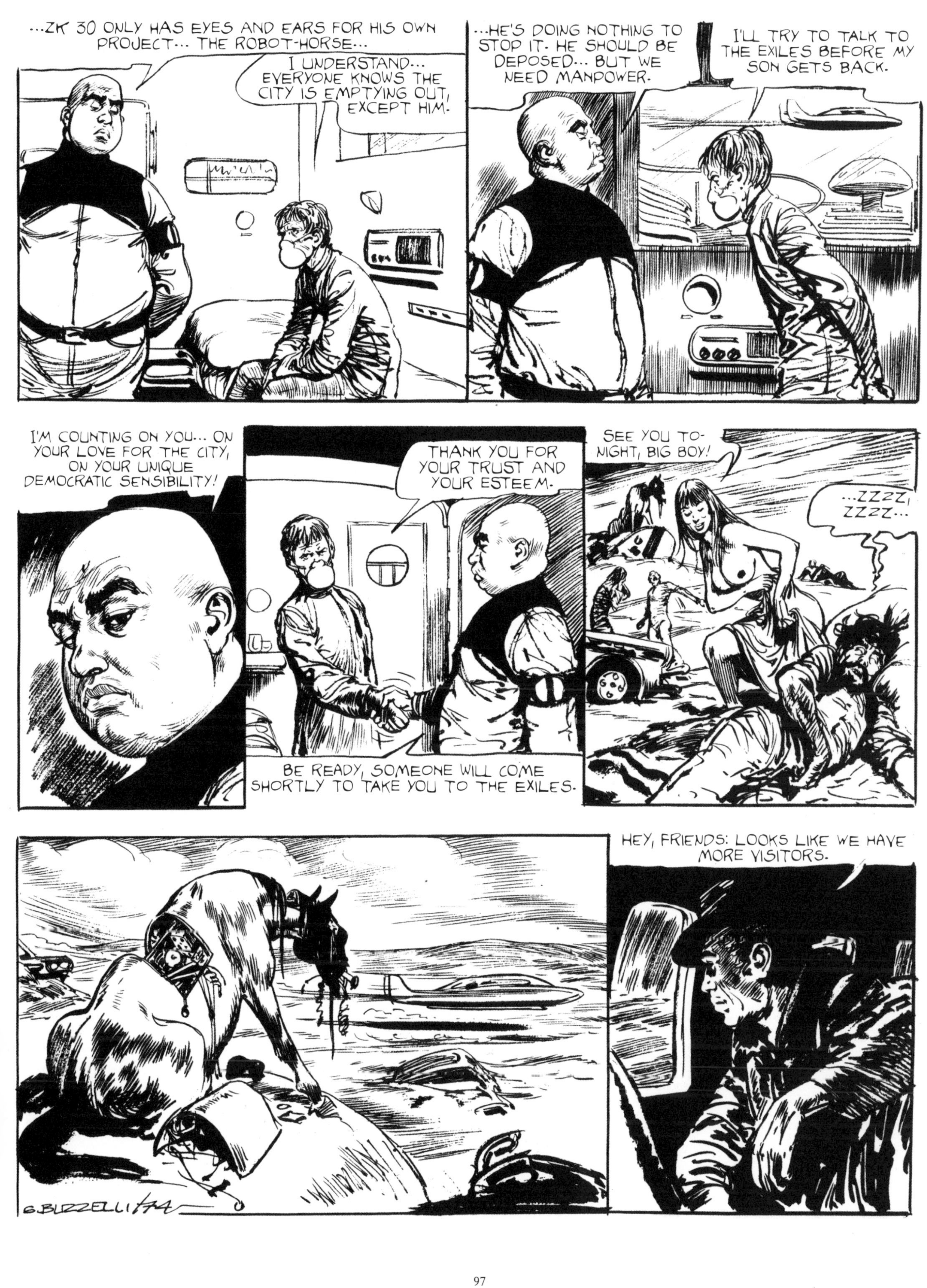
...ZK 30 ONLY HAS EYES AND EARS FOR HIS OWN PROJECT... THE ROBOT-HORSE...
I UNDERSTAND... EVERYONE KNOWS THE CITY IS EMPTYING OUT, EXCEPT HIM.
...HE'S DOING NOTHING TO STOP IT. HE SHOULD BE DEPOSED... BUT WE NEED MANPOWER.
I'LL TRY TO TALK TO THE EXILES BEFORE MY SON GETS BACK.
I'M COUNTING ON YOU... ON YOUR LOVE FOR THE CITY, ON YOUR UNIQUE DEMOCRATIC SENSIBILITY!
THANK YOU FOR YOUR TRUST AND YOUR ESTEEM.
BE READY, SOMEONE WILL COME SHORTLY TO TAKE YOU TO THE EXILES.
SEE YOU TO-NIGHT, BIG BOY!
...ZZZZ, ZZZZ...
HEY, FRIENDS: LOOKS LIKE WE HAVE MORE VISITORS.
G.BUZZELLI

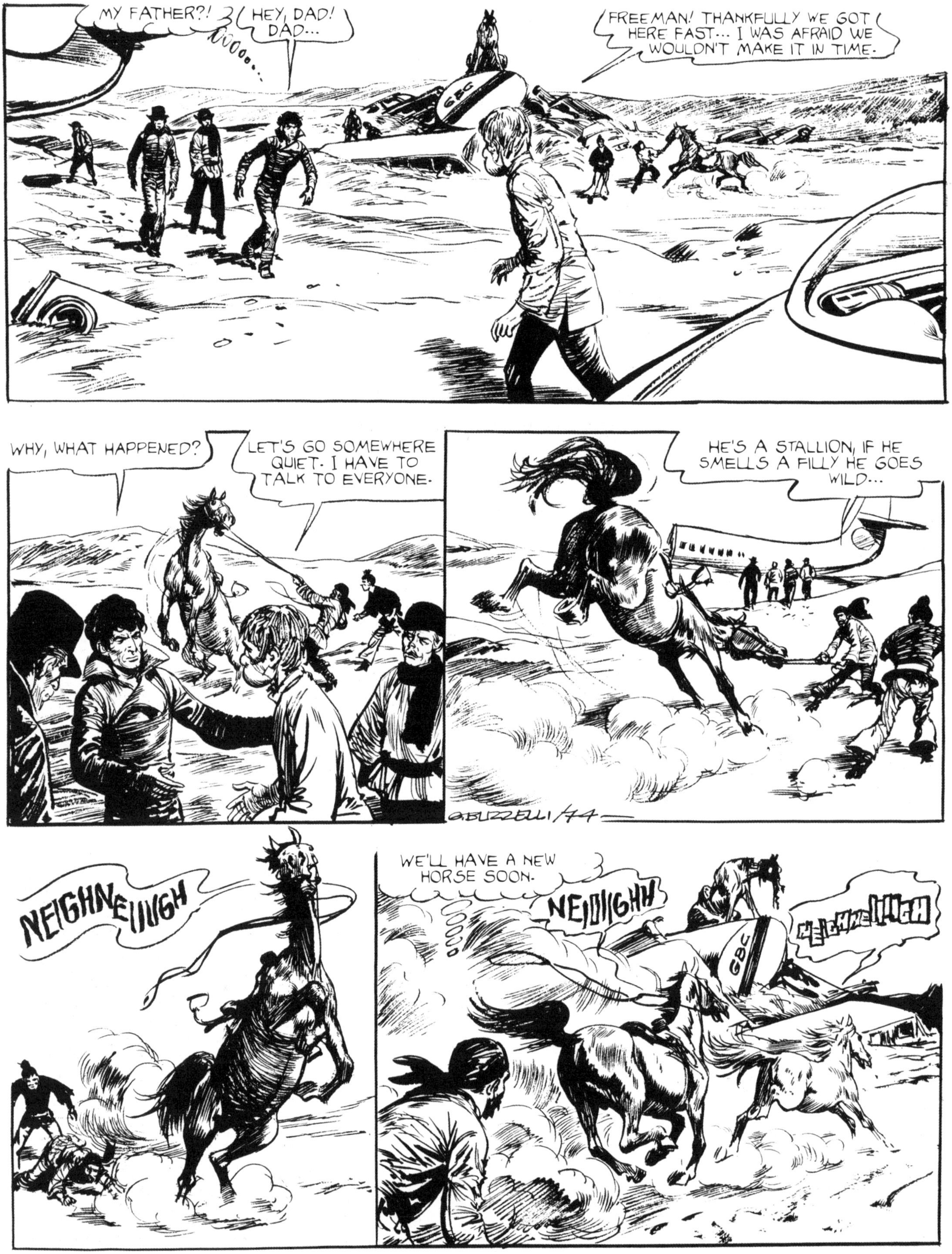
MY FATHER?!
HEY, DAD! DAD...
FREEMAN! THANKFULLY WE GOT HERE FAST... I WAS AFRAID WE WOULDN'T MAKE IT IN TIME.
WHY, WHAT HAPPENED?
LET'S GO SOMEWHERE QUIET. I HAVE TO TALK TO EVERYONE.
HE'S A STALLION, IF HE SMELLS A FILLY HE GOES WILD...
G.BUZZELLI/74
WE'LL HAVE A NEW HORSE SOON.
GBC

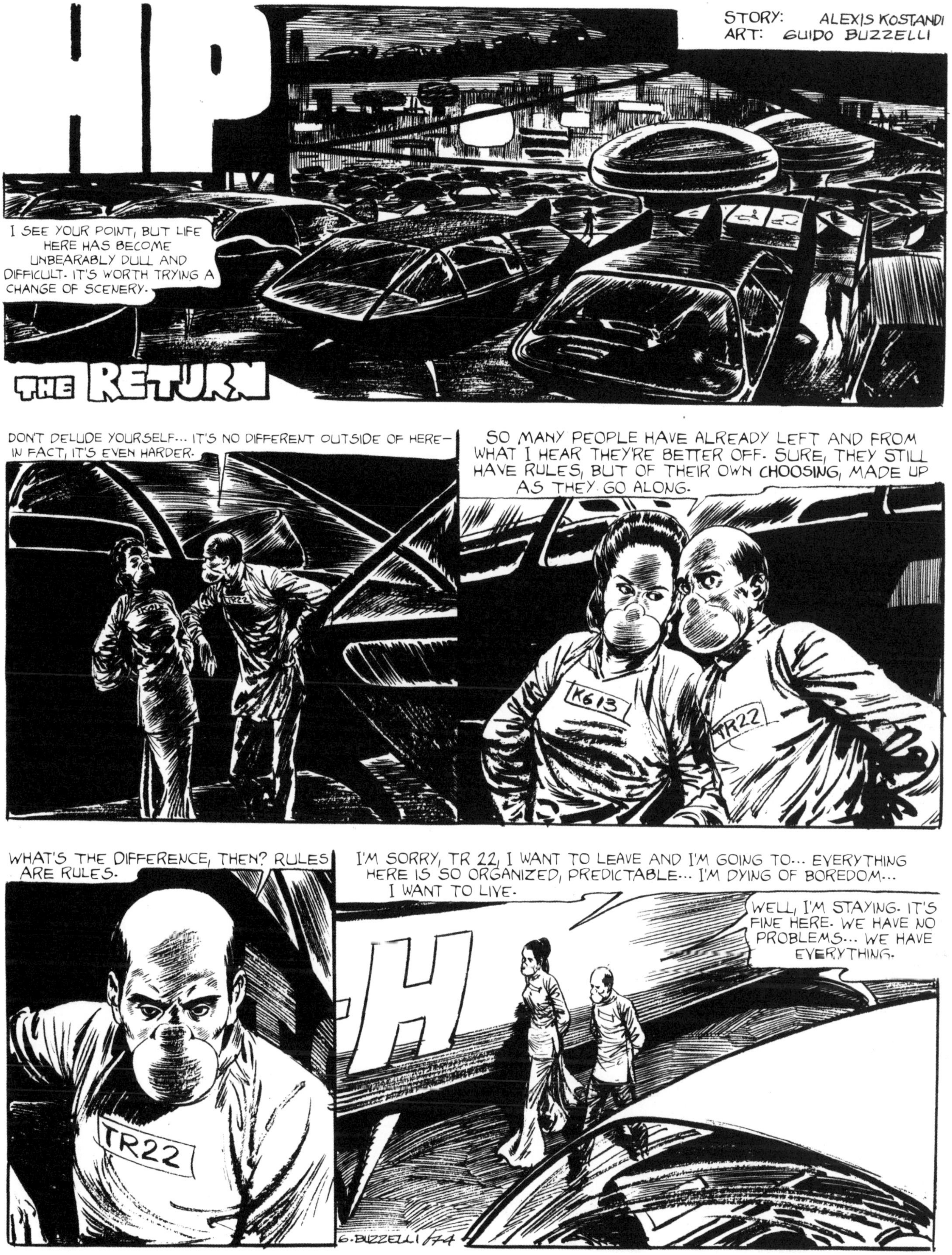
HP
STORY: ALEXIS KOSTANDI
ART: GUIDO BUZZELLI
I SEE YOUR POINT, BUT LIFE HERE HAS BECOME UNBEARABLY DULL AND DIFFICULT. IT'S WORTH TRYING A CHANGE OF SCENERY.
THE RETURN
DON'T DELUDE YOURSELF... IT'S NO DIFFERENT OUTSIDE OF HERE— IN FACT, IT'S EVEN HARDER.
TR22
SO MANY PEOPLE HAVE ALREADY LEFT AND FROM WHAT I HEAR THEY'RE BETTER OFF. SURE, THEY STILL HAVE RULES, BUT OF THEIR OWN CHOOSING, MADE UP AS THEY GO ALONG.
K613
TR22
WHAT'S THE DIFFERENCE, THEN? RULES ARE RULES.
TR22
I'M SORRY, TR 22, I WANT TO LEAVE AND I'M GOING TO... EVERYTHING HERE IS SO ORGANIZED, PREDICTABLE... I'M DYING OF BOREDOM... I WANT TO LIVE.
WELL, I'M STAYING. IT'S FINE HERE. WE HAVE NO PROBLEMS... WE HAVE EVERYTHING.
H
G. BUZZELLI /74

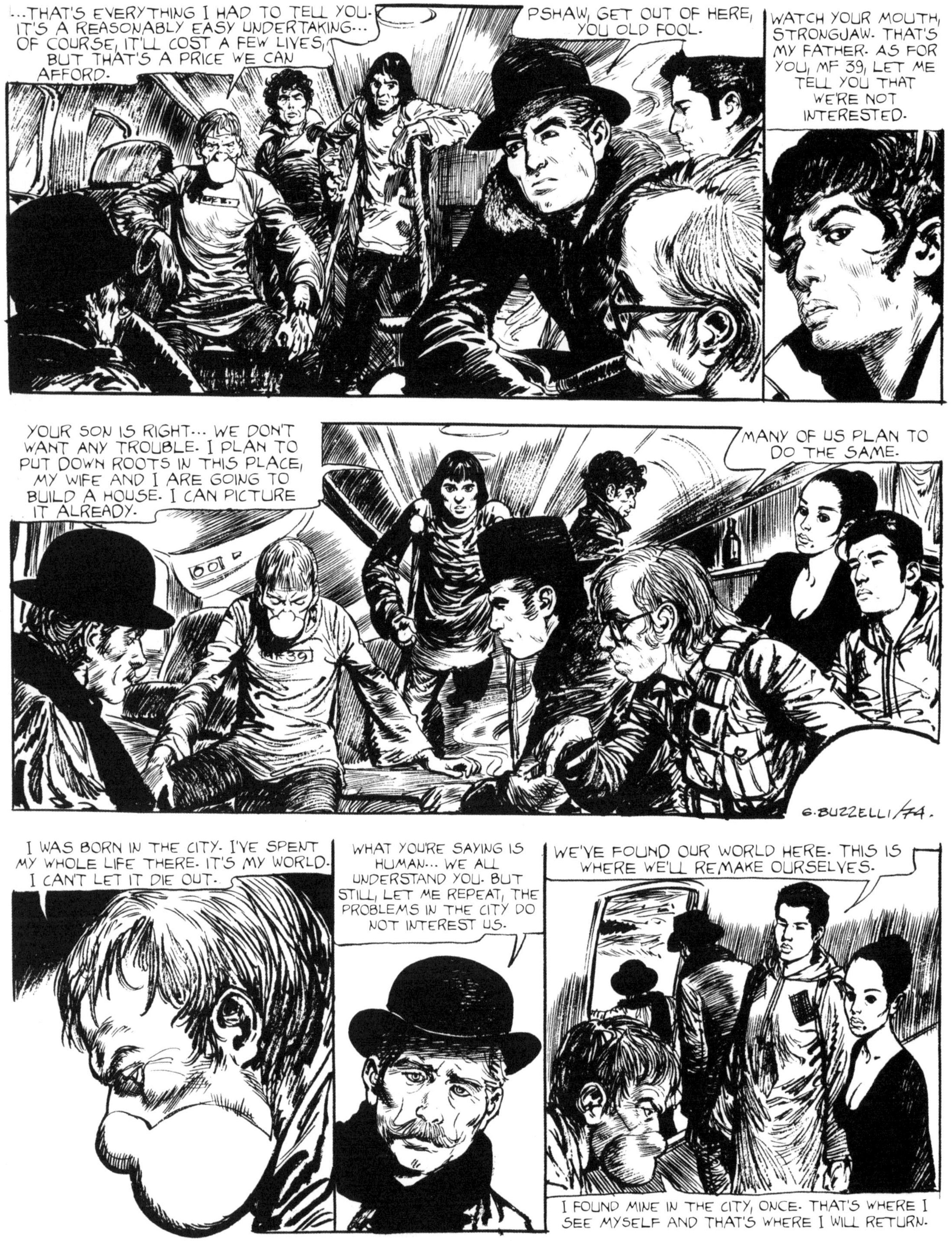
...THAT'S EVERYTHING I HAD TO TELL YOU. IT'S A REASONABLY EASY UNDERTAKING... OF COURSE, IT'LL COST A FEW LIVES, BUT THAT'S A PRICE WE CAN AFFORD.
PSHAW, GET OUT OF HERE, YOU OLD FOOL.
WATCH YOUR MOUTH, STRONGJAW. THAT'S MY FATHER. AS FOR YOU, MF 39, LET ME TELL YOU THAT WE'RE NOT INTERESTED.
YOUR SON IS RIGHT... WE DON'T WANT ANY TROUBLE. I PLAN TO PUT DOWN ROOTS IN THIS PLACE, MY WIFE AND I ARE GOING TO BUILD A HOUSE. I CAN PICTURE IT ALREADY.
MANY OF US PLAN TO DO THE SAME.
G. BUZZELLI /74.
I WAS BORN IN THE CITY. I'VE SPENT MY WHOLE LIFE THERE. IT'S MY WORLD. I CAN'T LET IT DIE OUT.
WHAT YOU'RE SAYING IS HUMAN... WE ALL UNDERSTAND YOU. BUT STILL, LET ME REPEAT, THE PROBLEMS IN THE CITY DO NOT INTEREST US.
WE'VE FOUND OUR WORLD HERE. THIS IS WHERE WE'LL REMAKE OURSELVES.
I FOUND MINE IN THE CITY, ONCE. THAT'S WHERE I SEE MYSELF AND THAT'S WHERE I WILL RETURN.

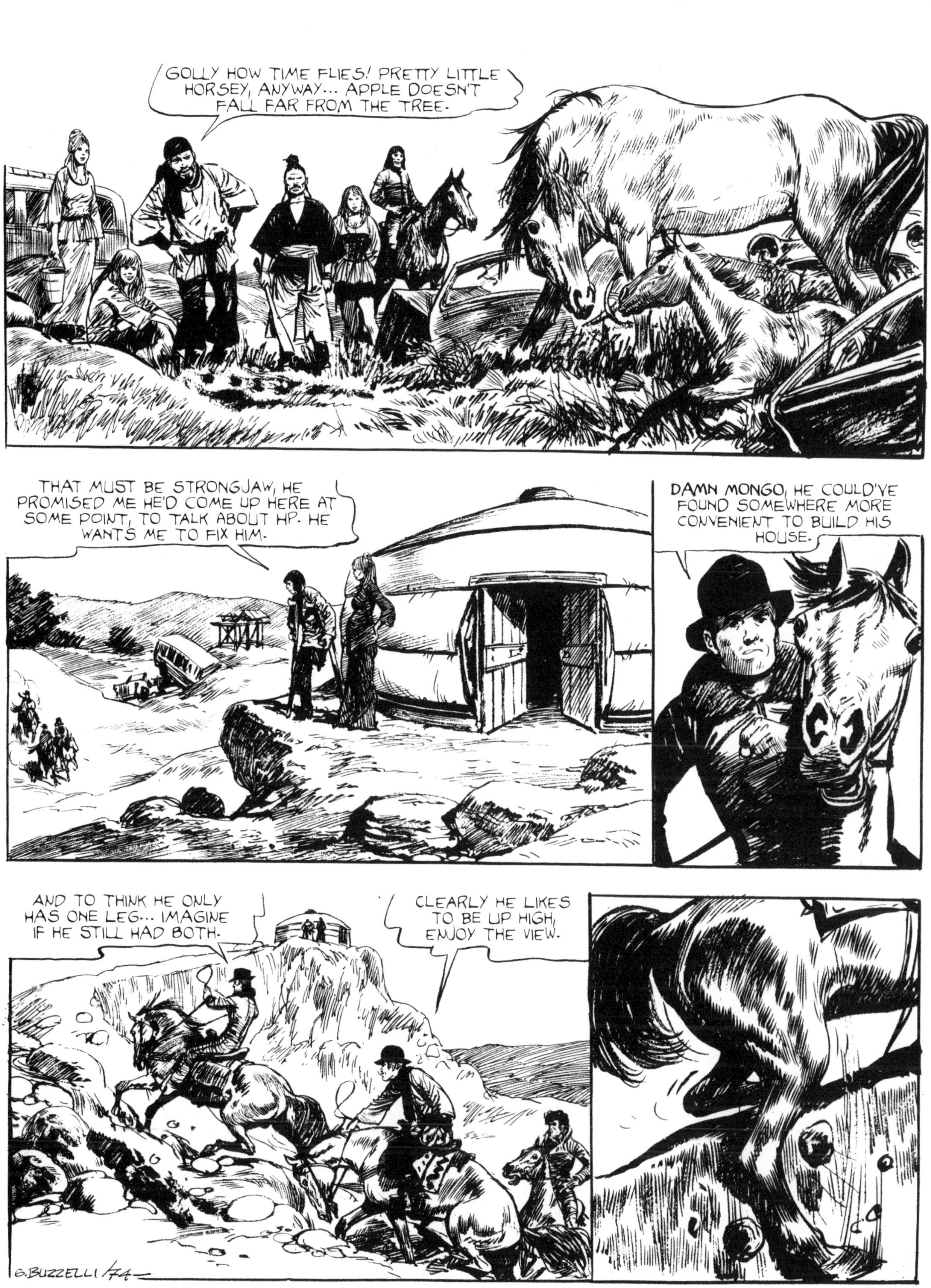
GOLLY HOW TIME FLIES! PRETTY LITTLE HORSEY, ANYWAY... APPLE DOESN'T FALL FAR FROM THE TREE.
THAT MUST BE STRONGJAW, HE PROMISED ME HE'D COME UP HERE AT SOME POINT, TO TALK ABOUT HP. HE WANTS ME TO FIX HIM.
DAMN MONGO, HE COULD'VE FOUND SOMEWHERE MORE CONVENIENT TO BUILD HIS HOUSE.
AND TO THINK HE ONLY HAS ONE LEG... IMAGINE IF HE STILL HAD BOTH.
CLEARLY HE LIKES TO BE UP HIGH, ENJOY THE VIEW.
G. BUZZELLI /74

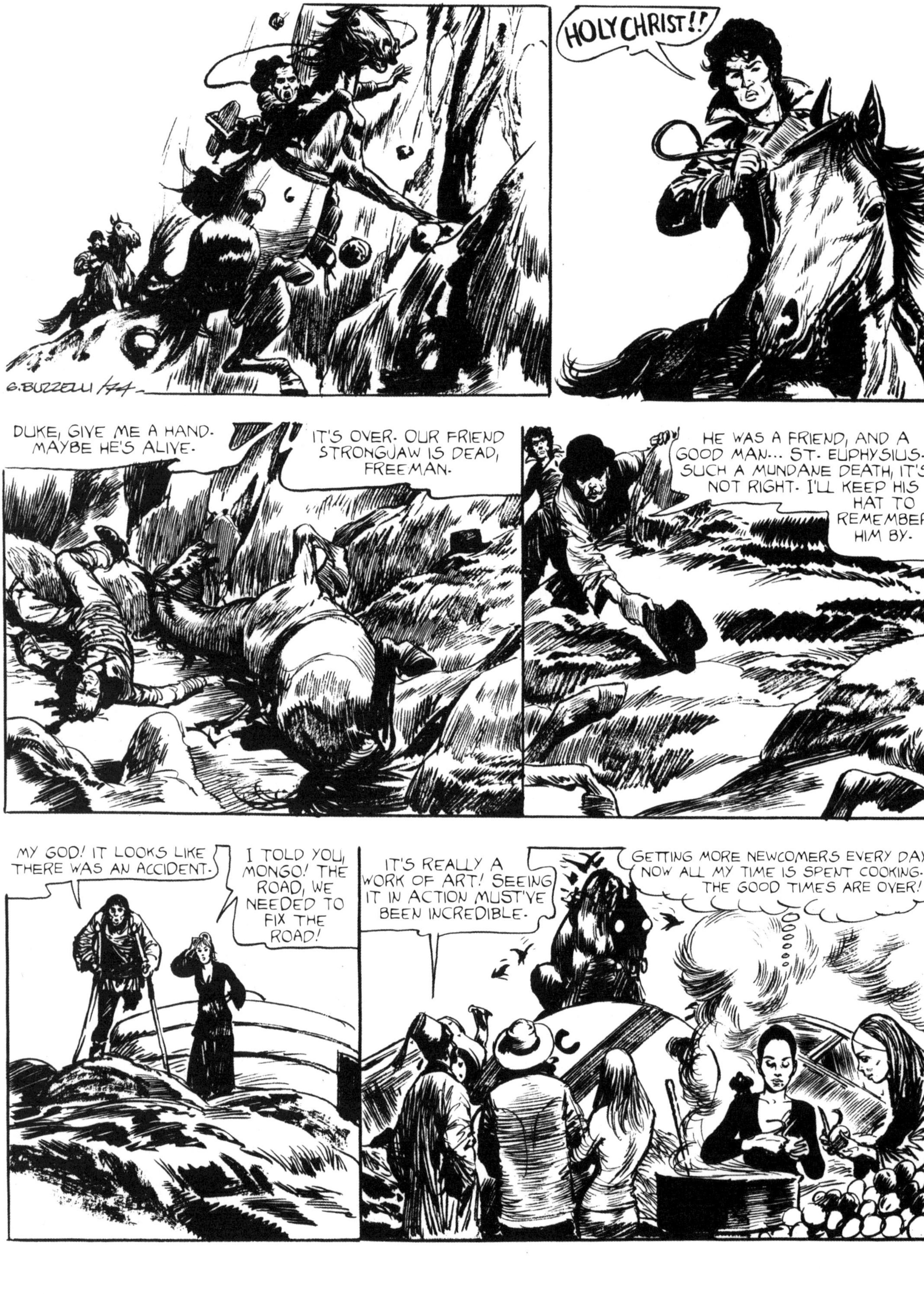
G. BUZZELLI
HOLY CHRIST!!
DUKE, GIVE ME A HAND. MAYBE HE'S ALIVE.
IT'S OVER. OUR FRIEND STRONGJAW IS DEAD, FREEMAN.
HE WAS A FRIEND, AND A GOOD MAN... ST. EUPHYSIUS... SUCH A MUNDANE DEATH, IT'S NOT RIGHT. I'LL KEEP HIS HAT TO REMEMBER HIM BY.
MY GOD! IT LOOKS LIKE THERE WAS AN ACCIDENT.
I TOLD YOU, MONGO! THE ROAD, WE NEEDED TO FIX THE ROAD!
IT'S REALLY A WORK OF ART! SEEING IT IN ACTION MUST'VE BEEN INCREDIBLE.
GETTING MORE NEWCOMERS EVERY DAY. NOW ALL MY TIME IS SPENT COOKING... THE GOOD TIMES ARE OVER!

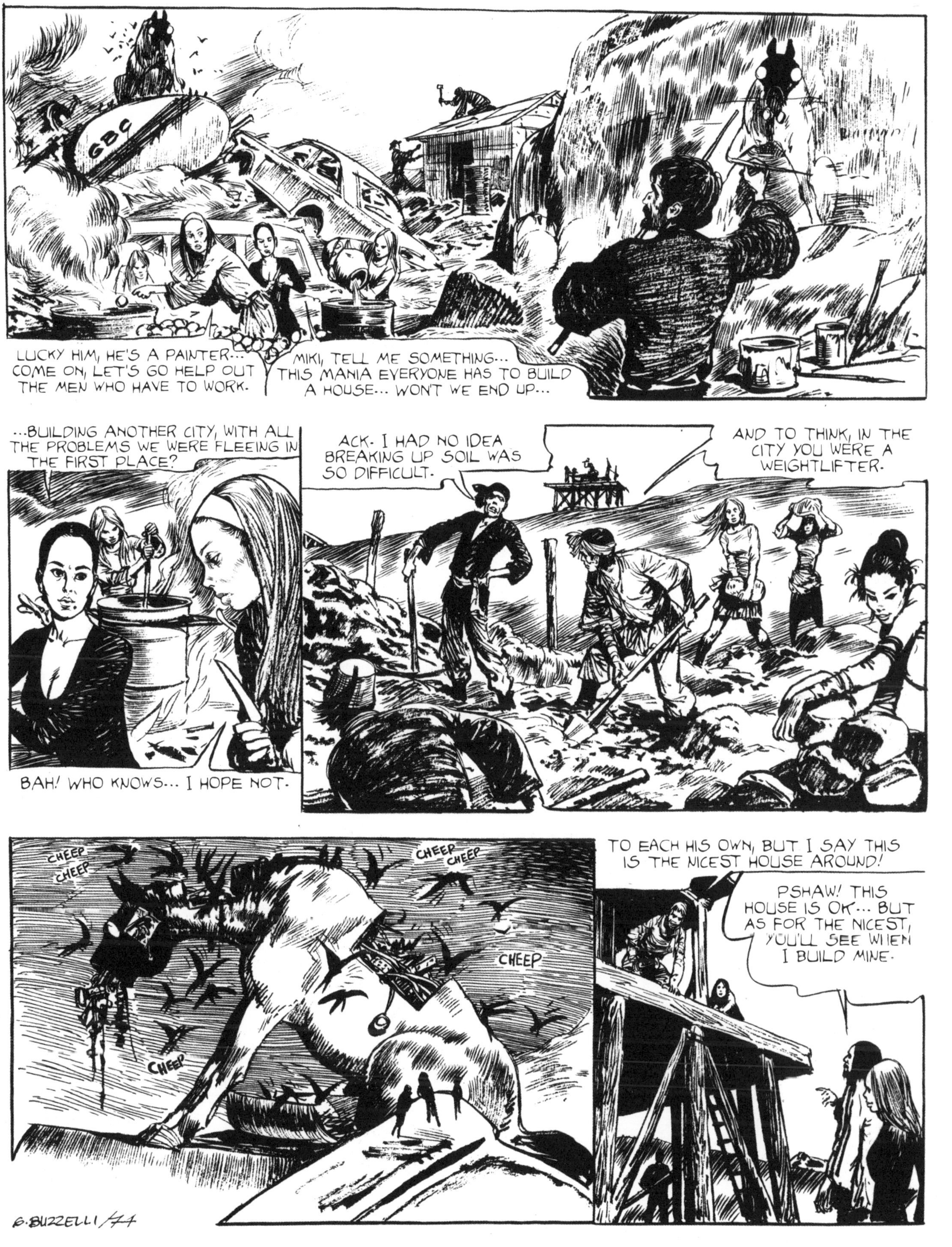
GBC
LUCKY HIM, HE'S A PAINTER... COME ON, LET'S GO HELP OUT THE MEN WHO HAVE TO WORK.
MIKI, TELL ME SOMETHING... THIS MANIA EVERYONE HAS TO BUILD A HOUSE... WON'T WE END UP...
...BUILDING ANOTHER CITY, WITH ALL THE PROBLEMS WE WERE FLEEING IN THE FIRST PLACE?
BAH! WHO KNOWS... I HOPE NOT.
ACK. I HAD NO IDEA BREAKING UP SOIL WAS SO DIFFICULT.
AND TO THINK, IN THE CITY YOU WERE A WEIGHTLIFTER.
CHEEP
CHEEP
CHEEP
CHEEP
CHEEP
CHEEP
G. BUZZELLI /74
TO EACH HIS OWN, BUT I SAY THIS IS THE NICEST HOUSE AROUND!
PSHAW! THIS HOUSE IS OK... BUT AS FOR THE NICEST, YOU'LL SEE WHEN I BUILD MINE.

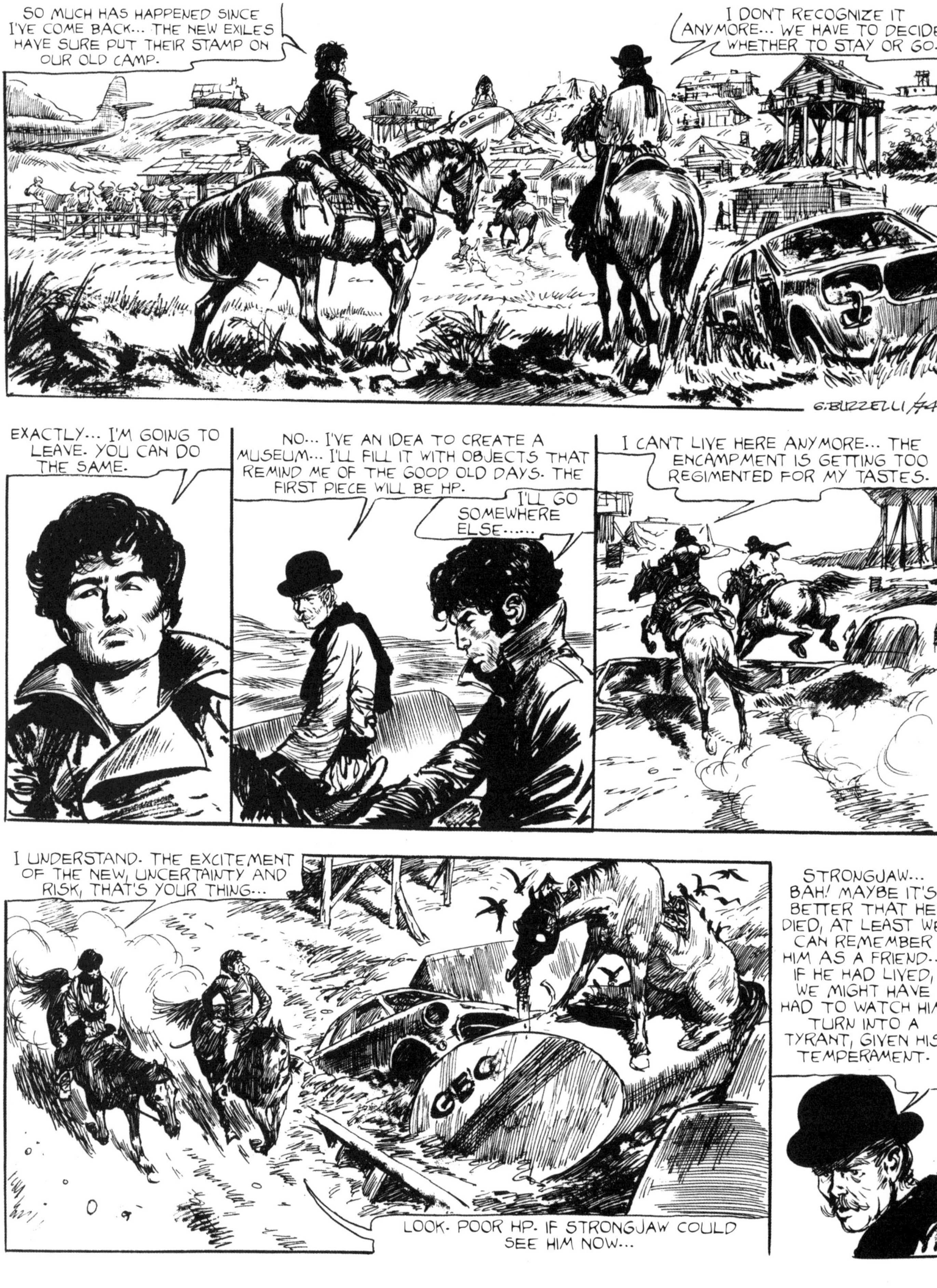
SO MUCH HAS HAPPENED SINCE I'VE COME BACK... THE NEW EXILES HAVE SURE PUT THEIR STAMP ON OUR OLD CAMP.
I DON'T RECOGNIZE IT ANYMORE... WE HAVE TO DECIDE WHETHER TO STAY OR GO.
G. BUZZELLI /74
EXACTLY... I'M GOING TO LEAVE. YOU CAN DO THE SAME.
NO... I'VE AN IDEA TO CREATE A MUSEUM... I'LL FILL IT WITH OBJECTS THAT REMIND ME OF THE GOOD OLD DAYS. THE FIRST PIECE WILL BE HP.
I'LL GO SOMEWHERE ELSE......
I CAN'T LIVE HERE ANYMORE... THE ENCAMPMENT IS GETTING TOO REGIMENTED FOR MY TASTES.
I UNDERSTAND. THE EXCITEMENT OF THE NEW, UNCERTAINTY AND RISK, THAT'S YOUR THING...
GBC
LOOK. POOR HP. IF STRONGJAW COULD SEE HIM NOW...
STRONGJAW... BAH! MAYBE IT'S BETTER THAT HE DIED, AT LEAST WE CAN REMEMBER HIM AS A FRIEND... IF HE HAD LIVED, WE MIGHT HAVE HAD TO WATCH HIM TURN INTO A TYRANT, GIVEN HIS TEMPERAMENT.

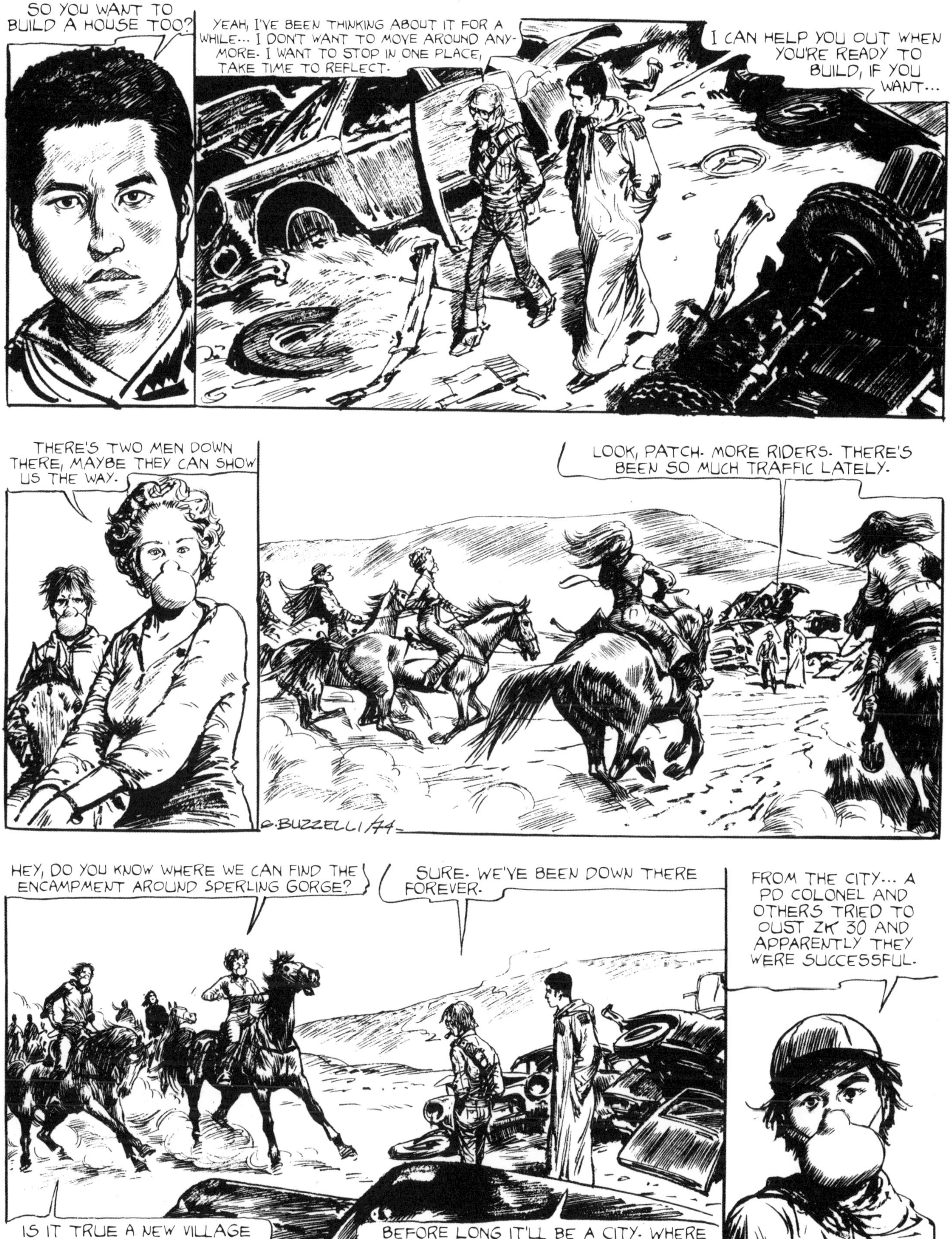
SO YOU WANT TO BUILD A HOUSE TOO?
YEAH, I'VE BEEN THINKING ABOUT IT FOR A WHILE... I DON'T WANT TO MOVE AROUND ANY-MORE. I WANT TO STOP IN ONE PLACE, TAKE TIME TO REFLECT.
I CAN HELP YOU OUT WHEN YOU'RE READY TO BUILD, IF YOU WANT...
THERE'S TWO MEN DOWN THERE, MAYBE THEY CAN SHOW US THE WAY.
LOOK, PATCH. MORE RIDERS. THERE'S BEEN SO MUCH TRAFFIC LATELY.
G. BUZZELLI /44
HEY, DO YOU KNOW WHERE WE CAN FIND THE ENCAMPMENT AROUND SPERLING GORGE?
SURE. WE'VE BEEN DOWN THERE FOREVER.
IS IT TRUE A NEW VILLAGE IS FORMING?
BEFORE LONG IT'LL BE A CITY. WHERE ARE YOU COMING FROM?
FROM THE CITY... A PD COLONEL AND OTHERS TRIED TO OUST ZK 30 AND APPARENTLY THEY WERE SUCCESSFUL.

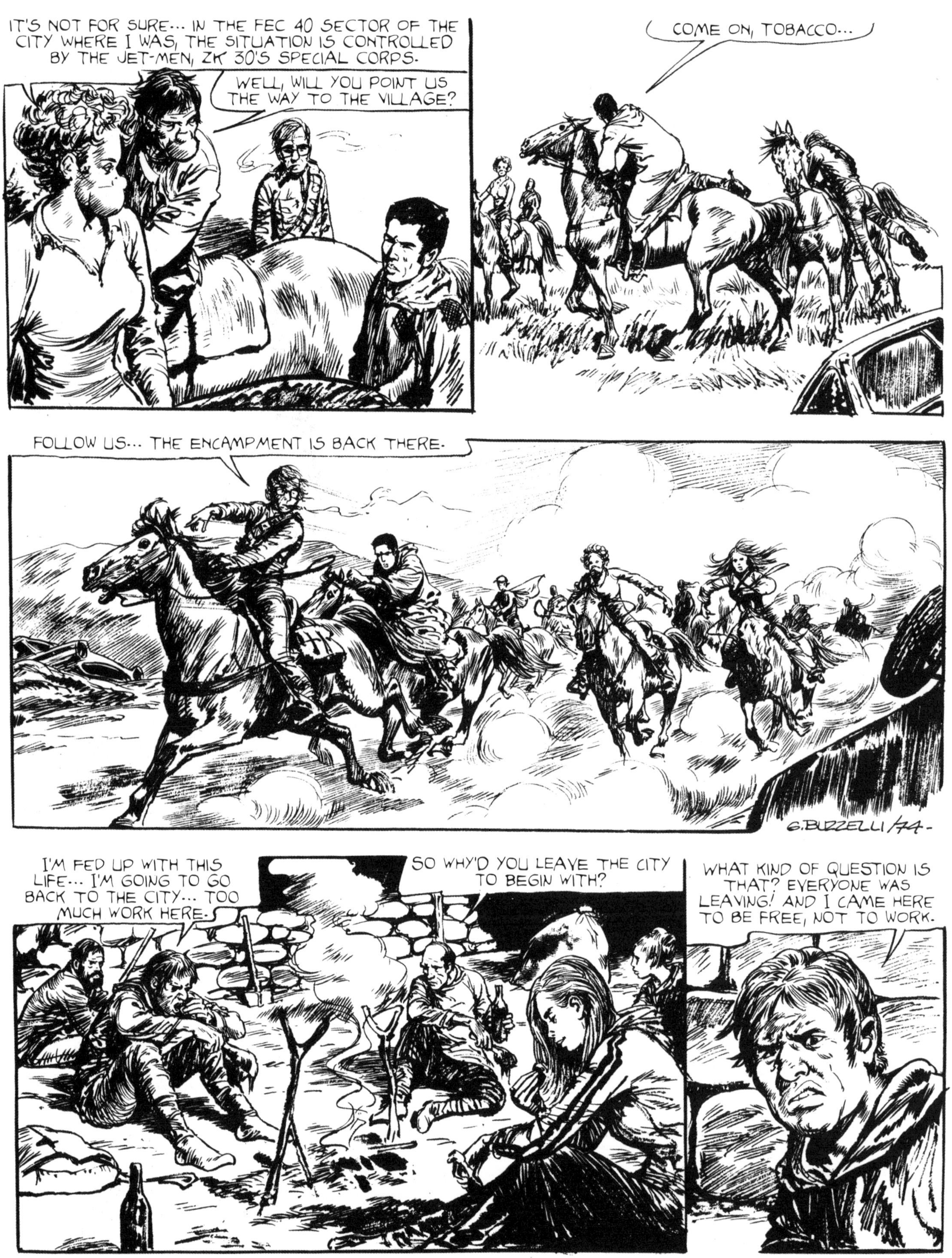
IT'S NOT FOR SURE... IN THE FEC 40 SECTOR OF THE CITY WHERE I WAS, THE SITUATION IS CONTROLLED BY THE JET-MEN, ZK 30'S SPECIAL CORPS.
WELL, WILL YOU POINT US THE WAY TO THE VILLAGE?
COME ON, TOBACCO...
FOLLOW US... THE ENCAMPMENT IS BACK THERE.
G. BUZZELLI /74.
I'M FED UP WITH THIS LIFE... I'M GOING TO GO BACK TO THE CITY... TOO MUCH WORK HERE.
SO WHY'D YOU LEAVE THE CITY TO BEGIN WITH?
WHAT KIND OF QUESTION IS THAT? EVERYONE WAS LEAVING! AND I CAME HERE TO BE FREE, NOT TO WORK.

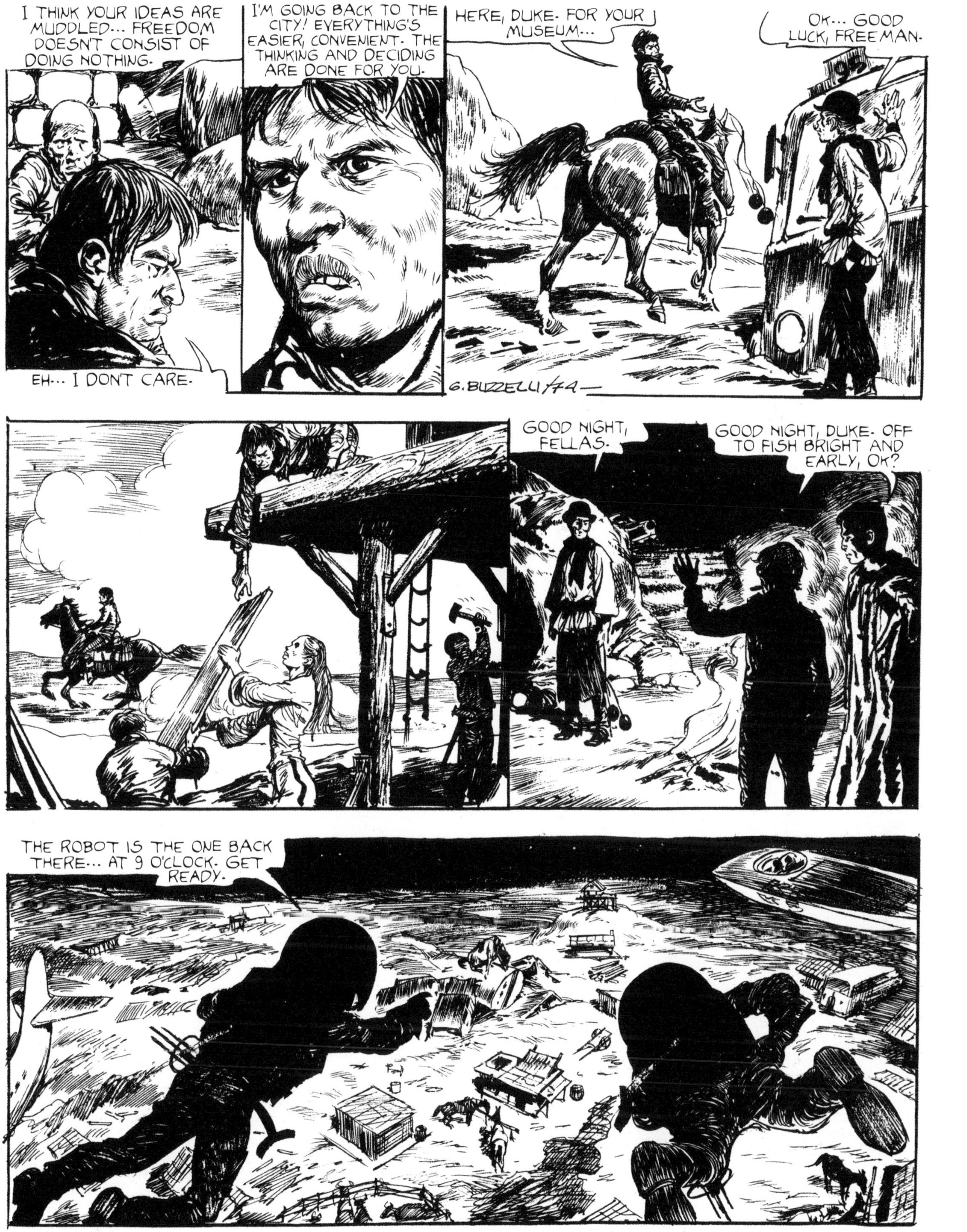
I THINK YOUR IDEAS ARE MUDDLED... FREEDOM DOESN'T CONSIST OF DOING NOTHING.
EH... I DON'T CARE.
I'M GOING BACK TO THE CITY! EVERYTHING'S EASIER, CONVENIENT. THE THINKING AND DECIDING ARE DONE FOR YOU.
HERE, DUKE. FOR YOUR MUSEUM...
G. BUZZELLI /74
OK... GOOD LUCK, FREEMAN.
GOOD NIGHT, FELLAS.
GOOD NIGHT, DUKE. OFF TO FISH BRIGHT AND EARLY, OK?
THE ROBOT IS THE ONE BACK THERE... AT 9 O'CLOCK. GET READY.

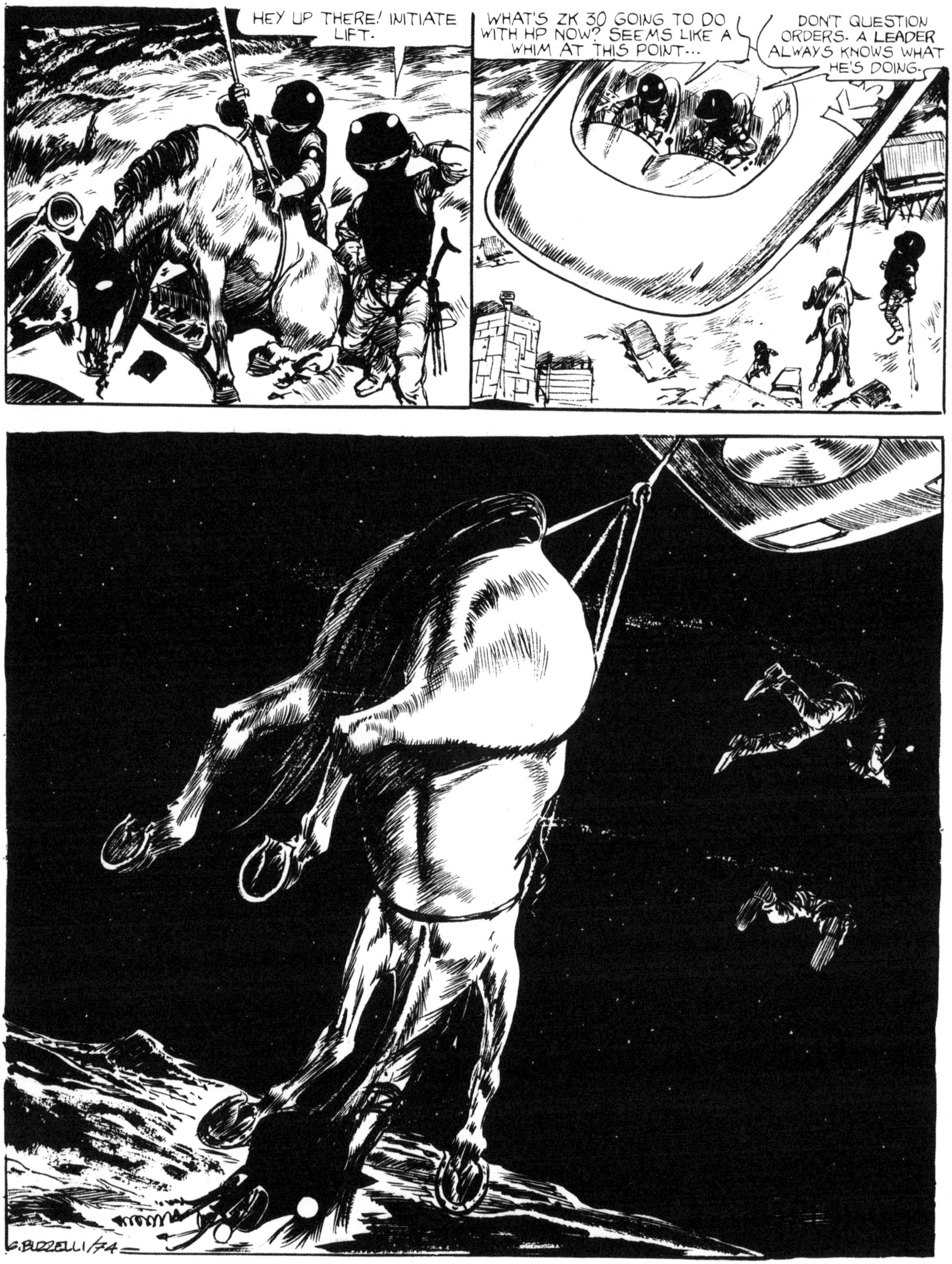
HEY UP THERE! INITIATE LIFT.
WHAT'S ZK 30 GOING TO DO WITH HP NOW? SEEMS LIKE A WHIM AT THIS POINT...
DON'T QUESTION ORDERS. A LEADER ALWAYS KNOWS WHAT HE'S DOING.
G. BUZZELLI/74

Morganna

(1975)

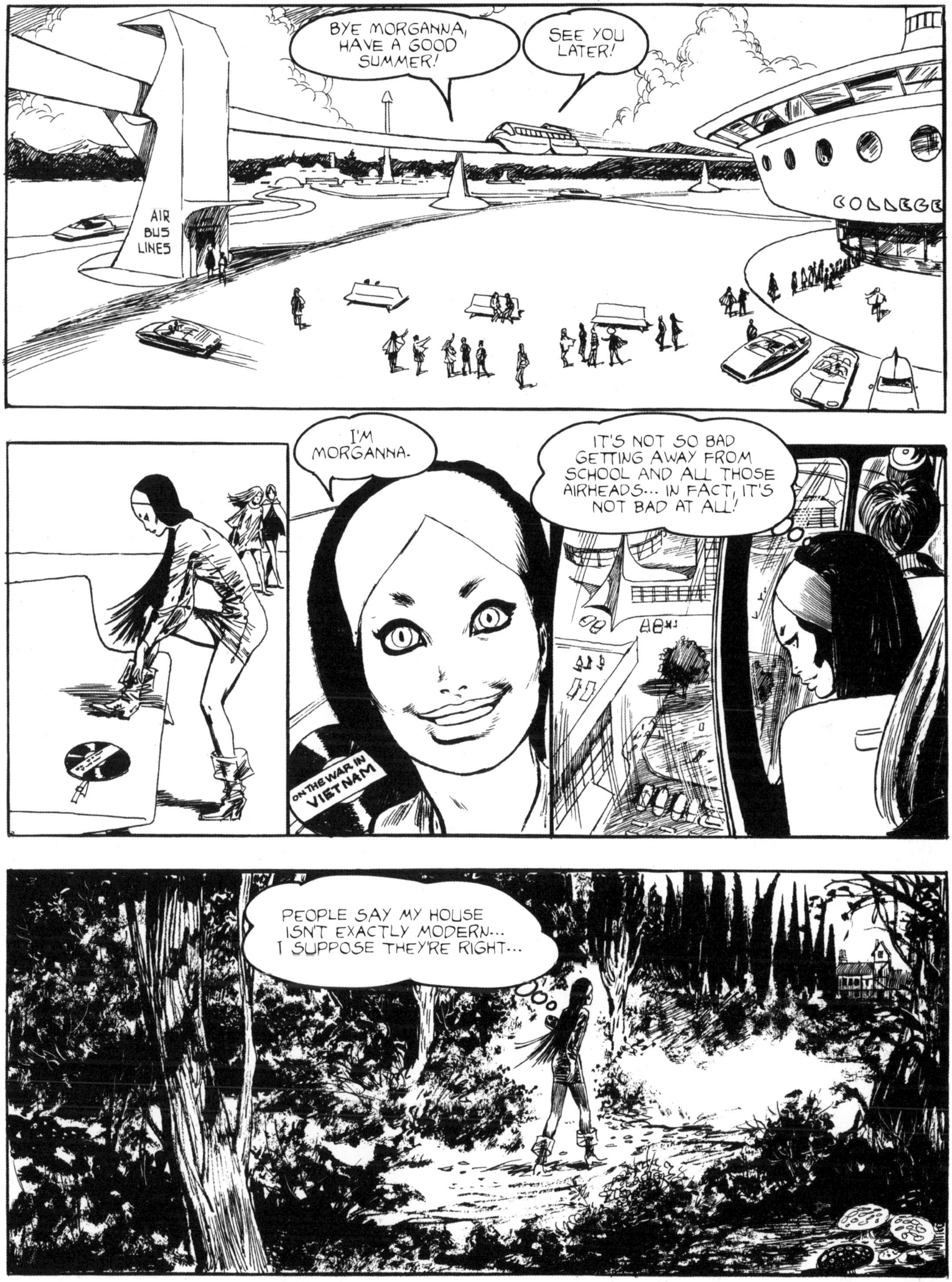
BYE MORGANNA, HAVE A GOOD SUMMER!
SEE YOU LATER!
AIR BUS LINES
COLLEGE
I'M MORGANNA.
ON THE WAR IN VIETNAM
IT'S NOT SO BAD GETTING AWAY FROM SCHOOL AND ALL THOSE AIRHEADS... IN FACT, IT'S NOT BAD AT ALL!
PEOPLE SAY MY HOUSE ISN'T EXACTLY MODERN... I SUPPOSE THEY'RE RIGHT...

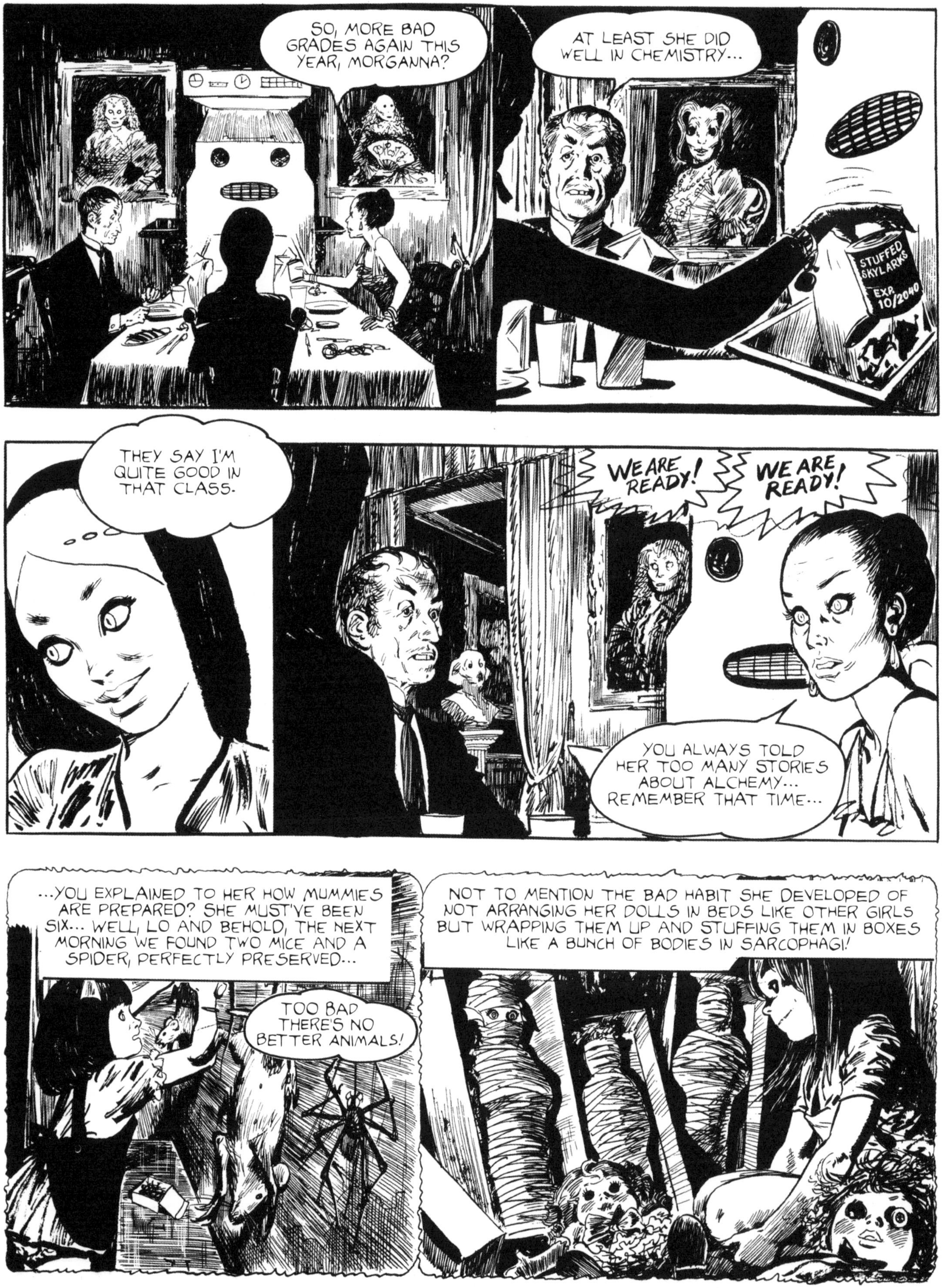

SO, MORE BAD GRADES AGAIN THIS YEAR, MORGANNA?
AT LEAST SHE DID WELL IN CHEMISTRY...
STUFFED SKYLARKS EXP. 10/2040
THEY SAY I'M QUITE GOOD IN THAT CLASS.
WE ARE READY!
WE ARE READY!
YOU ALWAYS TOLD HER TOO MANY STORIES ABOUT ALCHEMY... REMEMBER THAT TIME...
...YOU EXPLAINED TO HER HOW MUMMIES ARE PREPARED? SHE MUST'VE BEEN SIX... WELL, LO AND BEHOLD, THE NEXT MORNING WE FOUND TWO MICE AND A SPIDER, PERFECTLY PRESERVED...
TOO BAD THERE'S NO BETTER ANIMALS!
NOT TO MENTION THE BAD HABIT SHE DEVELOPED OF NOT ARRANGING HER DOLLS IN BEDS LIKE OTHER GIRLS BUT WRAPPING THEM UP AND STUFFING THEM IN BOXES LIKE A BUNCH OF BODIES IN SARCOPHAGI!

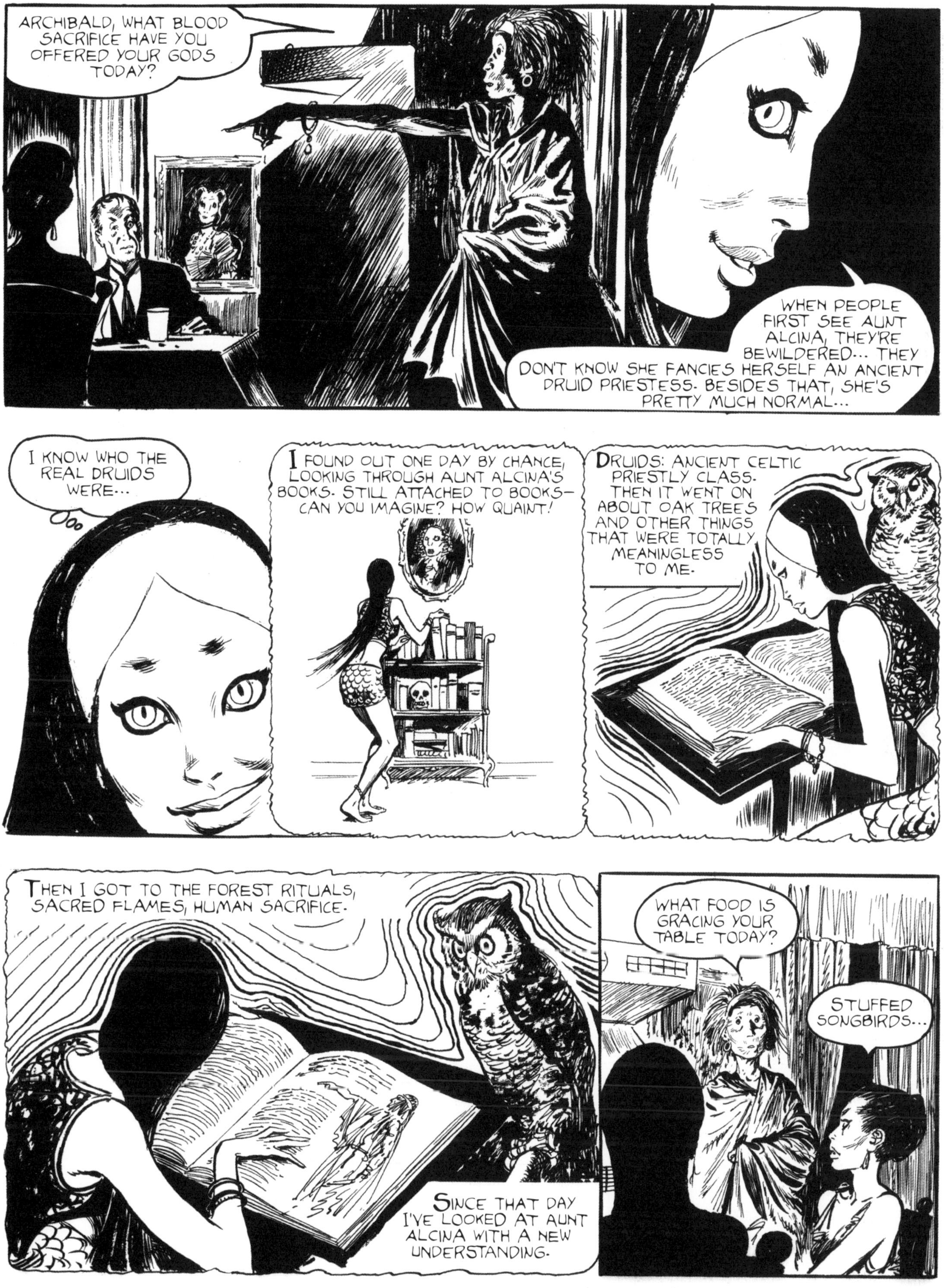
ARCHIBALD, WHAT BLOOD SACRIFICE HAVE YOU OFFERED YOUR GODS TODAY?
WHEN PEOPLE FIRST SEE AUNT ALCINA, THEY'RE BEWILDERED... THEY DON'T KNOW SHE FANCIES HERSELF AN ANCIENT DRUID PRIESTESS. BESIDES THAT, SHE'S PRETTY MUCH NORMAL...
I KNOW WHO THE REAL DRUIDS WERE...
I FOUND OUT ONE DAY BY CHANCE, LOOKING THROUGH AUNT ALCINA'S BOOKS. STILL ATTACHED TO BOOKS— CAN YOU IMAGINE? HOW QUAINT!
DRUIDS: ANCIENT CELTIC PRIESTLY CLASS. THEN IT WENT ON ABOUT OAK TREES AND OTHER THINGS THAT WERE TOTALLY MEANINGLESS TO ME.
THEN I GOT TO THE FOREST RITUALS, SACRED FLAMES, HUMAN SACRIFICE.
SINCE THAT DAY I'VE LOOKED AT AUNT ALCINA WITH A NEW UNDERSTANDING.
WHAT FOOD IS GRACING YOUR TABLE TODAY?
STUFFED SONGBIRDS...

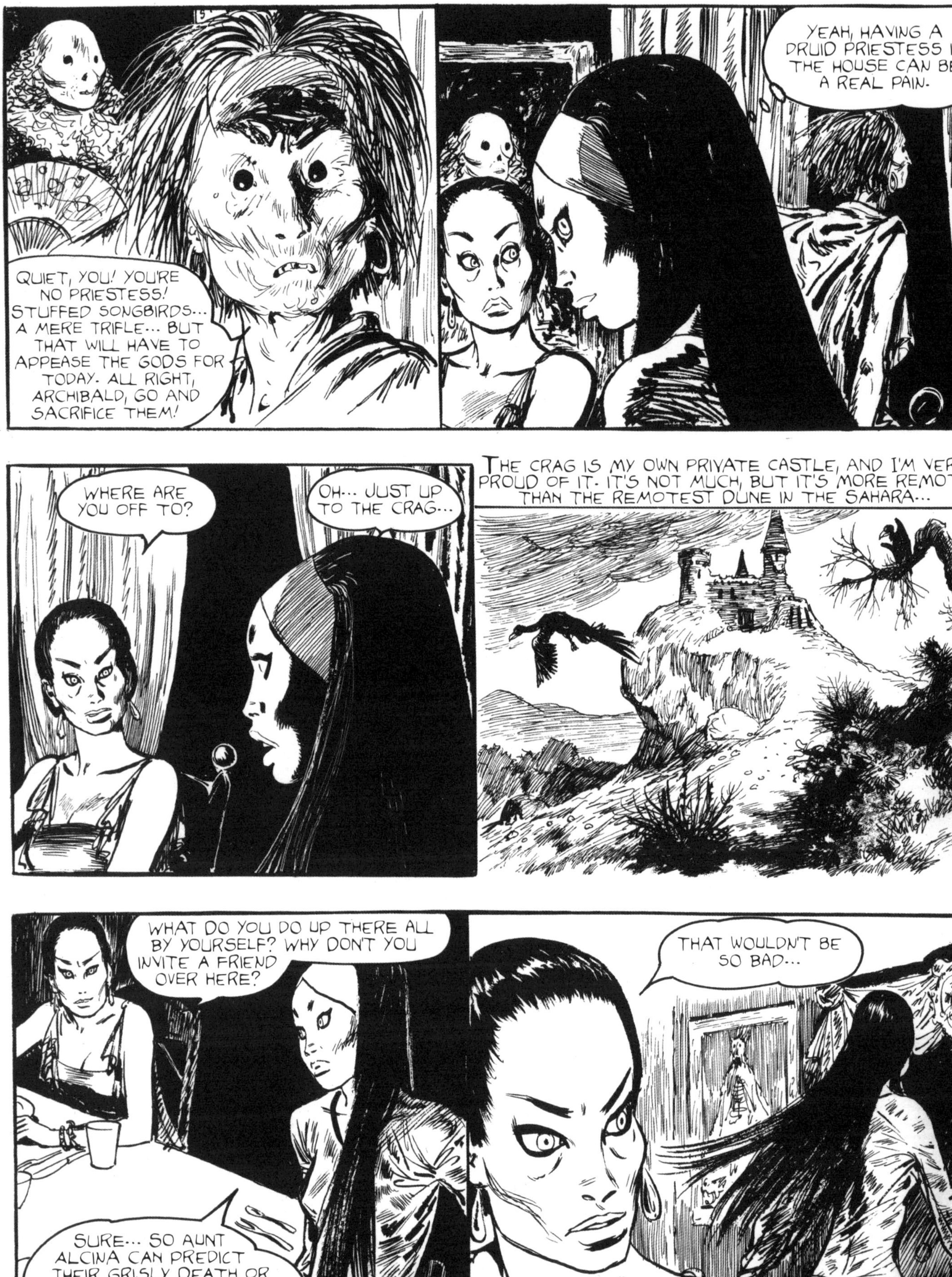
QUIET, YOU! YOU'RE NO PRIESTESS! STUFFED SONGBIRDS... A MERE TRIFLE... BUT THAT WILL HAVE TO APPEASE THE GODS FOR TODAY. ALL RIGHT, ARCHIBALD, GO AND SACRIFICE THEM!
YEAH, HAVING A DRUID PRIESTESS IN THE HOUSE CAN BE A REAL PAIN.
WHERE ARE YOU OFF TO?
OH... JUST UP TO THE CRAG...
THE CRAG IS MY OWN PRIVATE CASTLE, AND I'M VERY PROUD OF IT. IT'S NOT MUCH, BUT IT'S MORE REMOTE THAN THE REMOTEST DUNE IN THE SAHARA...
WHAT DO YOU DO UP THERE ALL BY YOURSELF? WHY DON'T YOU INVITE A FRIEND OVER HERE?
SURE... SO AUNT ALCINA CAN PREDICT THEIR GRISLY DEATH OR FORCE THEM TO TALK ABOUT HER GODS!
THAT WOULDN'T BE SO BAD...

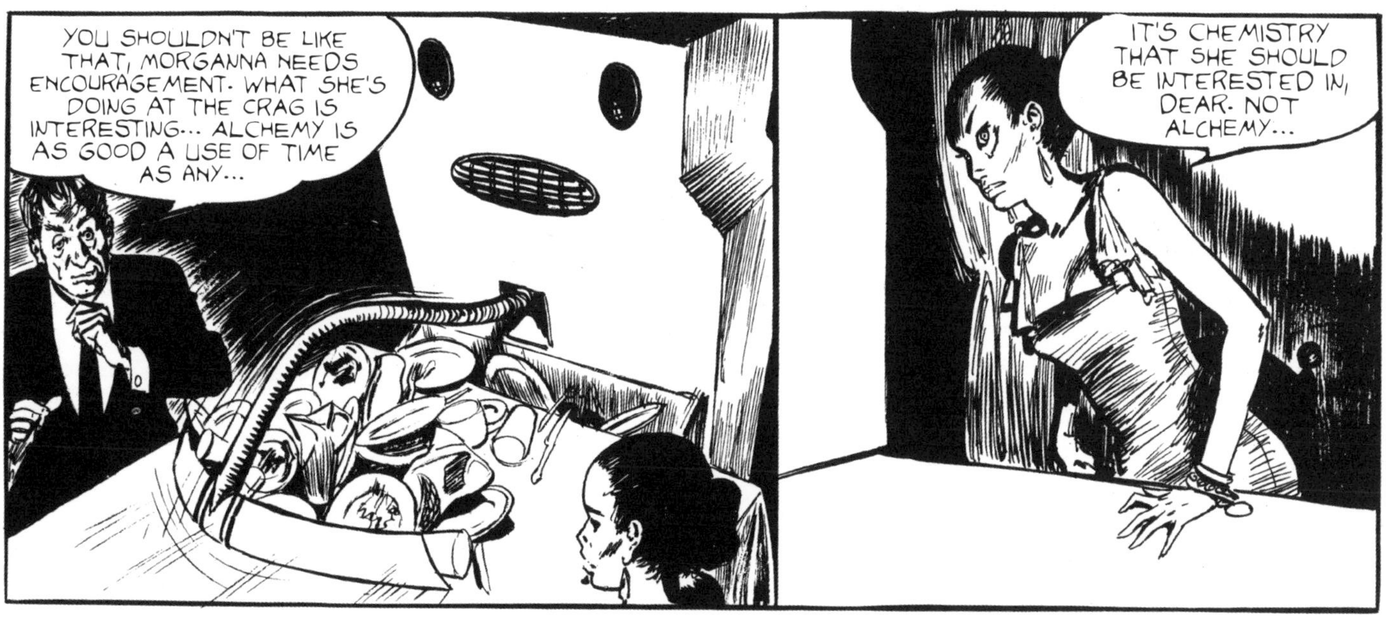
YOU SHOULDN'T BE LIKE THAT, MORGANNA NEEDS ENCOURAGEMENT. WHAT SHE'S DOING AT THE CRAG IS INTERESTING... ALCHEMY IS AS GOOD A USE OF TIME AS ANY...
IT'S CHEMISTRY THAT SHE SHOULD BE INTERESTED IN, DEAR. NOT ALCHEMY...

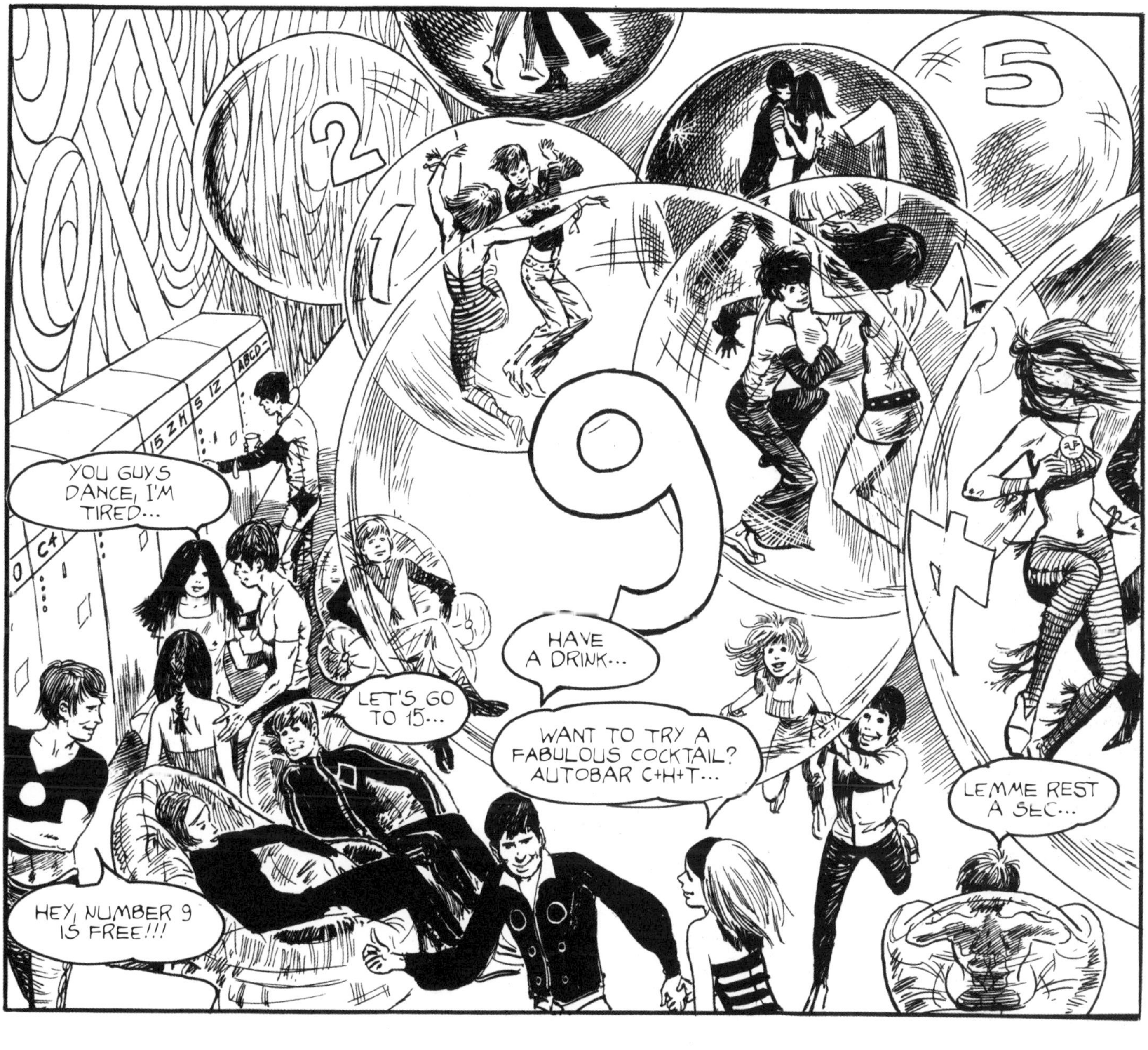
YOU GUYS DANCE, I'M TIRED...
LET'S GO TO 15...
HAVE A DRINK...
WANT TO TRY A FABULOUS COCKTAIL? AUTOBAR C+H+T...
LEMME REST A SEC...
HEY, NUMBER 9 IS FREE!!!

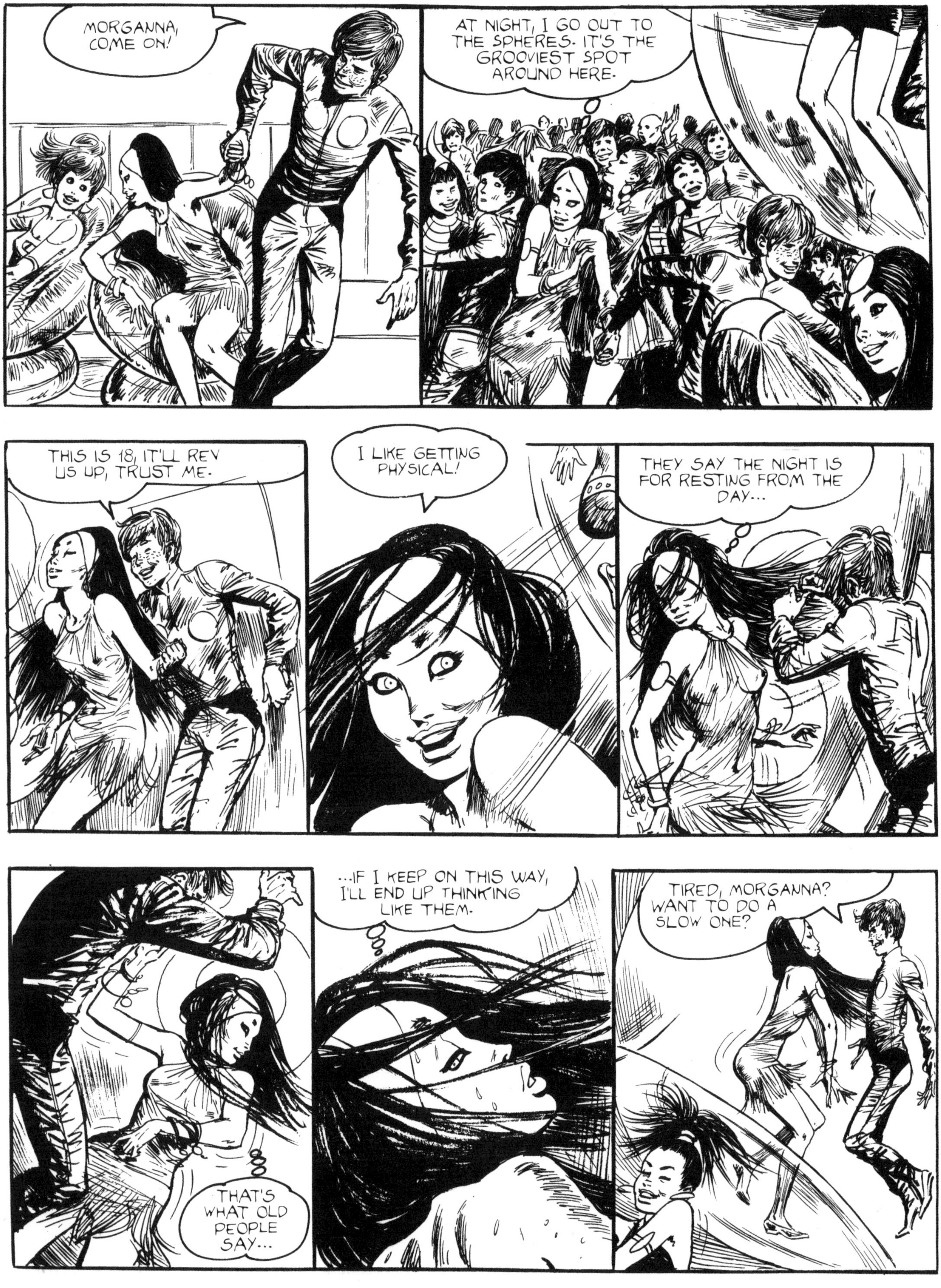
MORGANNA, COME ON!
AT NIGHT, I GO OUT TO THE SPHERES. IT'S THE GROOVIEST SPOT AROUND HERE.
THIS IS 18, IT'LL REV US UP, TRUST ME.
I LIKE GETTING PHYSICAL!
THEY SAY THE NIGHT IS FOR RESTING FROM THE DAY...
THAT'S WHAT OLD PEOPLE SAY...
...IF I KEEP ON THIS WAY, I'LL END UP THINKING LIKE THEM.
TIRED, MORGANNA? WANT TO DO A SLOW ONE?

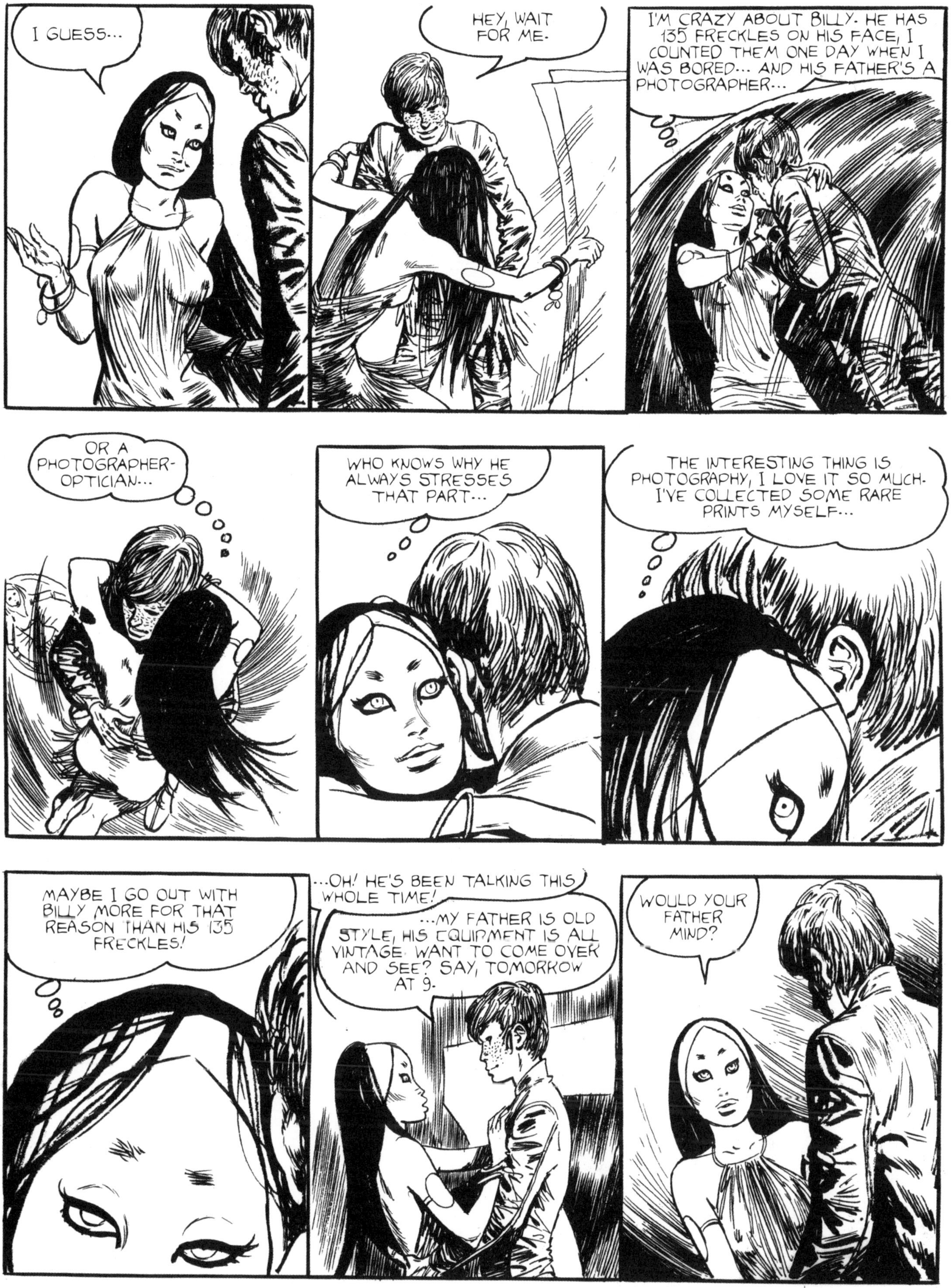
I GUESS...
HEY, WAIT FOR ME.
I'M CRAZY ABOUT BILLY. HE HAS 135 FRECKLES ON HIS FACE, I COUNTED THEM ONE DAY WHEN I WAS BORED... AND HIS FATHER'S A PHOTOGRAPHER...
OR A PHOTOGRAPHER-OPTICIAN...
WHO KNOWS WHY HE ALWAYS STRESSES THAT PART...
THE INTERESTING THING IS PHOTOGRAPHY, I LOVE IT SO MUCH. I'VE COLLECTED SOME RARE PRINTS MYSELF...
MAYBE I GO OUT WITH BILLY MORE FOR THAT REASON THAN HIS 135 FRECKLES!
...OH! HE'S BEEN TALKING THIS WHOLE TIME!
...MY FATHER IS OLD STYLE, HIS EQUIPMENT IS ALL VINTAGE. WANT TO COME OVER AND SEE? SAY, TOMORROW AT 9.
WOULD YOUR FATHER MIND?

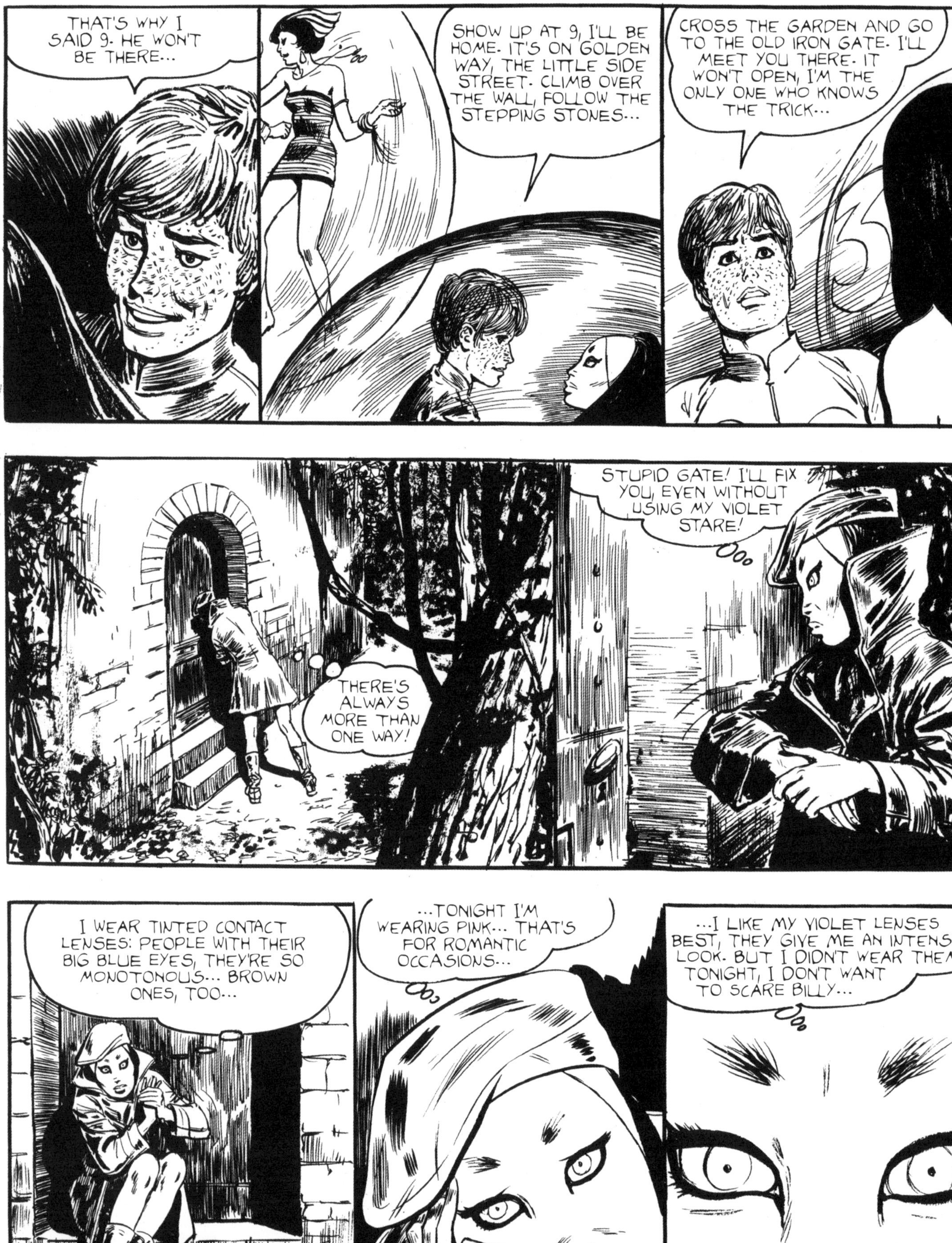
THAT'S WHY I SAID 9. HE WON'T BE THERE...
SHOW UP AT 9, I'LL BE HOME. IT'S ON GOLDEN WAY, THE LITTLE SIDE STREET. CLIMB OVER THE WALL, FOLLOW THE STEPPING STONES...
CROSS THE GARDEN AND GO TO THE OLD IRON GATE. I'LL MEET YOU THERE. IT WON'T OPEN, I'M THE ONLY ONE WHO KNOWS THE TRICK...
THERE'S ALWAYS MORE THAN ONE WAY!
STUPID GATE! I'LL FIX YOU, EVEN WITHOUT USING MY VIOLET STARE!
I WEAR TINTED CONTACT LENSES: PEOPLE WITH THEIR BIG BLUE EYES, THEY'RE SO MONOTONOUS... BROWN ONES, TOO...
...TONIGHT I'M WEARING PINK... THAT'S FOR ROMANTIC OCCASIONS...
...I LIKE MY VIOLET LENSES BEST, THEY GIVE ME AN INTENSE LOOK. BUT I DIDN'T WEAR THEM TONIGHT, I DON'T WANT TO SCARE BILLY...

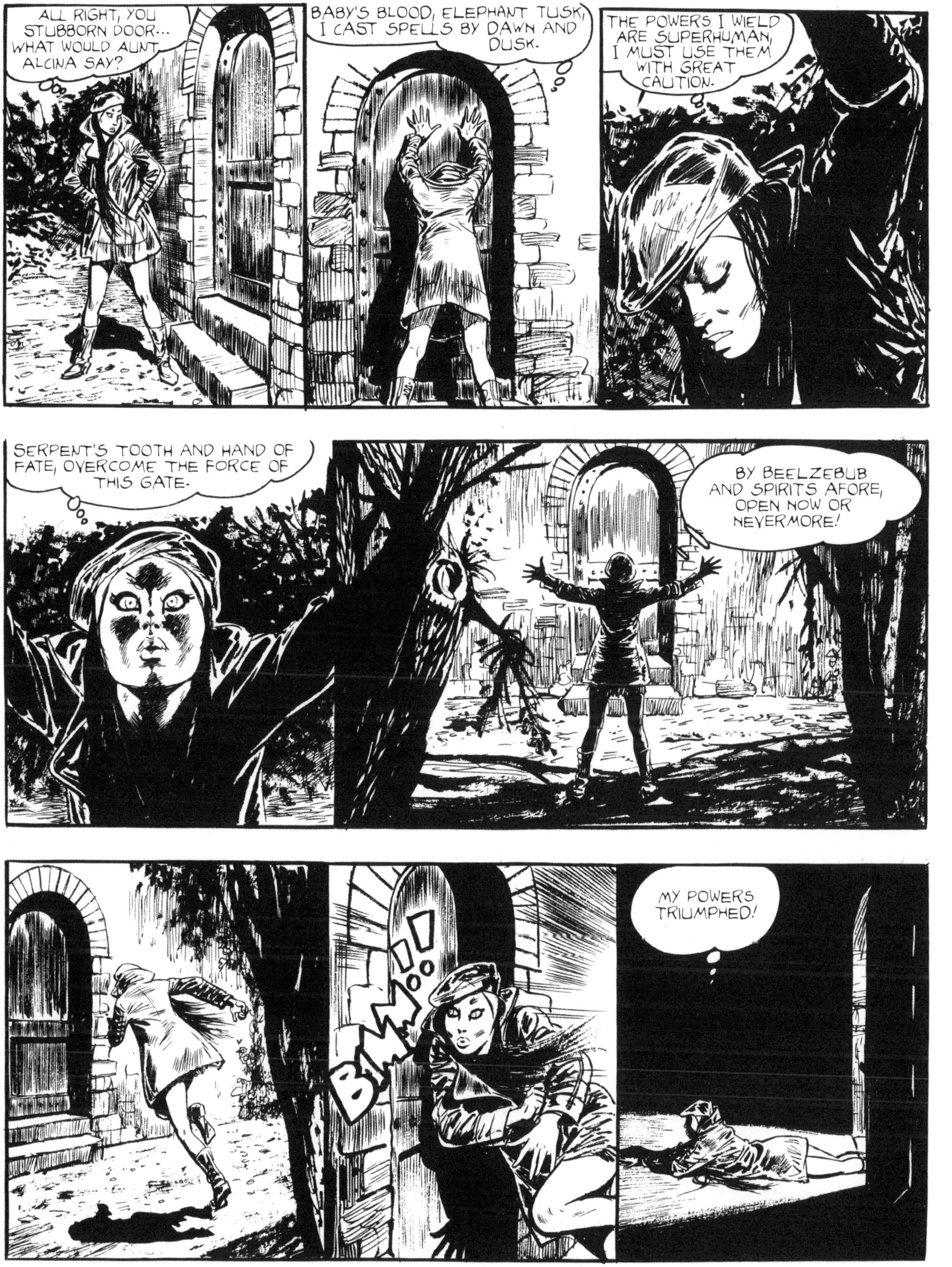
ALL RIGHT, YOU STUBBORN DOOR... WHAT WOULD AUNT ALCINA SAY?
BABY'S BLOOD, ELEPHANT TUSK, I CAST SPELLS BY DAWN AND DUSK.
THE POWERS I WIELD ARE SUPERHUMAN, I MUST USE THEM WITH GREAT CAUTION.
SERPENT'S TOOTH AND HAND OF FATE, OVERCOME THE FORCE OF THIS GATE.
BY BEELZEBUB AND SPIRITS AFORE, OPEN NOW OR NEVERMORE!
BOOM!!!
MY POWERS TRIUMPHED!

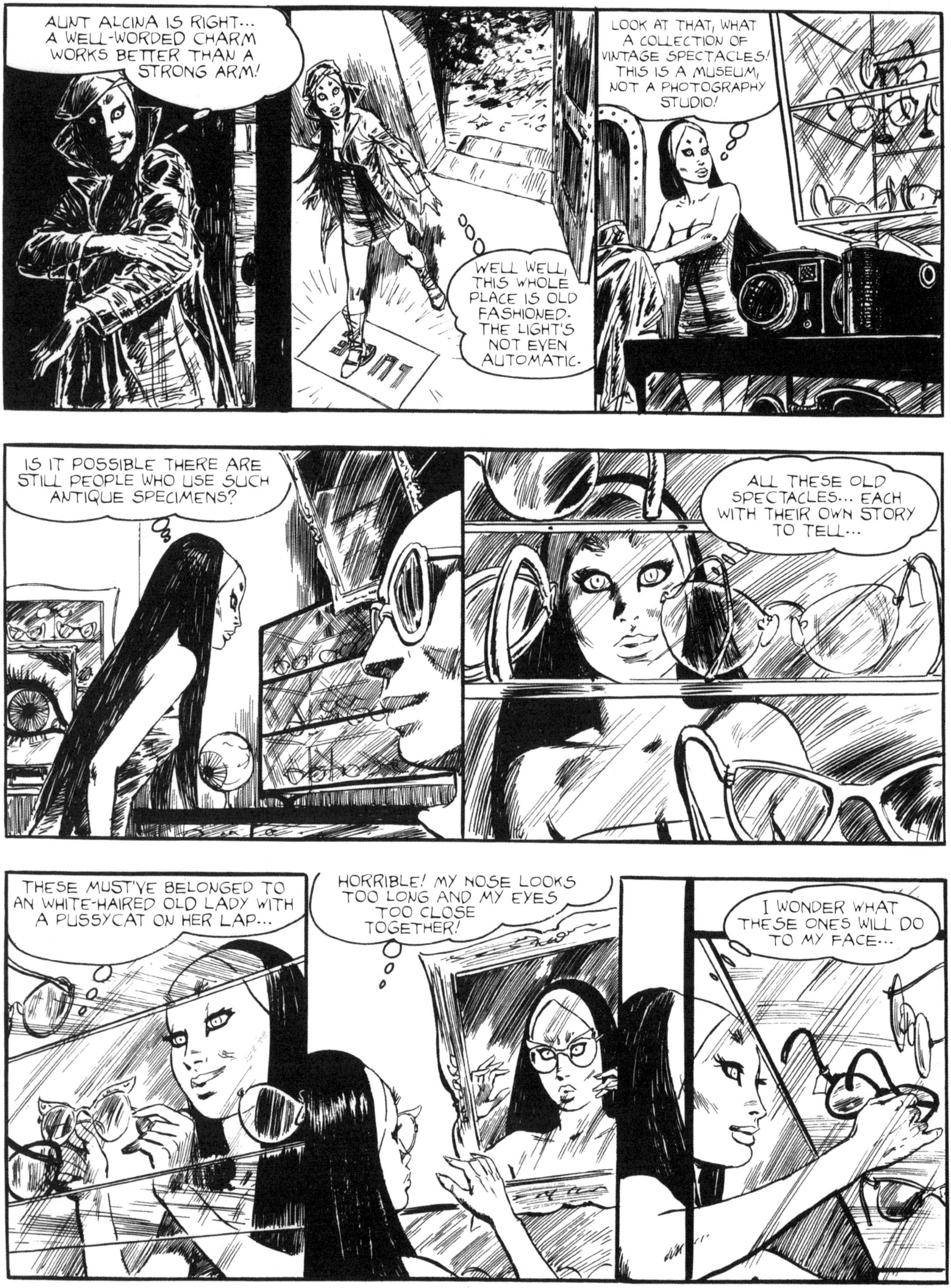
AUNT ALCINA IS RIGHT... A WELL-WORDED CHARM WORKS BETTER THAN A STRONG ARM!
WELL WELL, THIS WHOLE PLACE IS OLD FASHIONED. THE LIGHT'S NOT EVEN AUTOMATIC.
LOOK AT THAT, WHAT A COLLECTION OF VINTAGE SPECTACLES! THIS IS A MUSEUM, NOT A PHOTOGRAPHY STUDIO!
IS IT POSSIBLE THERE ARE STILL PEOPLE WHO USE SUCH ANTIQUE SPECIMENS?
ALL THESE OLD SPECTACLES... EACH WITH THEIR OWN STORY TO TELL...
THESE MUST'VE BELONGED TO AN WHITE-HAIRED OLD LADY WITH A PUSSYCAT ON HER LAP...
HORRIBLE! MY NOSE LOOKS TOO LONG AND MY EYES TOO CLOSE TOGETHER!
I WONDER WHAT THESE ONES WILL DO TO MY FACE...

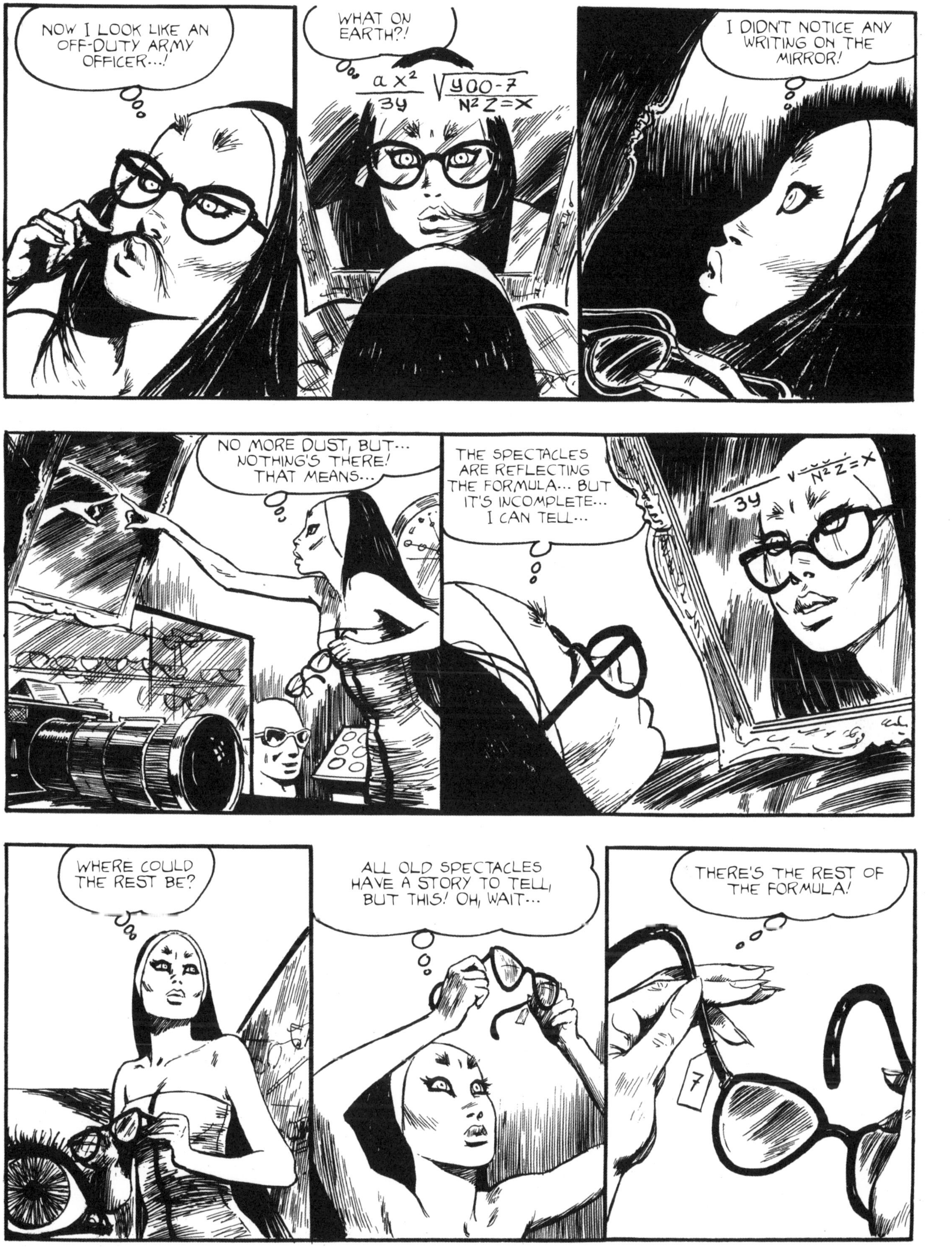
NOW I LOOK LIKE AN OFF-DUTY ARMY OFFICER...!
WHAT ON EARTH?!
I DIDN'T NOTICE ANY WRITING ON THE MIRROR!
NO MORE DUST, BUT... NOTHING'S THERE! THAT MEANS...
THE SPECTACLES ARE REFLECTING THE FORMULA... BUT IT'S INCOMPLETE... I CAN TELL...
WHERE COULD THE REST BE?
ALL OLD SPECTACLES HAVE A STORY TO TELL, BUT THIS! OH, WAIT...
THERE'S THE REST OF THE FORMULA!
7

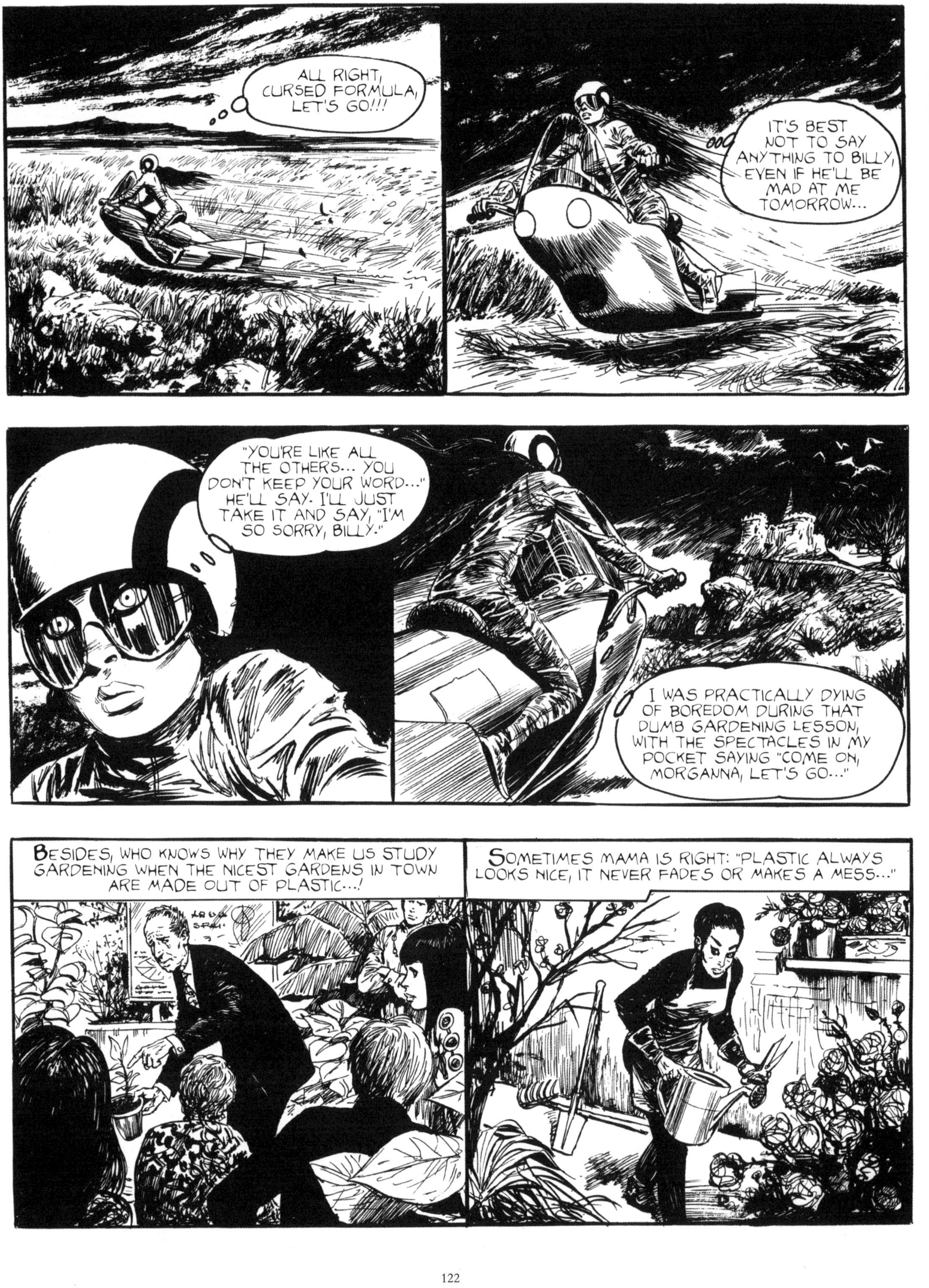
ALL RIGHT, CURSED FORMULA, LET'S GO!!!
IT'S BEST NOT TO SAY ANYTHING TO BILLY, EVEN IF HE'LL BE MAD AT ME TOMORROW...
"YOU'RE LIKE ALL THE OTHERS... YOU DON'T KEEP YOUR WORD..." HE'LL SAY. I'LL JUST TAKE IT AND SAY, "I'M SO SORRY, BILLY."
I WAS PRACTICALLY DYING OF BOREDOM DURING THAT DUMB GARDENING LESSON, WITH THE SPECTACLES IN MY POCKET SAYING "COME ON, MORGANNA, LET'S GO..."
BESIDES, WHO KNOWS WHY THEY MAKE US STUDY GARDENING WHEN THE NICEST GARDENS IN TOWN ARE MADE OUT OF PLASTIC...!
SOMETIMES MAMA IS RIGHT: "PLASTIC ALWAYS LOOKS NICE, IT NEVER FADES OR MAKES A MESS..."

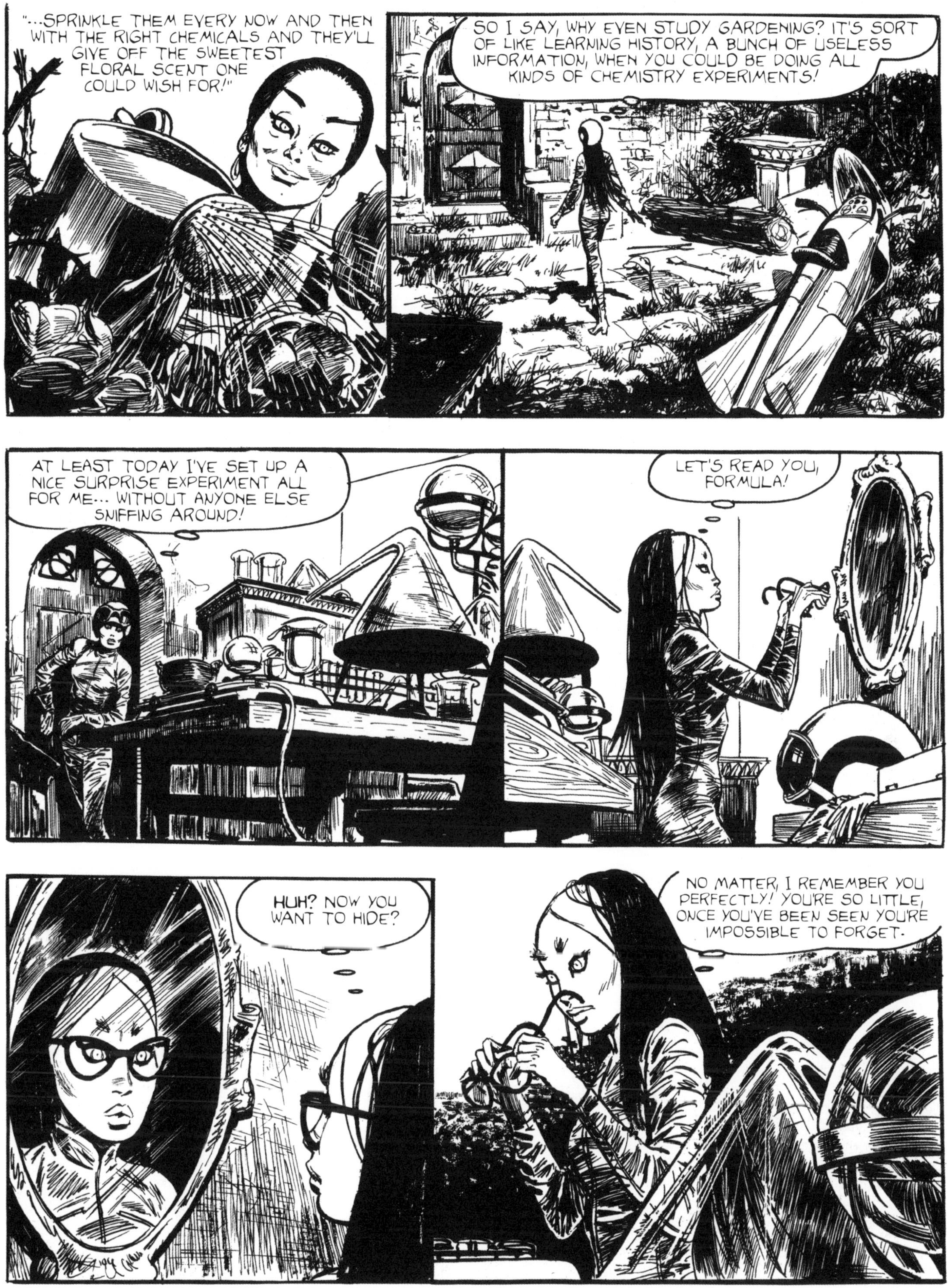
"...SPRINKLE THEM EVERY NOW AND THEN WITH THE RIGHT CHEMICALS AND THEY'LL GIVE OFF THE SWEETEST FLORAL SCENT ONE COULD WISH FOR!"
SO I SAY, WHY EVEN STUDY GARDENING? IT'S SORT OF LIKE LEARNING HISTORY, A BUNCH OF USELESS INFORMATION, WHEN YOU COULD BE DOING ALL KINDS OF CHEMISTRY EXPERIMENTS!
AT LEAST TODAY I'VE SET UP A NICE SURPRISE EXPERIMENT ALL FOR ME... WITHOUT ANYONE ELSE SNIFFING AROUND!
LET'S READ YOU, FORMULA!
HUH? NOW YOU WANT TO HIDE?
NO MATTER, I REMEMBER YOU PERFECTLY! YOU'RE SO LITTLE, ONCE YOU'VE BEEN SEEN YOU'RE IMPOSSIBLE TO FORGET.

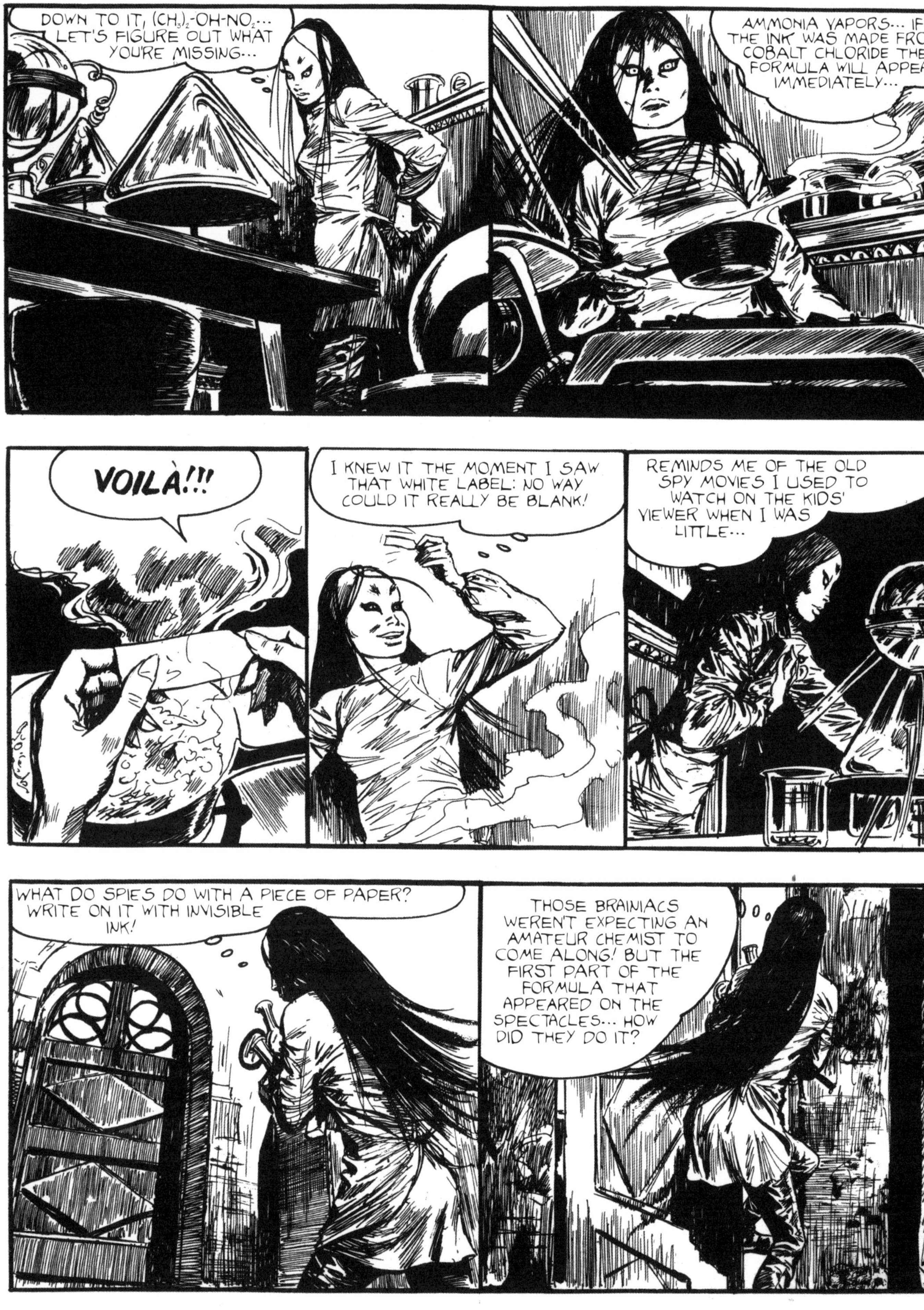
DOWN TO IT, $(CH_3)_2$-OH-NO_2... LET'S FIGURE OUT WHAT YOU'RE MISSING...
AMMONIA VAPORS... IF THE INK WAS MADE FROM COBALT CHLORIDE THE FORMULA WILL APPEAR IMMEDIATELY...
VOILÀ!!!
I KNEW IT THE MOMENT I SAW THAT WHITE LABEL: NO WAY COULD IT REALLY BE BLANK!
REMINDS ME OF THE OLD SPY MOVIES I USED TO WATCH ON THE KIDS' VIEWER WHEN I WAS LITTLE...
WHAT DO SPIES DO WITH A PIECE OF PAPER? WRITE ON IT WITH INVISIBLE INK!
THOSE BRAINIACS WEREN'T EXPECTING AN AMATEUR CHEMIST TO COME ALONG! BUT THE FIRST PART OF THE FORMULA THAT APPEARED ON THE SPECTACLES... HOW DID THEY DO IT?

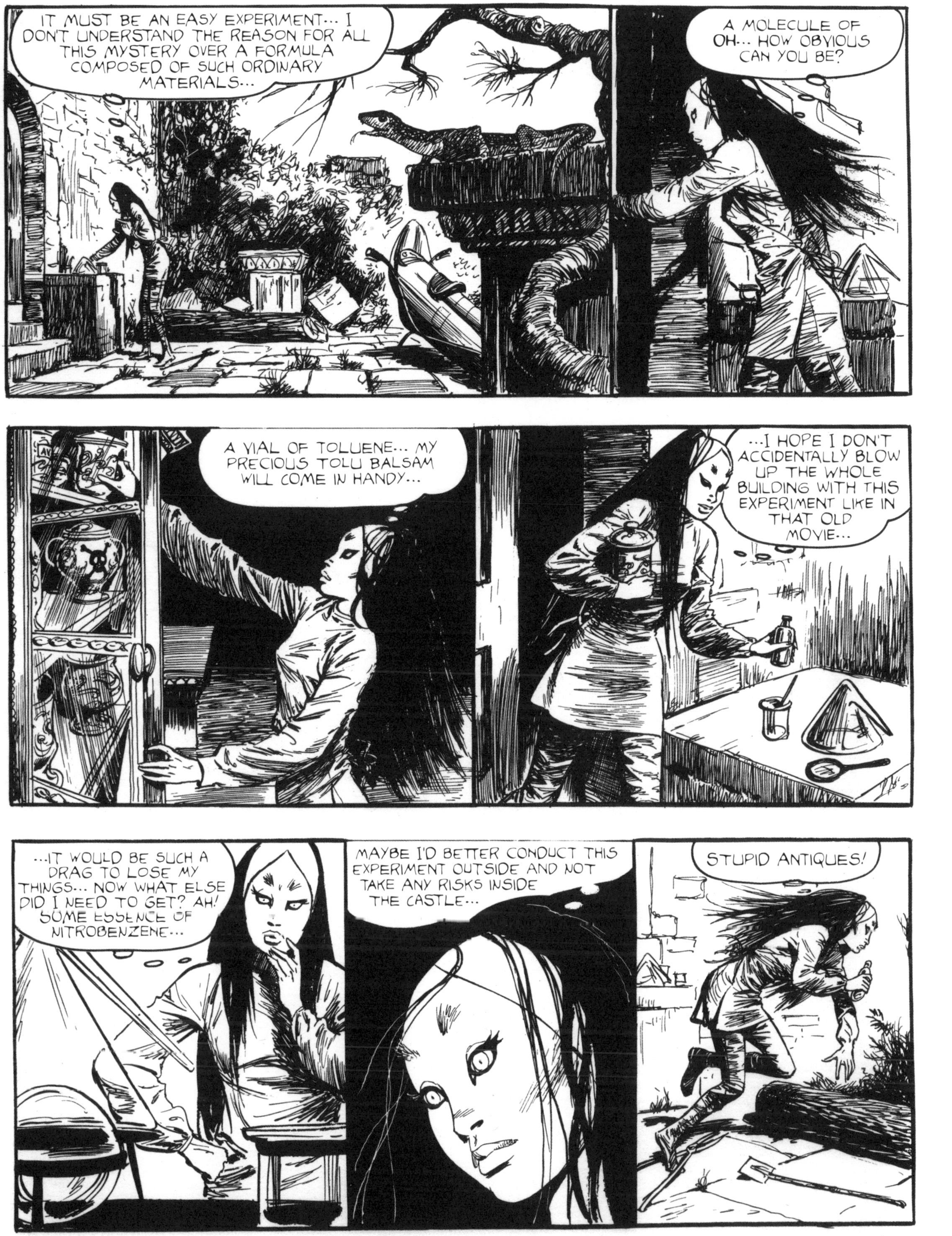
IT MUST BE AN EASY EXPERIMENT... I DON'T UNDERSTAND THE REASON FOR ALL THIS MYSTERY OVER A FORMULA COMPOSED OF SUCH ORDINARY MATERIALS...
A MOLECULE OF OH... HOW OBVIOUS CAN YOU BE?
A VIAL OF TOLUENE... MY PRECIOUS TOLU BALSAM WILL COME IN HANDY...
...I HOPE I DON'T ACCIDENTALLY BLOW UP THE WHOLE BUILDING WITH THIS EXPERIMENT LIKE IN THAT OLD MOVIE...
...IT WOULD BE SUCH A DRAG TO LOSE MY THINGS... NOW WHAT ELSE DID I NEED TO GET? AH! SOME ESSENCE OF NITROBENZENE...
MAYBE I'D BETTER CONDUCT THIS EXPERIMENT OUTSIDE AND NOT TAKE ANY RISKS INSIDE THE CASTLE...
STUPID ANTIQUES!

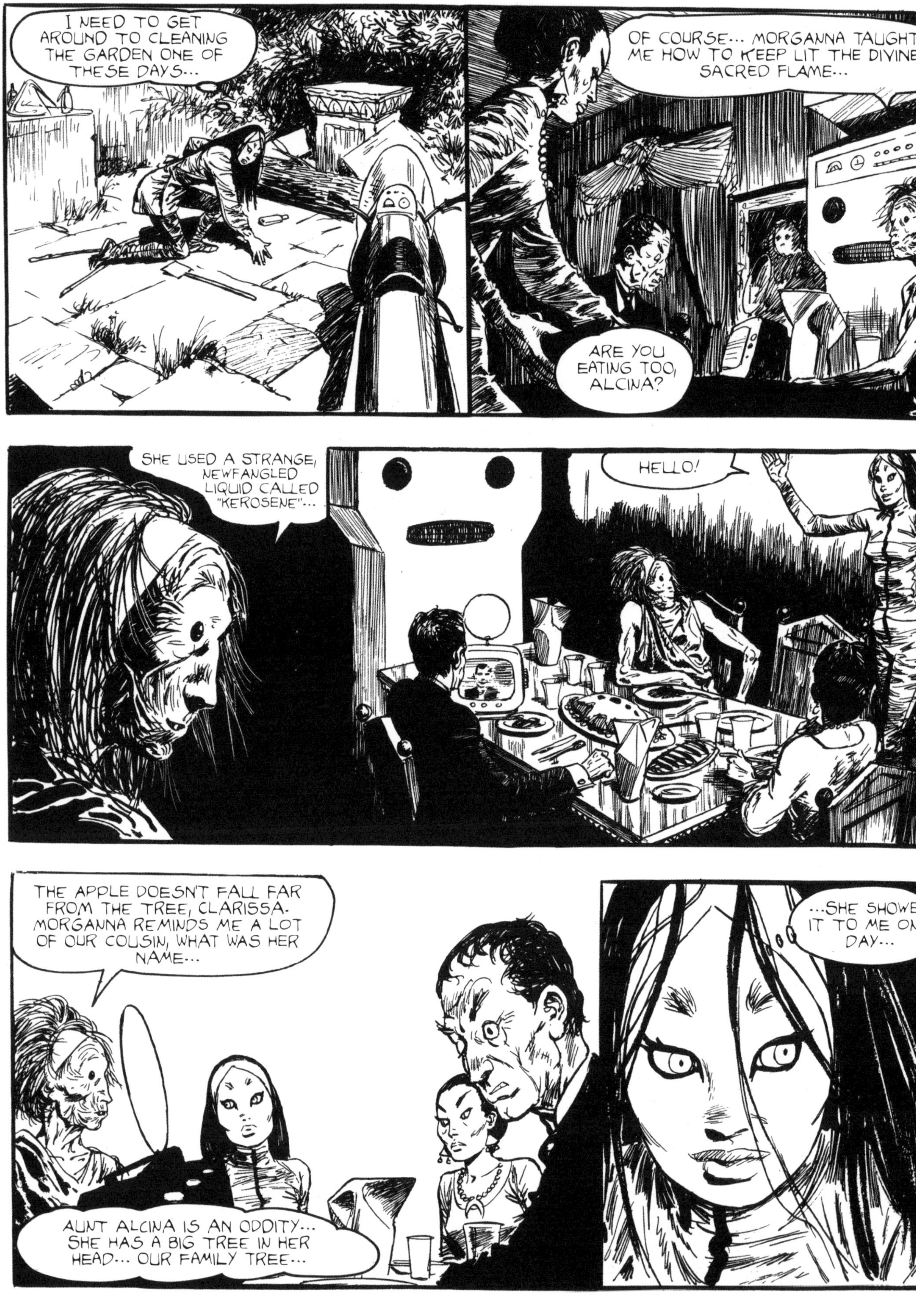
I NEED TO GET AROUND TO CLEANING THE GARDEN ONE OF THESE DAYS...
OF COURSE... MORGANNA TAUGHT ME HOW TO KEEP LIT THE DIVINE SACRED FLAME...
ARE YOU EATING TOO, ALCINA?
SHE USED A STRANGE, NEWFANGLED LIQUID CALLED "KEROSENE"...
HELLO!
THE APPLE DOESN'T FALL FAR FROM THE TREE, CLARISSA. MORGANNA REMINDS ME A LOT OF OUR COUSIN, WHAT WAS HER NAME...
AUNT ALCINA IS AN ODDITY... SHE HAS A BIG TREE IN HER HEAD... OUR FAMILY TREE...
...SHE SHOWED IT TO ME ONE DAY...

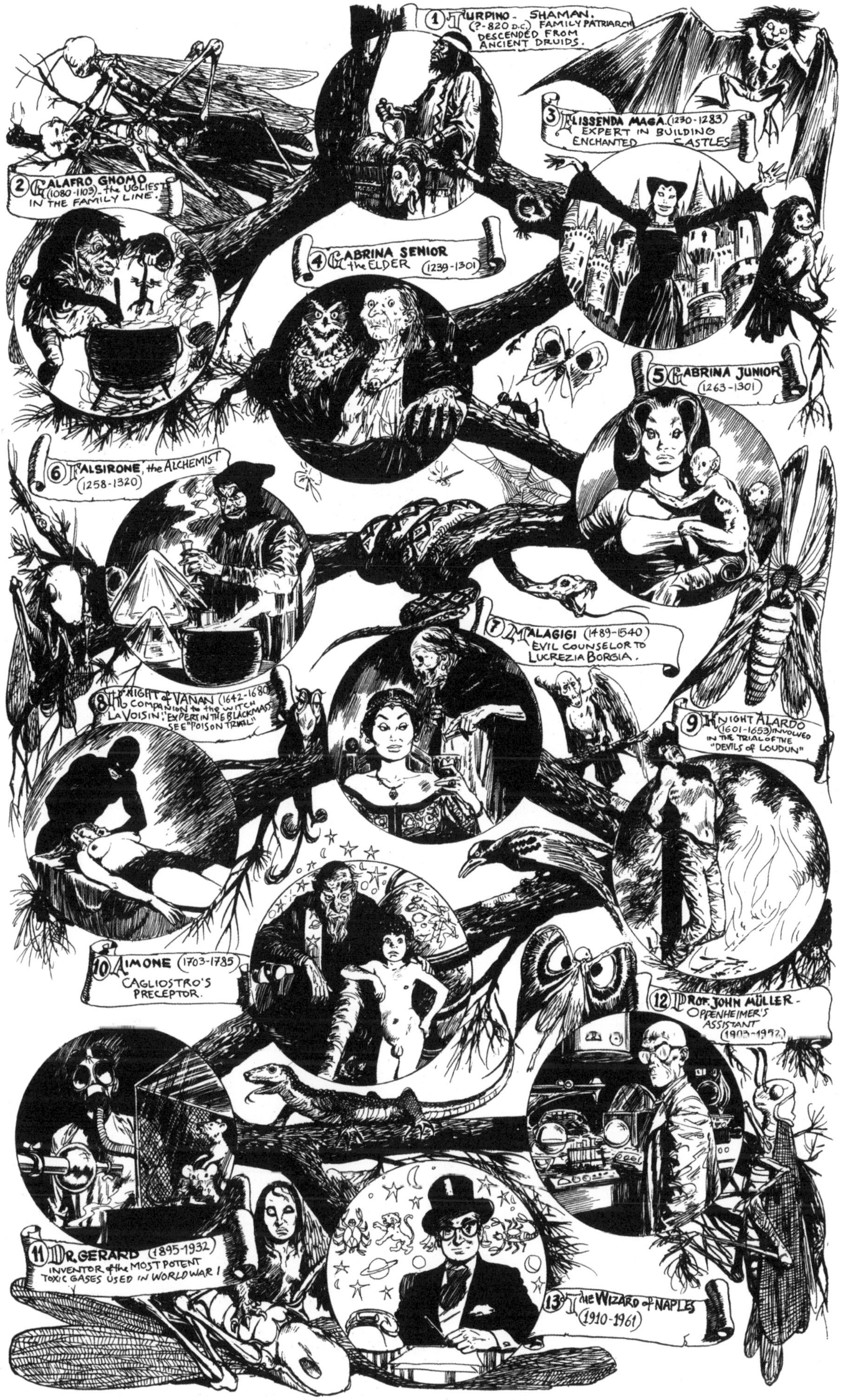

1 TURPINO - SHAMAN. (?-820 D.C.) FAMILY PATRIARCH DESCENDED FROM ANCIENT DRUIDS.
2 GALAFRO GNOMO (1080-1103) - the UGLIEST IN THE FAMILY LINE.
3 ELISSENDA MAGA (1230-1283) EXPERT IN BUILDING ENCHANTED CASTLES
4 GABRINA SENIOR the ELDER (1239-1301)
5 GABRINA JUNIOR (1263-1301)
6 FALSIRONE, the ALCHEMIST (1258-1320)
7 MALAGIGI (1489-1540) EVIL COUNSELOR TO LUCREZIA BORGIA.
8 KNIGHT of VANAN (1642-1680) COMPANION to the WITCH LA VOISIN; "EXPERT IN THE BLACKMASS" SEE "POISON TRIAL"
9 KNIGHT ALARDO (1601-1653) INVOLVED IN THE TRIAL OF THE "DEVILS of LOUDUN"
10 AIMONE (1703-1785) CAGLIOSTRO'S PRECEPTOR.
11 DR GERARD (1895-1932) INVENTOR of the MOST POTENT TOXIC GASES USED IN WORLD WAR I
12 PROF. JOHN MÜLLER - OPPENHEIMER'S ASSISTANT (1903-1952)
13 THE WIZARD of NAPLES (1910-1961)

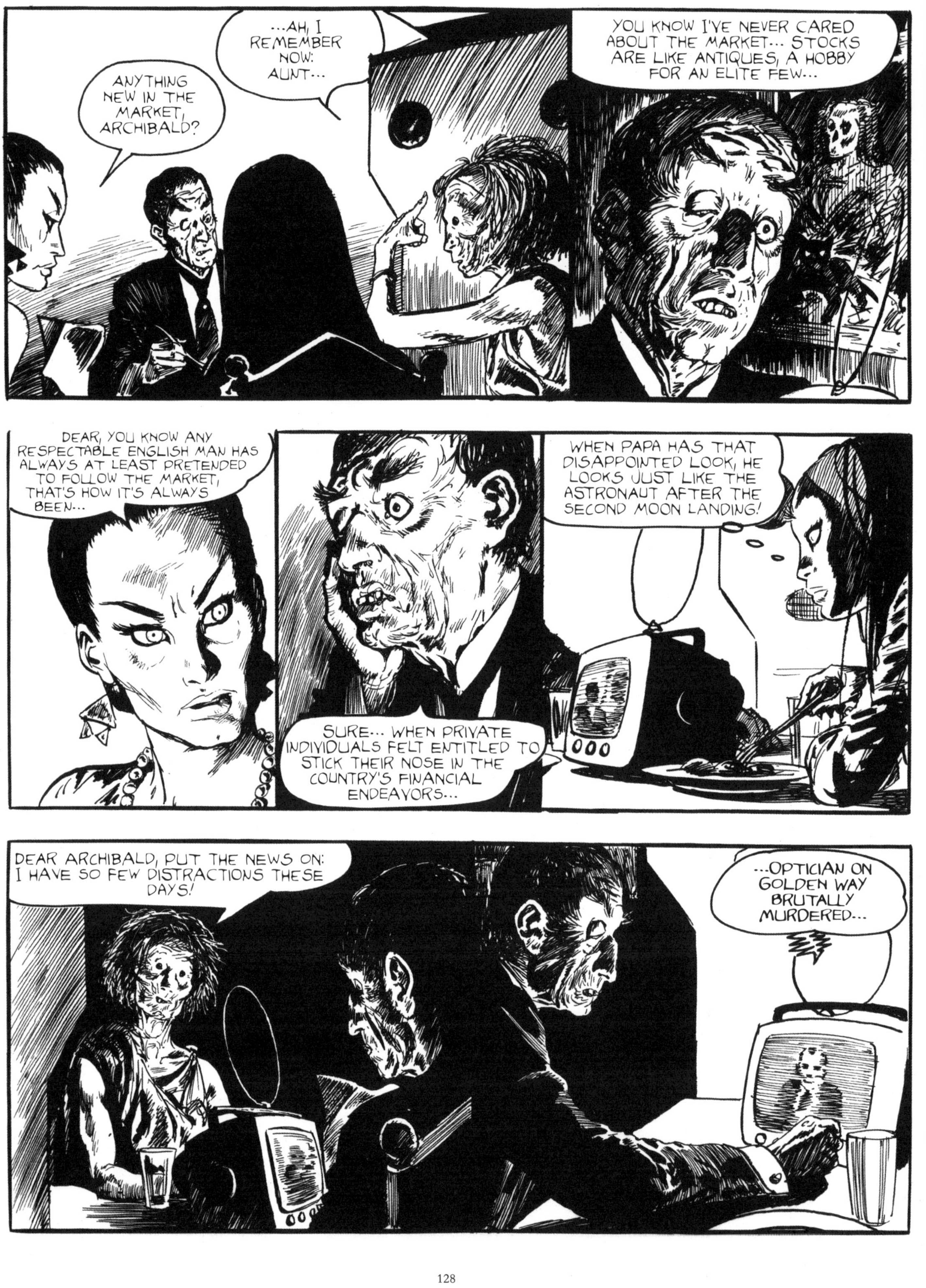
ANYTHING NEW IN THE MARKET, ARCHIBALD?
...AH, I REMEMBER NOW: AUNT...
YOU KNOW I'VE NEVER CARED ABOUT THE MARKET... STOCKS ARE LIKE ANTIQUES, A HOBBY FOR AN ELITE FEW...
DEAR, YOU KNOW ANY RESPECTABLE ENGLISH MAN HAS ALWAYS AT LEAST PRETENDED TO FOLLOW THE MARKET, THAT'S HOW IT'S ALWAYS BEEN...
SURE... WHEN PRIVATE INDIVIDUALS FELT ENTITLED TO STICK THEIR NOSE IN THE COUNTRY'S FINANCIAL ENDEAVORS...
WHEN PAPA HAS THAT DISAPPOINTED LOOK, HE LOOKS JUST LIKE THE ASTRONAUT AFTER THE SECOND MOON LANDING!
DEAR ARCHIBALD, PUT THE NEWS ON: I HAVE SO FEW DISTRACTIONS THESE DAYS!
...OPTICIAN ON GOLDEN WAY BRUTALLY MURDERED...

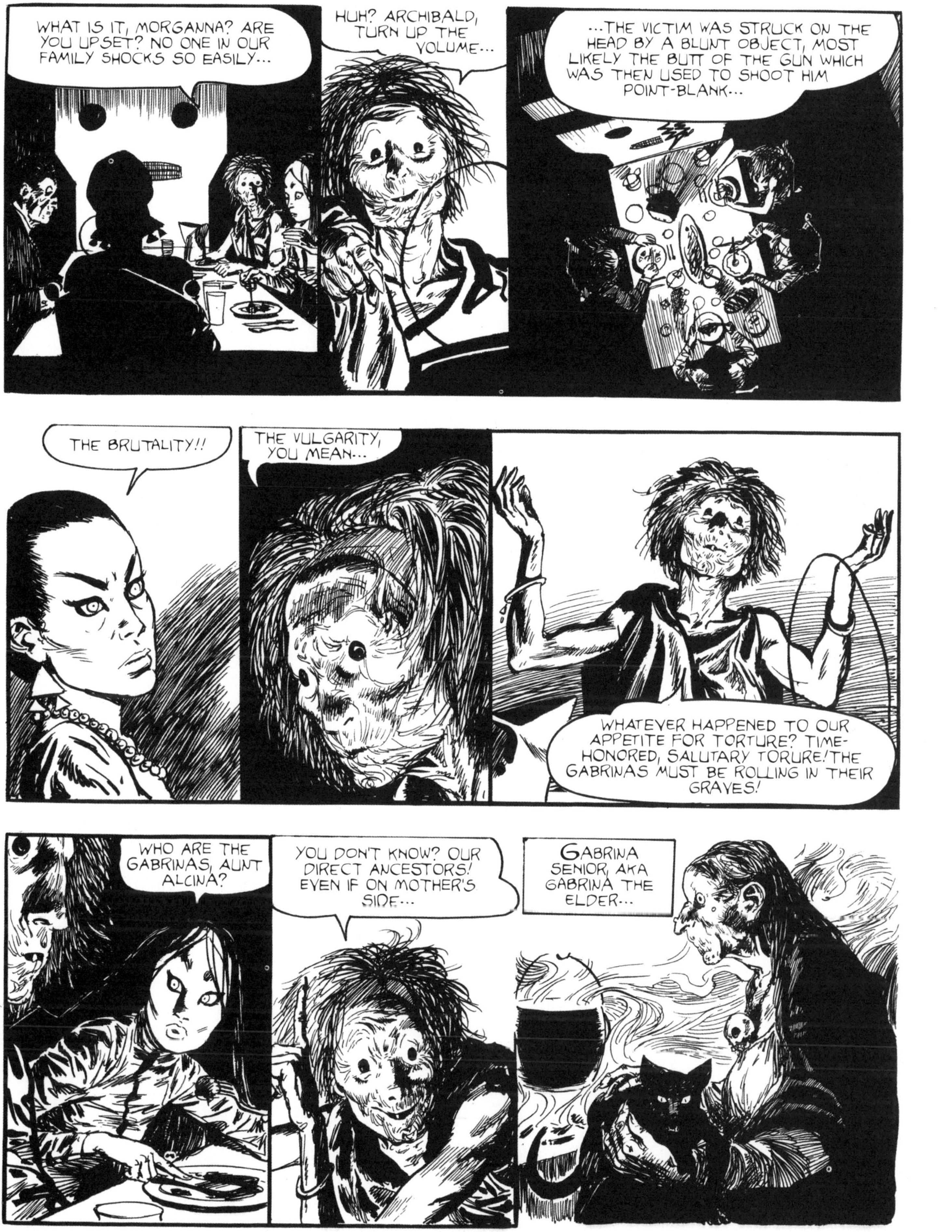
WHAT IS IT, MORGANNA? ARE YOU UPSET? NO ONE IN OUR FAMILY SHOCKS SO EASILY...
HUH? ARCHIBALD, TURN UP THE VOLUME...
...THE VICTIM WAS STRUCK ON THE HEAD BY A BLUNT OBJECT, MOST LIKELY THE BUTT OF THE GUN WHICH WAS THEN USED TO SHOOT HIM POINT-BLANK...
THE BRUTALITY!!
THE VULGARITY, YOU MEAN...
WHATEVER HAPPENED TO OUR APPETITE FOR TORTURE? TIME-HONORED, SALUTARY TORURE! THE GABRINAS MUST BE ROLLING IN THEIR GRAVES!
WHO ARE THE GABRINAS, AUNT ALCINA?
YOU DON'T KNOW? OUR DIRECT ANCESTORS! EVEN IF ON MOTHER'S SIDE...
GABRINA SENIOR, AKA GABRINA THE ELDER...

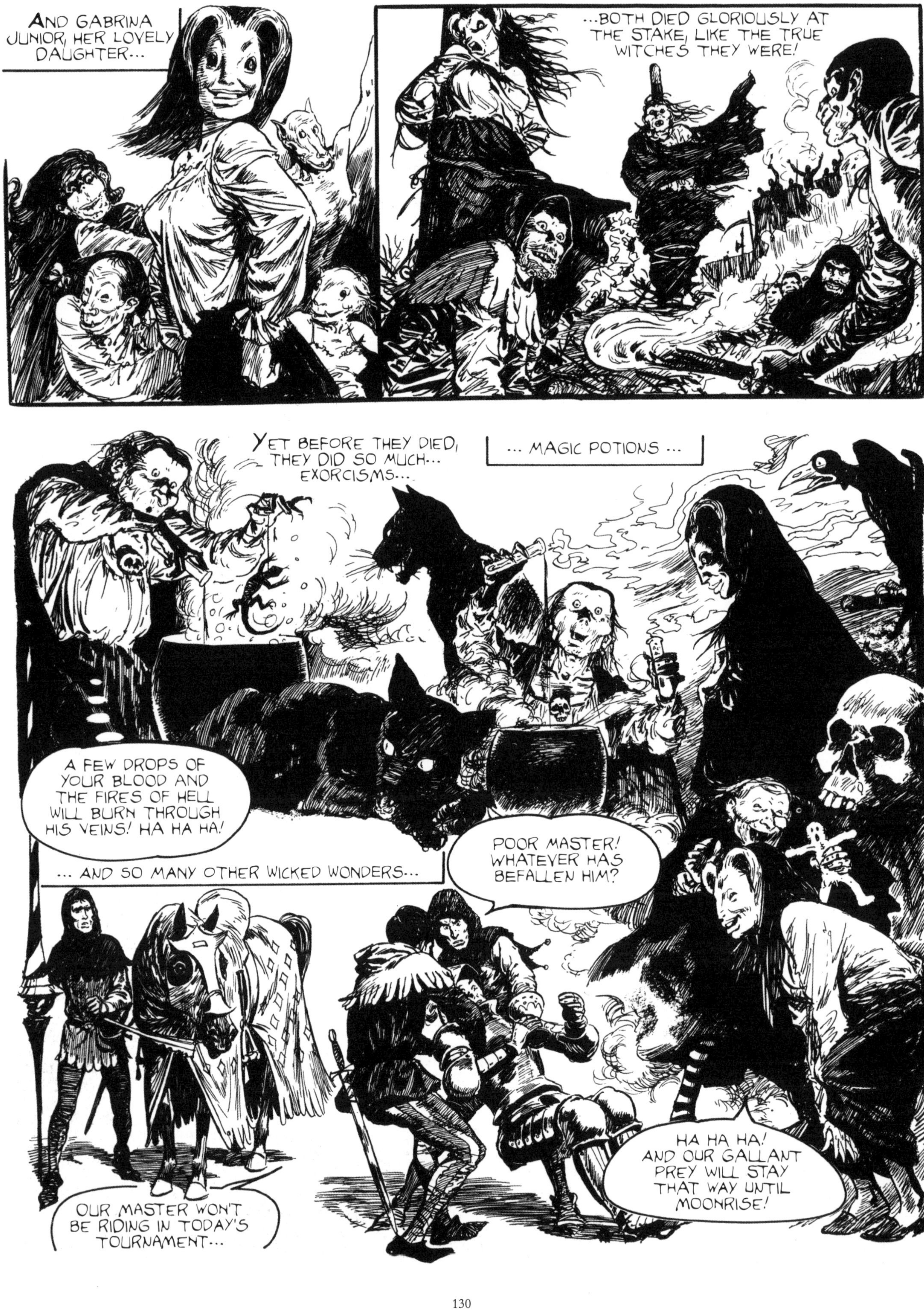
AND GABRINA JUNIOR, HER LOVELY DAUGHTER...
...BOTH DIED GLORIOUSLY AT THE STAKE, LIKE THE TRUE WITCHES THEY WERE!
YET BEFORE THEY DIED, THEY DID SO MUCH... EXORCISMS...
... MAGIC POTIONS ...
A FEW DROPS OF YOUR BLOOD AND THE FIRES OF HELL WILL BURN THROUGH HIS VEINS! HA HA HA!
... AND SO MANY OTHER WICKED WONDERS...
POOR MASTER! WHATEVER HAS BEFALLEN HIM?
OUR MASTER WON'T BE RIDING IN TODAY'S TOURNAMENT...
HA HA HA! AND OUR GALLANT PREY WILL STAY THAT WAY UNTIL MOONRISE!

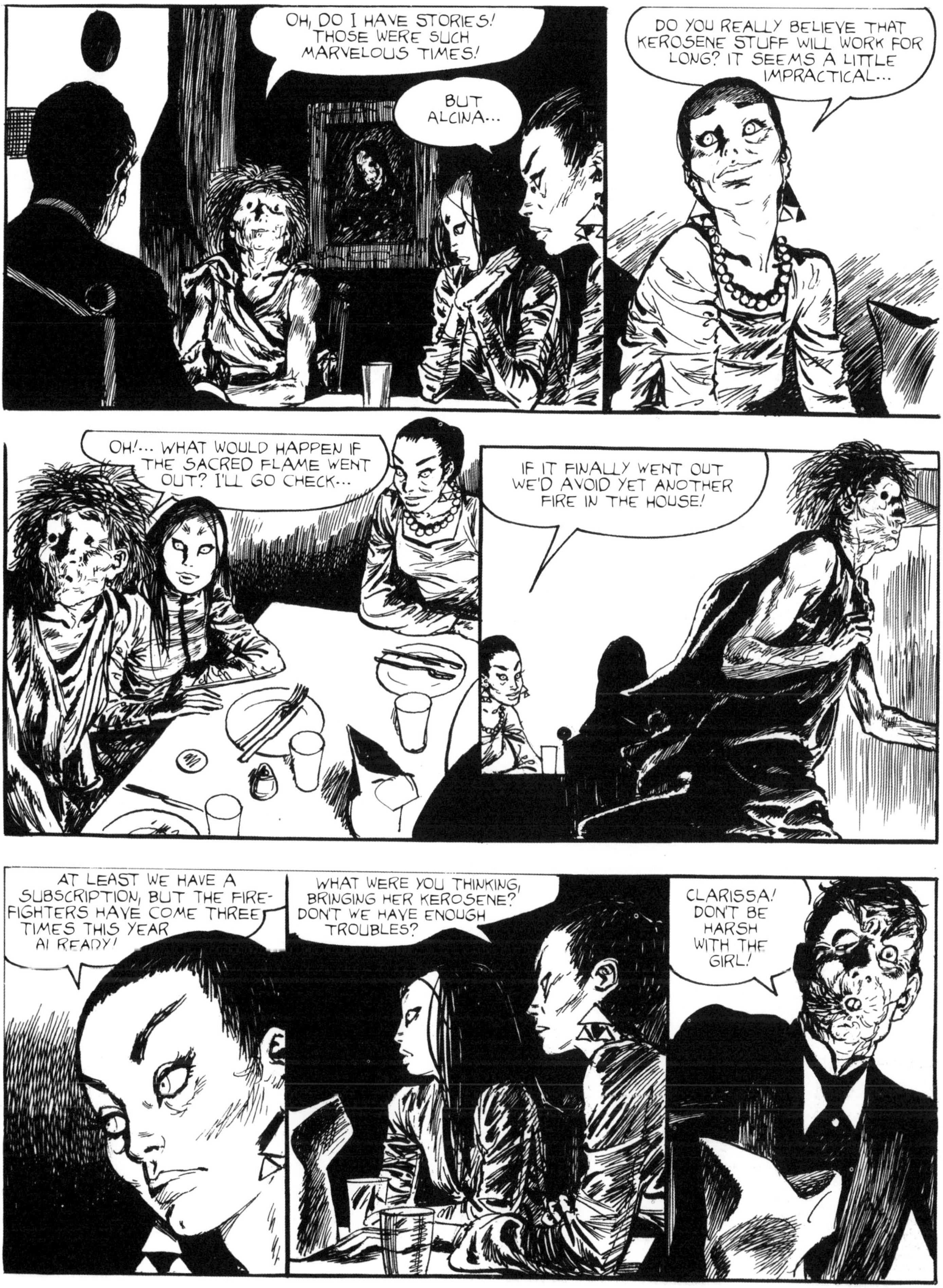
OH, DO I HAVE STORIES! THOSE WERE SUCH MARVELOUS TIMES!
BUT ALCINA...
DO YOU REALLY BELIEVE THAT KEROSENE STUFF WILL WORK FOR LONG? IT SEEMS A LITTLE IMPRACTICAL...
OH!... WHAT WOULD HAPPEN IF THE SACRED FLAME WENT OUT? I'LL GO CHECK...
IF IT FINALLY WENT OUT WE'D AVOID YET ANOTHER FIRE IN THE HOUSE!
AT LEAST WE HAVE A SUBSCRIPTION, BUT THE FIRE-FIGHTERS HAVE COME THREE TIMES THIS YEAR ALREADY!
WHAT WERE YOU THINKING, BRINGING HER KEROSENE? DON'T WE HAVE ENOUGH TROUBLES?
CLARISSA! DON'T BE HARSH WITH THE GIRL!

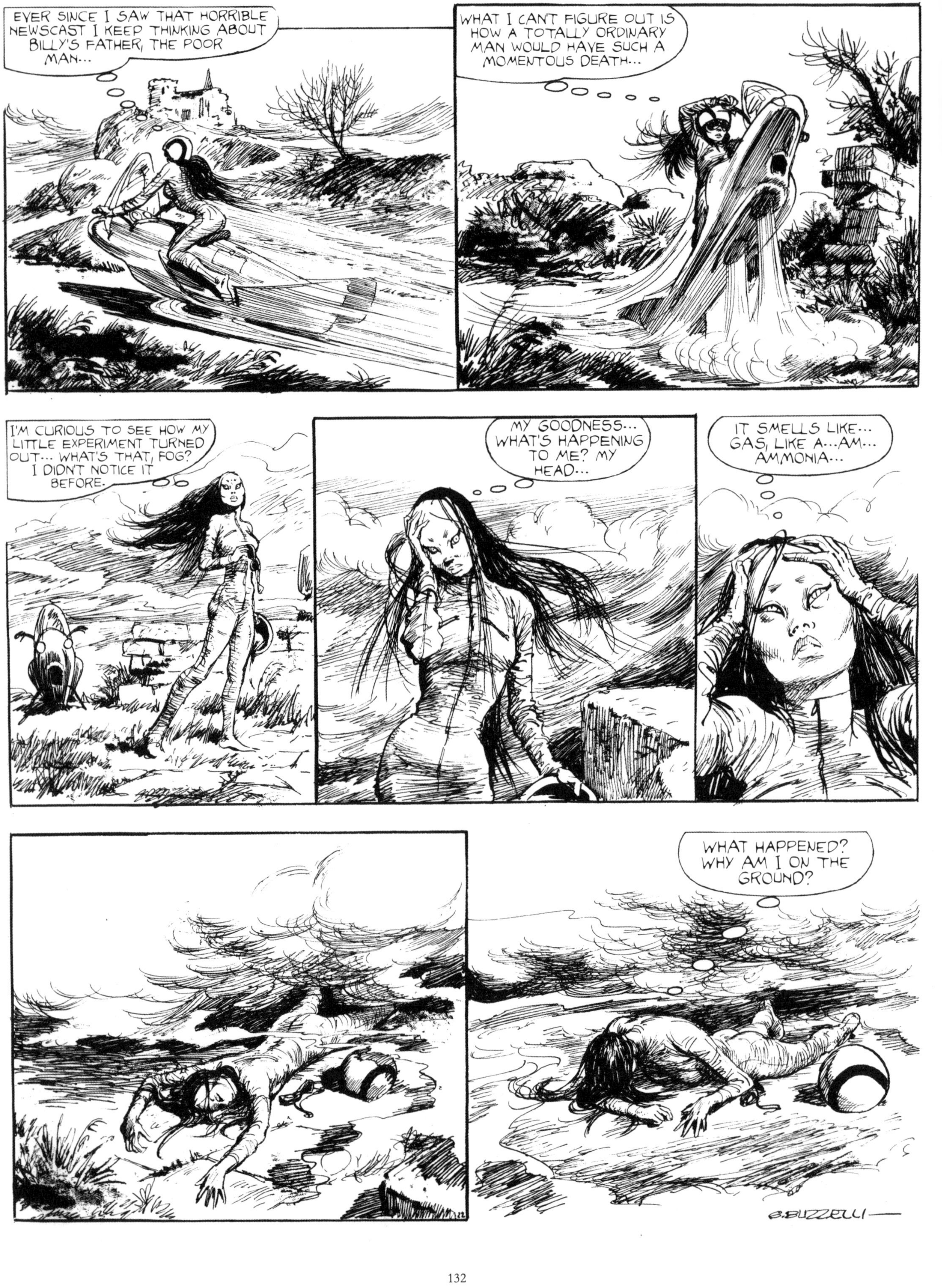
EVER SINCE I SAW THAT HORRIBLE NEWSCAST I KEEP THINKING ABOUT BILLY'S FATHER, THE POOR MAN...
WHAT I CAN'T FIGURE OUT IS HOW A TOTALLY ORDINARY MAN WOULD HAVE SUCH A MOMENTOUS DEATH...
I'M CURIOUS TO SEE HOW MY LITTLE EXPERIMENT TURNED OUT... WHAT'S THAT, FOG? I DIDN'T NOTICE IT BEFORE.
MY GOODNESS... WHAT'S HAPPENING TO ME? MY HEAD...
IT SMELLS LIKE... GAS, LIKE A...AM... AMMONIA...
WHAT HAPPENED? WHY AM I ON THE GROUND?
G. BUZZELLI

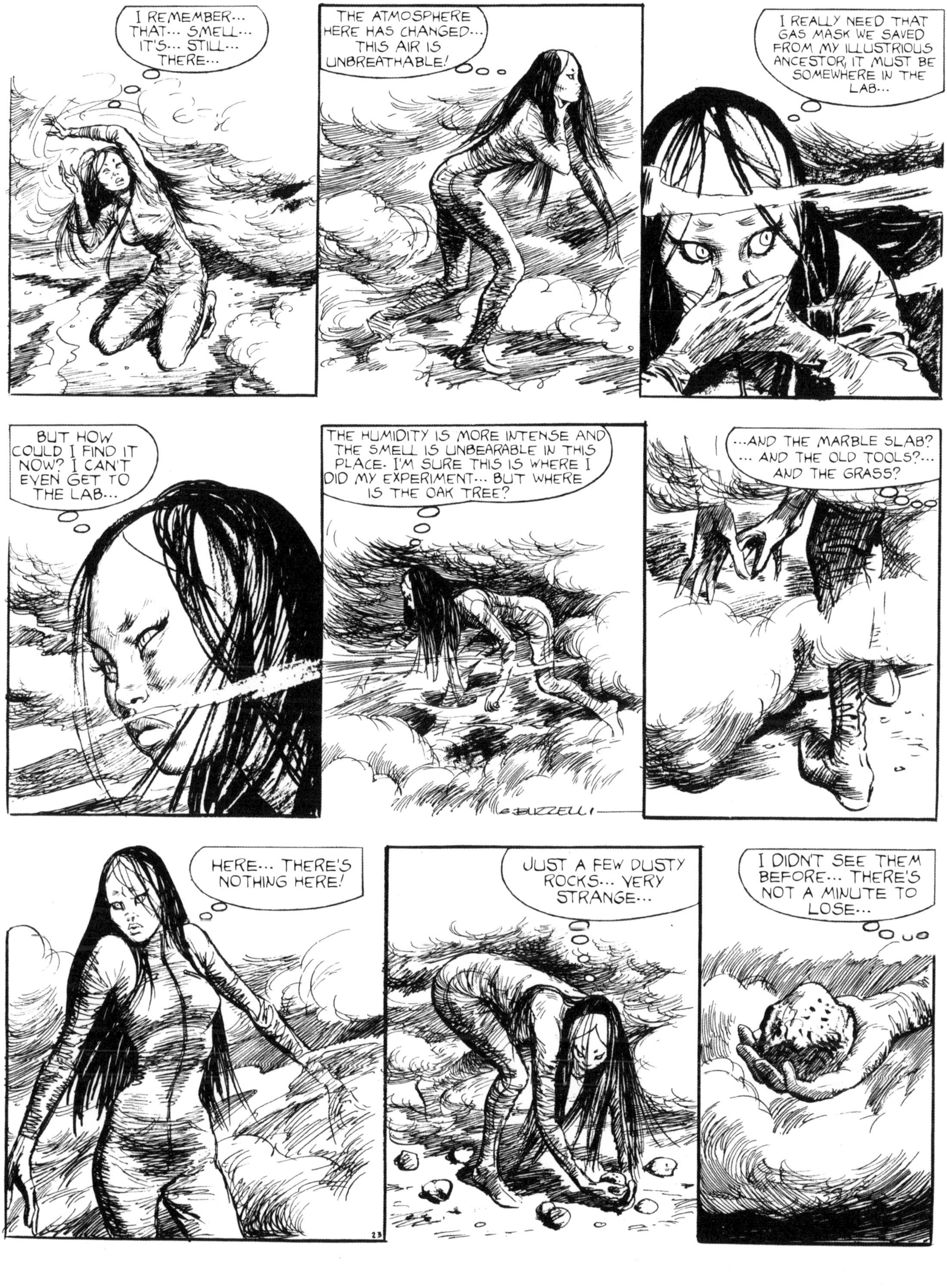
I REMEMBER... THAT... SMELL... IT'S... STILL... THERE...
THE ATMOSPHERE HERE HAS CHANGED... THIS AIR IS UNBREATHABLE!
I REALLY NEED THAT GAS MASK WE SAVED FROM MY ILLUSTRIOUS ANCESTOR, IT MUST BE SOMEWHERE IN THE LAB...
BUT HOW COULD I FIND IT NOW? I CAN'T EVEN GET TO THE LAB...
THE HUMIDITY IS MORE INTENSE AND THE SMELL IS UNBEARABLE IN THIS PLACE. I'M SURE THIS IS WHERE I DID MY EXPERIMENT... BUT WHERE IS THE OAK TREE?
...AND THE MARBLE SLAB? ... AND THE OLD TOOLS?... AND THE GRASS?
G BUZZELLI
HERE... THERE'S NOTHING HERE!
23
JUST A FEW DUSTY ROCKS... VERY STRANGE...
I DIDN'T SEE THEM BEFORE... THERE'S NOT A MINUTE TO LOSE...

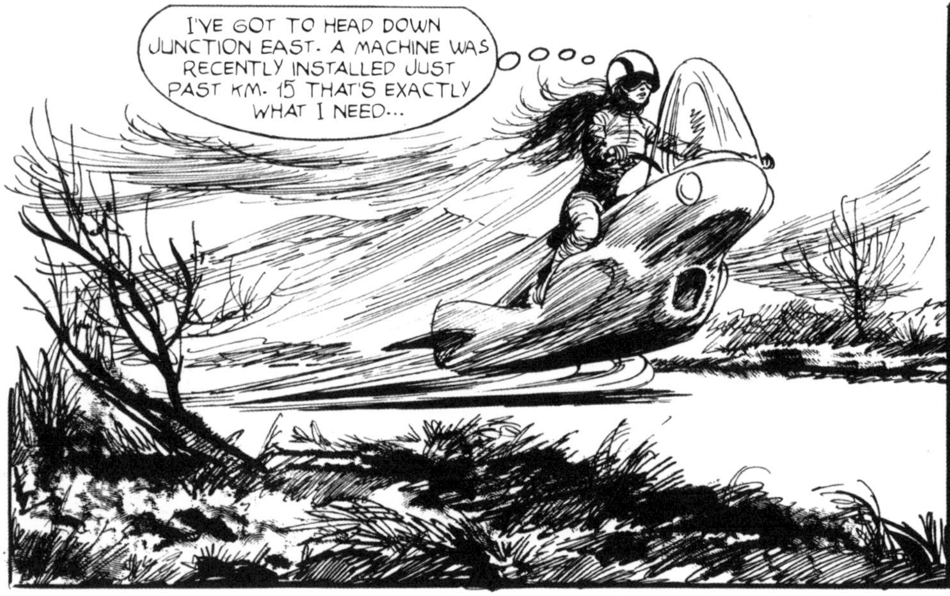
I'VE GOT TO HEAD DOWN JUNCTION EAST. A MACHINE WAS RECENTLY INSTALLED JUST PAST KM. 15 THAT'S EXACTLY WHAT I NEED...

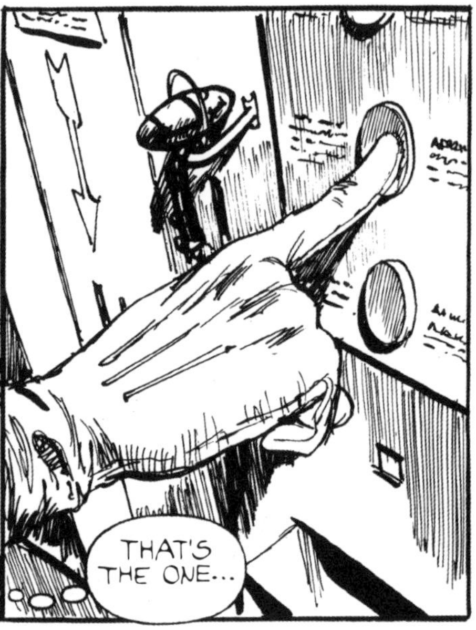
THAT'S THE ONE...

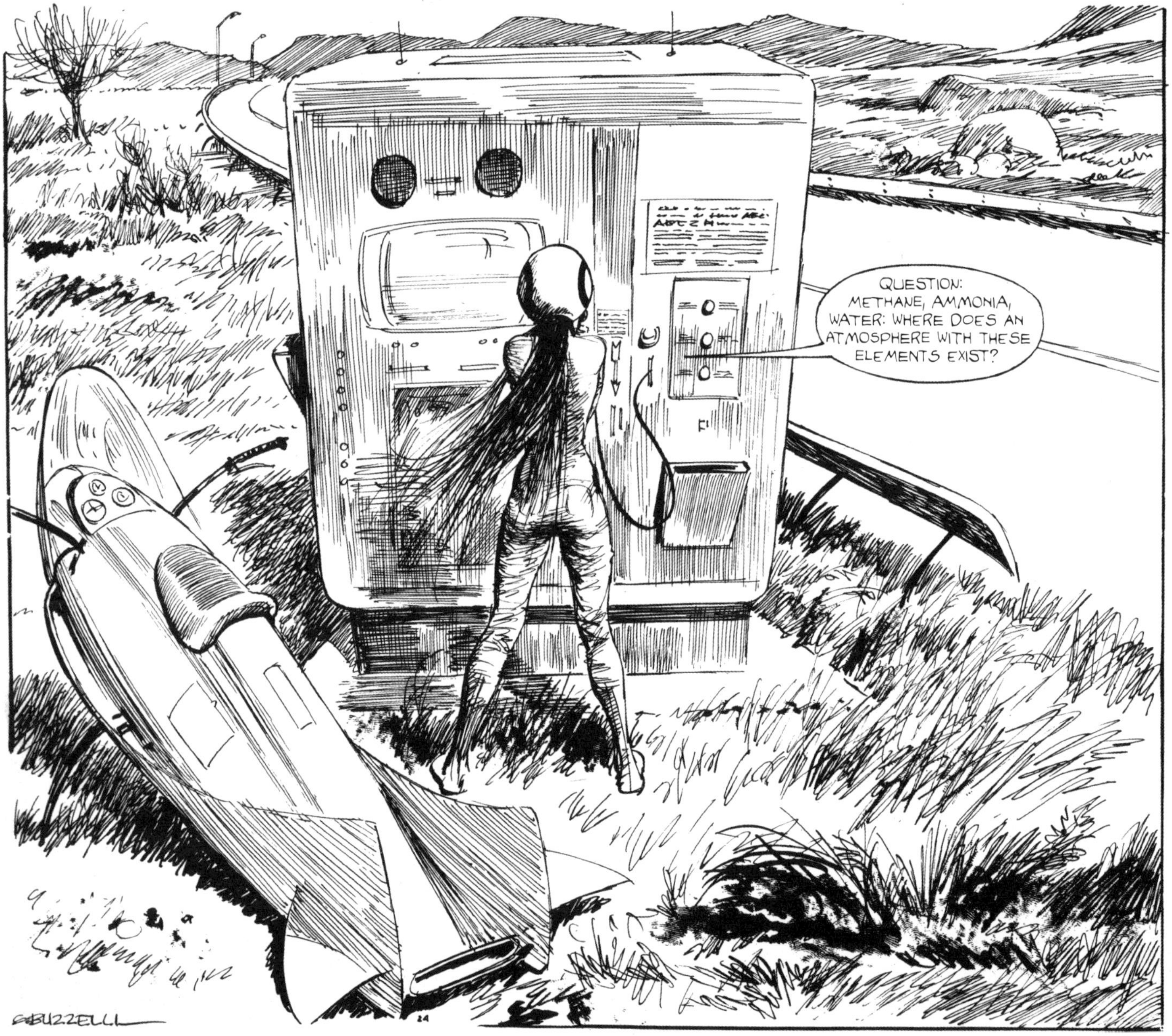
QUESTION: METHANE, AMMONIA, WATER: WHERE DOES AN ATMOSPHERE WITH THESE ELEMENTS EXIST?

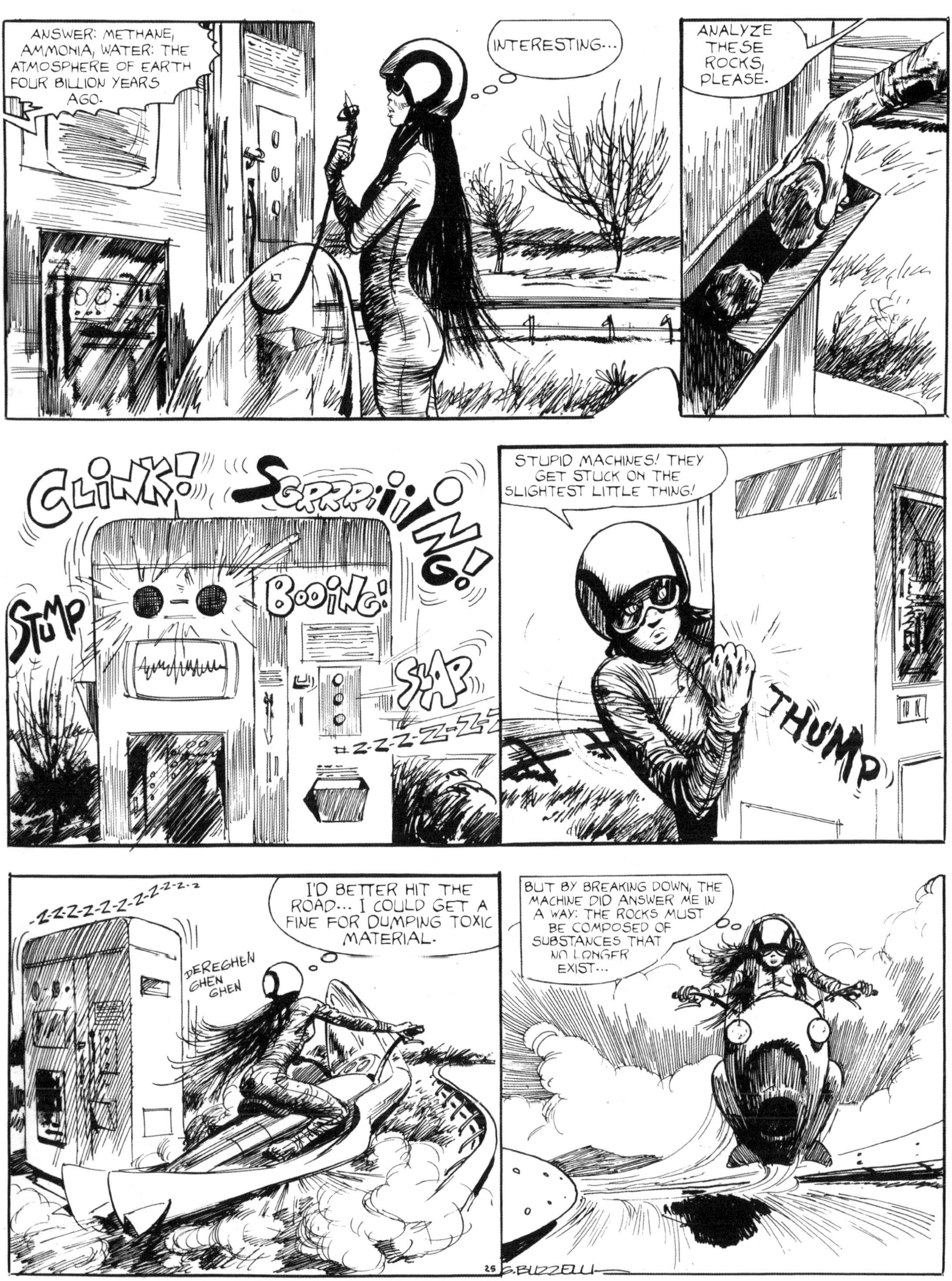
ANSWER: METHANE, AMMONIA, WATER: THE ATMOSPHERE OF EARTH FOUR BILLION YEARS AGO.
INTERESTING...
ANALYZE THESE ROCKS, PLEASE.
CLINK!
SGRRRIIIING!
STUMP
BOOING!
SLAP
-Z-Z-Z-Z-Z-Z
STUPID MACHINES! THEY GET STUCK ON THE SLIGHTEST LITTLE THING!
THUMP
-Z-Z-Z-Z-Z-Z-Z-Z-Z-Z-Z-Z-Z
I'D BETTER HIT THE ROAD... I COULD GET A FINE FOR DUMPING TOXIC MATERIAL.
DEREGHEN GHEN GHEN
BUT BY BREAKING DOWN, THE MACHINE DID ANSWER ME IN A WAY: THE ROCKS MUST BE COMPOSED OF SUBSTANCES THAT NO LONGER EXIST...
25
G. BUZZELLI

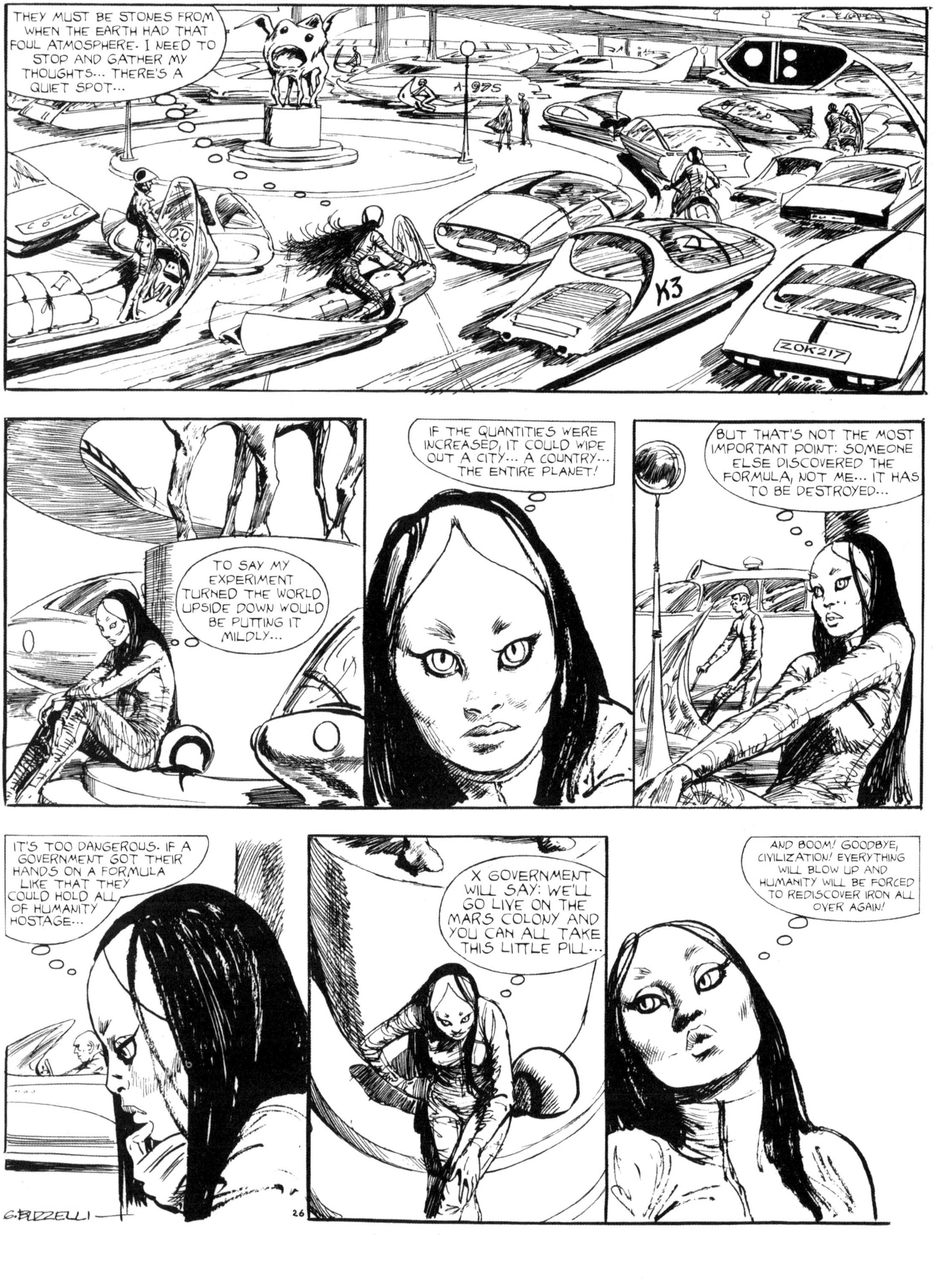
THEY MUST BE STONES FROM WHEN THE EARTH HAD THAT FOUL ATMOSPHERE. I NEED TO STOP AND GATHER MY THOUGHTS... THERE'S A QUIET SPOT...
A-975
K3
ZOK217
TO SAY MY EXPERIMENT TURNED THE WORLD UPSIDE DOWN WOULD BE PUTTING IT MILDLY...
IF THE QUANTITIES WERE INCREASED, IT COULD WIPE OUT A CITY... A COUNTRY... THE ENTIRE PLANET!
BUT THAT'S NOT THE MOST IMPORTANT POINT: SOMEONE ELSE DISCOVERED THE FORMULA, NOT ME... IT HAS TO BE DESTROYED...
IT'S TOO DANGEROUS. IF A GOVERNMENT GOT THEIR HANDS ON A FORMULA LIKE THAT THEY COULD HOLD ALL OF HUMANITY HOSTAGE...
X GOVERNMENT WILL SAY: WE'LL GO LIVE ON THE MARS COLONY AND YOU CAN ALL TAKE THIS LITTLE PILL...
AND BOOM! GOODBYE, CIVILIZATION! EVERYTHING WILL BLOW UP AND HUMANITY WILL BE FORCED TO REDISCOVER IRON ALL OVER AGAIN!
G. BUZZELLI
26

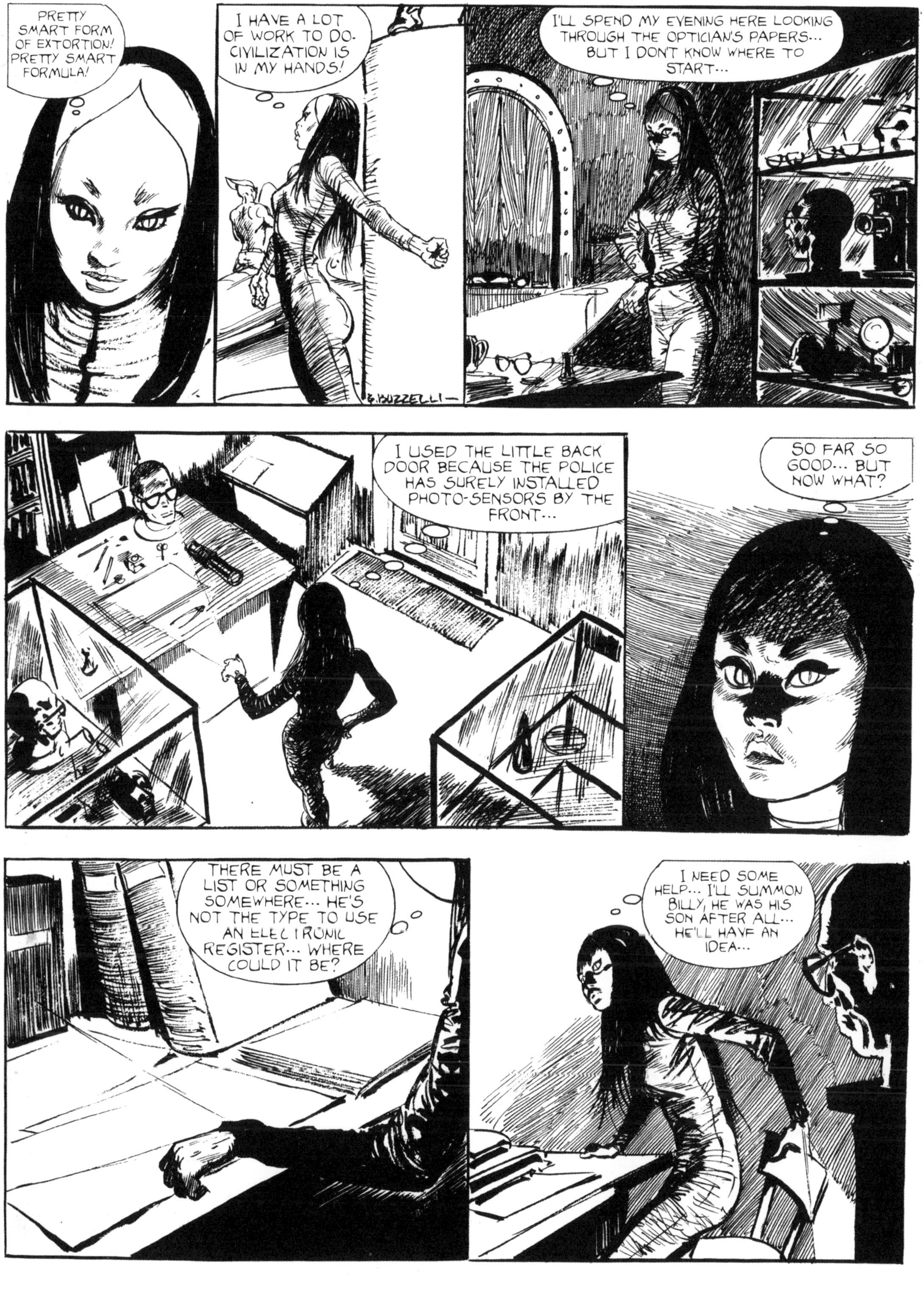
PRETTY SMART FORM OF EXTORTION! PRETTY SMART FORMULA!
I HAVE A LOT OF WORK TO DO- CIVILIZATION IS IN MY HANDS!
G. BUZZELLI
I'LL SPEND MY EVENING HERE LOOKING THROUGH THE OPTICIAN'S PAPERS... BUT I DON'T KNOW WHERE TO START...
I USED THE LITTLE BACK DOOR BECAUSE THE POLICE HAS SURELY INSTALLED PHOTO-SENSORS BY THE FRONT...
SO FAR SO GOOD... BUT NOW WHAT?
THERE MUST BE A LIST OR SOMETHING SOMEWHERE... HE'S NOT THE TYPE TO USE AN ELECTRONIC REGISTER... WHERE COULD IT BE?
I NEED SOME HELP... I'LL SUMMON BILLY, HE WAS HIS SON AFTER ALL... HE'LL HAVE AN IDEA...

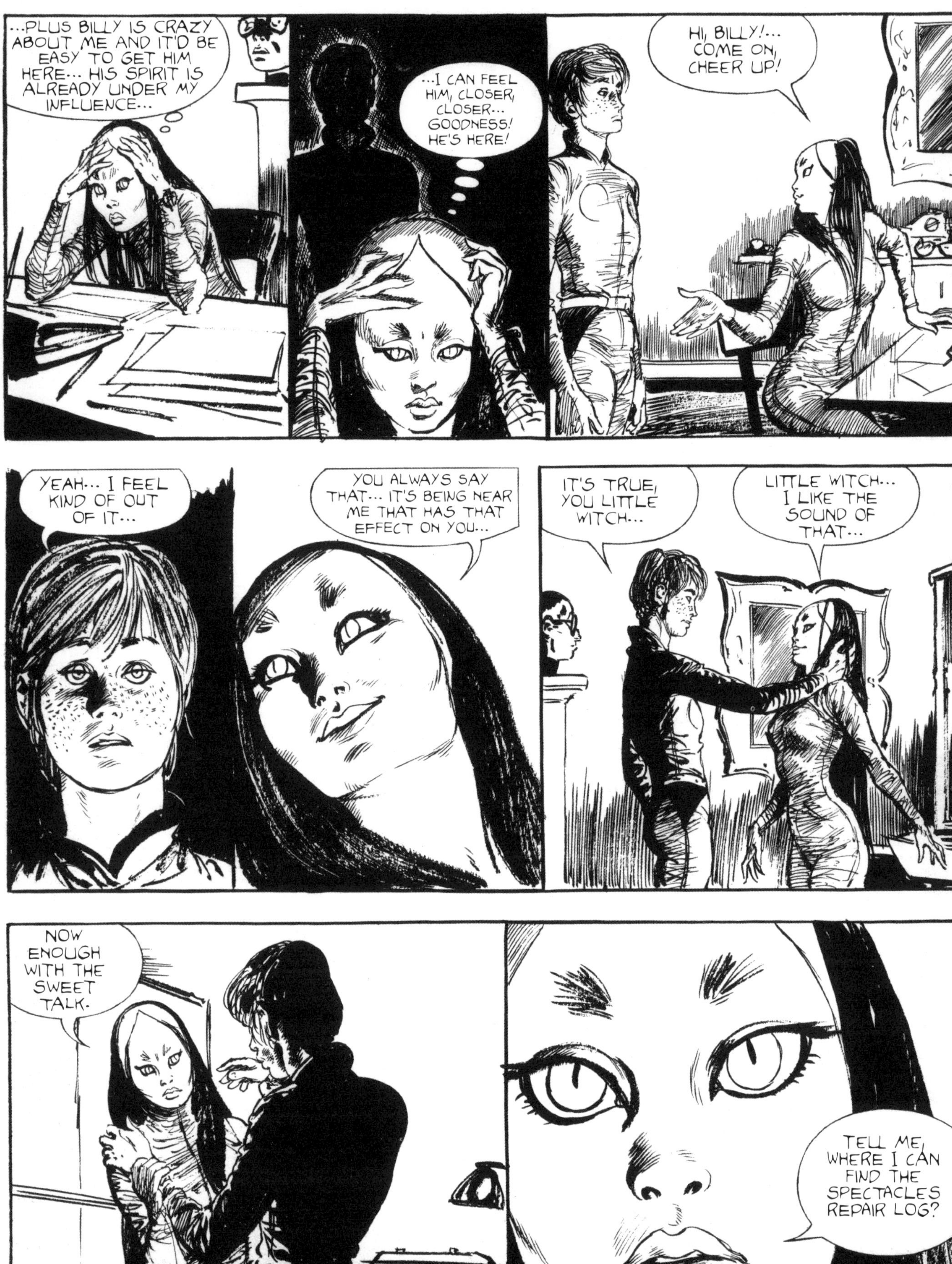
...PLUS BILLY IS CRAZY ABOUT ME AND IT'D BE EASY TO GET HIM HERE... HIS SPIRIT IS ALREADY UNDER MY INFLUENCE...
...I CAN FEEL HIM, CLOSER, CLOSER... GOODNESS! HE'S HERE!
HI, BILLY!... COME ON, CHEER UP!
YEAH... I FEEL KIND OF OUT OF IT...
YOU ALWAYS SAY THAT... IT'S BEING NEAR ME THAT HAS THAT EFFECT ON YOU...
IT'S TRUE, YOU LITTLE WITCH...
LITTLE WITCH... I LIKE THE SOUND OF THAT...
NOW ENOUGH WITH THE SWEET TALK.
TELL ME, WHERE I CAN FIND THE SPECTACLES REPAIR LOG?
G. BUZZELLI

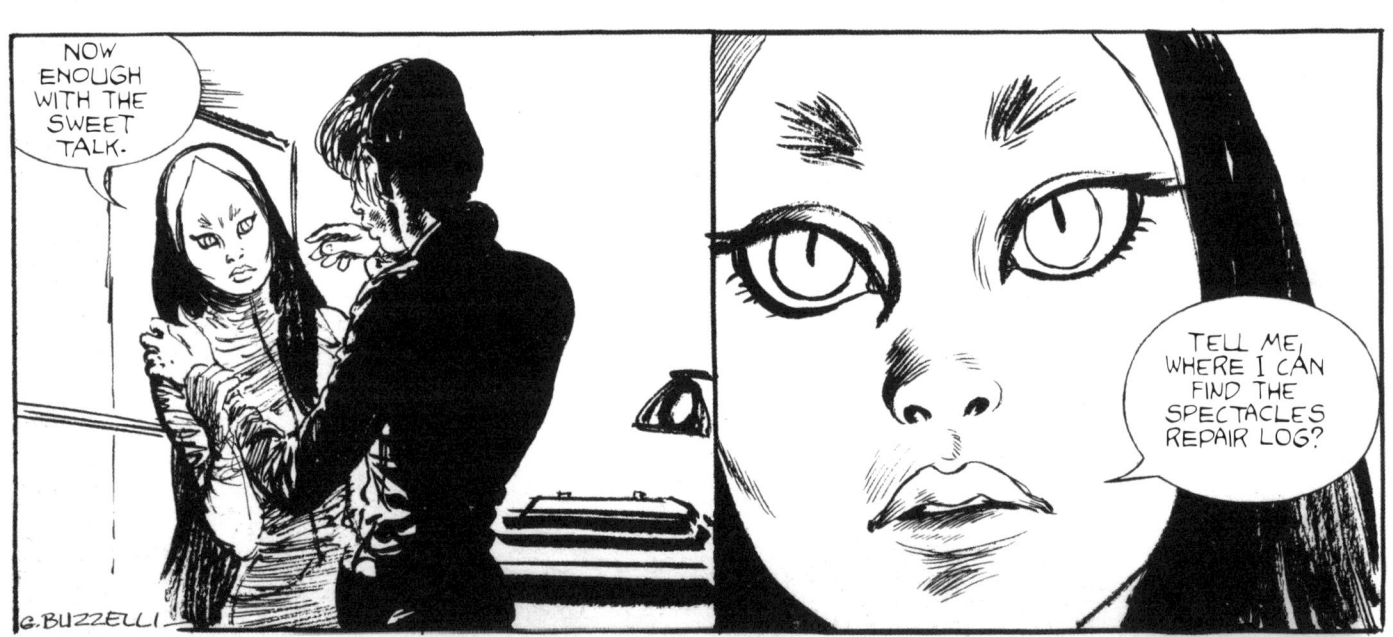

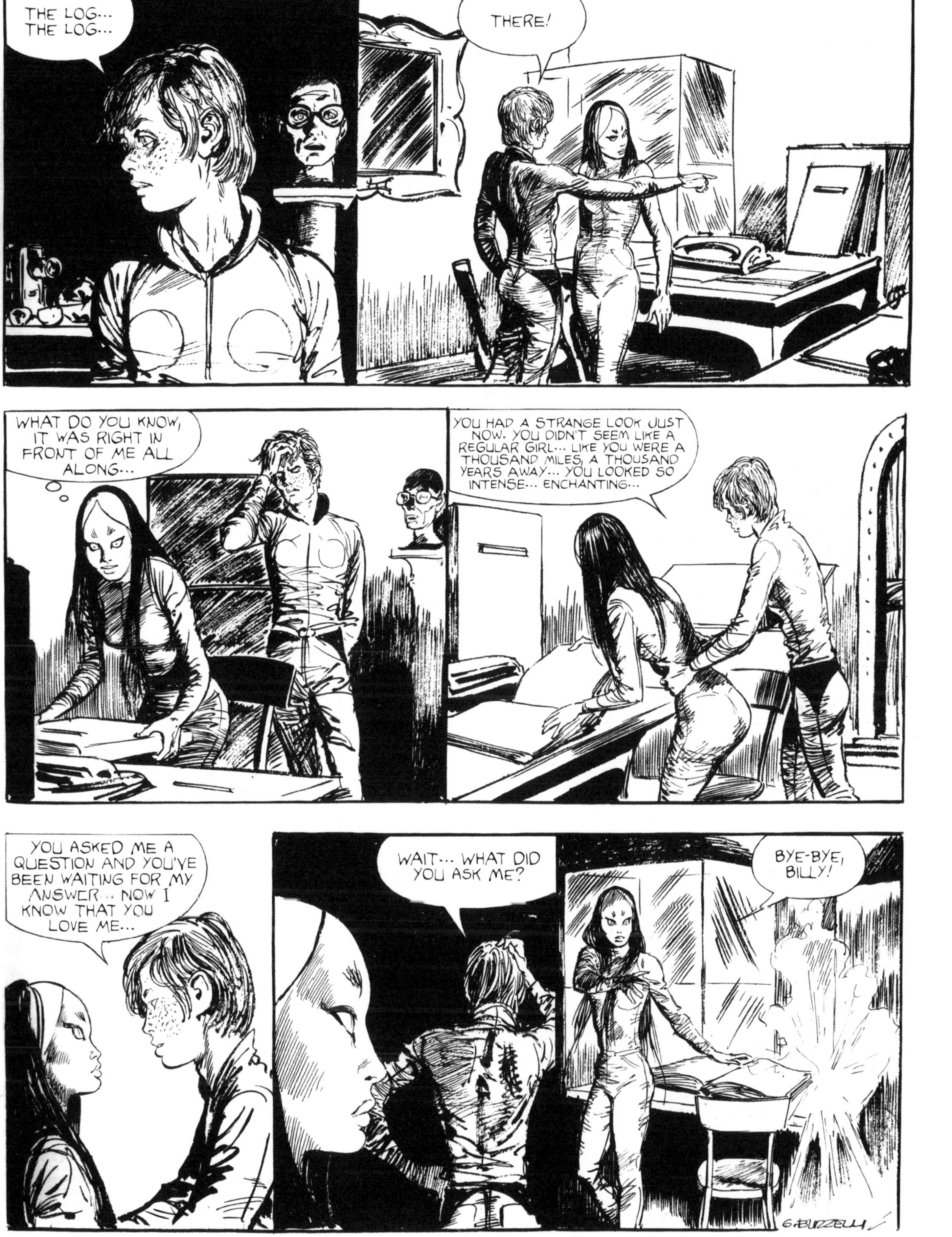
THE LOG... THE LOG...
THERE!
WHAT DO YOU KNOW, IT WAS RIGHT IN FRONT OF ME ALL ALONG...
YOU HAD A STRANGE LOOK JUST NOW. YOU DIDN'T SEEM LIKE A REGULAR GIRL... LIKE YOU WERE A THOUSAND MILES, A THOUSAND YEARS AWAY... YOU LOOKED SO INTENSE... ENCHANTING...
YOU ASKED ME A QUESTION AND YOU'VE BEEN WAITING FOR MY ANSWER... NOW I KNOW THAT YOU LOVE ME...
WAIT... WHAT DID YOU ASK ME?
BYE-BYE, BILLY!
G. BUZZELLI

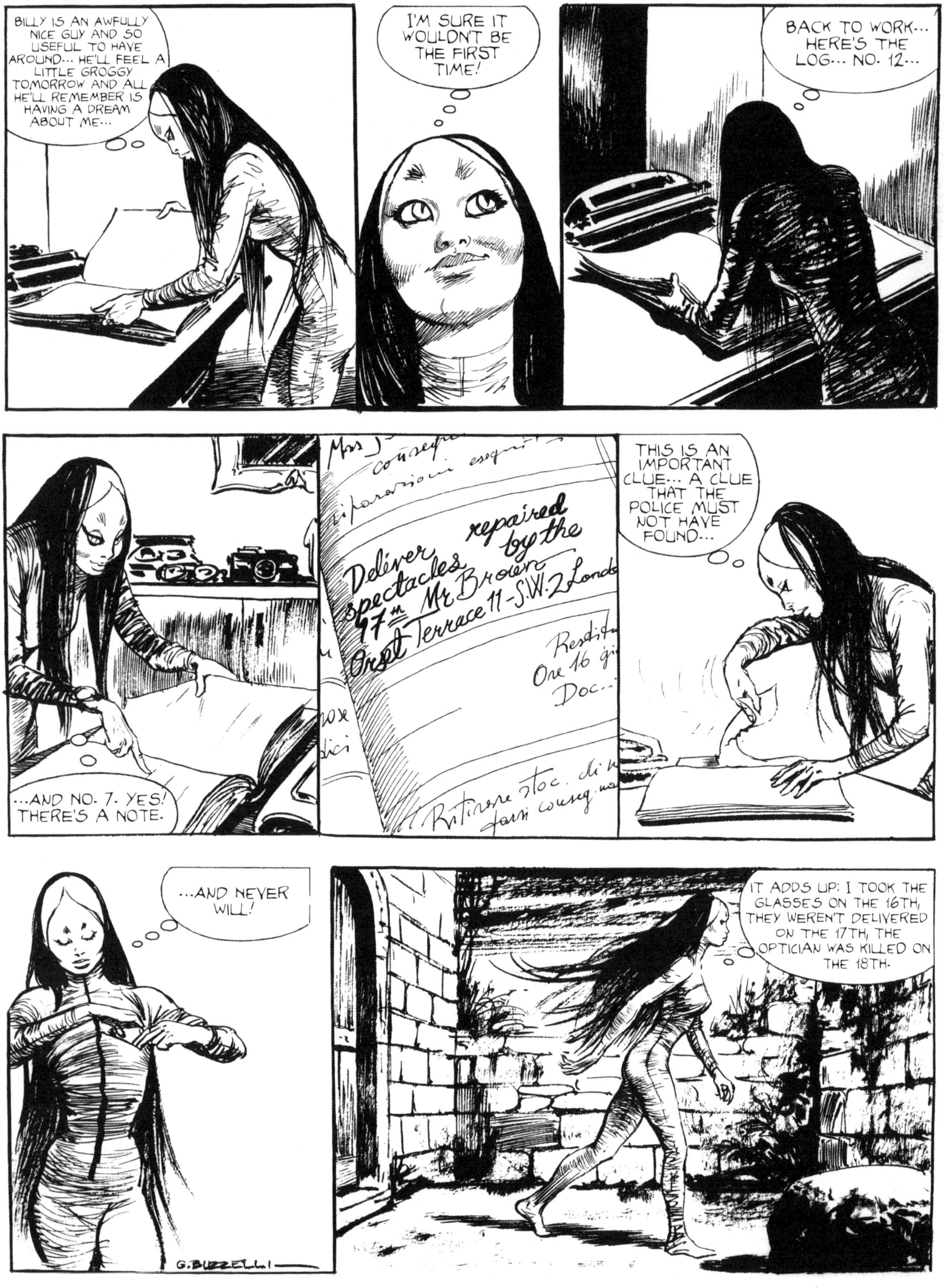
BILLY IS AN AWFULLY NICE GUY AND SO USEFUL TO HAVE AROUND... HE'LL FEEL A LITTLE GROGGY TOMORROW AND ALL HE'LL REMEMBER IS HAVING A DREAM ABOUT ME...
I'M SURE IT WOULDN'T BE THE FIRST TIME!
BACK TO WORK... HERE'S THE LOG... NO. 12...
...AND NO. 7. YES! THERE'S A NOTE.
Deliver repaired
spectacles by the
17th Mr Brown
Orset Terrace 11-S.W.2
THIS IS AN IMPORTANT CLUE... A CLUE THAT THE POLICE MUST NOT HAVE FOUND...
...AND NEVER WILL!
G. BUZZELLI
IT ADDS UP: I TOOK THE GLASSES ON THE 16TH, THEY WEREN'T DELIVERED ON THE 17TH, THE OPTICIAN WAS KILLED ON THE 18TH.

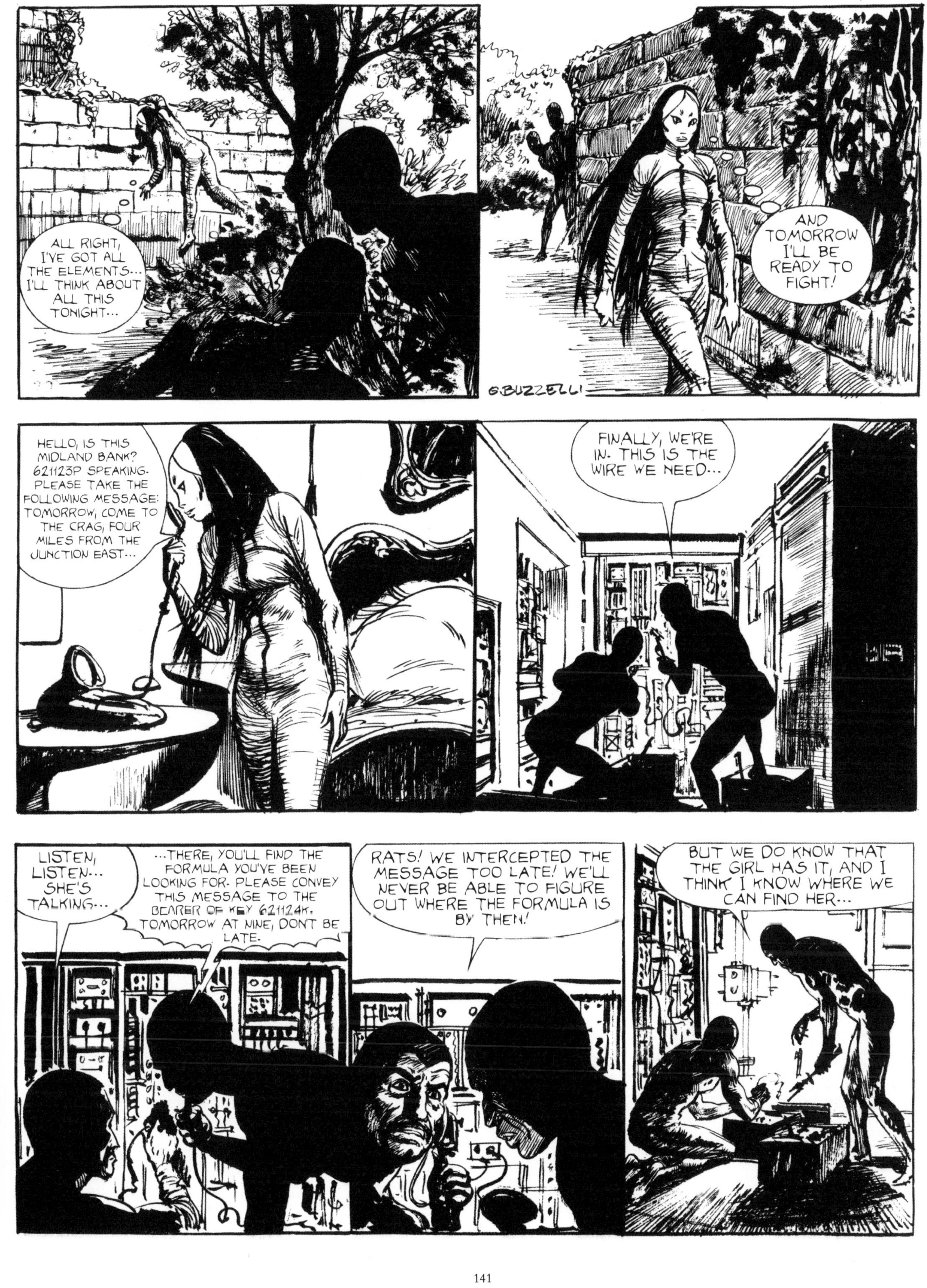
ALL RIGHT, I'VE GOT ALL THE ELEMENTS... I'LL THINK ABOUT ALL THIS TONIGHT...
AND TOMORROW I'LL BE READY TO FIGHT!
G.BUZZELLI
HELLO, IS THIS MIDLAND BANK? 621123P SPEAKING. PLEASE TAKE THE FOLLOWING MESSAGE: TOMORROW, COME TO THE CRAG, FOUR MILES FROM THE JUNCTION EAST...
FINALLY, WE'RE IN. THIS IS THE WIRE WE NEED...
LISTEN, LISTEN... SHE'S TALKING...
...THERE, YOU'LL FIND THE FORMULA YOU'VE BEEN LOOKING FOR. PLEASE CONVEY THIS MESSAGE TO THE BEARER OF KEY 621124K, TOMORROW AT NINE, DON'T BE LATE.
RATS! WE INTERCEPTED THE MESSAGE TOO LATE! WE'LL NEVER BE ABLE TO FIGURE OUT WHERE THE FORMULA IS BY THEN!
BUT WE DO KNOW THAT THE GIRL HAS IT, AND I THINK I KNOW WHERE WE CAN FIND HER...

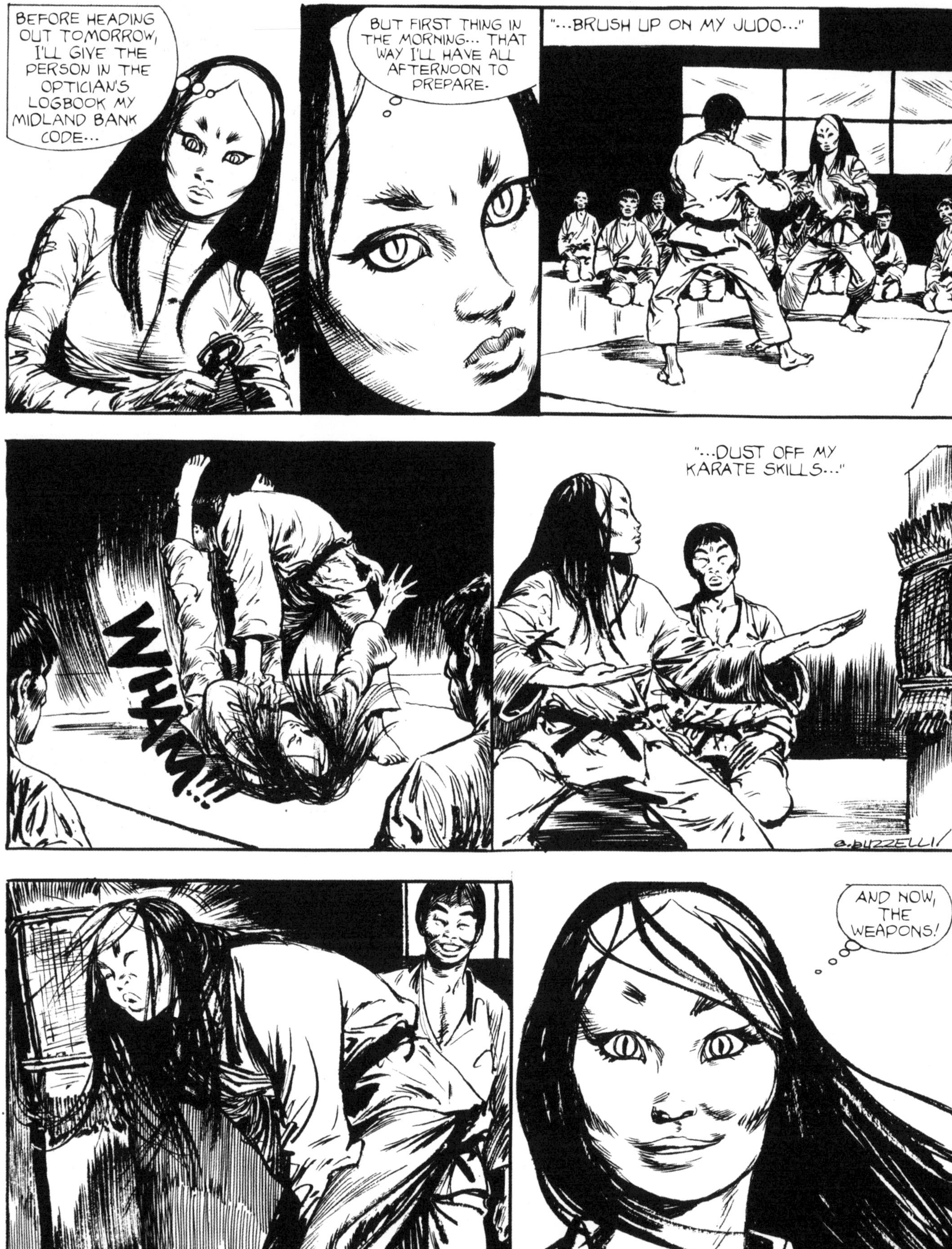
BEFORE HEADING OUT TOMORROW, I'LL GIVE THE PERSON IN THE OPTICIAN'S LOGBOOK MY MIDLAND BANK CODE...
BUT FIRST THING IN THE MORNING... THAT WAY I'LL HAVE ALL AFTERNOON TO PREPARE.
"...BRUSH UP ON MY JUDO..."
WHAM!!!
"...DUST OFF MY KARATE SKILLS..."
G. BUZZELLI
AND NOW, THE WEAPONS!

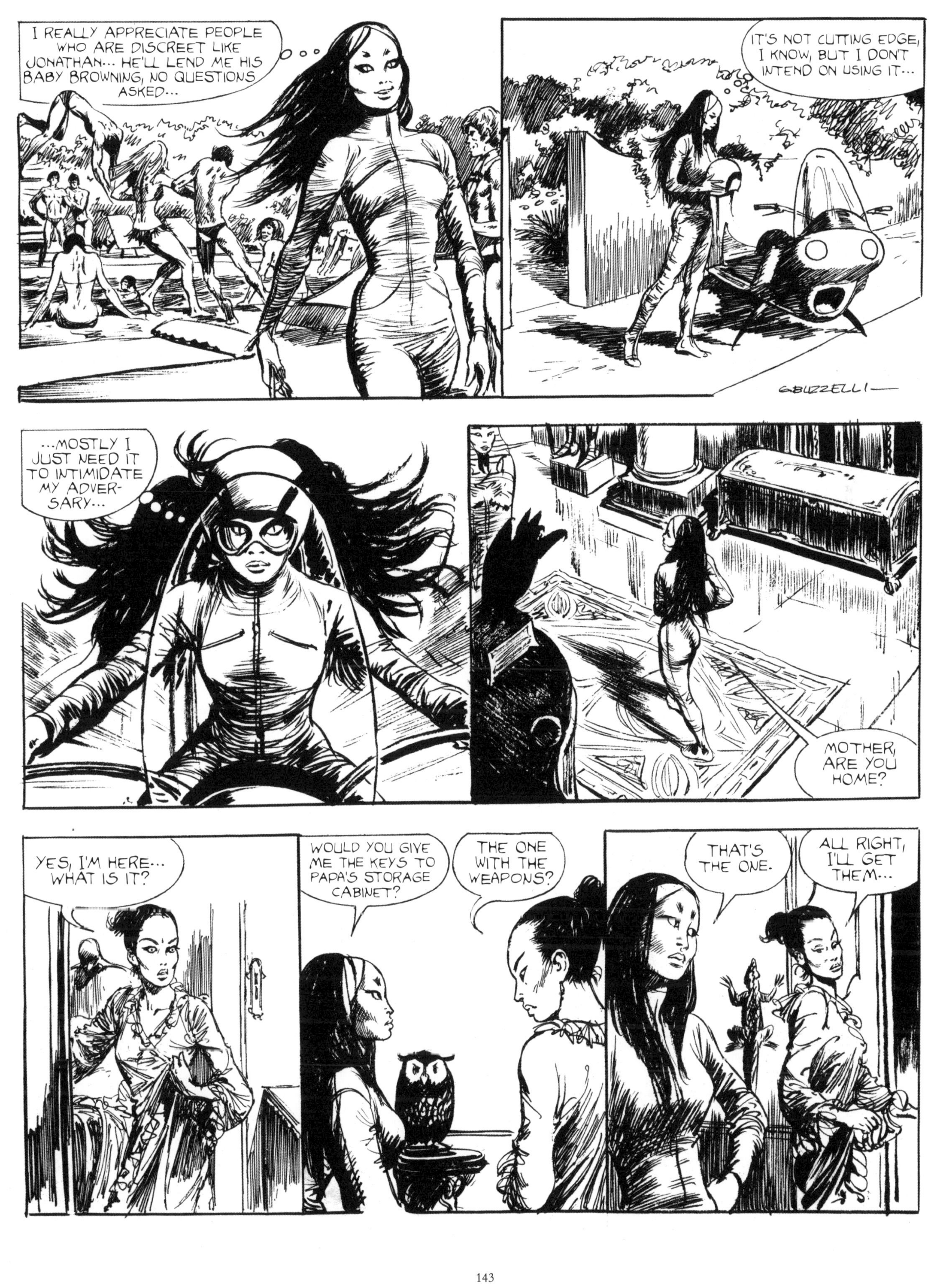
I REALLY APPRECIATE PEOPLE WHO ARE DISCREET LIKE JONATHAN... HE'LL LEND ME HIS BABY BROWNING, NO QUESTIONS ASKED...
IT'S NOT CUTTING EDGE, I KNOW, BUT I DON'T INTEND ON USING IT...
GBUZZELLI
...MOSTLY I JUST NEED IT TO INTIMIDATE MY ADVER-SARY...
MOTHER, ARE YOU HOME?
YES, I'M HERE... WHAT IS IT?
WOULD YOU GIVE ME THE KEYS TO PAPA'S STORAGE CABINET?
THE ONE WITH THE WEAPONS?
THAT'S THE ONE.
ALL RIGHT, I'LL GET THEM...

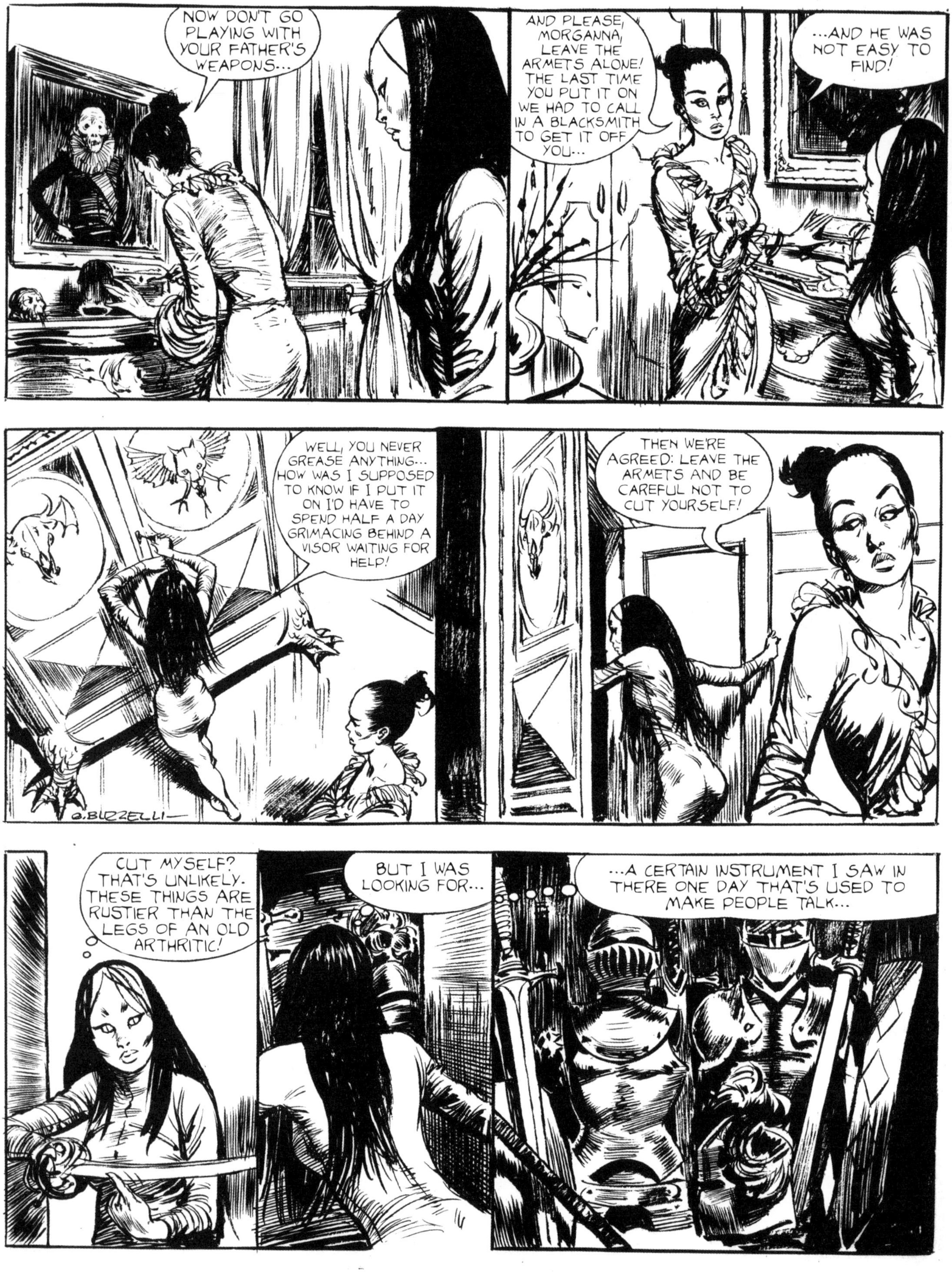
NOW DON'T GO PLAYING WITH YOUR FATHER'S WEAPONS...
AND PLEASE, MORGANNA, LEAVE THE ARMETS ALONE! THE LAST TIME YOU PUT IT ON WE HAD TO CALL IN A BLACKSMITH TO GET IT OFF YOU...
...AND HE WAS NOT EASY TO FIND!
WELL, YOU NEVER GREASE ANYTHING... HOW WAS I SUPPOSED TO KNOW IF I PUT IT ON I'D HAVE TO SPEND HALF A DAY GRIMACING BEHIND A VISOR WAITING FOR HELP!
G. BUZZELLI
THEN WE'RE AGREED: LEAVE THE ARMETS AND BE CAREFUL NOT TO CUT YOURSELF!
CUT MYSELF? THAT'S UNLIKELY. THESE THINGS ARE RUSTIER THAN THE LEGS OF AN OLD ARTHRITIC!
BUT I WAS LOOKING FOR...
...A CERTAIN INSTRUMENT I SAW IN THERE ONE DAY THAT'S USED TO MAKE PEOPLE TALK...

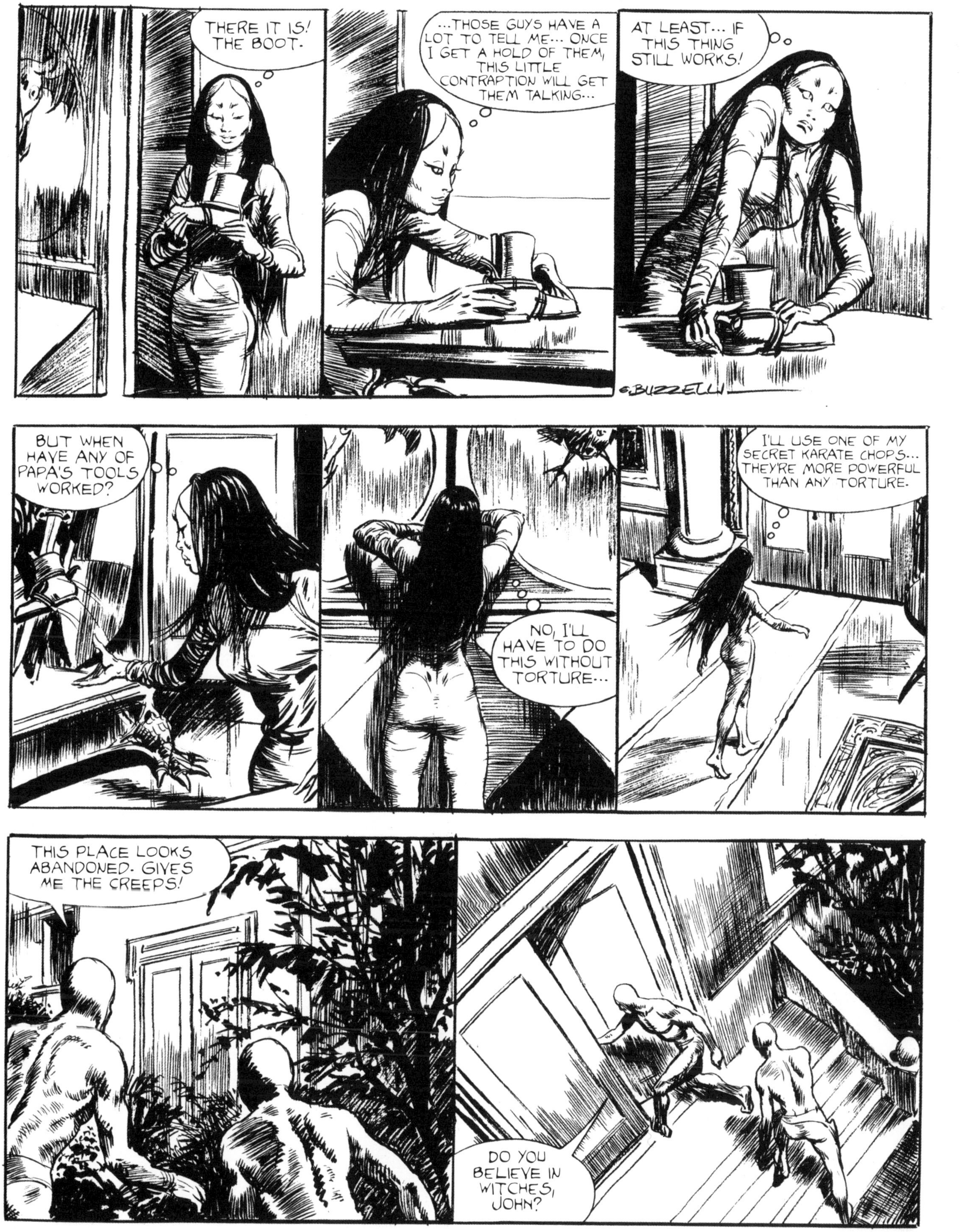
THERE IT IS! THE BOOT.
...THOSE GUYS HAVE A LOT TO TELL ME... ONCE I GET A HOLD OF THEM, THIS LITTLE CONTRAPTION WILL GET THEM TALKING...
AT LEAST... IF THIS THING STILL WORKS!
BUZZELLI
BUT WHEN HAVE ANY OF PAPA'S TOOLS WORKED?
NO, I'LL HAVE TO DO THIS WITHOUT TORTURE...
I'LL USE ONE OF MY SECRET KARATE CHOPS... THEY'RE MORE POWERFUL THAN ANY TORTURE.
THIS PLACE LOOKS ABANDONED. GIVES ME THE CREEPS!
DO YOU BELIEVE IN WITCHES, JOHN?

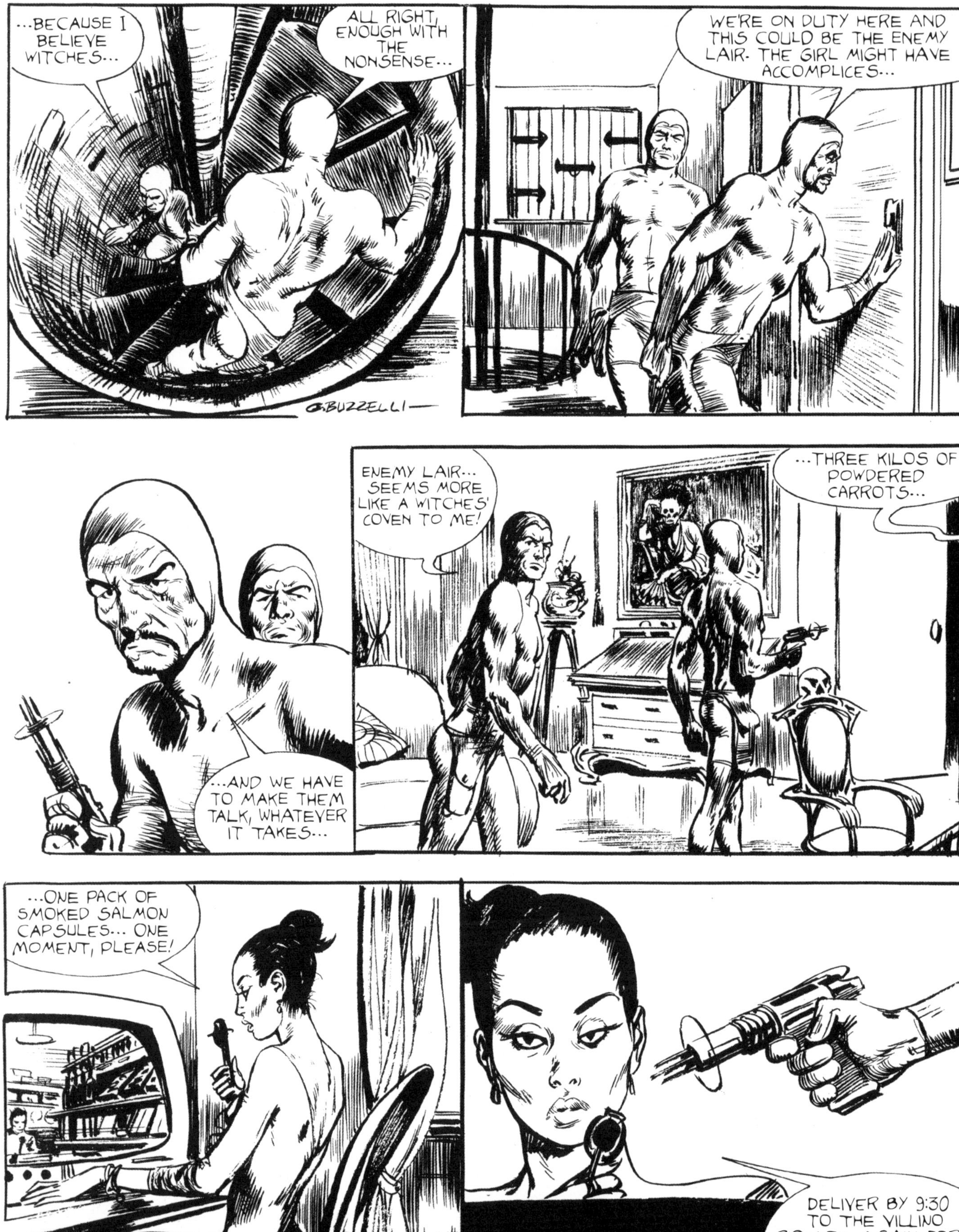
...BECAUSE I BELIEVE WITCHES...
ALL RIGHT, ENOUGH WITH THE NONSENSE...
G. BUZZELLI
WE'RE ON DUTY HERE AND THIS COULD BE THE ENEMY LAIR. THE GIRL MIGHT HAVE ACCOMPLICES...
...AND WE HAVE TO MAKE THEM TALK, WHATEVER IT TAKES...
ENEMY LAIR... SEEMS MORE LIKE A WITCHES' COVEN TO ME!
...THREE KILOS OF POWDERED CARROTS...
...ONE PACK OF SMOKED SALMON CAPSULES... ONE MOMENT, PLEASE!
DELIVER BY 9:30 TO THE VILLINO RIDENTE. AGAIN, FOR CUSTOMER NO. 341600 B. OYER AND OUT.

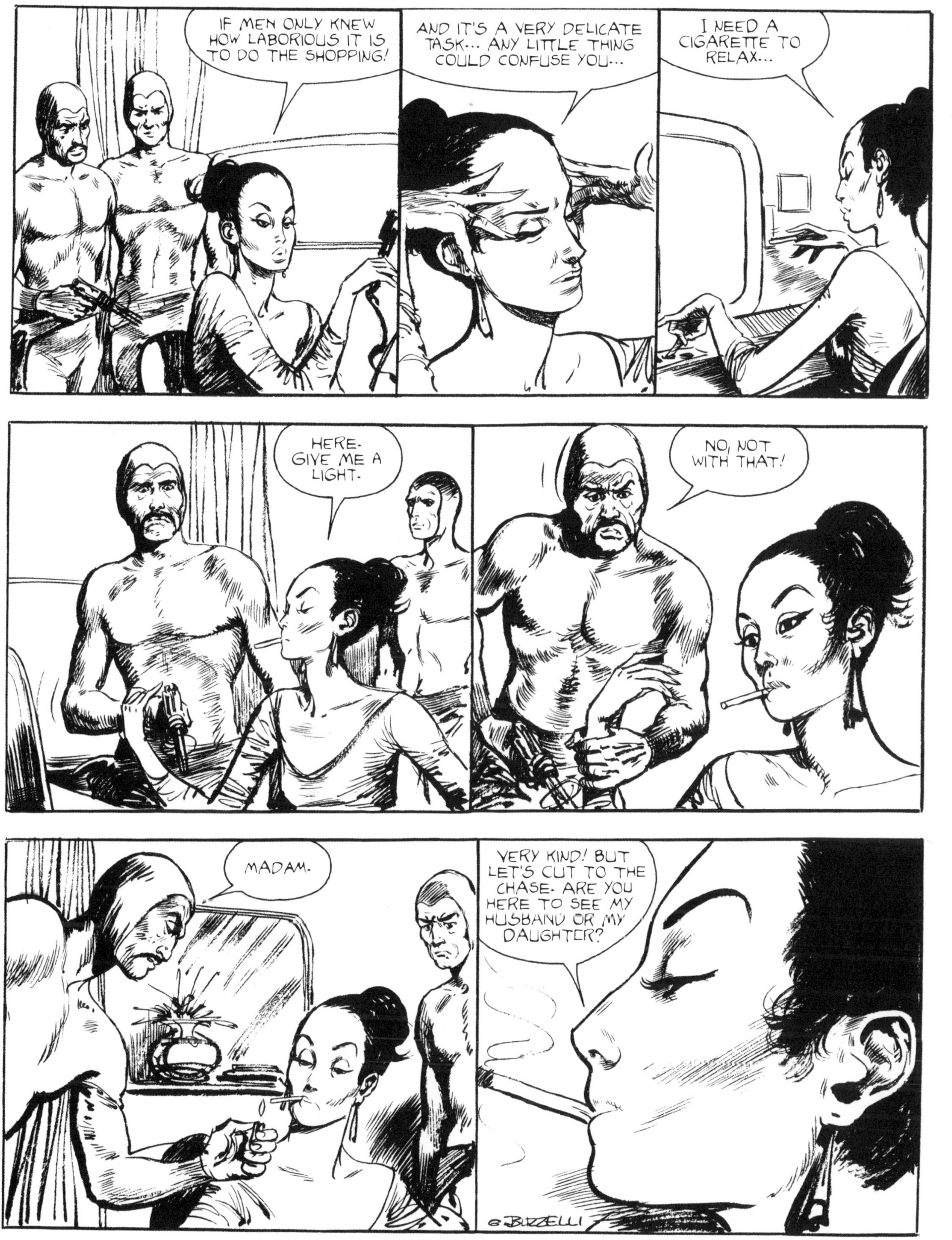
IF MEN ONLY KNEW HOW LABORIOUS IT IS TO DO THE SHOPPING!
AND IT'S A VERY DELICATE TASK... ANY LITTLE THING COULD CONFUSE YOU...
I NEED A CIGARETTE TO RELAX...
HERE. GIVE ME A LIGHT.
NO, NOT WITH THAT!
MADAM.
VERY KIND! BUT LET'S CUT TO THE CHASE. ARE YOU HERE TO SEE MY HUSBAND OR MY DAUGHTER?
G. BUZZELLI

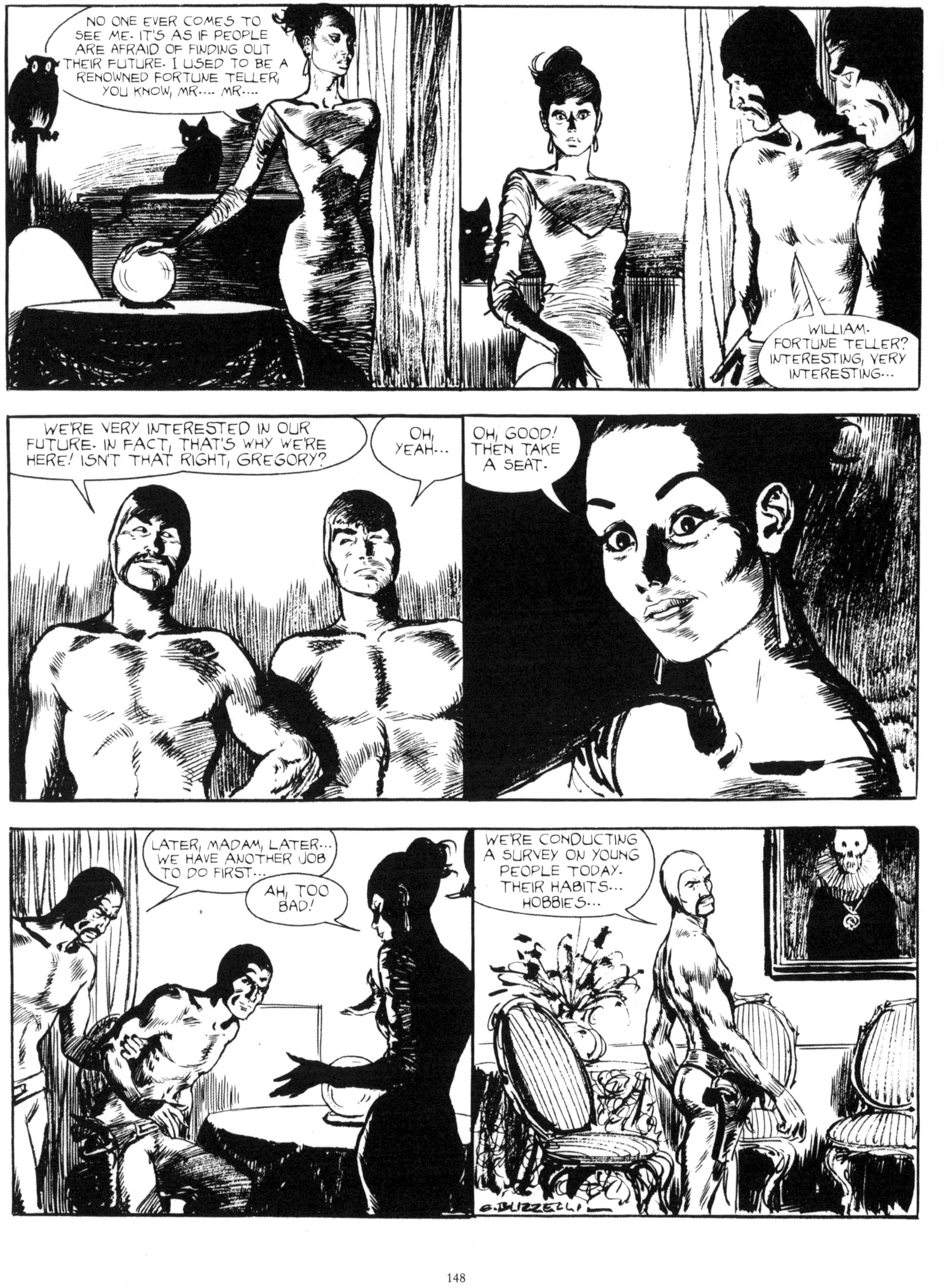
NO ONE EVER COMES TO SEE ME. IT'S AS IF PEOPLE ARE AFRAID OF FINDING OUT THEIR FUTURE. I USED TO BE A RENOWNED FORTUNE TELLER, YOU KNOW, MR.... MR....
WILLIAM. FORTUNE TELLER? INTERESTING, VERY INTERESTING...
WE'RE VERY INTERESTED IN OUR FUTURE. IN FACT, THAT'S WHY WE'RE HERE! ISN'T THAT RIGHT, GREGORY?
OH, YEAH...
OH, GOOD! THEN TAKE A SEAT.
LATER, MADAM, LATER... WE HAVE ANOTHER JOB TO DO FIRST...
AH, TOO BAD!
WE'RE CONDUCTING A SURVEY ON YOUNG PEOPLE TODAY. THEIR HABITS... HOBBIES...
G. BUZZELLI

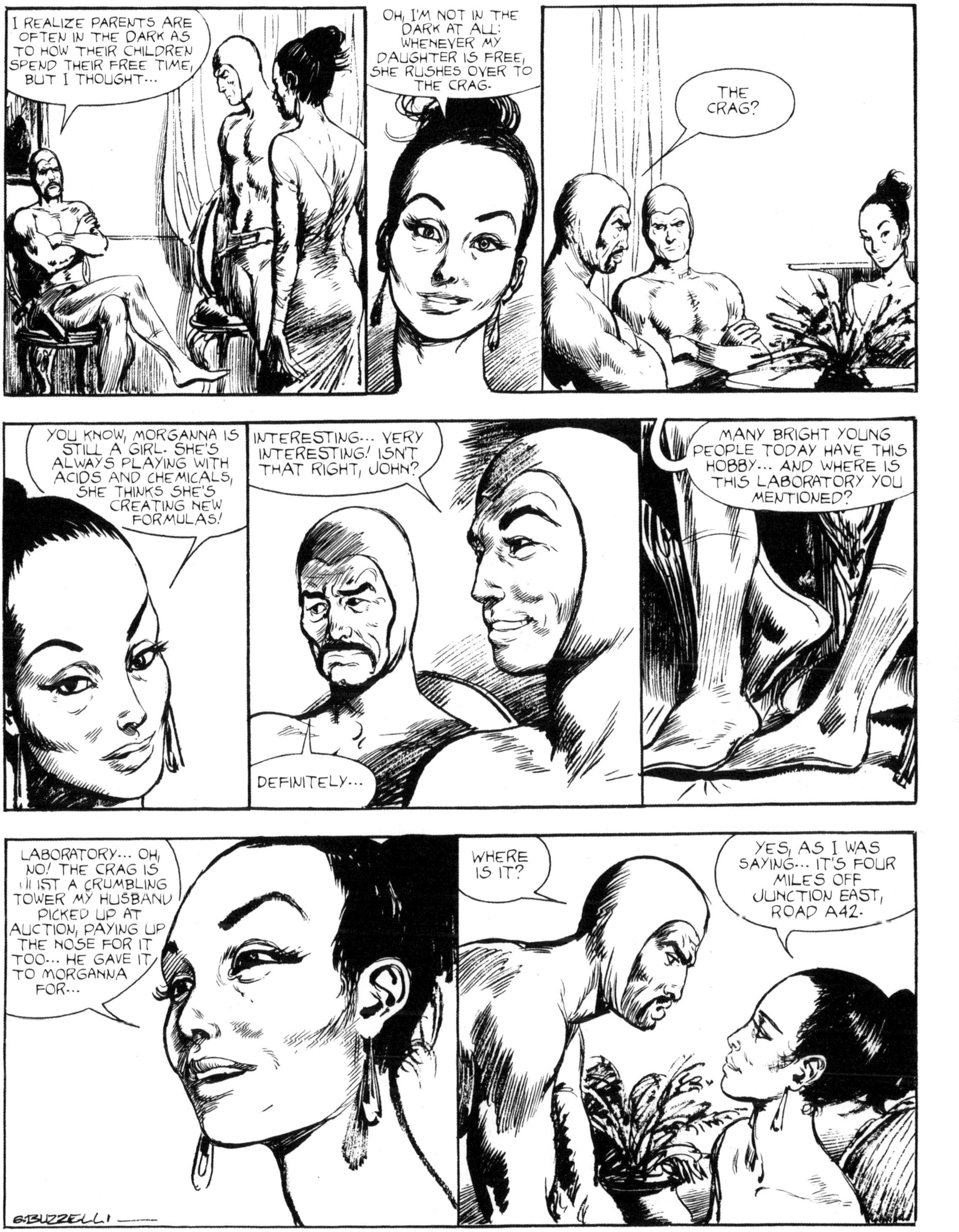

I REALIZE PARENTS ARE OFTEN IN THE DARK AS TO HOW THEIR CHILDREN SPEND THEIR FREE TIME, BUT I THOUGHT...
OH, I'M NOT IN THE DARK AT ALL: WHENEVER MY DAUGHTER IS FREE, SHE RUSHES OVER TO THE CRAG.
THE CRAG?
YOU KNOW, MORGANNA IS STILL A GIRL. SHE'S ALWAYS PLAYING WITH ACIDS AND CHEMICALS, SHE THINKS SHE'S CREATING NEW FORMULAS!
INTERESTING... VERY INTERESTING! ISN'T THAT RIGHT, JOHN?
DEFINITELY...
MANY BRIGHT YOUNG PEOPLE TODAY HAVE THIS HOBBY... AND WHERE IS THIS LABORATORY YOU MENTIONED?
LABORATORY... OH, NO! THE CRAG IS JUST A CRUMBLING TOWER MY HUSBAND PICKED UP AT AUCTION, PAYING UP THE NOSE FOR IT TOO... HE GAVE IT TO MORGANNA FOR...
G.BUZZELLI
WHERE IS IT?
YES, AS I WAS SAYING... IT'S FOUR MILES OFF JUNCTION EAST, ROAD A42.

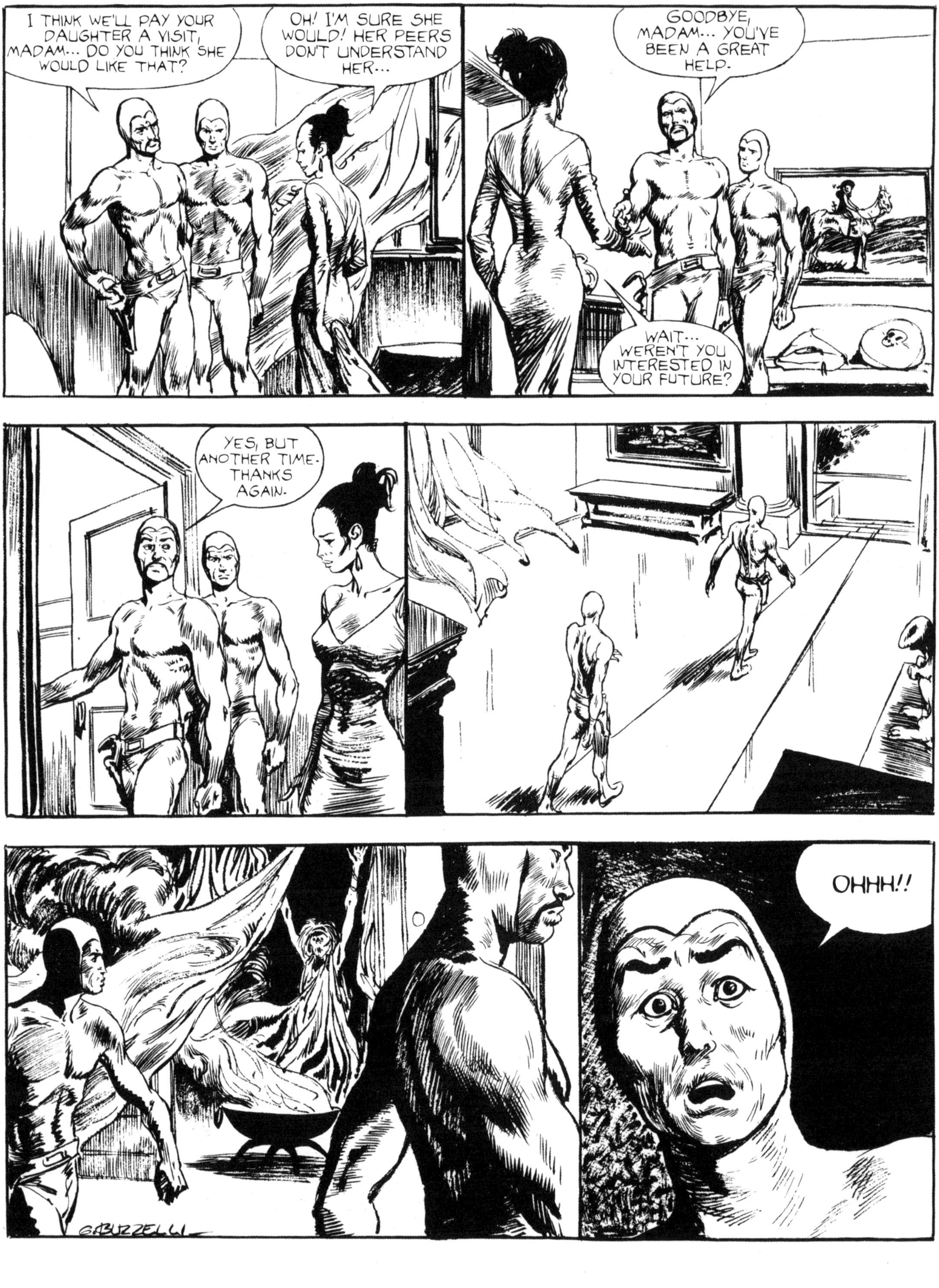

I THINK WE'LL PAY YOUR DAUGHTER A VISIT, MADAM... DO YOU THINK SHE WOULD LIKE THAT?
OH! I'M SURE SHE WOULD! HER PEERS DON'T UNDERSTAND HER...
GOODBYE, MADAM... YOU'VE BEEN A GREAT HELP.
WAIT... WEREN'T YOU INTERESTED IN YOUR FUTURE?
YES, BUT ANOTHER TIME. THANKS AGAIN.
GABURZELLI
OHHH!!

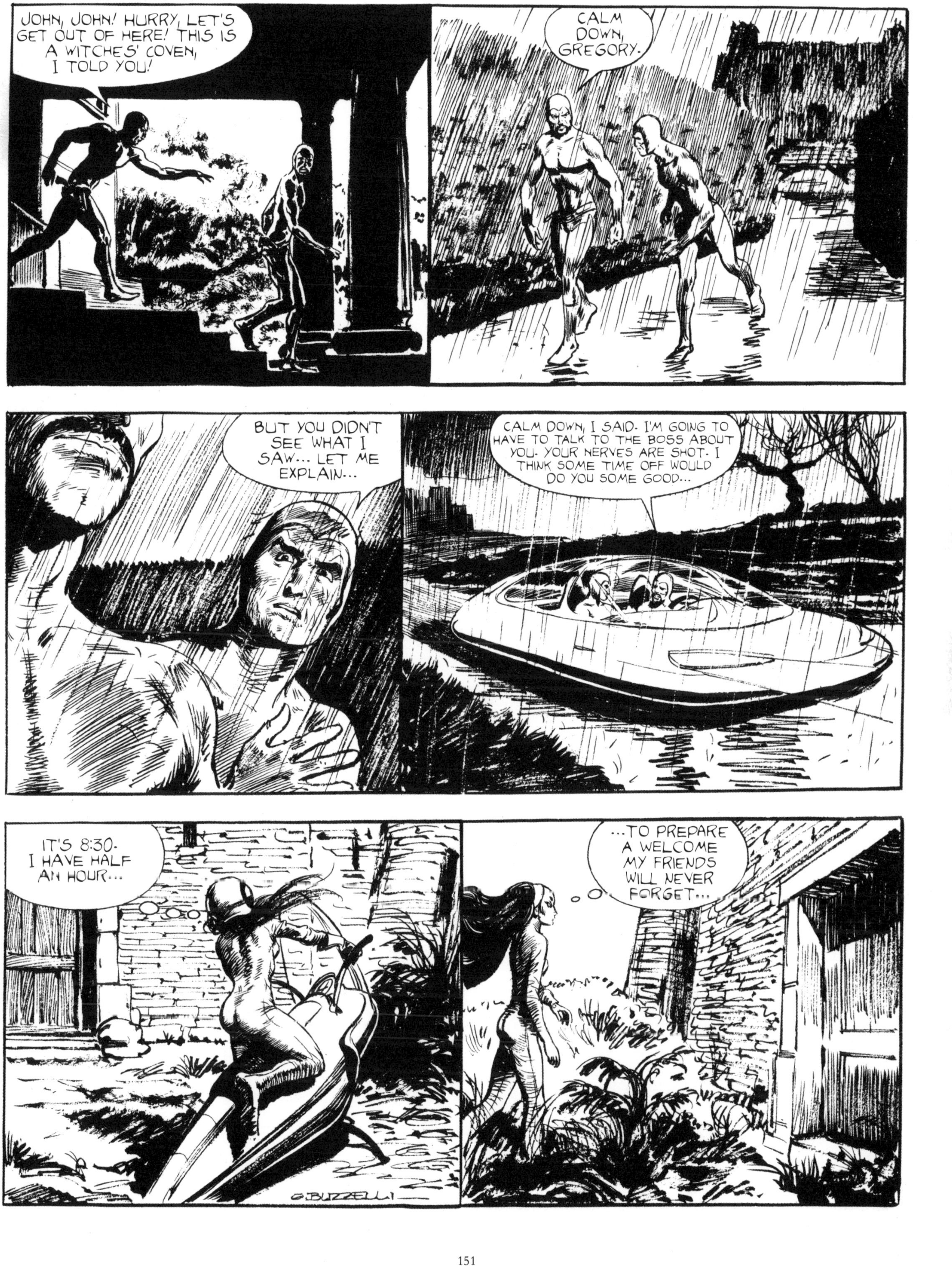

JOHN, JOHN! HURRY, LET'S GET OUT OF HERE! THIS IS A WITCHES' COVEN, I TOLD YOU!
CALM DOWN, GREGORY.
BUT YOU DIDN'T SEE WHAT I SAW... LET ME EXPLAIN...
CALM DOWN, I SAID. I'M GOING TO HAVE TO TALK TO THE BOSS ABOUT YOU. YOUR NERVES ARE SHOT. I THINK SOME TIME OFF WOULD DO YOU SOME GOOD...
IT'S 8:30. I HAVE HALF AN HOUR...
...TO PREPARE A WELCOME MY FRIENDS WILL NEVER FORGET...
G. BUZZELLI

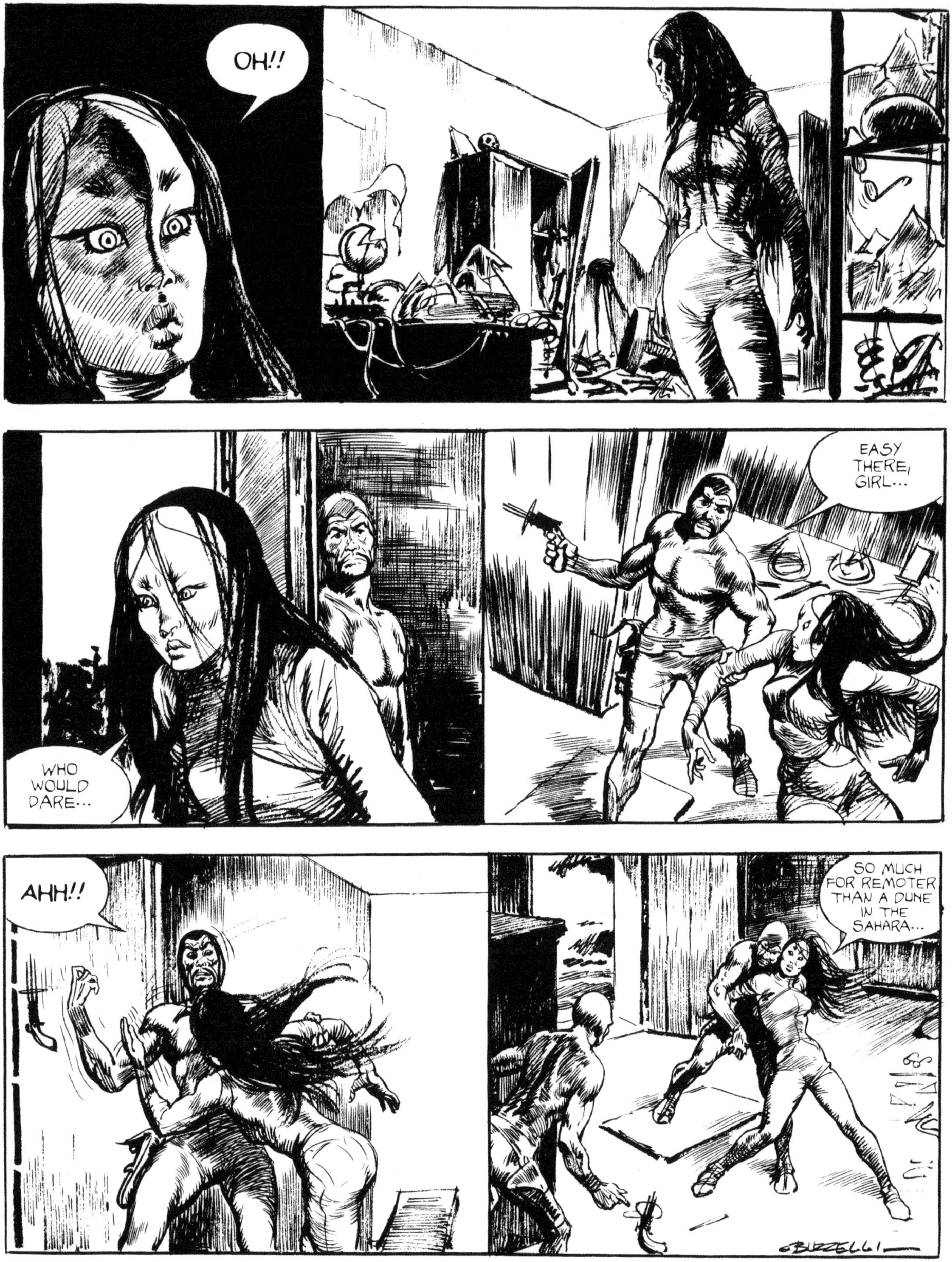
OH!!
WHO WOULD DARE...
EASY THERE, GIRL...
AHH!!
SO MUCH FOR REMOTER THAN A DUNE IN THE SAHARA...
BUZZELLI

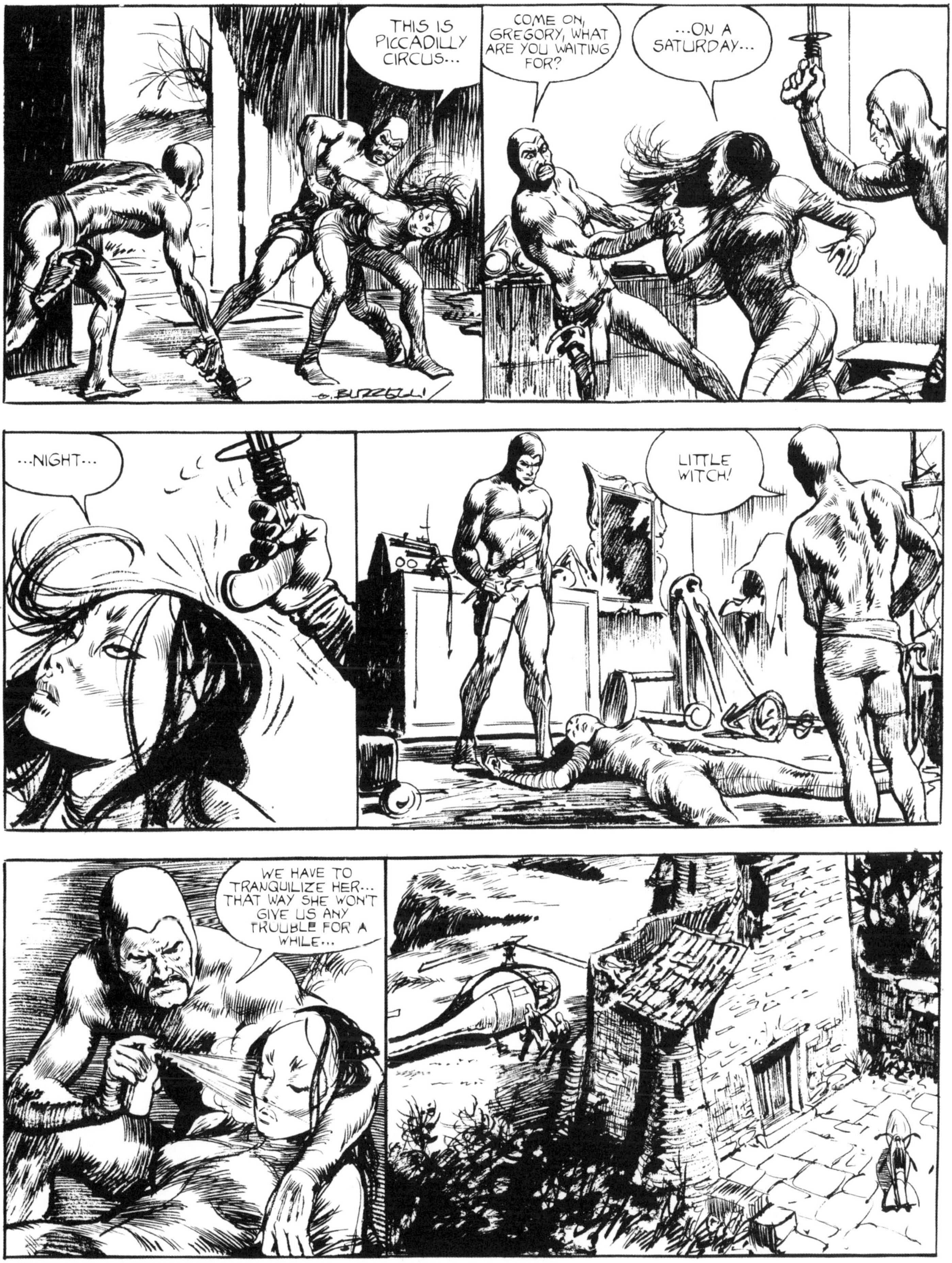
THIS IS PICCADILLY CIRCUS...
G. BUZZELLI
COME ON, GREGORY, WHAT ARE YOU WAITING FOR?
...ON A SATURDAY...
...NIGHT...
LITTLE WITCH!
WE HAVE TO TRANQUILIZE HER... THAT WAY SHE WON'T GIVE US ANY TROUBLE FOR A WHILE...

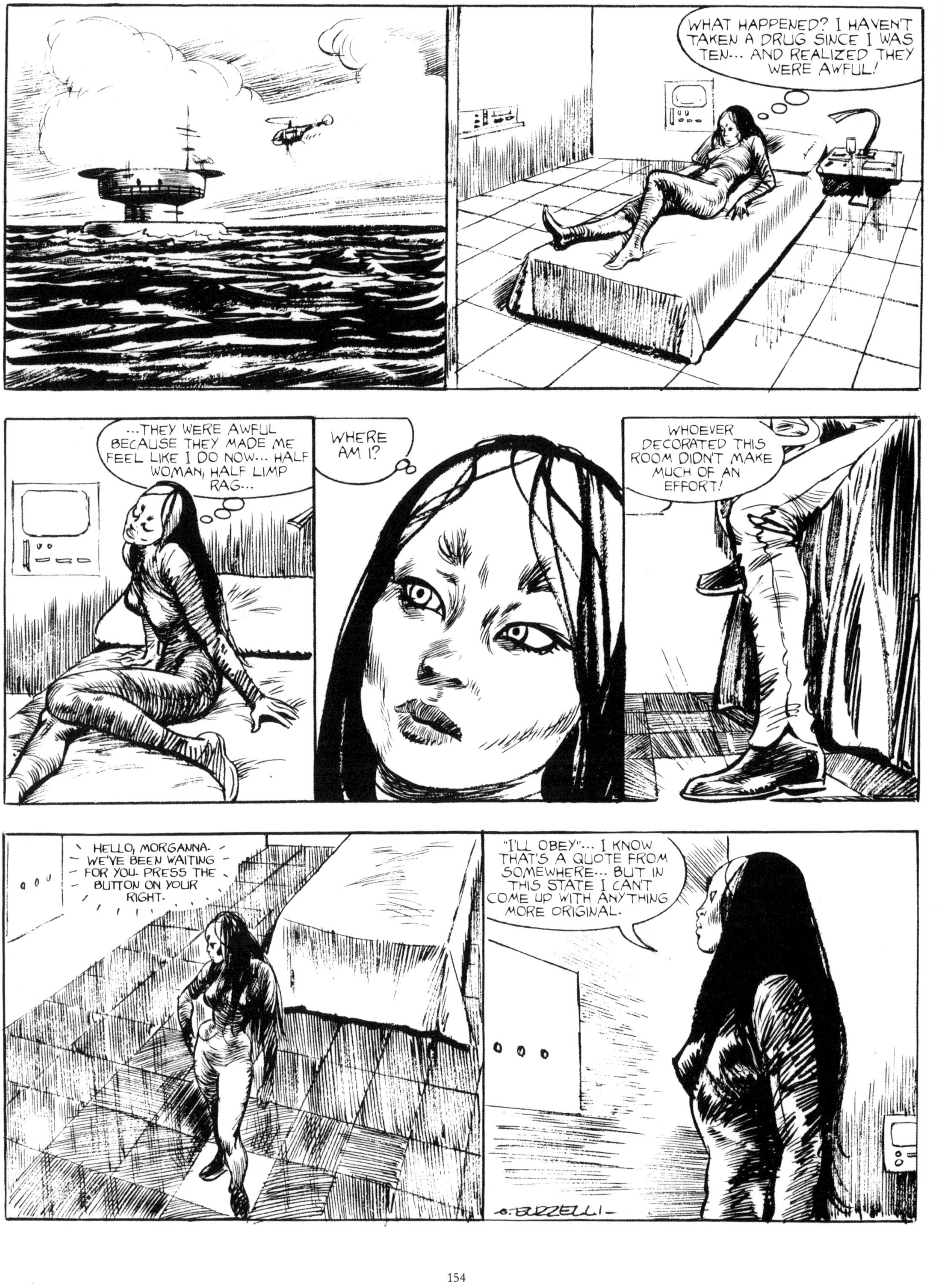
WHAT HAPPENED? I HAVEN'T TAKEN A DRUG SINCE I WAS TEN... AND REALIZED THEY WERE AWFUL!
...THEY WERE AWFUL BECAUSE THEY MADE ME FEEL LIKE I DO NOW... HALF WOMAN, HALF LIMP RAG...
WHERE AM I?
WHOEVER DECORATED THIS ROOM DIDN'T MAKE MUCH OF AN EFFORT!
HELLO, MORGANNA. WE'VE BEEN WAITING FOR YOU. PRESS THE BUTTON ON YOUR RIGHT.
"I'LL OBEY"... I KNOW THAT'S A QUOTE FROM SOMEWHERE... BUT IN THIS STATE I CAN'T COME UP WITH ANYTHING MORE ORIGINAL.
G. BUZZELLI

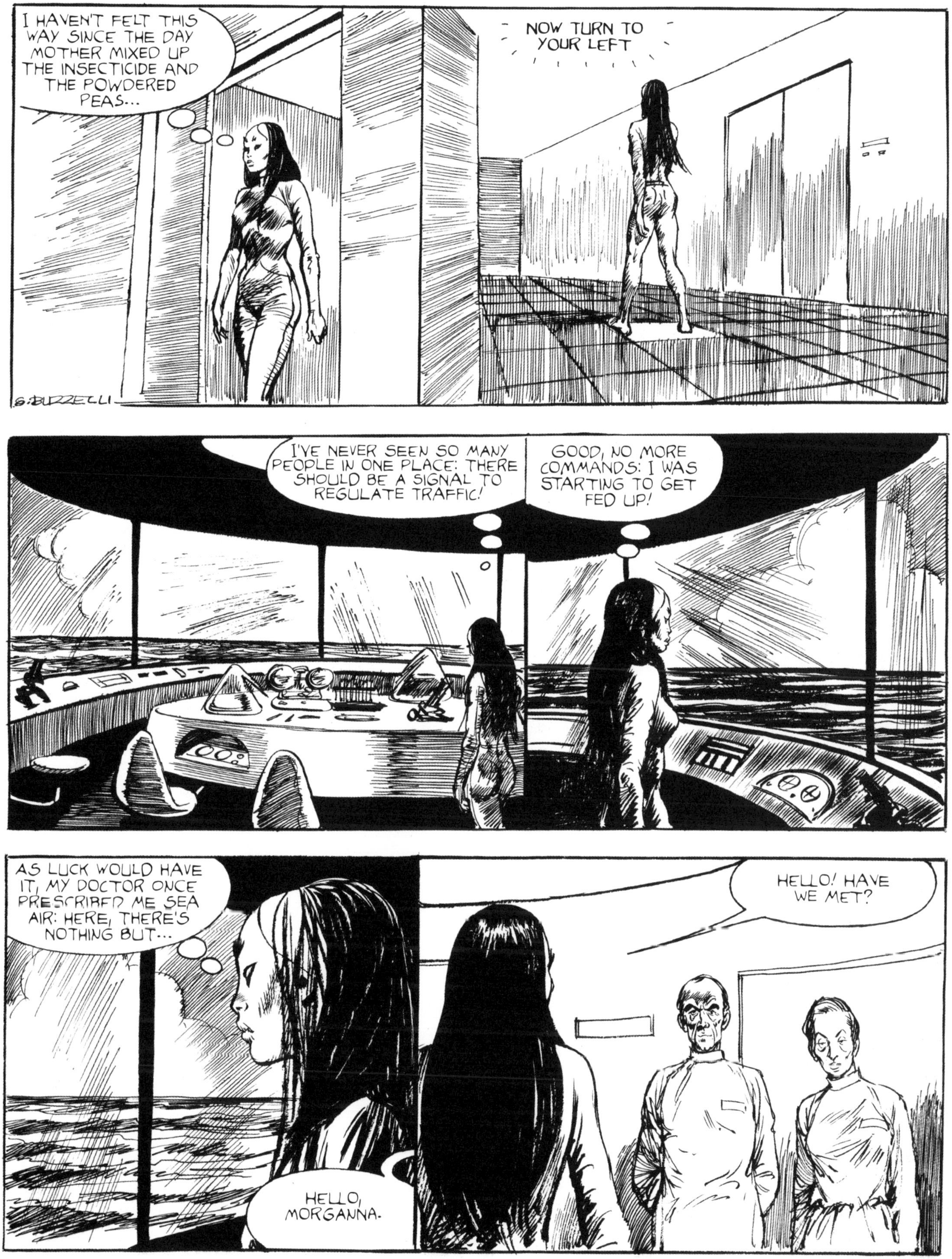
I HAVEN'T FELT THIS WAY SINCE THE DAY MOTHER MIXED UP THE INSECTICIDE AND THE POWDERED PEAS...
S. BUZZELLI
NOW TURN TO YOUR LEFT
I'VE NEVER SEEN SO MANY PEOPLE IN ONE PLACE: THERE SHOULD BE A SIGNAL TO REGULATE TRAFFIC!
GOOD, NO MORE COMMANDS: I WAS STARTING TO GET FED UP!
AS LUCK WOULD HAVE IT, MY DOCTOR ONCE PRESCRIBED ME SEA AIR: HERE, THERE'S NOTHING BUT...
HELLO! HAVE WE MET?
HELLO, MORGANNA.

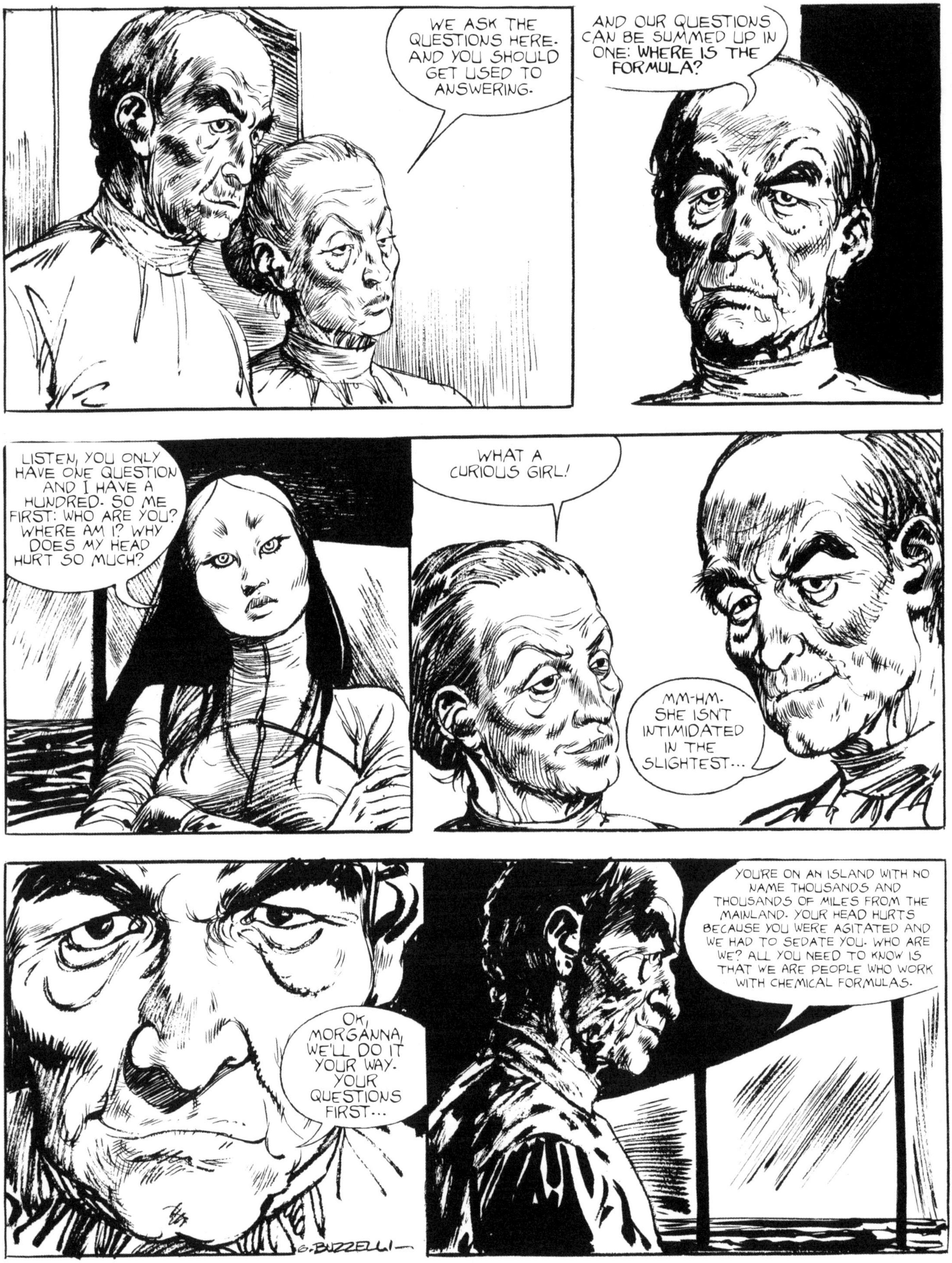
WE ASK THE QUESTIONS HERE. AND YOU SHOULD GET USED TO ANSWERING.
AND OUR QUESTIONS CAN BE SUMMED UP IN ONE: WHERE IS THE FORMULA?
LISTEN, YOU ONLY HAVE ONE QUESTION AND I HAVE A HUNDRED. SO ME FIRST: WHO ARE YOU? WHERE AM I? WHY DOES MY HEAD HURT SO MUCH?
WHAT A CURIOUS GIRL!
MM-HM. SHE ISN'T INTIMIDATED IN THE SLIGHTEST...
OK, MORGANNA, WE'LL DO IT YOUR WAY. YOUR QUESTIONS FIRST...
G. BUZZELLI
YOU'RE ON AN ISLAND WITH NO NAME THOUSANDS AND THOUSANDS OF MILES FROM THE MAINLAND. YOUR HEAD HURTS BECAUSE YOU WERE AGITATED AND WE HAD TO SEDATE YOU. WHO ARE WE? ALL YOU NEED TO KNOW IS THAT WE ARE PEOPLE WHO WORK WITH CHEMICAL FORMULAS.

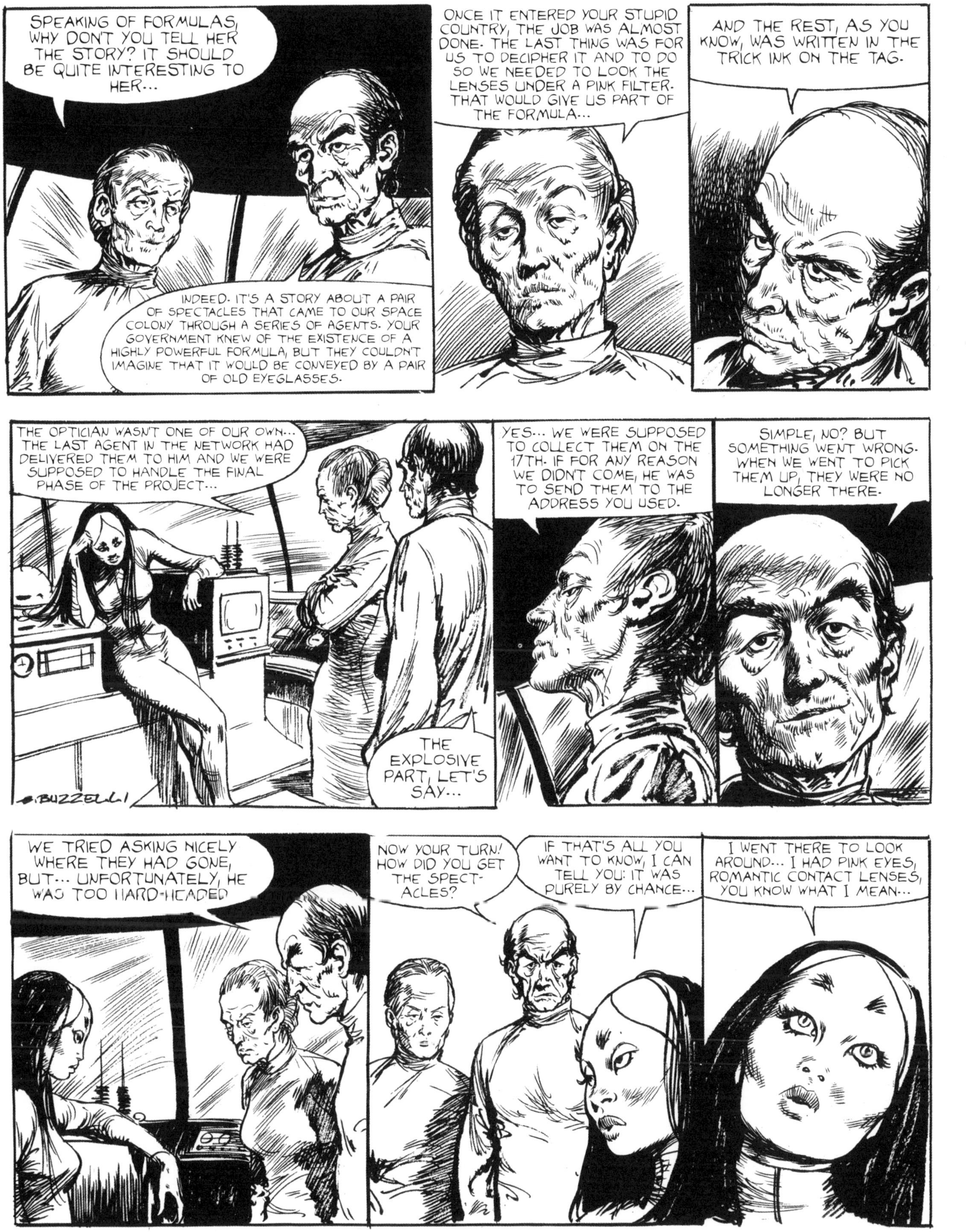
SPEAKING OF FORMULAS, WHY DON'T YOU TELL HER THE STORY? IT SHOULD BE QUITE INTERESTING TO HER...
INDEED. IT'S A STORY ABOUT A PAIR OF SPECTACLES THAT CAME TO OUR SPACE COLONY THROUGH A SERIES OF AGENTS. YOUR GOVERNMENT KNEW OF THE EXISTENCE OF A HIGHLY POWERFUL FORMULA, BUT THEY COULDN'T IMAGINE THAT IT WOULD BE CONVEYED BY A PAIR OF OLD EYEGLASSES.
ONCE IT ENTERED YOUR STUPID COUNTRY, THE JOB WAS ALMOST DONE. THE LAST THING WAS FOR US TO DECIPHER IT AND TO DO SO WE NEEDED TO LOOK THE LENSES UNDER A PINK FILTER. THAT WOULD GIVE US PART OF THE FORMULA...
AND THE REST, AS YOU KNOW, WAS WRITTEN IN THE TRICK INK ON THE TAG.
THE OPTICIAN WASN'T ONE OF OUR OWN... THE LAST AGENT IN THE NETWORK HAD DELIVERED THEM TO HIM AND WE WERE SUPPOSED TO HANDLE THE FINAL PHASE OF THE PROJECT...
THE EXPLOSIVE PART, LET'S SAY...
YES... WE WERE SUPPOSED TO COLLECT THEM ON THE 17TH. IF FOR ANY REASON WE DIDN'T COME, HE WAS TO SEND THEM TO THE ADDRESS YOU USED.
SIMPLE, NO? BUT SOMETHING WENT WRONG. WHEN WE WENT TO PICK THEM UP, THEY WERE NO LONGER THERE.
WE TRIED ASKING NICELY WHERE THEY HAD GONE, BUT... UNFORTUNATELY, HE WAS TOO HARD-HEADED
NOW YOUR TURN! HOW DID YOU GET THE SPECT-ACLES?
IF THAT'S ALL YOU WANT TO KNOW, I CAN TELL YOU: IT WAS PURELY BY CHANCE...
I WENT THERE TO LOOK AROUND... I HAD PINK EYES, ROMANTIC CONTACT LENSES, YOU KNOW WHAT I MEAN...

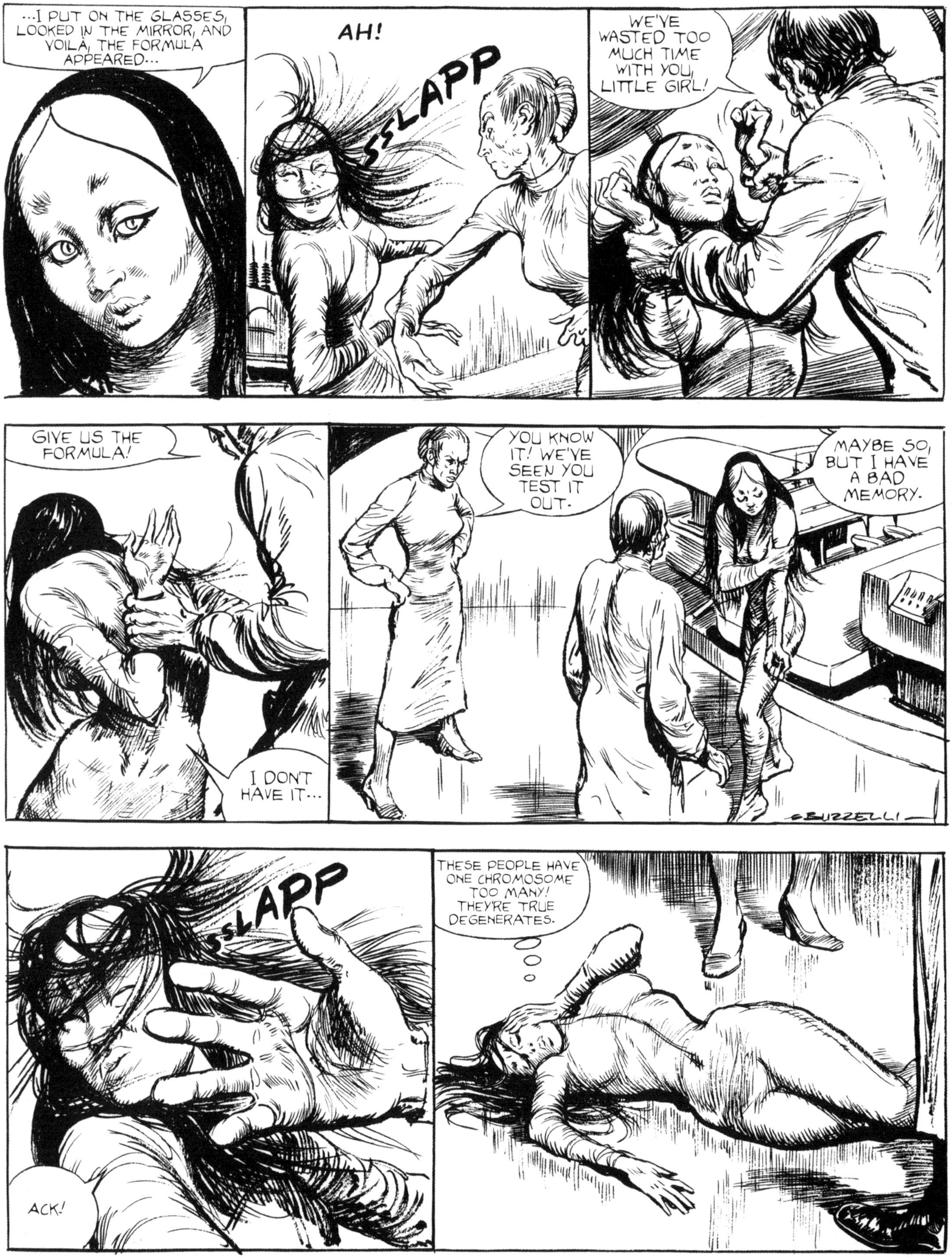
...I PUT ON THE GLASSES, LOOKED IN THE MIRROR, AND VOILÀ, THE FORMULA APPEARED...
AH!
SSLAPP
WE'VE WASTED TOO MUCH TIME WITH YOU, LITTLE GIRL!
GIVE US THE FORMULA!
I DON'T HAVE IT...
YOU KNOW IT! WE'VE SEEN YOU TEST IT OUT.
MAYBE SO, BUT I HAVE A BAD MEMORY.
G. BUZZELLI
SSLAPP
ACK!
THESE PEOPLE HAVE ONE CHROMOSOME TOO MANY! THEY'RE TRUE DEGENERATES.

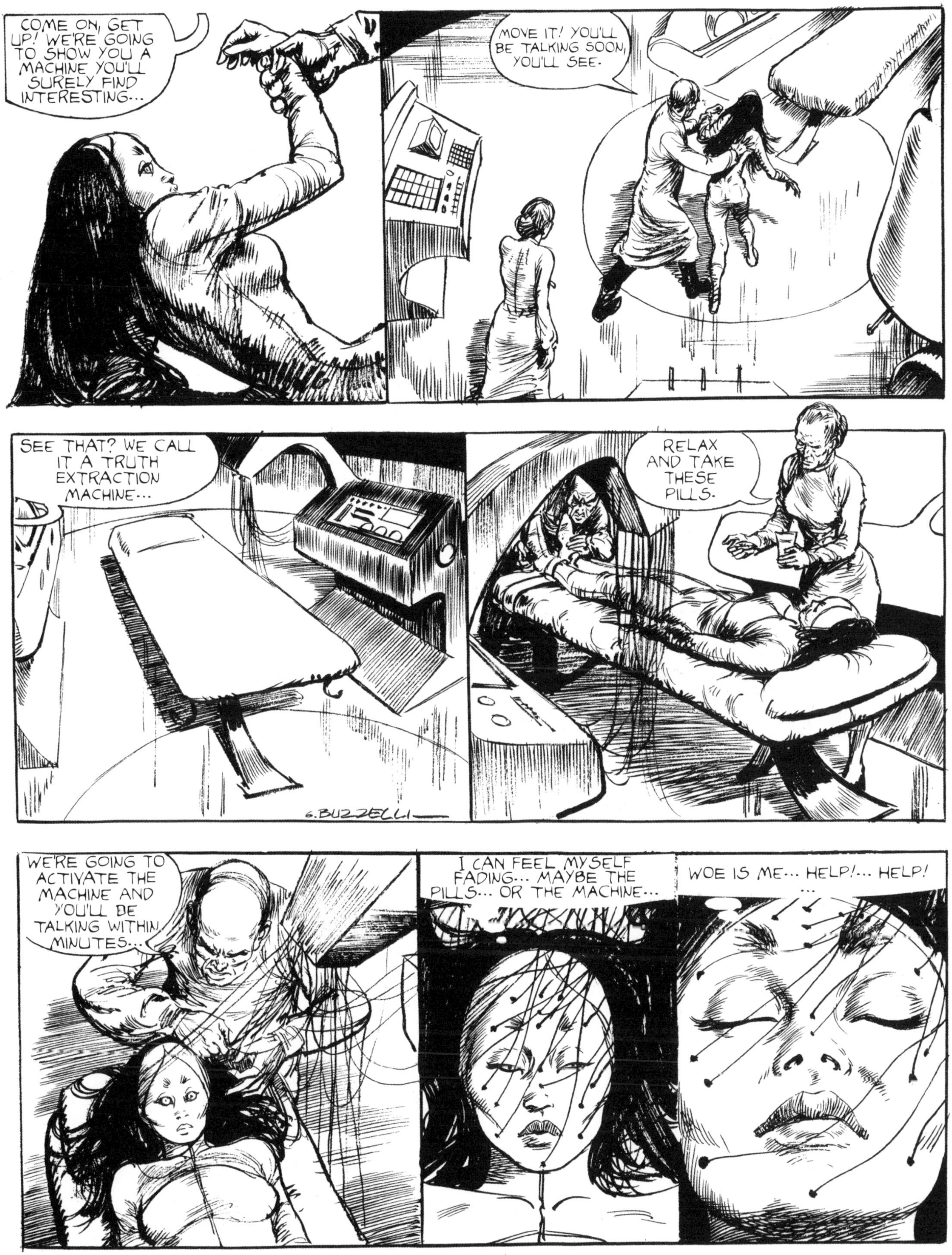
COME ON, GET UP! WE'RE GOING TO SHOW YOU A MACHINE YOU'LL SURELY FIND INTERESTING...
MOVE IT! YOU'LL BE TALKING SOON, YOU'LL SEE.
SEE THAT? WE CALL IT A TRUTH EXTRACTION MACHINE...
RELAX AND TAKE THESE PILLS.
G. BUZZELLI
WE'RE GOING TO ACTIVATE THE MACHINE AND YOU'LL BE TALKING WITHIN MINUTES...
I CAN FEEL MYSELF FADING... MAYBE THE PILLS... OR THE MACHINE...
WOE IS ME... HELP!... HELP! ...

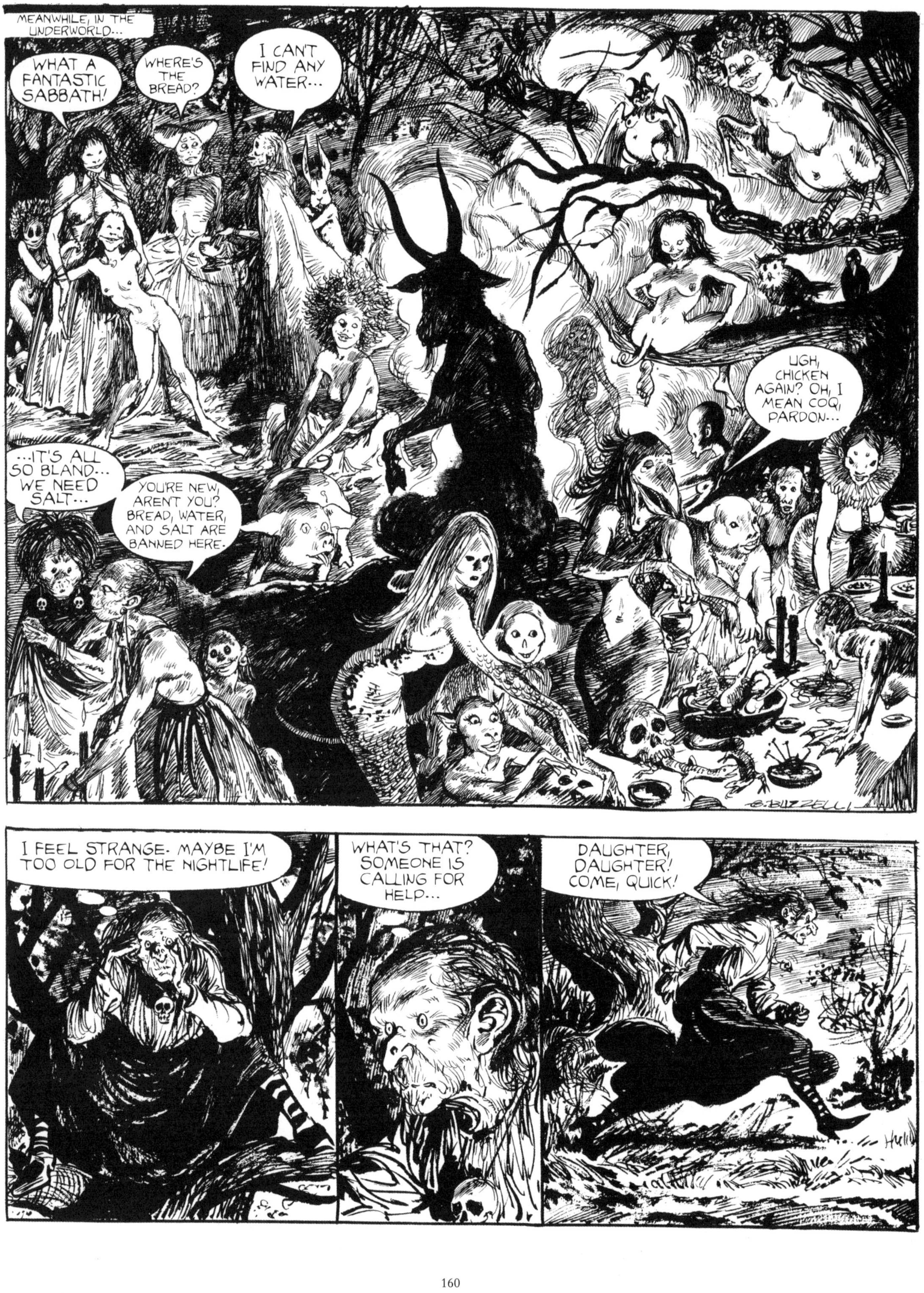
MEANWHILE, IN THE UNDERWORLD...
WHAT A FANTASTIC SABBATH!
WHERE'S THE BREAD?
I CAN'T FIND ANY WATER...
UGH, CHICKEN AGAIN? OH, I MEAN COQ, PARDON...
...IT'S ALL SO BLAND... WE NEED SALT...
YOU'RE NEW, AREN'T YOU? BREAD, WATER, AND SALT ARE BANNED HERE.
G. BUZZELLI
I FEEL STRANGE- MAYBE I'M TOO OLD FOR THE NIGHTLIFE!
WHAT'S THAT? SOMEONE IS CALLING FOR HELP...
DAUGHTER, DAUGHTER! COME, QUICK!

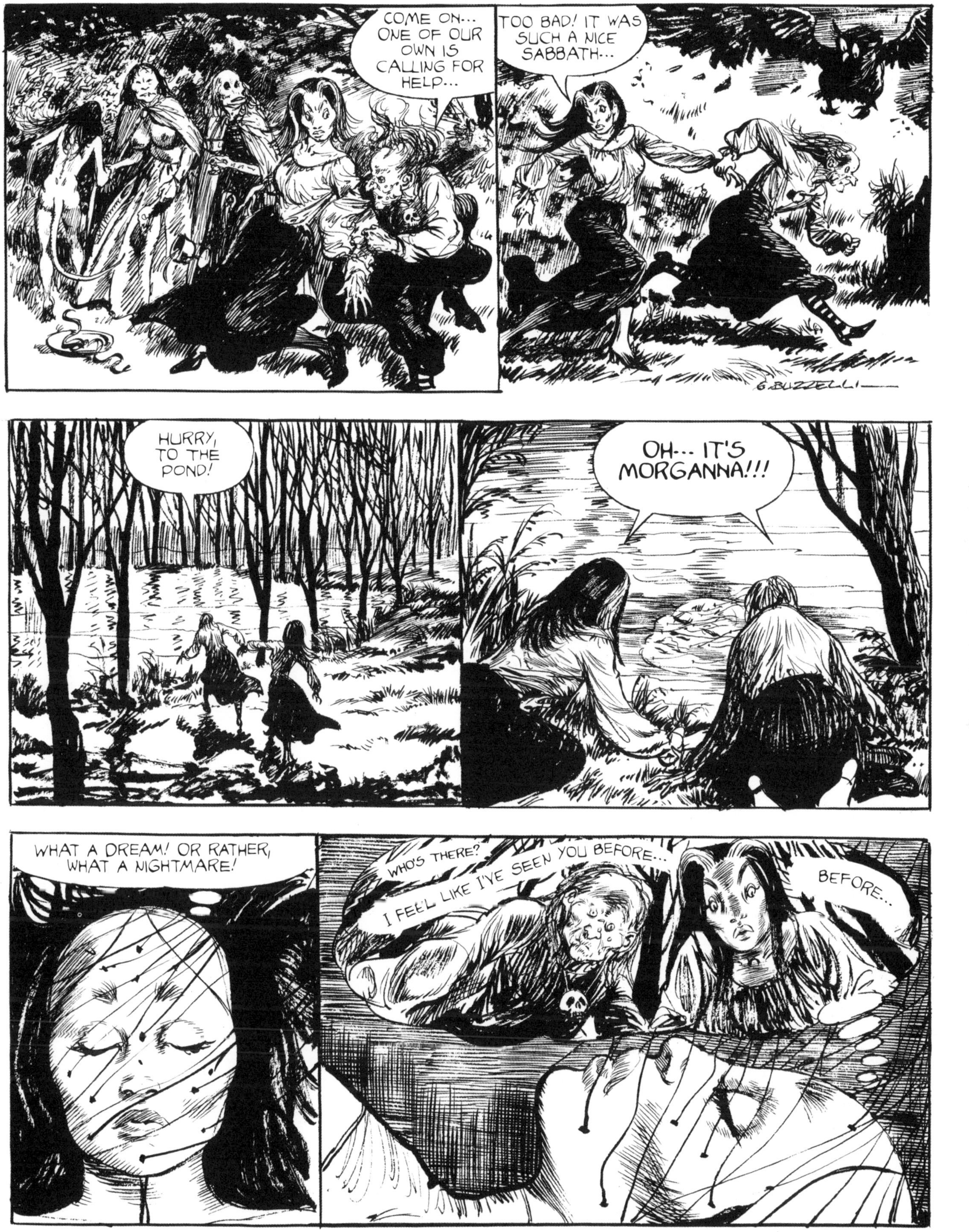
COME ON... ONE OF OUR OWN IS CALLING FOR HELP...
TOO BAD! IT WAS SUCH A NICE SABBATH...
G. BUZZELLI
HURRY, TO THE POND!
OH... IT'S MORGANNA!!!
WHAT A DREAM! OR RATHER, WHAT A NIGHTMARE!
WHO'S THERE?
I FEEL LIKE I'VE SEEN YOU BEFORE...
BEFORE...

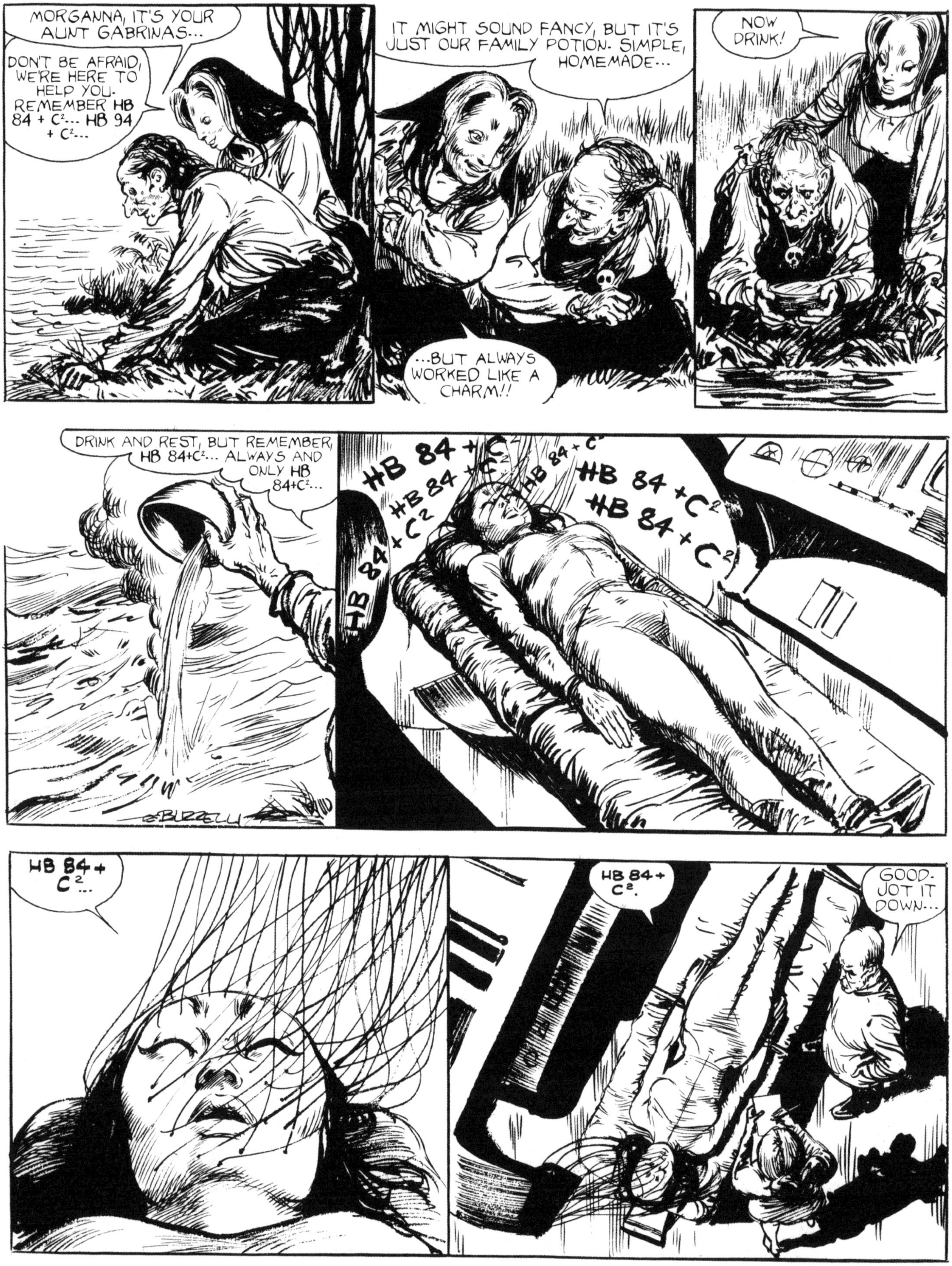
MORGANNA, IT'S YOUR AUNT GABRINAS...
DON'T BE AFRAID, WE'RE HERE TO HELP YOU. REMEMBER HB 84 + C^2... HB 94 + C^2...
IT MIGHT SOUND FANCY, BUT IT'S JUST OUR FAMILY POTION. SIMPLE, HOMEMADE...
...BUT ALWAYS WORKED LIKE A CHARM!!
NOW DRINK!
DRINK AND REST, BUT REMEMBER, HB 84+C^2... ALWAYS AND ONLY HB 84+C^2...
BUZZELLI
HB 84 + C^2
HB 84 + C^2
HB 84 + C
HB 84 + C^2
HB 84 + C^2
HB 84 + C^2
HB 84 + C^2...
HB 84 + C^2.
GOOD. JOT IT DOWN...

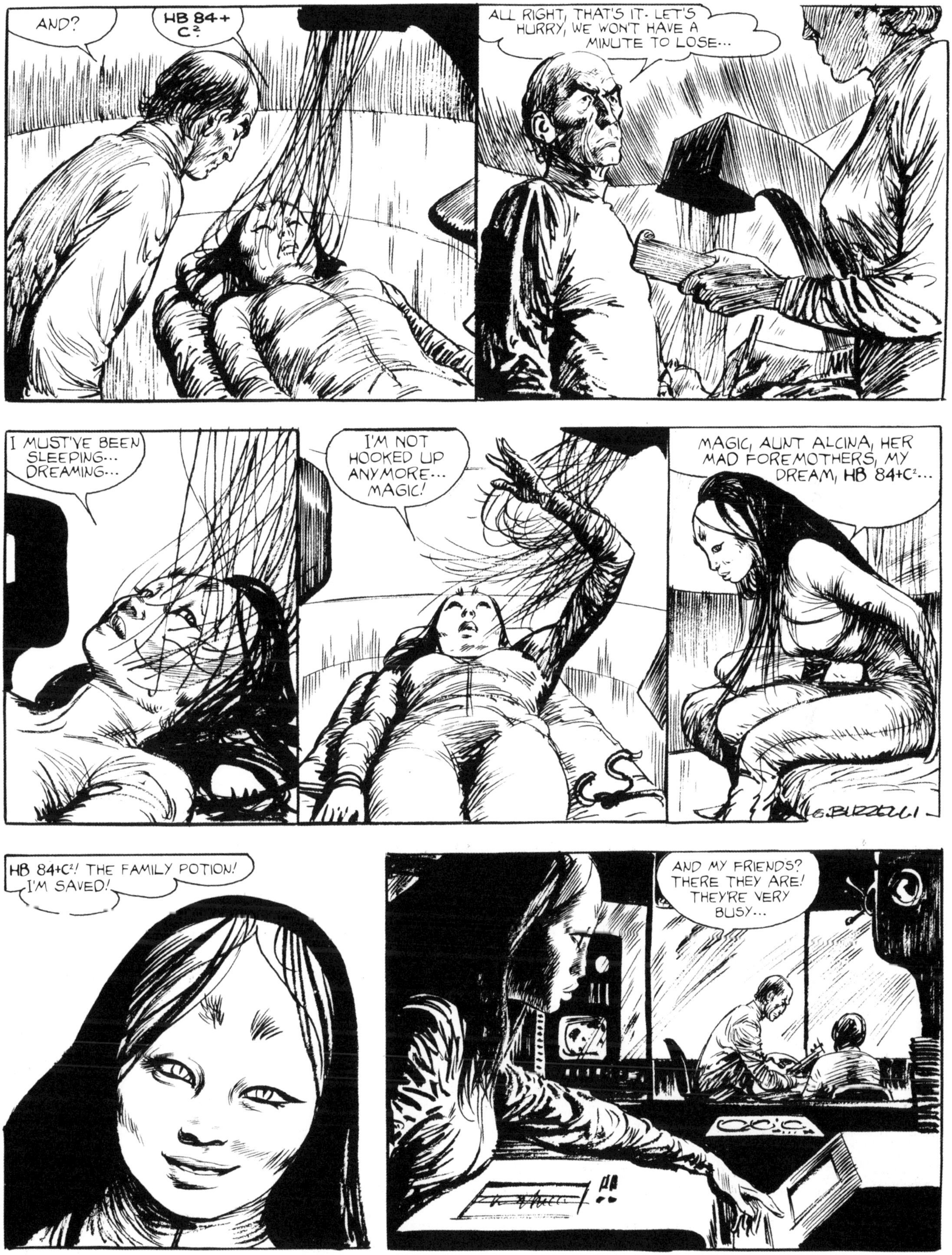
AND?
HB 84+ C^2.
ALL RIGHT, THAT'S IT. LET'S HURRY, WE WON'T HAVE A MINUTE TO LOSE...
I MUST'VE BEEN SLEEPING... DREAMING...
I'M NOT HOOKED UP ANYMORE... MAGIC!
MAGIC, AUNT ALCINA, HER MAD FOREMOTHERS, MY DREAM, HB 84+C^2...
HB 84+C^2! THE FAMILY POTION! I'M SAVED!
AND MY FRIENDS? THERE THEY ARE! THEY'RE VERY BUSY...

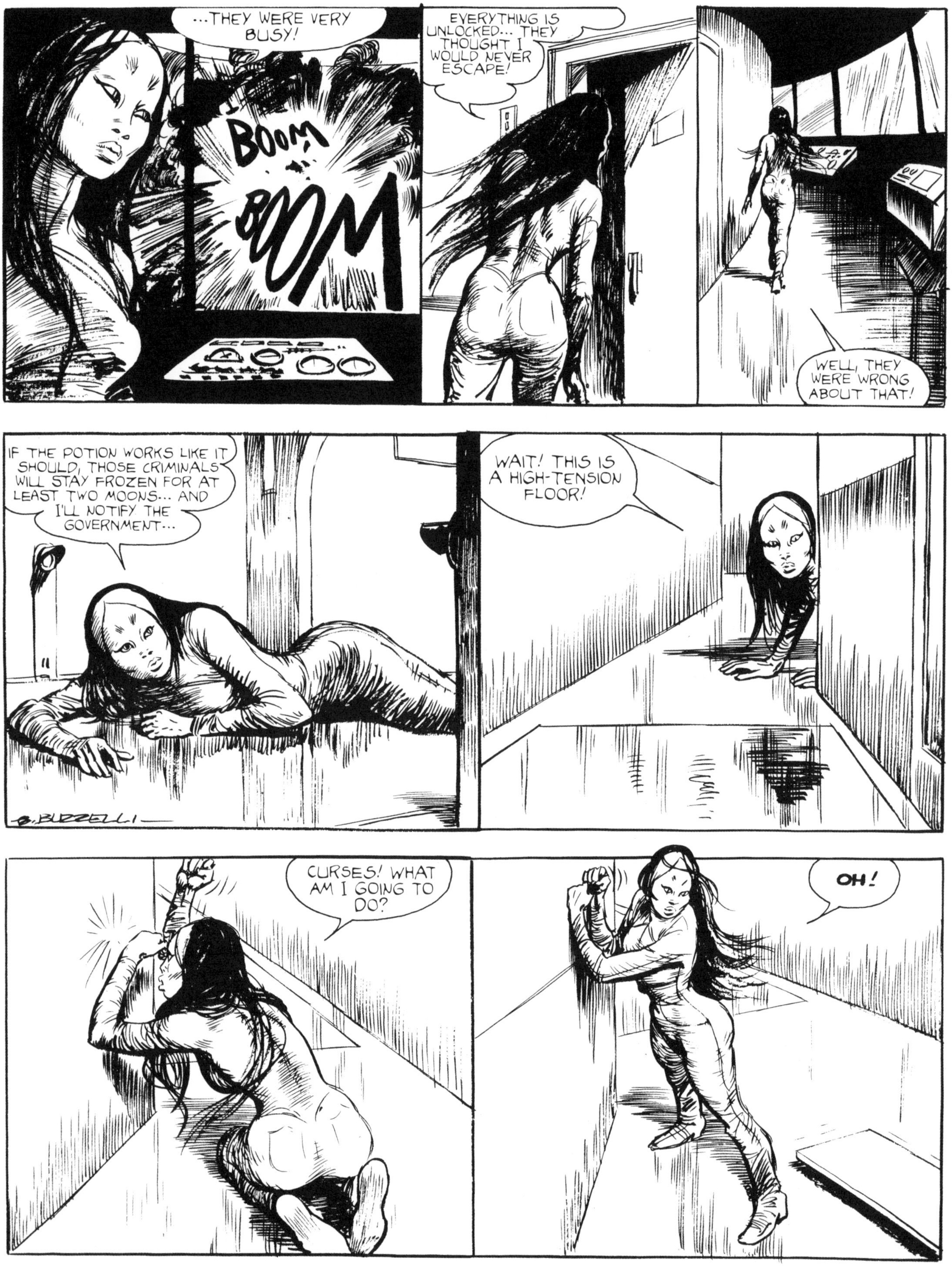
...THEY WERE VERY BUSY!
BOOM
BOOM
EVERYTHING IS UNLOCKED... THEY THOUGHT I WOULD NEVER ESCAPE!
WELL, THEY WERE WRONG ABOUT THAT!
IF THE POTION WORKS LIKE IT SHOULD, THOSE CRIMINALS WILL STAY FROZEN FOR AT LEAST TWO MOONS... AND I'LL NOTIFY THE GOVERNMENT...
B. BUZZELLI
WAIT! THIS IS A HIGH-TENSION FLOOR!
CURSES! WHAT AM I GOING TO DO?
OH!

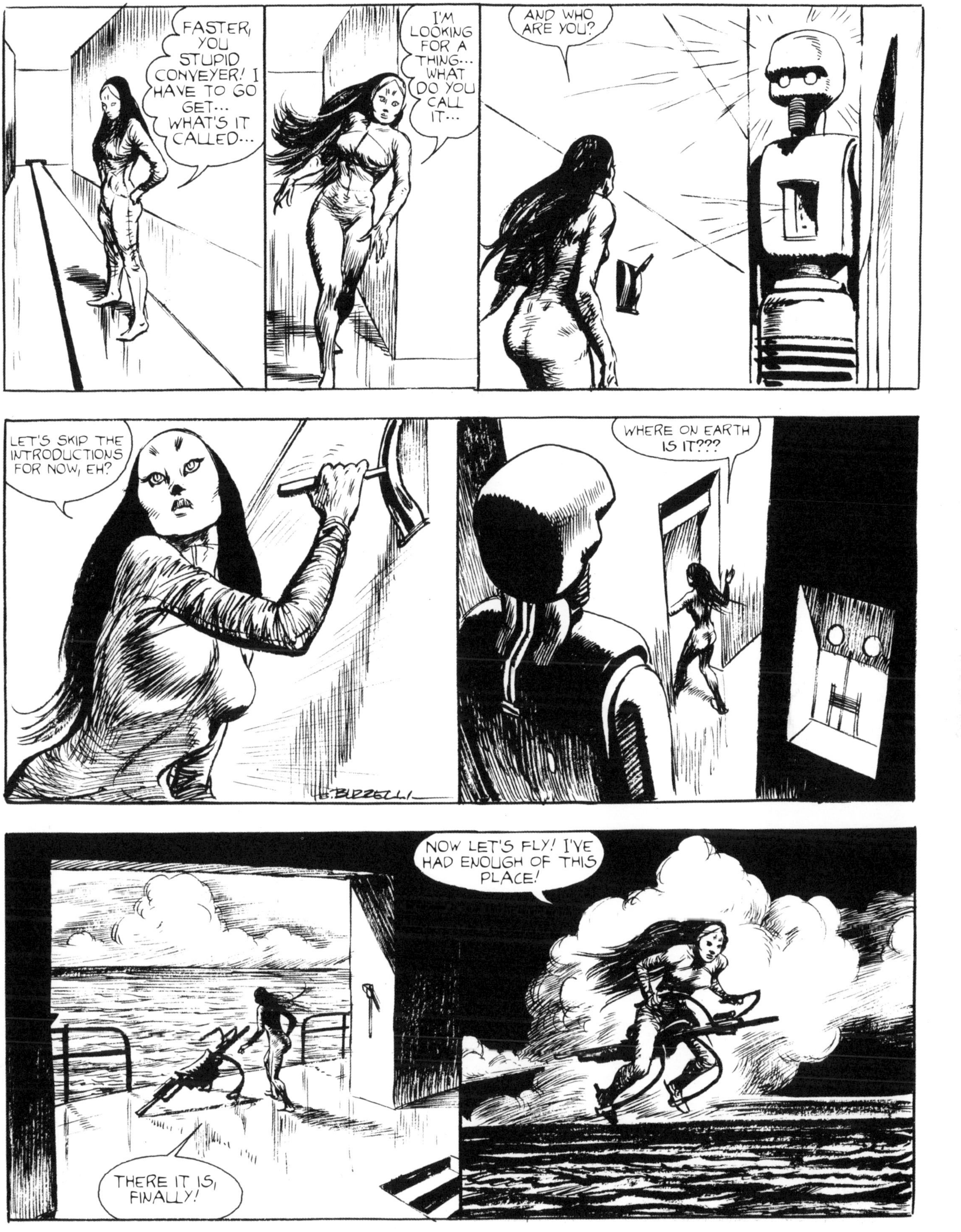
FASTER, YOU STUPID CONVEYER! I HAVE TO GO GET... WHAT'S IT CALLED...
I'M LOOKING FOR A THING... WHAT DO YOU CALL IT...
AND WHO ARE YOU?
LET'S SKIP THE INTRODUCTIONS FOR NOW, EH?
E. BUZZELLI
WHERE ON EARTH IS IT???
THERE IT IS, FINALLY!
NOW LET'S FLY! I'VE HAD ENOUGH OF THIS PLACE!

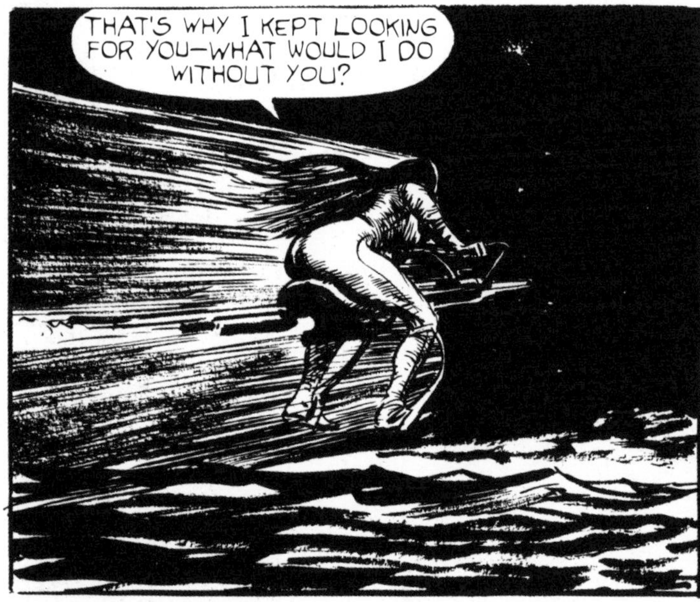
THAT'S WHY I KEPT LOOKING FOR YOU—WHAT WOULD I DO WITHOUT YOU?
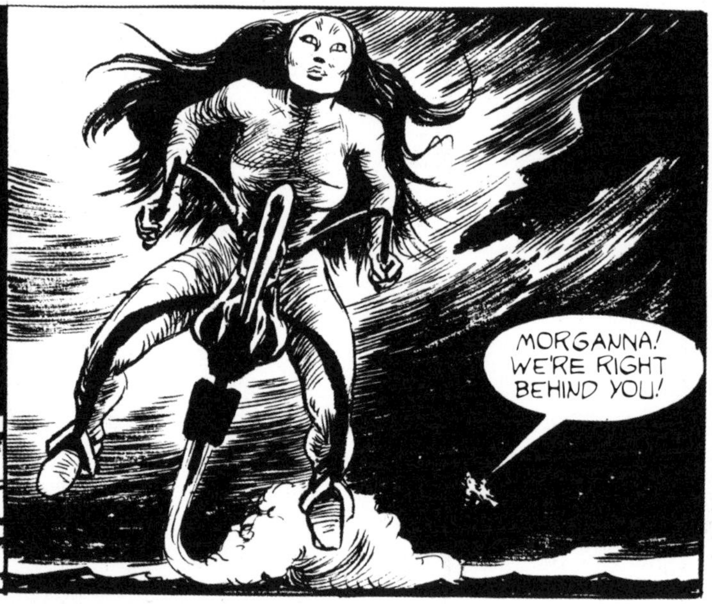
MORGANNA! WE'RE RIGHT BEHIND YOU!
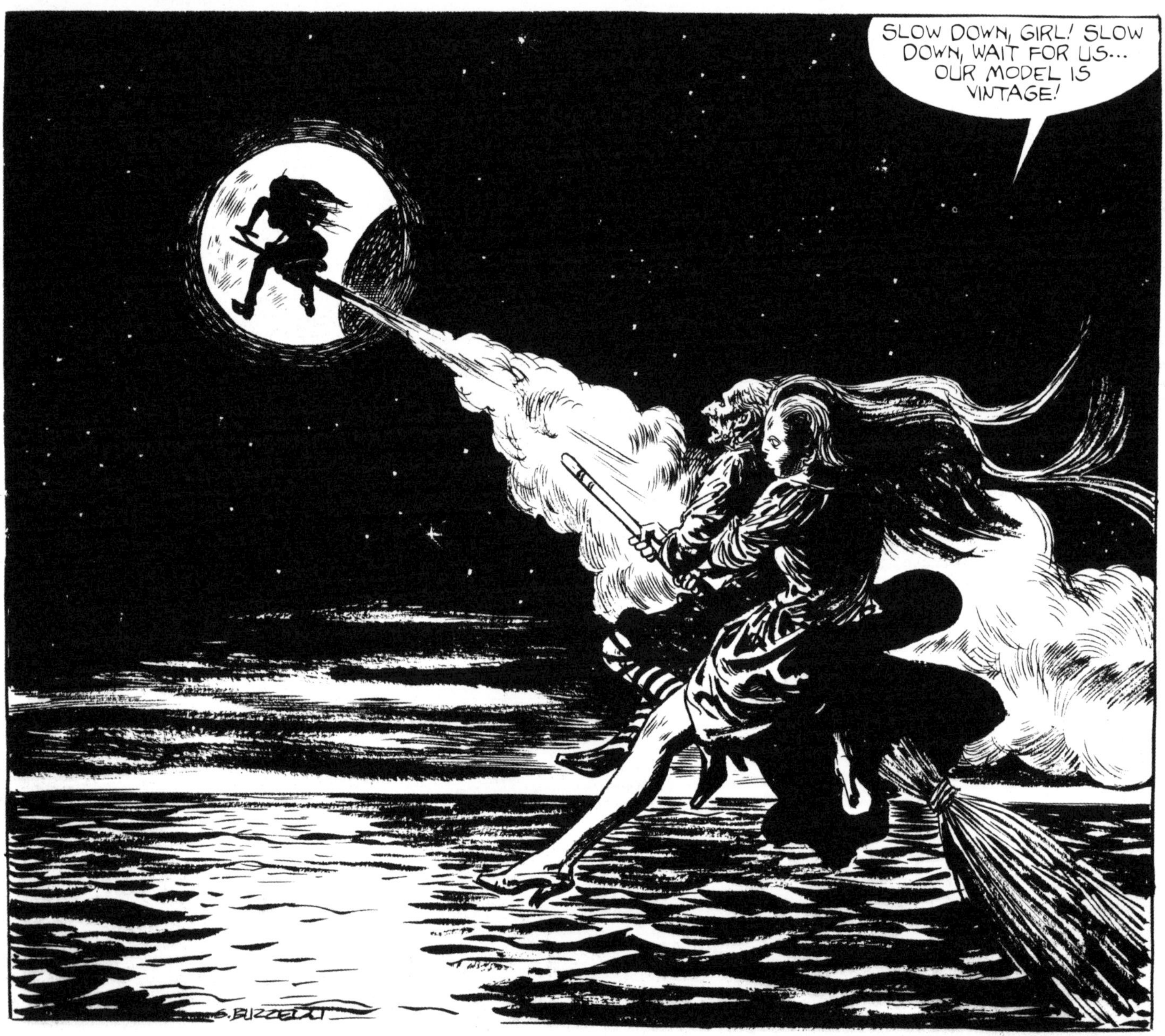
SLOW DOWN, GIRL! SLOW DOWN, WAIT FOR US... OUR MODEL IS VINTAGE!

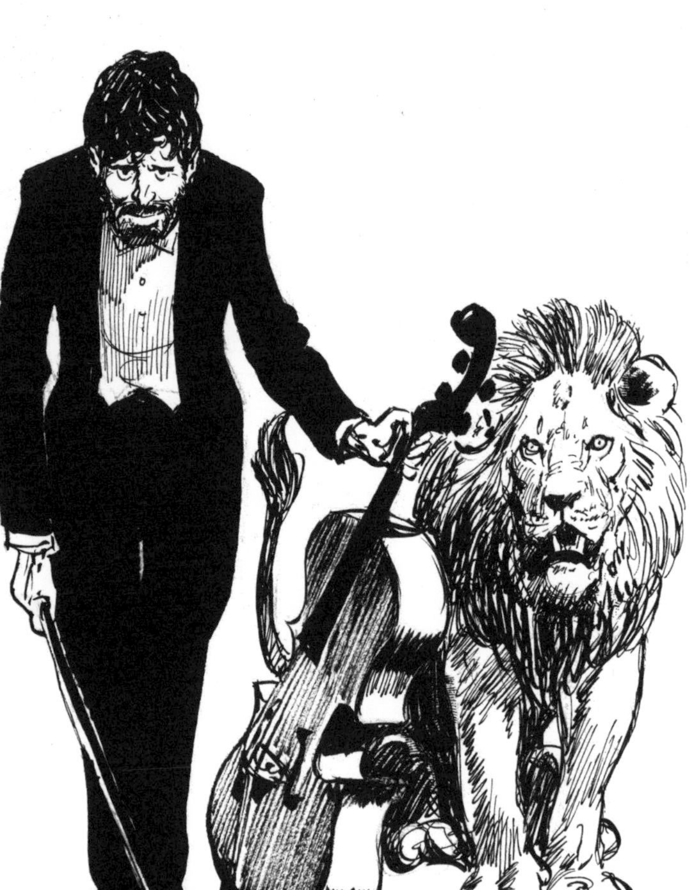

HAILED IN ITALY AND FRANCE, Buzzelli has been called "the Michelangelo of monsters," "the Goya of comics," "the patron saint of all Italian cartoonists." A pioneer active from the 1950s-1980s, today virtually unknown in English, Guido Buzzelli horrifies, fascinates, entertains, provokes, with his unique blend of surrealism and dynamism. Displaying a range of influences from Westerns and science fiction to Renaissance art and futurism, Buzzelli's stories are a delightful, quasi-postmodern mishmash of high and low showing an intricate hand and stylish narrative skill.

What I admire most in his work is the evident impulse to exploit the full powers of the imagination using fantasy to draw beyond what reality can produce. And yet all in the service of subtle but mordant social commentary: on our complicated relationship with technology, our so-called civilization and the notion of progress, our proclivity for barbarism and warfare. In short, Buzzelli depicts the monstrous in the human, and the human in the monstrous—and almost always with a more or less secret self-portrait, perhaps an artist painting in the background or sometimes an alter-ego protagonist.

"Comics is theater in paper and ink, made for pockets and libraries, where the actors stand motionless waiting for someone to turn the pages and bring them to life," is how Buzzelli once described his idea of the graphic narrative art. A modern master, not to be missed.

—Jamie Richards

Buzzelli Collected Works Vol. 2
HP